TEETHMARKS

110652570

EILEEN BATTERSBY

TEETHMARKS ON MY TONGUE

A NOVEL

DALKEY ARCHIVE PRESS

Copyright © 2016 by Eileen Battersby

First edition, 2016

All rights reserved

Lines quoted from "They Flee From Me" by Sir Thomas Wyatt (1503–1542) are taken from Richard Tottel's version as used in his *Miscellany* (1557) and subsequently referred to in *The Literature of Renaissance England* by John Hollander and Frank Kermode (Oxford University Press, 1973). Much gratitude to Paul Simon for expressing his pleasure at having his songs referenced.

Library of Congress Cataloging-in-Publication Data

Names: Battersby, Eileen, author.
Title: Teethmarks on my tongue / by Eileen Battersby.
Description: First edition. | Victoria, TX : Dalkey Archive Press, 2016.
Identifiers: LCCN 2016031188 | ISBN 9781628971477 (softcover : acid-free paper)
Subjects: LCSH: Self-actualization (Psychology) in women--Fiction. | Self-realization in women--Fiction. | Teenage girls--Fiction. | Psychological fiction. | GSAFD: Bildungsromans.
Classification: LCC PR6102.A793 T44 2016 | DDC 823/.92--dc23
LC record available at https://lccn.loc.gov/2016031188

ILLINOIS
ARTS
COUNCIL
AGENCY

Partially funded by a grant by the Illinois Arts Council, a state agency

Victoria, TX / McLean, IL / Dublin

Dalkey Archive Press publications are, in part, made possible through the support of the University of Houston-Victoria and its programs in creative writing, publishing, and translation.

Printed on permanent/durable acid-free paper

3 1327 00623 8224

Declan Kiberd

"A young American woman's passionate and moving search for the lost frontier among the artworks and crazy-boys of Europe. The effect is as if Scout Finch had been set down as an innocent abroad in the world of Daisy Miller."

Jennifer Johnston

"This is a book filled with clues, not just clues for those people who fill in crossword puzzles or who struggle with chess problems, but those who are searchers for the truth about life and death and how we fill in our time between these realities. These readers will find pleasure at every turn of the pages."

Dedication

For My Beloved Kate (1982–2013). Courageous, kind, dignified, astute, and possessed of a will of iron, the very best horse in the Universe and then some . . . not a moment passes . . .

. . . . .And for Ashley, a very special little black and white dog, who found me on a train and whose love was as tenacious as it was profound and irreplaceable.

PART ONE

THEY ASK YOU WHERE YOU WERE, what you were doing. What they really want to find out is what you are thinking, but they can't ask that, not yet, not at the beginning. Instead they will peer at your face, avoiding your eyes, focus on your shoulder or the funny parting in your hair, and try and guess at your inner thoughts, or more pertinently, what you know; how much you hurt. The policemen came to the house and stood looking at Father as if he was about to pay them. They were solemn like undertakers; they were respectful, almost embarrassed when they mentioned they would be "retrieving" the footage. Perhaps they had come anticipating tears and loud wailing? All they got was our mute astonishment. That must have been pretty unsettling; no hysteria, no rage. My face felt rigid with shock; disbelief, a cold, helpless feeling. I stared back at them, it was so unreal. How preposterously limp that all sounds now, but that's what it was like.

Father gazed at the blank TV screen. Mrs. Faulkner must have turned the set off, and when he spoke, it was as if he had been walking along a tunnel for a long time. He put his hands in his pockets and rocked back and forth, from the balls of his feet to his heels, the rubber squealing on the waxed tiles, only to repeat . . . no, more like recite. Why, that's exactly what he did . . . recite, intone in a daze . . . oblivious to us standing there watching him; he chanted over and over: "Planned like a dance routine, planned like a dance routine. Those greedy cameras, busy catching it all and her skirt billowing on the breeze . . ." He

puffed out his cheeks, half-whistled and looked . . . preoccupied,
processing what he had just witnessed and was intrigued, not
distressed, but truly intrigued. Mother had finally recaptured
his attention.

I could remember asking, "What's happened? Why are
they screaming?" my voice thin and high, the words landing hollow in the room, no one paying me heed. Little figures on the screen were running, automobiles stopped all
over the place and people climbed out, rushing, just leaving those car doors wide open and adding to the chaos.

Mayhem, that word, kept dancing in my brain. My only
clear response was . . . mayhem. Only I couldn't visualize the
word; I had forgotten how it looked written down. Then I
noticed the white dress and it was slowly filling up with red, as
the woman on the television in a slow motion free fall, dropped
the big fancy box she had been carrying even though it seemed
so light and it drifted on the air, weightless. That wonderful,
every-day-is-Christmas box just falling away, gradually revealing the white floaty fabric behind it becoming soaked, filling
up with dark blood. The camera was trained on that tragic,
tragic woman as closely as the gunman must have been and
she folded, fell, collapsed and I saw her face clench, become
all small and tight . . . and then a part of her head came loose
and fell away, pursued by minute pieces of grit that turned
out to be fragments of bone and brain and her bright yellow
hair contracted, slick with darkening blood, and soon turned
into a thick hank, like a wet piece of hemp pulled from some
murky old river. Mother, alone and dying outside her favorite
department store, and with the world watching on in horror.

So many bullets; most likely six. Did I count? Perhaps? I'd
like to think I didn't . . . It takes six shots to empty a gun, but
she was dead and all with the very first one.

You think that there is someone who can stop the clock, that big clock that's always racing away off into the distance . . . high tailing it, what a funny, cartoon phrase . . . Someone must be able to stop that mean ticking and somehow rewind time. Her left leg was juddering with a life of its own; the neat tan leather high-heeled shoe still on her foot and blood seeping out all around her. Mother lying flat in the street, it was in fact the sidewalk; everyone looking at her. Her eyes, wide and empty; beyond surprise. Such a deal of matted hair smeared across her forehead and with her own blood. Then it struck me that what we had just seen on the screen, on the news, had already been witnessed by whoever was there in the street. It could have happened an hour or more before we knew. Those onlookers had known Mother was dead before we did. She had been a victim, before she became the late Mrs. Stockton Defoe, before she became Mother. While I was edging down the stairs, attempting to appear as if I had just taken a bath, instead of trying to recover from a fall I wanted kept secret, Mother had been dying, had died, been randomly gunned down in the street by some madman on a rampage.

Maybe if I had gone shopping with her, she'd still be alive? Perhaps the bullets would've hit me? She hadn't said anything that morning about a shopping trip. Not a word. Why, she'd gone out before I even saw her, and that fact alone—that she had not asked me to come along—was some small consolation. Had she invited me and I'd shrugged a "no" like so many times . . . well I would never have been able to deal with the shame, the heavy slab of guilt. I would have needed to kill myself, just vanish; disappear . . . crawl away and die.

Someone, I don't know who, a relative, or one of Father's clients had once given me a lovely Victorian doll; it looked antique and was probably valuable. It had a delicately pale china face, not the kind of doll you play with; more one to look at, barely touch, just gaze at and build dreams and stories around. The thick, black hair was real, it had come from a horse, or so Father had once said. "Which horse?" I'd wanted to know, was it one of ours? But he just laughed and pushed my question away, like he always did, and said she was an enchanted mare who grew her mane every night specially to accommodate dolls who needed lots of good quality hair only did not much like eating green vegetables.

I had called the doll Queen Emmy Lou and pretended she was a Southern belle, the Queen of the Mississippi. Her throne was a shelf in my bedroom and she was so beautiful, dressed in blue velvet with a fur muff and her crown was a picture hat sporting a jaunty, gray feather. She had dark brown eyes like shiny marbles, with no pupils. The maid was dusting and when she knocked her over, had just said "tsk, tsk," went on about her work and was not remotely upset—never even said she was sorry, although she should have. I had always been so careful. Queen Emmy Lou fell right on her face, which shattered, and the only sound was the soft thud of her landing on the carpet and you could look into her head and see where the hair was attached, like one of those handmade rugs when you check on the obverse side, and see all the meticulously executed knots. The sight of Mother made me think of my broken doll from long ago, I could remember picking up the brittle splinters of the face. I placed Queen Emmy Lou into a drawer where she lay in state like a doomed princess and each time I looked I'd first close my eyes and pray that God would've fixed her. He never did.

I had wanted some orange juice that day, the day of my fall, the day of the killing; otherwise I could have been upstairs in my room, lying on the floor or maybe on my bed, listening to "Bridge Over Troubled Water" as I had intended. Had I not been thrown, though, I would have still been down in the stable yard and would only have been told about Mother's death, had the devastation of it broken to me, formally, by Father in the dignified voice he could summon in a thrice. But instead I had seen it happen, well, had watched a recording of it as if it had been staged deliberately for a publicity stunt advertizing one of those blockbuster movies. I had seen Mother die on the TV news and had never gotten to say goodbye.

On finally heaving my battered self up out of the bath, I'd caught sight of a ghostly shape looming through the steam that had clouded Mother's full-length mirror. It was me. The glass became wet under my fingers when I tried to wipe it clear and get a closer peek. My hip was already turning blue and yellow; green, cerise, every sort of color. What with the cuts, abrasions, the half-moon of the kick to the ribs, I looked as if the air had been let out of me. It was too painful to even bend down and pick up my clothes because a thunderous surge of blood had rushed to my head and for a moment I thought the pressure would cause me to pass out clean away on the floor. So I'd kicked my things together into a soggy heap and dropped a towel over the mess . . .

Slowly making my way down the stairs, my bones creaking loud enough to waken the dead, I held my breath . . . and of course, on cue, along came Mrs. Faulkner striding erect across the hall, straighter than a marine guard of honor. She seemed set to ignore me as was her way, only then, pretty much against her will, she paused and half-turned, asking had I seen the injured stag. I hadn't seen any stag. Apparently he had wandered into the yard, completely disoriented, meek as a lamb, lame down one side, "and Mr. Porter had the mind to put him into one of the wooden loose boxes beside the sand arena," she said importantly. Who was this Mr. Porter I had asked, although far more taken with the notion of a deer being in the yard. Mrs. Faulkner rarely spoke to anyone, but she looked directly at me with a faint smile, and seemed to enjoy informing me that Mr. Porter was Billy Bob's proper name. "You should always address your elders by their full and formal name," she'd retorted, adding primly that it was the polite way of doing things. Then she told me that he, Mr. Porter, had told her that I had had a little mishap but had gotten up and caught the critter. Critter? Was that her word or Billy Bob's? I wonder . . . certainly not mine. Who knows? I didn't much care. "I'm fine, I'm fine," I mumbled, realizing that old Galileo had been startled by the stag. Most horses spook at deer. The fall suddenly made sense; it could be explained, he hadn't been to blame for his sequence of bucks and spins, or for the tiny matter of him stomping all over me . . . I felt better, well at least my mind did.

Cheered slightly by that useful explanation I had then followed Mrs. Faulkner into the kitchen; glad I was behind her and didn't have to try and walk as if normal instead of being partly flattened and hurting all over. That is the last thing I recall of "ordinary" that day. Father had been standing, looking at the television, saying, "Dead. Just killed. Struck down. Obliterated and for no earthly reason. Gone. Slain. Would you look at that?" and there was a hint of amazement about the way he stood there, making him seem younger and different, more animated, if only for an instant.

The police had come quietly up the drive barely disturbing the gravel; two cars and following close behind, the county sheriff, he was friendly with Father. He had two racehorses in training and he and Father had gone together to Claiborne a few times to visit Secretariat at stud and then later on in retirement. Jamie Hodge, the sheriff, was a fat man with small little eyes and an unusually beautiful speaking voice, very soothing, rather old-fashioned in intonation. He looked menacing, because of his size and his bald bullet head atop no neck to speak of, but he was sweet and kindly, I always, always liked him. He whispered, "William, William," and, quite lovingly, had held out both his hands to Father who stared blankly back at him and then seemed to remember who he was and, as if they had already been in deep conversation, without even greeting him, remarked, it looked like a scene from an opera. "How could one human do that to another? To kill your fellow man with such . . . such . . ." He didn't finish, just stopped and shrugged . . . There was no anger, only genuine wonder. The room was silent; no one spoke. Father had seen to that.

*

Would the new girl have been so drawn to me had I not been near the center of a horrible story, what the newscasters had taken to calling a "crime of passion." Maybe if Mother had died in a car crash or from a disease or during an operation or something mundane and well, not so shocking . . . But I could tell Mitzi wasn't like that, she was sympathetic and kind, not some nosy parker wanting to feast on horrors. It must have been a surprise though, her coming from a crazy place like Santa Monica and finding this, well me. Maybe she was speechless at discovering that awful stuff happened elsewhere as well, even in stuffy old Richmond, where she'd probably imagined we all sat around drinking mint juleps, languidly discussing the Civil War. She kept saying that it was all down to bad luck and fate and karma, one of her favorite words as I found out. She told me a story about a woman who'd been hit by lightning in Santa Barbara. One of the customers in their bakery had arrived to collect a cake. He'd just heard, so he passed it on as people do . . . the unfortunate woman had been found, still just about alive, and was purple, completely purple. Her skin had been all burnt by the hot flash and was already flaking away, like paper or ashes. The lady's neighbors had heard her dog barking away for hours, and had finally gone to investigate. She did die, that woman, and I imagined her just lying there at peace, with her hair all fanned out around her head like a halo. She would have looked like a ghost, I decided, not a victim like Mother.

But the first thing Mitzi actually got to know about me was the science stuff, because of the competition. The school had made a big to-do and put a gigantic poster of Galileo up behind the stage in the assembly hall. It was magnificent only Mitzi said he looked like a wizard or a magician on account of his dark robes and the high collar, I hadn't thought of him that way, as some sort of Disney Merlin, and it made me laugh. But for her, on maybe her second or third day at our school, the first sight she had of me was of my being tongue-tied when asked to explain the project. There I was, unable to speak, and with the science teacher talking each time I made an effort to say something. It was a nightmare, like being asked to reveal your private thoughts, and coming not that long after Mother when everybody at school was still treating me as a traumatized casualty.

My passion, the very thing I'd brooded over for hours, well years, always reading about it and finding out things that were never mentioned in class and collecting stuff; I had so many books and charts, journals, my telescopes . . . when it came to explaining my project, something I knew all about way before anyone ever mentioned the competition, there I was sounding as if I barely spoke English. What an impression she must have gotten, and I can imagine how everyone would have tried to help, by telling her the complete and entire story. None of them would have been mean, I know that, I was lucky . . . lucky in some ways, even though I didn't always see it like that. The girls were great, even before Mother, I was always the class nerd and because I'm quiet—and different—was handled with care. Any time I see that printed on a package, I have to smile; it makes me think I'm the piece of glass wrapped up inside.

After Mother though I could sense that people were waiting for me to have a breakdown, it just hadn't happened and even I was beginning to wonder why not. Was there something wrong with me? The best way of explaining it is to imagine a plane being kept in a holding zone, not being able to land until the way is clear and somehow the space never does become free. Leaving it stuck up there in the sky.

After the competition the TV station was interested in doing a report and the interviewer had to sign something agreeing not to ask me about anything except the project. But when the crew came to the school, they could see I was not a natural communicator, so the principal did most of the talking, heaping praise upon me, while I looked down at my hands as if I'd committed a crime. Nothing could induce me to look into the camera, not in full color.

*

Mitzi was standing at the counter in the school cafeteria and it was plain to see that she was mildly jumpy, being confident yet also new and all. She looked around, probably wondering where she was going to sit, or more like who she would go over to and ask if they'd mind her joining them. Aside from her new girl's nerves she was sociable and had no difficulty in mixing with people. Me? I'd gulp and scurry to an underpopulated corner, which is where I was when she noticed me looking over, so she waved. I must have done something, attempted a long distance smile, always safe, and resumed reading.

A few minutes later, a bright "Hi there" caused me to look up and there stood Mitzi with a lunch tray. Then she gasped, blurting out, "Your eyes, they're . . ." and I shot back, loudly, in an exaggerated plantation accent, "Yes sir, this here green one's made of glass. You want to hold it?" She shrieked and her beans and bacon hot mash slid off the tray, as did the tall chocolate malt. It all happened split-second quick.

*

Poor Mitzi; the look on her face. I rarely attempt jokes although I love laughing. Lots of things make me guffaw, often the oddest little situation. Sometimes I look around and no one else is even smiling while I could be on the verge of collapse. Panic and crisis also set me off, as do melodramas and anything corny. But I've never been a practical joker and am not even all that keen on slapstick or overly visual gags so I really don't know what made me do that thing with the eye complete with the pop sound created by pulling my finger out of my mouth. By then I had completely forgotten about the stupid article in the newspaper and the "Helen spelt wrong on a big black horse . . ." Mitzi was new and from a place most of us connected to the movies; everyone took an instant liking to her, although the girls also protected me. Well, it was a sordid and despicable business, difficult to explain for lots of reasons, none of them helped by the fact that the murderer was if not exactly insane, clearly disturbed and there was a great deal of medication involved and the law has a convoluted way of going about things. I was delighted when Mitzi came over to me, and it was my fault that her lunch made such a mess of my prized possession, a *National Geographic* atlas of the solar system. I knew that Mitzi and I would be friends, and I'd never had a friend before. It was exciting, the beginning of something I had often dreamed of happening. She had a kind of freshness, an open-faced goodness, very direct and she was spontaneous when the others, the more girly types, were serious about makeup and spending lunch break crowding around the mirrors in the rest room, sighing over boys. As for my joke, it could have gone better but it was nowhere as bad as Father's Dixie quip that had even shocked Caleb Montgomery, the most sanguine lawyer in the South. No, I don't have a glass eye, but if I did, it would be the right color. My eyes are not a matching pair. Taken individually they're fine; not too small, not too big and bulgy and not crossed either. But together, they're ill-matched, not a couple. I mean, not a pair and it took over my life.

Mother had, with her customary sensitivity, once observed quite memorably, "You know, honey, it's scary, real scary—those eyes, they absolutely ruin your face. Maybe you should check out some contacts?" She had informed me that they, contacts, come in all kinds of colors, and that I could get matching ones. "Yes, I do believe that you should decide on a color," she had said in full seriousness. "You could buy yourself a pair of matching blue eyes." She meant well, she just never thought too deeply, about anything, not even about my defect which is what it was to me and still is, like being cheated by nature . . . Mother used to find my silences disturbing, but then she put it down to my being an intellectual—her phrase, not mine. "Helen's real bright," she'd say with an expression of astonished pleasure. She never took any credit for this and would announce with a spirited flourish that all she could bequeath me were her good looks and more than once, to me alone but also while in company, she would beam before conceding, "I guess you kind of missed out there!" No kidding. I always hated my eyes, one brown, the other a vivid green which has on occasion been referred to as "startling." It's the kind of thing you either believe makes you special, or it grieves you to death. Me, I hated it and felt downright afflicted.

*

And at what point should I begin my story? Most accounts of personal tribulation tend to share a common theme—parents as the enemy. Mine weren't. They did happen to be my earliest experience of humans and through them, particularly on account of Father, I was inclined to look at people, to observe them, try and read their faces for clues instead of engaging directly with them. There was always a hint of tension at home, you'd hardly notice it, but it was there. We were not close . . . we barely knew each other. Yet we were always civil: "Good Day" in the hall, "Have the papers arrived?" or in the kitchen, at breakfast, "May I have the syrup?", "Please pass the milk," courteous at all times, excepting for my father's irony which struck at varying levels, depending on his mood.

Mother's chatter was a continuous stream of chatty consciousness, directed at no one in particular. We all three of us shared what you'd call a fine residence and it had an atmosphere similar to one of those boarding houses in Paris or Berlin—two cities in which my daydreams usually took place. Father was aloof; rather taken with his notion of himself as old money—which we weren't exactly, but near enough. Nor did he sit in judgment of sinners; he had never been an attorney or a legal man. He was referred to as The Judge because like his father and grandfather before him, he had a shrewd, almost "sexually astute" eye for a fine horse—Mr. Montgomery always said that and it could cause a stir, depending on the company. Father was a veterinarian, deferred to throughout the state of Virginia and beyond, as the leading authority on joint conditions as well as bone and related injuries. He believed in time and patience as a cure depending on a single crucial factor—the injured individual's temperament. He referred to his patients as "individuals" and had far more sympathy for them than for the owners. Bloodlines and breeding were among his passions and his opinion was the one to seek out. He had bred some fine Thoroughbreds, including Monticello, who would have become very famous only for having the bad luck to come along at the same time as a rare genius, Secretariat, the magnificent race horse that's always included in lists of the 100 Greatest American Athletes of All Time. My grandfather had bred a winner of the Kentucky Derby, the Holy Grail for Father, who was very tall and imposing-looking—very much in keeping with his lofty notions. Mother was tiny, a doll. I'm a bit over average height but with slightly longer-than-usual legs; useful when it comes to riding horses.

Aside from horses, Father had two other obsessions: Thomas Jefferson—hence Monticello; and Edgar Allan Poe, who had been fostered in Richmond as a child and later returned to the town. As for Mother, Father regarded her as a domestic pet that had somehow become part of his household. She was nervy, determined to be happy and she played the part of the Southern belle with an abandon that bordered on parody. She was in fact from Toledo, Ohio. But I'll get back to that. Mother cultivated a Gone with the Wind accent and usually sounded far more Southern than Father. I remember a new maid who had for a while bit her lip whenever Mother spoke, until the maid—I forget her name—realized that she wasn't being mocked; Mrs. Stockton Defoe really did speak that way, leastways did most of the time.

Father would look on and smile his small, tight smile and declare that he had married "an adopted daughter of the South."

Her days were busy with hairdressers, beauty treatments and shopping; she had what she called "Zen sessions" and practiced yoga and mostly just stayed out of Father's way, reminding me of a puppy dodging a broom sweeping the floor. I was always thinking of puppies because I was never allowed to have one. Mother didn't want pets despite her showing little interest in our home, which was managed by our housekeeper, Mrs. Faulkner, who regarded life in general with a forlorn seriousness, and our household in particular, with a grim dedication. She acted as if it was her special mission to get us through the hours, the seasons, and the long, long years. Instead of taking orders from Mother, Mrs. Faulkner was in charge and she reported on the plans for the day; the chores, repairs, purchases, services. Mother would respond as if these lists had all been her idea. On hearing that a room was about to be painted, or a carpet lifted, she would agree enthusiastically, adding that it was about time. Father held firm views about many things, including wallpaper. Our walls were painted. Some rooms were yellow, there was a great deal of yellow; we had strong blues, and subtle greens and grays. It was a handsome house, filled with light from the large windows. There were many paintings and period prints as well as elegantly mounted photographs, usually of horses. I don't remember any pictures of people, not so surprising considering . . . Father had also acquired or maybe inherited—I'm not sure—three minor works by the famous English horse artist Stubbs, the man who painted Whistlejacket.

As long as I could remember there was a large print of a horse in my bedroom, it was military in aspect, war-like even though there was no rider. Discipline, not freedom, is what it always made me think of. I was paging through a large art book one day, and there it was, that drawing from my room, the original was kept in Windsor Castle, near London, England. It was by Leonardo da Vinci. We had several genuine Wyeth paintings; my grandfather had known him. Most of them were hung in the drawing room—Mother loved hosting her little gatherings there. Her lunch parties and high teas were where she got to demonstrate her efforts at becoming incontestably Southern. She wore white gauze like dresses and her hysterical laughter rose high above the murmur of conventional conversation. The wives would come, not out of friendship to Mother but because it apparently meant something socially to be invited to the Judge's house, even if the invitation had nothing to do with him.

I was left to my own devices; in a house full of books—leather-bound volumes about history and wars; science and horses, and quite a collection of nineteenth-century fiction, Jane Austen, Balzac, Trollope, Dickens, Walter Scott, Thomas Hardy, and best of all, the Russians: Turgenev and Dostoyevsky—Father's interests. It was easy for me to keep occupied, I was never bored.

And of course there was also the stable yard, a kind of wonderland with horses, three full-time workers and a live-in guru, round-faced old Billy Bob, who lived for these big, mysterious, beautiful creatures. He couldn't have been as old as he looked, but he hobbled about like a Civil War veteran and spoke to each Thoroughbred in his charge as if it was his only child. He never changed his clothes and lived in a black suit jacket, shiny with the grime of living, not a single surviving button. His yellowish shirt had once been white. His pants were stretched across his belly but sagged at the backside, and his broken boots were the kind of objects that catch a painter's eye. True, he smelled a smell so pungent as to be beyond mere odor; his personal aroma was a unique mixture of dirt and sweat, tobacco and alcohol and the pine, minty hot liniment he was forever rubbing into the love of his life, his charge, Father's aged, once almost-great racehorse, Monticello, crippled with arthritis but lovingly supported by Billy Bob's devotion.

*

Watching Billy Bob with Monticello was my introduction to affection, he taught me more about empathy than either of my parents ever did. How Billy Bob adored that beautiful, chronically-lame chestnut. Father couldn't even look at the horse, I think it hurt him—I know it hurt him—to see Monticello shuffle about, slow and tentative, but Father was content in knowing that the horse was alive and being loved by someone who was a lot better at loving than he could ever be. As long as Monticello wanted to live he was free to do so, Billy Bob would see to that, and with Father's blessing along with the best of veterinary treatments and medications.

There was no doubting Father's profound depth of feeling for his horse. As for Mother, he barely tolerated her, no more no less. If it had once been otherwise, which it must have been, I never saw it. He inhabited his world, from which she was excluded; she craved his attention, his approval and yes they were indeed an odd pair, as odd as my eyes about which I never minded until my ninth birthday when I discovered I was a freak. Father

seldom asked about my riding but when I won my first big competition at state level, he had a pair of long boots made for me,
ordered in from a famous firm in England that had the Queen's
approval. They were handmade with a last to my measurement
which had been taken from a mold made from a pair of my
boots. The English leather was soft and dark reddish, almost the
same rich color as Monticello. Such beautiful boots; so elegant
with an aura of the eighteenth century and all that tradition of
horsemanship, an art spanning the ages. I regard those boots as
romantic because for me, horses are romance heroes, powerful
but passive, vulnerable. Monticello's helpless, courageous dignity
had a kind of nobility I've yet to see in any human. I have to be
careful; people take offence when I make comments like that.
All Father said when he gave me the boots was that he'd heard
I had ridden well, and that he hoped they'd fit. And that was
pretty much that.

It didn't bother me. I knew how lucky I was; working stables
just out through the kitchen door. There was no spending my
weekends mucking out at a local riding stable in exchange for
a lesson on a school horse. I had my choice of talented, testing
youngsters, and rode whatever horse Billy Bob reckoned would
suit. Father was often left with horses as bad debts. If an injured
horse was abandoned when the bills got too high, Father didn't
seem to notice and the horse just settled into the yard attached
to the practice. I enjoyed the facilities of what had formerly been
an extensive training operation; my grandfather, the one who
had bred the derby winner, had been a serious trainer. Although
born into this, Father decided to become a veterinarian specializing in horses. When he was young students from Virginia and
Maryland had to attend the University of Georgia as it was the
nearest veterinary faculty so it had looked like Father had turned

his back on his father's passion—but no he hadn't. He only had a different way of doing things.

Just beyond the kitchen, a short walk through an orchard garden, down a path lined by trees was the yard, my private paradise. There was stabling for about sixty and although I can't recall the yard ever being more than about half-full, that still meant thirty horses—several of whom were more than willing to be ridden by me. Billy Bob was there and he knew everything about horses—and they seemed to know that this little man could read their minds and identify their needs. It was perfect and I took full advantage of all of it. Any pressure on me was entirely of my own making. I didn't even have to worry about getting to the local events. There was always a yardman to help me load and to drive me, until I could manage the jeep myself. My interest in learning to drive was about logistics, not teenage independence. It soon became obvious to me that I needed to be able to drive because I didn't like being a passenger on the way to a competition—I wanted to be on my own to prepare my head. I always got very nervous, my heart would race and I found singing helped, it calmed me. Most of all I was aware that the drive from home to the university, Thomas Jefferson's, of course, at Charlottesville, was about seventy miles—I had to be confident of managing the journey alone and towing a trailer when the time came.

The little rituals involved in preparing for the shows, grooming, getting the tack ready, ironing my shirts—the one thing I hated, although more often than not, they were already done for me and back in my drawer—were almost as much fun as the actual event. Competing was great, it surprised me. There was no certainty, not like exams. It was a challenge. I had set my goal; I wanted to be a member of the University of Virginia equestrian team. It wouldn't be easy; this is horse country with many wealthy fathers backing their sons and their daughters; fathers more than willing to source good horses from abroad. Fathers far more competitive than mine; perhaps it would have been different had I been a son involved in racing. Father could then have watched as one of his horses was ridden to a derby triumph. I don't know; I never knew what went on inside Father's head.

Sometime in the future I reckoned I would find myself a quiet career in a university physics department; lecturing and tutoring while I explored the night skies in search of a forgotten star, or a constellation more beautiful than heaven itself. All very vague, I know, but from early on at school I tried to read everything I could about Galileo, his study of comets, and Kepler, and before them, further back to Copernicus who had influenced Galileo; all of these discoveries resented by angry popes who regarded science as an insult to God.

My bedroom was full of charts of night skies as seductive as paintings but far more convincing as I knew them to be accurate. I even had a poster of Galileo's drawings of the Milky Way and the Pleiades thumb-tacked to my ceiling, along with a great photograph of star clusters taken from space. Yellow and red and formed about fifty million years ago, in the right corner was the white patch of a much younger cluster, only about four million years old. Wonderful stuff, I imagined the excitement felt by Galileo. Of course I was privileged. Father maintained a detached interest in my science obsessions. He would surprise me at times like the day he tossed a paperback to me as he walked into the kitchen. It was early morning, I was going riding and was sitting down eating cereal, half-reading the cornflakes box as I swallowed and gulped noisily, without chewing. The book flopped down on the table with a slap; it was the Brecht play about the life of Galileo. Father presenting me with that play proved to me that he did regard these heroes of mine as real people who had once lived. No I was lucky, the world of the arts and culture, sport, history, were free and open for me to wander into. I never took any of it for granted, leastways I didn't think I did, but it was all there—ready to be explored if I was interested and I was. Yet people were to pity me for a tragedy that never quite openly distressed me. It numbed me for sure and left me sort of paralyzed emotionally. The images remained vivid if unreal, like a theater performance but one without sound. Faces had moved in silence, registering horror. Mouths were wide open making words, without a soundtrack like in a nightmare and I couldn't figure out what they were saying. Most of all there was the weird choreography which made it seem as though it had been planned to shock the passing traffic as well as the pedestrians who just happened to find themselves there, aware that maybe any one of them could have been shot dead as dead—only for luck being on their side.

My telescopes were mounted on tripods. The most powerful one was aligned with the window that opened on to a small balcony. How could I complain? I had so much without anyone, aside from Mrs. Faulkner, suggesting I was spoiled. All I'd needed was a friend and when Mitzi came over to me that day, I knew I had found one—or better still she'd picked me.

Mother had mistaken my telescopes for cameras and was awfully embarrassed on the evening she had ventured into my lair, asking me to take her photograph, "One you can keep in here, you know. Get it enlarged and put it in a frame, wouldn't that be sweet? Our secret snap-shot and taken by you." Her smile froze when I told her they weren't cameras. She blustered then, waving her hands and saying how she despaired of me, what with my big teeth and my funny eyes, my silence and "all that time spent down in the stables, with those dangerous animals and their excrement and the dirt and the dust, it can't be healthy."

She said my bedroom was a splendid place, "but mighty austere." Her using the word "austere" surprised her as it did me, because it was so precise and described it exactly. Such an interesting insight, not really something she'd say.

During a few months, when I was about thirteen or maybe fourteen, she would plan epic shopping sprees that usually culminated in a late lunch at a fancy restaurant named The Clock Tower. There'd be a pianist, one of several, on duty playing familiar tunes from the movies; tinkling, light playing in a style that would drive Father into a frenzy. Poor Mother, how she would smile with delight when she recognized the Lara theme from *Doctor Zhivago*, or that famous love song from *The Godfather*, a movie she had not enjoyed because of the violence. She wanted everything to be nice; a world full of flowers, beautiful clothes, and romance all nicely choreographed, not like real life.

*

Staring at my bedroom ceiling was what I did, for hours. Those posters of the constellations would somehow come to life; I imagined a comet bursting across the skies, a messenger from the heavens, some wayward god in the shape of a rogue star born of gases seething there somewhere, within the furious poetry of Copernicus's solar system. It was easy to get carried away, I guess, because I had learned a jumble of stuff from reading on my own, which made it more exciting. My room was on the corner of the house with large windows on two sides, and a small, walk-out balcony opening out from one of them. If I was lonely, which I suppose I was, I was never unhappy. But now as I think about Mother what I most remember is her picturesque misery, a mixture of hysteria and nervy despair. At times she moved about as if she had been physically beaten. During those dark phases she wore a large pair of men's pajamas, her own, not Father's. They had come from Scotland, some famous outfitters in the city of Edinburgh, and were made of something called *Black Watch* flannel—a soft and comforting fabric; the black and dark green set off her wide pale face and her guileless blue eyes. On her "mope days" her hair hung down, straight, no fancy waves, no clips or intricate French braid, no heavy scent of hairspray lingering in her wake. She shuffled about in slippers, whereas on her good days she always wore high heels, even in the house, clickety-clack, clacking on the polished wooden floors. The sound irritated Father who would complain about the unnecessary wear and tear she was "inflicting upon" the eighteenth-century timbers his grandfather had salvaged from an old church in Delaware. Before that they had been part of the deck of a sailing ship, a New England schooner. Father loved history, its continuity, and I inherited that from him.

I don't know when I began to suspect that she was seeing someone, a man I mean, not a therapist. Though, she did have plenty of shrinks. One character who pretended he came from Paris, France, but turned out to be a Midwesterner, from Illinois perhaps, had recommended that she should invest in a tank and fill it with seaweed, then lie in it for as long as she could take either the heat or the cold—I can't rightly recall which. Father found this hilarious and laughed loudly on hearing it. "I think my dear," he said in the kindly voice he would use to ease his clients through a crisis, "that he may be telling you to drown yourself. And that is one way of curing whatever it is from which you think you are suffering." Mother gazed at him and then me, wondering if she should smile happily and take it in good sport, which to be fair she did, and she laughed along with him in that eager-to-please way she always had.

A gentleman friend was inevitable. Mother loved attention. Attention was as important to her as affection, probably more so, and Father's irritatingly paternalistic attitude toward her was more insulting than aggression could ever be. She craved approval, admiration. She never invited kisses lest they muss her makeup. I couldn't imagine her engaged in sexual activity: it would have required a gymnastic commitment beyond her. Her petite body was at its most confident when upright, strapped into tight, uncomfortable-looking clothes. Yet there was also her collection of chiffon summer outfits, girls' dresses, which she favored for the luncheons she gave or for school events she attended usually with her blonde hair flowing down loose while the other mothers wore stiff jackets and sensible skirts, blouses with high collars, their faces creased with worry and household responsibility. Mother was more like a visitor in her own home. She would hold me at arm's length, examine my hair, urge me to use sunscreen, "even though your skin is so much darker than mine" and buff the top of my head.

By the time I was nine years old I was taller than her, so she took to blowing me hasty kisses before clacking off, clickety-clack, to wherever it was she was going.

For a while, on our enforced shopping expeditions, the ones I mentioned her planning when I think I was about fourteen, she would hold my hand, always complaining about the rough-ness of it. If she said it once, she must have said it one hundred times, "Well you haven't yet picked up any warts from those fool horses; and I do declare, for this we must be truly grateful."

Our hand-holding ended abruptly for good when she was stealing a glance at herself in the large display window of one of the pretentious department stores she frequented with the

devotion of a worshipper at prayer in a temple. There we were—
me at least a head taller and noticeably broader, wearing blue
jeans and a sweater, my brown hair hanging down around my
face to beyond my shoulders and her, all dressed up as if in a
Hollywood movie from another era. She gasped, startled at the
absurdity of our contrasting appearances and looked around, up
and down the street, checking for witnesses; before dropping my
hand, so much bigger than her thin, narrow one with its sharp
rings and the feel of fragile bird-bones.

At times I could sense her disappointment in herself for never
having been an involved mother. One day as she was driving us
back home after yet another white- linen-tablecloth high tea, I
asked her to pull over outside a drug store. She was surprised,
I rarely requested anything. But I needed sanitary pads. I got
out without asking for money, I had a twenty-dollar bill in my
pocket; it had been there for days. I ran to the store, waiting
at the entrance while a defiant-looking woman forced a dandy
stroller with its lace parasol out into the still sharp, late afternoon sunlight. Her rough movement woke the baby, who looked
startled and paused before beginning to wail.

When I got back to the car, Mother was also crying and
could barely speak. She asked me when my periods had begun,
I couldn't rightly remember as I was never ill or sore with them.
Some of the girls at school saw it as a badge of honor and put
forth the pain suffered as proof they had become women. For me
periods were just messy inconveniences, very heavy and lasting
about a week, maybe longer. "A year or so," I ventured, more to
give her an answer although I figure that it was roughly correct,
sometime during the previous summer, when it was hot and
there we were again, heading back into the warm weather. I had
said a year; it could have been ten months. It didn't matter, not
to me. But it did to her. "I should have told you about them,"

she had sobbed. "I should have told you. Prepared you better, prepared you . . ." Her voice had tailed off as if she was lost in thought. Then she became aware of me again and peered closely at my face like she suddenly realized that something important had happened to her, not to me, to her. That she had missed out on something. "It's a big deal," she said sadly, delicately patting her tears, a pulse fluttering at her neck. "You've grown up without me noticing." I could sense her sadness, and it was a sincere sadness, different from the irritated disappointment she had shown on the day she suggested I would enjoy watching reruns of that old TV serial, *Star Trek*. "It's all about space ships and aliens, weird planets and stuff, honey you'll love it." I must have looked horrified or something, all I had muttered pompously was that science fiction wasn't quite my idea of astral physics. But I doubt she had even heard me.

I didn't feel particularly grown-up, not then, not even now. To be honest about it, I was never that introspective or particularly interested in me; or about how I did in anything, except the riding because being a good rider was never enough. It was challenging, unpredictable and horses have minds of their own, along with very quick reactions. The more I improved, the more testing the horses became.

As for the periods, well they were a surprise and had begun unexpectedly. I woke up one morning, sticky with blood. Of course, I wondered had I somehow ruptured myself riding so much. I'm sure we had been taught about the female cycle in biology but clearly I must have missed that class. I was never too taken with human physiology. I did like botany, only my real love was physics, and had been from first discovering the drama to be beheld through a telescope and my holy trinity: Copernicus, Kepler, and Galileo. Their medieval world and their various disputes with the Church and God's teaching transfixed me. Much as I would have loved to I could not step back in time. More than 500 years separated me from those visionaries—if you date it from 1473, the birth of Copernicus; they were dust and yet I could examine the same skies that they had mapped and all that thrilled me.

It was also about that time that I took to drinking entire pitchers of orange juice, mainly at night. I never much cared for orange juice in the morning, but by evening I had a persistent craving for it. Perhaps the years wearing braces had tainted my taste for it, all that metal in my mouth had conspired to ruin the flavor of many things. But once the braces came off I rediscovered orange juice. My addiction worried Mother; she would fret and warn me that I would develop a stomach ulcer, "from all that sistic (she meant citric) acid." I never corrected her, consuming so much vitamin C my face should have glowed in the dark. Mrs. Faulkner always kept a supply of ice tea ready in the refrigerator for Father's clients and would at times run out of pitchers. She usually ended up in my room hunting them down.

*

Pride cometh before a fall. That may well be so. But I've never been proud and I was feeling very humble as I sat slumped in the bath, in water so hot my head felt ready to burst and the rest of me was as sore as I reckoned it was possible to be while still alive and outside of a hospital bed. The steam was doing its job, distracting me as I wondered how on earth I was going to haul my body out of Mother's sunken bath. I had thought it would be easier to get out of it in my then pulverized state. But the sides looked steeper than I had imagined causing me to think that perhaps I should have used my own conventional tub instead. At least there would be less chance of being caught by Mother who might have felt inclined to ask some questions.

Caution best describes my approach to most things. And I lay in that bath, counting up the fancy dress boxes from Mother's favorite department store, all stacked in a corner of the room. They were gorgeous presentation boxes, made of a padded cardboard, lovely to touch; pale gray with bands of dark rose and muted pink. Often they would be strewn about, as Mother delightedly displayed her finds of the day. There had been a day when she had gone out and bought the exact same outfit she had purchased some weeks earlier and not gotten around to wearing. When I was smaller I used to be captivated by the arrival of those beautiful, scented boxes, but soon realized that they only contained grown-up fashion, not toys or big dolls dressed in fairy princess costumes, and I lost interest. Mother would deposit the packaging and all those sheets of silvery tissue paper on the floor. After a shopping mission, while Mother posed before her full-length mirror, assessing each item, deciding its future, of which combination it could be part, Mrs. Faulkner quietly appeared and gathered the boxes, eventually taking them away, or sometimes immediately, but she hadn't gotten around to collecting boxes on that terrible day. There looked to be fancy debris left over from a couple of recent excursions, if none from that afternoon. I noticed boxes and wrapping on the floor, as I languished in the bath, contemplating my immediate dilemma: Galileo's wild display and why it had happened.

The more I rode that young black horse of treacherous disposition, the more I discovered about uncertainty. He was taciturn; unforgiving—as Billy Bob put it, "That damn horse has a mind of his own. No, make that two minds and youse gotta figure out the both of them." We got along, Galileo and me, up to a point.

He had been going to be sold as a yearling in a private deal and when that fell through, Father, having bred him out of one of his favorite brood mares, refused to allow him be sent to the sales as a reject. There was a principle involved, he had announced with a flourish, and Father was never a man to ignore principle.

One of Billy Bob's many contacts had arrived up from a big yard in Georgia, where I think Billy Bob used to work. This man whose voice I never even heard, was to start Galileo. He was a good enough rider; but the silent horseman was more decisive than subtle; you could see pretty quick that he had an even shorter fuse than the horse did. After about a month, or maybe six weeks, the fellow finished up and went back on home, leaving the young horse off to the fields to think about all the stuff he had learned. Then one fine day, while I was in the arena, riding one of Father's hunting mares, I noticed Billy Bob lurking down at the fence, watching us. I knew he would have something interesting to say, he always did. He knew how to do the best with a horse and recognized that each one is different. The mare I was riding had been a successful show jumper up to a certain level but then became mysteriously lame. The owner had sent her to Father but after a surprisingly short time considering his initial concern, had lost all interest in her recovery and phoned, leaving a curt instruction. "I'm thinking you can shoot her, she's had her chance and all." Even the secretary, who relayed the message, seemed disgusted. Father decided the mare would spend some months standing in, as long as it took, to allow her recover. "Her performance won't improve, she is at her limit. But with time she will heal," he had predicted. And he was right.

She was the classic nice horse; easy to ride and happy to be ridden. She took to me, probably because she had been pushed around like so many horses, regarded as a machine with no feelings. It makes me sick but don't let me get started. She was a bit flat I guess, not a show horse but then she had been a good jumper, nothing fancy but effective and willing. She had a very nasty white scar on each of her fronts; it was easy to guess why she had them and a long-healed ugly bow tendon on the left front as well as matching capped hocks behind. Anyhow she was now set up for life, Father was good to horses.

Billy Bob waited until we were finished working and I was riding out of the arena. He then shambled over in that unassuming walk of his that created the impression both his ankles had been broken sometime in the past and reaching up to pat the mare's neck, began his sales pitch. "I've been thinking, Missy Helen," he said, "you gotten strong and you really on the way to being mighty damn good now, so why not push yourself some? Git riding that young black fella when he come back in. He'll make you good, real good." Billy Bob radiated benevolence and he was excited by his proposal.

So was I, it would be a great test of my riding, I would have to get better, riding a horse that good would be the making of any rider and I had a secret weapon—Billy Bob. Yet again I thought of how lucky I was. Very few girls would have a horse like that just hanging around in their father's yard. Father being so indifferent to the commercial aspect of having horses, could concentrate on producing a small, select number of them. It was an elite sideline all tied up with the family tradition of breeding the best. For us it was not about money. The horse wasn't going anywhere and Father would never again speak to the man who had backed out of the private deal. Billy Bob would help me, I was thrilled and after I had returned the mare to her stall, I went down to the paddock to look at the black horse. Admittedly he was really a very dark bay, but he looked black and that was good enough for me. Father had mentioned naming him The Raven—more Poe stuff. But I had my own name for him; I would call him Galileo. Aside from a small white star, he had no markings and was exquisite, very fine and just over 16.2, "the big side of medium," as Father always said. The first time I sat on that horse I thought I was stepping way ahead of myself, but old Billy Bob just kept smiling, his dentures hopping with the thrill of his latest project. "You can ride him, you can ride him. Just keep your hands soft and not too much leg or he'll fly. Know what I mean?"

I did; I had found out real quick that he could indeed fly without warning. The first time I meant to squeeze him, it was more like a kick, he had responded by going from trot to gallop with no canter transition in between. I lurched forwards like a beginner and grabbed on to his mane. It sure was embarrassing but useful; it showed me exactly how quickly he could move. I rode him as if he was made of glass. A bird could have landed on my head and I would never have noticed; I was focused that hard on being relaxed and had entered a place known as abject terror—but if I could learn from the fear, I would become really good—or at least that was my reasoning. I had a purpose. Aside from simply trying to remain alive, I had this thrilling horse and I had Billy Bob—between the two of them I had been given the clichéd chance of a lifetime, only an idiot would turn it down.

Galileo wasn't perfect. He had two off-putting habits; he snorted very loudly while tossing his head around and he often just stomped the ground with a ferocity which was new to me. Billy Bob laughed it off. I went along with it and the first few weeks of riding the horse was so nervous I took to song to cover my fear, even when he bucked I sang, more shouting than singing, anything that came into my head, even the national anthem, not an easy tune to sing at the best of times.

It was obvious that he was still at the stage where he needed a rider who knew more than him, and far more than me. He was willing and responsive, moved like a dressage horse, yet was still

capable of being startled by whatever it was that had sent me flying not so much over the jump but, far more painfully, into it. A
hind leg had also got me, right in the ribs, and I wasn't quite sure
which pains came from my fall and which were added by being
kicked, and he had walked on various parts of me, but it was all
very hazy. Maybe I was concussed? I did see stars, a great many
of them. It must have looked hilarious, I yelped with laughter
at the thought of it, before wincing in pain. My ribs hurt and
laughing made them even worse.

One thing I was certain of though as I lay gazing at Mother's
elegant dress boxes—two of which were particularly large and
may well have held more of those loathsome fur coats to which
she was partial—was that my first reaction after discovering that
I was still alive had been: did anyone see it? There was no denying that I was Mother's daughter after all, worried about what
others would say. I hadn't noticed Billy Bob watching us, as he
often did, standing at the fence, squiring his Monticello, out for
a walk. That adorable horse always looked magnificent, his coat
shining, silky red mane perfect, ears pricked, a king, regal, until
he began to move in that slow, painful shuffle. Billy Bob would
inch along with him, coaxing him and telling him over and over,
"You is the best horse, the finest horse in the universe, God's Man
and all and more. Best horse in the universe," I was hoping that
Billy Bob had not witnessed the spectacle. It wasn't pride, not at
all; I just didn't want to be advised against riding Galileo.

After such a disaster I needed to climb back on, it would be
easy to lose my nerve, not just for riding him, any horse. It was
something I had heard many times, especially from older women.
They would tell each other how they had hunted and jumped
and then one fine day realized that suddenly they'd become
scared, and had crossed the dread imaginary line, often without

even having had a fall, and lost their nerve. Once the horse feels the rider tense up, it's all over—leastways for the human.

Shivers ran through me. The water was still hot, but I was shaking. Maybe this was shock? God, what next? I thought. I know, Mother will appear with more shopping, yet another dress to try on and study from all angles, posing like a Spanish dancer, raising her arms above her head, stamping her feet. I opened the hot faucet, more steamy water gushed out. I lay back, imagining the assorted pains, one by one, drifting out of me. That didn't happen. Perhaps I dozed off? Suddenly the water was cold and the bubbles had vanished. Time to run a fresh bath, I reached for another of Mother's many jars and bottles of bubble bath and salts and tipped half the contents of one with pinkish gravel in it, down into the bath. It hit the enamel beneath me. Another jar had an eye-catching label, proclaiming in bold print that it was a Natural De-Stressor, it looked like green goo. In it went with more hot water. It was still bright outside. Had Galileo forgotten the entire episode? Was he eating his hay? Did he reckon he'd won some stupid battle with me?

He had stood watching in the arena as I crawled to my feet and somehow reached for his reins and led him back to the stable, attempting to walk normally. After I removed his tack, I slid the saddle onto a low rack and just carried the bridle up to the house with me as I couldn't reach its usual hook for pain. There was no chance I could brush him. It took incredible effort bending down to unfasten his tendon boots, although for once he didn't lift his feet and snort at me . . . Galileo was quiet, not contrite, but quiet. I hadn't reprimanded him; I hadn't even raised my voice in the arena and was silent in the stable, too shook to speak.

Walking semi-normally to the house required immense concentration. I hoped no one would come along, I felt like a cartoon character that had been squashed flat by a steam roller. Father was having a telephone conversation in his den; all I could hear was his voice with long pauses in between. Mrs. Faulkner was busy in the kitchen, preparing supper. If this was a novel or a movie she would have appeared at my side, her face creased with sympathy, a tray of orange juice in one hand and a discreet bottle of powerful pain killers in the other. But it was real life, I was so sore and weak and ready to burst out laughing before beginning to scream with pain. Maybe go to the bathroom, right there on the hall carpet. I'd limped to the staircase and grabbed the banister, edging my way up the steps, one at a time and still urgently needing to pee but holding on.

Having decided that Mother's bath would be easier to struggle out of, I headed toward her quarters; her bathroom was more like a large dressing area within a sitting room that just happened to also have a bath in it. My eyes stared back at me, I looked insane. My face was streaked with dirt and tears, although I hadn't realized I had been crying. My hair was flattened from my riding helmet that I had dropped along the way. Perhaps it was back in the tack room? I didn't know. My nose was bleeding, as were my teeth. I peered closely in the mirror, and then rinsed my mouth out. Perhaps due to shock my expensive teeth somehow looked bigger than usual but still perfect, none missing, no chips. It was my lip that was cut. Scratches and small cuts had appeared on my face. I looked away and then fell over as I was attempting to sit on the edge of the bath. I needed to take my boots off, luckily I was wearing an old pair of short ones but it still took a long time to push them off. My sweaty socks then obligingly came off with them. I collapsed on to the toilet but the lid had slapped down and well I peed over it and couldn't help noticing that my urine looked awfully yellow on the white floor tiles.

My sweater was tricky to remove as I couldn't raise my arms; I did get out of my jodhpurs but still had on a shirt and my "Iron Maiden" no-nonsense sports bra, all straps, to prize off along with my panties.

The first time I tried to fill the bath the faucet was so tight I couldn't move it. There was no chance Mother's frail and delicate wrists had closed it so firmly. Then I realized she wouldn't have cleaned the bath and it probably only seemed tight because I was so feeble. Good old bad temper came to my assistance and out blasted the hot water. Which bubble bath would be most likely to fix me? I wondered, powder, liquid, or gel.

I lurched heavily down into the bath, a dead weight, causing the water to shift and then began removing my underwear. If I remain very still, the pain will seep away, I had thought. It didn't.

What day was it? Where was Mother? What were the chances of her walking in? What would I say? I was too sore to think. She would probably breeze in, remind me not to forget to use conditioner and breeze out again. She had been buoyant, far less needy. Come to think of it, she was out a lot around that time. She'd had her reasons.

*

Back upstairs in my bedroom after the horrors in the kitchen; the policemen's visitation and everything else, I struggled with sliding *Bridge Over Troubled Water* out of its sleeve. That's when I noticed how much my hands were shaking. Finally I managed to position the record on the turntable, aware that although I had wanted to listen to it for my own comfort, the playing of it had by then become a personal tribute to Mother's memory.

She had followed Simon and Garfunkel from their folk club beginnings, having been introduced to their music by an early suitor of hers from Queens who had been a musician and half-knew Paul Simon. I had only discovered Simon and Garfunkel long after they had broken up; in fact it was all the fuss over the *Graceland* album that first alerted me to Paul Simon and from that—on to his backlist which I then investigated with my customary relentless zeal. Soon I knew most of the songs by heart. Mother had been surprised and smilingly emotional when she walked into my room, drawn by tunes familiar to her which she had never associated with me. She began to sing along in her thin, breathy girl's voice and told me about the pilgrimage she had undertaken in 1981, traveling all alone to New York for that famous reunion concert in Central Park. It was early fall and I would have been about eleven and back at school. I didn't know she'd gone, I would never have noticed. I can still visualize that soft, faraway look on her face when she described being among an audience of 500,000, all gathered together on a September evening "in a park in the middle of one of the world's greatest cities" she'd whispered. Mother loved New York. Soon after that when she gave me the *Bookends* album, she said she was "passing on a sacred text," which I guess she was. As some critic or other once proclaimed, "America," Paul Simon's seductive anthem of an innocence lost and gone forever, is the most famous track.

But before we, the chief mourners, had dispersed on that night of the killing, Father going into his study, having canceled three consultations with anxious trainers; me pausing in the cloakroom off the hall, before returning upstairs, Mrs. Faulkner had stepped toward us and considering her legendary reticence, unexpectedly spoke. I often relive the moment she suddenly materialized that evening, so silently, breaking the spell we were under. She had been standing in the shadows—or would

have been had there been any—conscious of being caught on
the edge of a human tragedy that had nothing to do with her.
Mother had been little more than an absentee employer. They
barely exchanged a word: Mrs. Faulkner recited her lists for the
day; and Mother, an ineffectual figurehead to be sure, ever eager
to convey the impression that she had of course been thinking
along the exact same lines—which she most certainly had not—
always agreed fullheartedly, just short of clapping her hands with
delight. They hadn't known each other at all. Yet the horrific circumstances of Mother's very public death had certainly distressed
Mrs. Faulkner, whose restrained bewilderment touched me in a
way I had not foreseen.

Perhaps as a crime, it was not that unusual. Richmond for
all its surface civility had a shameful reputation for violence,
ranking at that time about ninth on the national average. One
of the policemen said that when he and his colleagues had come
to our house. It was as if he was trying to make us feel a bit
better. Old hatreds tend to fester long and slow in the South.
Mother's killing was not about hate though, it was caused by passion, admittedly a perverted love that may have been provoked,
taunted, exploited, and frustrated before being dragged down a
million little alleyways of her boredom and his hurt. As I saw
it, at least initially, she had encouraged it and then settled into
treating their arrangement with a casual lightheartedness as if to
reverse by proxy the multiple humiliations Father had dealt her
and well, this tentative, ritualized revenge appeared to have cost
Mother her life.

The truth did out as it usually does and it seemed that, except
for Father and me, a sizeable number of observers had known all
about Mother's affair. It was not her first, though it was clearly
the most complicated as we were to discover. Several of her quasi-
intimates had been there as this one had begun, then flourished

and went from coy and cute and something salacious to gossip about, to a serious situation, before ending so tragically. Father had been given many hints by well-wishers, some concerned, others gloating, and had countered, declaring, "My, my; is that a fact?" ensuring that his apparent amusement deflected the scandal, and it did, leastways for a while. Mother's beau was the son of a local millionaire. The young man, Walter Welter, was rich and idle; ideally suited to pursuing an old-style summer courtship. He drove a vintage roadster; it was cream in color and had a novelty Klaxon—a 1920s varsity one like something F. Scott Fitzgerald may have once coveted, or perhaps had considered writing about. The besotted Walt would present Mother with gifts, and wait for hours in uptown fashion showrooms as she tried on evening gowns—a hobby of hers. He almost always arrived bearing flowers and baskets of fruit, particularly plums and apricots, apples that shone as if polished   which he would have had the time to do. He was twenty-nine, thirteen years her junior, almost as big as the sixteen-year age gap between Mother and Father, who was fifty-eight when she was murdered. I hadn't known how old my parents were until I read it in the newspaper.

Highly unsettling, to be reading about your parents I mean; I found out things about them at the same time as total strangers would have, assuming they'd been reading the same reports. That was when I discovered that what I had always believed to be one of Father's little witticisms, the one about him marrying a debutante, was close on true. Mother had been a minor beauty queen and had progressed to the finals of Miss America—I thank God that she didn't win, how Father would have taunted her of former glories. Nor had I ever known that he had been married before and that his first wife had also been killed, except her death was an accident. She had broken her neck while hunting and Father, having ordered her horse be shot on the spot, had held her in his arms as she died. Mother would have regarded that catastrophe as tremendously romantic; it may even have helped her think, if only for a while, that it was the reason that she had fallen in love with Father, a widower who had endured deep personal sorrow.

*

I can only speculate as to how much Mrs. Faulkner had known before the reporters had gotten busy but when she stepped toward us that evening and uttered, like the good Baptist woman she was, "May the Lord have mercy on her soul," she conferred a quiet dignity on the madness. She just turned then and slowly walked out of the hall and back into the kitchen. I could hear the screen door close behind her and her footsteps fade on the path outside as she left for the night. The crickets seemed louder than usual. I had gone into the little cloakroom, the one with the hunting prints and the antique pair of riding boots kept in shape by wooden boot trees, and raised the toilet lid but dropped it straight away because I didn't need to use it. Instead I again tried to pull the boot trees free but as always couldn't, they were jammed fast, almost fused with the leather. I stood at the sink and opened both faucets, and splashed water on my face. Then I said out loud to my reflection, "Mother died today. My mother is dead." Perhaps I had half-expected my hair to have turned white with the shock? I think it is shock that makes that happen, although prolonged grieving probably does age a person more cruelly, I don't know. My hair was still brown, but my ill-matched eyes were wide and scared looking. I wondered what Mother's last thought had been and did she know that her "ridiculous boy"—that apparently, again according to the newspapers, was her pet name for the obsessive Walt—had slain her. Did she smile at him as he approached? Did she think he was going to make a grand announcement, drop on one knee and declare his undying love while ordering her, "at once and for all," to leave Father. Had she been about to laugh and tease him a bit, offer him another chance, before dashing off with him again for one last drive in the roadster? Did she realize she was going to die? Did she cry out in fear or surprise or both? What did she feel when the first bullet hit her and the world turned black? Was she relieved it was finally over and that at long last she wouldn't have to try so hard to be happy?

I lay on my bed, gazing at the ceiling, looking at the stars in the posters and the charts, the photographs of outer space, the heavens. Then turned on my side and stared at an enlarged, close-up picture of Saturn, its rings shimmering as the evening faded, night was closing in. The image was pinned to my wall, beside the bed. I liked seeing Saturn in the pale light of morning, the first thing to meet my eyes when I woke. It had been Galileo who had noticed something odd about that planet. I tried to recall the name of the Dutch astronomer who had eventually proven that there was a ring around Saturn. My mind was blank and I panicked until the name came back to me; Christiaan Huygens. Anytime I forget something I know, I get real upset. It's as if information is a lifeline for me. My memory is a precious retreat. Huygens had built a telescope far more powerful than the one Galileo had used. Relieved that I had retrieved the name, I rolled over, onto my back and continued examining my ceiling. The rings of Saturn, each a vast halo composed of hundreds of sharply defined ringlets, all there only millions of miles away.

Pretty soon it would be dark and I could gaze at the actual sky, not as dramatic as the more specific depiction on the posters and enlarged closeup photographs, but vast, so immense.

Mother would not be coming home, no busy clickety-clack on the polished wood. Simon and Garfunkel sang on. I hadn't been thinking of title songs and tracks when I had first heard "Bridge Over Troubled Water," it was the song alone that had struck me and it was being sung by a woman. Her name was Nana Mouskouri, she had a lilting soprano, slightly accented and apparently she was very famous, a smiling Greek superstar who looked like a friendly librarian equipped with substantial black-framed spectacles. It had been the song that I had liked; it resembled an easeful Baptist hymn. I mentioned it at school and about three girls sat me down during recess to explain its origins. It must have been a major novelty being able to impart information to the resident class know-it-all. My musical interests were not exactly contemporary; Bach, Beethoven, Schubert and Chopin, a lot of Brahms, dominated my record collection. My music appreciation essay got an A but the teacher didn't ask me to read it out to the class. It would not have gone as well as the two papers on Bob Dylan had or the several homages to Leonard Cohen, and although the four on Neil Young all sounded pretty much the same, each was applauded enthusiastically in a way my celebration of Bach's pioneering use of counterpoint and his response to French and Italianate influences might not have been. The girls were always nice to me, even when their eyes would glaze over as I was called upon to outline yet another historical event or explain a particularly interesting scientific fact, recite the Latin homework or maybe solve a math problem on the blackboard. Everyone seemed to indulge my interest in space and the solar system as if it was an endearing eccentricity to be nurtured. When the picture of me and Galileo was in the paper, no one laughed or mentioned the misspelling of my name. They just applauded and treated me as if I was special and not merely different. Mitzi's interest in me was never resented; the girls seemed pleased that she was able to understand me and that we got along so well, even though she was a lot more like them.

After Mother's murder, my classmates were real kind. Such befuddled sympathy was shown to me by girls I had known yet not known throughout my schooling. It was so heartfelt it made me cry in a way that her death somehow had not. I'm ashamed to admit, I felt so sorry for her, for the squalor and the cruelty of her death, the apparently infantile lover, but it was the sorrow of one human for another, not the heart-wrenching desolation of having lost a parent.

"Sail on, silvergirl, / Sail on by. / Your time has come to shine / All your dreams are on their way." Mother had no dreams now, but she was shining in a grotesque kind of way, all the compassionate descriptions of her idiot lover who agreed that "yes" he had killed her and "yes" he had loved her and "yes" he too wanted to die so that they would be together for ever, appeared to further diminish her. There seemed to be no need for a trial, what with Walt, convinced he had struck some profound blow in the name of love eternal, bragging about having slain Mother and his reasoning on the subject being written about by a squadron of understanding reporters intent on immortalizing his every banal utterance—there must not have been any other news going on just then. Meanwhile his family were busy proving he was insane and that it had all been a mistake. Father offered no opinions. He stood aloof and had taken to gazing at people, rarely replying as he studied their faces, looking for clues in which he had but marginal interest.

So much attention; heavy automobiles proceeded slowly up the avenue and many visitors, mainly women, got out, dressed in black or navy, a few even wore veils, all come to commiserate with Father. It was then that I first perceived how much his detached manner seemed to attract the matrons of this world.

How odd it was to see them cradle his large, long hands in their gloved ones and simper up into his face, pause slightly, before collapsing into discreetly lady-like sobs. Father looked on, perfectly still and attentive until whoever it was that was weeping before him moved reluctantly away, allowing another bereft female to take her place and commence a share of the lamentation. It was a pageant put on for Father, while Mother was merely a conduit. That angered me some. When it was my turn for the women to hug me and stroke my hair, they were doing it to impress Father, not offer me comfort. Very few of them even knew my name, none asked. The Richmond widow women were out in their numbers; Father was suddenly available, and in need of a companion by their reasoning, if not his.

*

Before the trial got going though, there would have to be a funeral. Father commenced retreating into his study. When he shut the door, it remained closed. Only Mr. Caleb Montgomery, his lawyer and close friend, a thin, loosely-put-together individual who always brought to mind *The Legend of Sleepy Hollow*, disregarded that door. During that strange interlude following Mother's death, he would arrive at the house, walk straight on in through to the hall, no knocking, and hand his coat and fancy walking stick to Mrs. Faulkner, without a, "Good morning. How you doing?" demand a pot of coffee and "Some of your mighty fine pie" of her, and march over to Father's study.

On one particular day I'd gone back up to my room, going riding seemed disrespectful in the circumstances, so had eating, although Mrs. Faulkner tried to fortify me with grilled cheese sandwiches, the only food I could face. I planned on reading or just thinking. It was humid; time had become hazy, slowed right down. There was no breeze.

After a while Mrs. Faulkner tapped on my door and announced I was wanted downstairs. By then I had already made my visit, the previous afternoon I think, to the funeral parlor to see Mother. That had been unsettling: Mother lying there in white satin, her face pinker than I remembered; her hair more yellow. A little spray of violets had been artfully placed on the pillow beside her head, I guess to conceal the part of her skull that was damaged or missing. The undertakers had given her an inane smile, slightly exposing her front teeth. Her hands were joined. There was a sickly sweetish smell, I thought of Snow White in her glass box. A man in a dark suit appeared beside me. "Your momma looks right pretty, don't she?" he asked, expecting my approval of his work. I don't know if I said anything, just walked on out of the room, as if the floor was tilted slightly forward, and I feared I would fall over. My feet were sinking into the thick pile carpet and I needed to go to the bathroom.

It was to transpire that Father had not viewed Mother, but I didn't know that until weeks later. He just told me as if he was commenting on the news of the day. In fact he had come into the kitchen and was looking at the morning's baking, all lined up on a side counter still oven-warm; plain stuff, apple pies, bread, sourdough biscuits, nothing fancy, not of the decorative quality that Mitzi's family were to introduce to us all. Father examined the baking, as if he alone had been entrusted with a prize to award, only was not convinced that these conventional efforts merited it. I was reading a biography of Copernicus; it was opened on the page with a picture caption about the publication of his theory of the Sun-centered Universe. Father picked up the hefty tome. He liked to peruse any open book he happened upon. Neither of us spoke. Then he said that he could recall exactly when my interest in space had begun. He took me by surprise making a nostalgic comment like that and he peered directly at me and said that he could see me still, as I had been, a small child dressed in "some fancy outfit your mother would have purchased when she still saw you as a doll to wrap," he laughed, as I did. Mother never had hidden her disappointment at my lack of "commitment" to fashionable clothing. "There you were, out there on that front porch," said Father, "and you stepped down and out on to the lawn, into the bright light of day." He paused, and I hoped he wouldn't cry, I wouldn't know what to do, but he didn't. Instead he looked away, into the past, before turning back to me. My exact words, he recalled with a rueful expression on his face, had been, "I wonder where the sun goes when it goes down?"

He watched for my reaction. Try as I might I could not rec-ollect saying anything about the sun, but I knew I had always wondered about it. So many Christmas Eve nights I'd also tried to stay awake to hear the reindeer on the roof and a few times imagined hearing distant bells, the jangle of the sleigh as Santa Claus approached. "You were a clever child, very clever, you still have curiosity. It is a wondrous quality." I was touched by Father's words and his sincerity. Although we weren't close, I was aware that we were equally repressed; too reserved, self-reliant—him with his secrets, me with my dreams—I knew he was proud of me. As a daughter I was about as close to being a son as I could be without actually being a boy. That morning was when he admitted that he never had looked at Mother all laid out in the funeral parlor. He had gotten to the door of the room she was in and he told me that he could see the open casket and the white material, the pillow, her hair, but he didn't look at her face. "And, to think that I told you that you should," he said, and he seemed to regret his instruction. Then he stood silent for a moment, lost in his thoughts and said he always believed that there was something distinctly unnatural about a face being readjusted to meet its maker.

Well he had told me to view her, and I obeyed. The casket was closed for the service, on his request. And yes, the service, that was why I had been summoned down to the study. Mr. Montgomery had decided to discuss the funeral arrangements with Father and me.

*

St Paul's Episcopal Church it was. There had been no discussion; I could have guessed Father would have chosen it. It had a special place in history; General Lee had been given a pew there. He had walked up the aisle on that famous April morning after the surrender and knelt down beside the black man whose dramatic gesture in making the first move to communion had made clear to all present that the old South was finally dead. Lee had always maintained that slavery was a far greater evil for the white man than the black, so it was fitting that he had led the white part of the congregation to the altar rail in St Paul's. I had never really regarded it as a church; for me it was an historic building symbolizing Richmond's past and so had been erected in Capitol Square according to the Greek revival style beloved by Thomas Jefferson. A tall spire had once dominated the building, but had been damaged and later removed as a hazard following a hurricane in 1900, and that splendid little dome only dates from then.

Our class had visited St Paul's, about three years before Mother was killed, as part of a history tour. I knew the church

and its famous memorial stained-glass windows, most depicting angels, commemorating departed parents and children—
because of the project we later did, not through attending services. Father hadn't prayed there either. He admired the building
for its aesthetics as well as its prime location across the road from
Jefferson's state capital and the federal court house that had, since
the killing, acquired an entirely new relevance for us. Mother had
never stepped foot inside St Paul's, or any other historic building. She used to say that history gave her the creeps, "Just the
thought of all those dead people piled up somewhere under the
ground, pushing their way back toward the living makes my skin
feel like little black ants are crawling all over me." She certainly
had a singular way of looking at things.

Mr. Montgomery was pacing courtroom-style about the
study, convinced he alone was dictating proceedings. Not that he
was facing any opposition. Father was sitting at the desk watching his friend but saying little. Father looked tired, drained; or
maybe it was just that he had gotten old, and it was showing—
him being not all that far off of sixty, as I was suddenly aware,
having read it in the newspapers. And to me that was old—
Robert E. Lee had been all of sixty-three when he died and I
remember looking at those early photographs and thinking he
must have been ancient when he was in his forties during the mid
to late 1850s. Now in the context of the funeral, I thought again
and figured that Lee had been fifty-eight when he followed the
black man up the aisle in 1865, the same age as Father was when
Mother was . . . when she died. True, Lee looked almost Biblical
but everyone looked older in nineteenth-century photographs,
what with the stiff hair and the high collars. Every face I looked
at, male or female, appeared to be a variation of Queen Victoria's.

Still, Father was old and had, through no fault of his own,
seen off two wives. Kepler had died at fifty-eight—easy to see the

way in which my mind works . . . The discussion in Father's study had moved on to the choice of music. He became animated and said that he was considering playing Fauré's Pavane. He reckoned he could get a decent tune out of the church organ but then slapped the flat of his hand down on the desk, causing the old leather blotter to sigh at the disturbance. "Even better, we could get a small piano in . . ." He looked eagerly at Mr. Montgomery, then at me—I was standing near the door, my backside and ribs continuing to remind me of my little tumble off Galileo—and as if drawing us into his plans, Father concluded he would indeed be happier playing a piano.

Well Mr. Montgomery's face was a study in various shades of red. I knew his thoughts were running along the same lines as mine and it was easy to predict what he was going to say next. "You can't do that William, it'll never work, as sure as day follows night, it will . . ." The skinny lawyer, a born dandy to the soles of his immaculate, handmade brogues, paused as if to gather himself for the effort he felt required to rein in Father's monomania. He reminded Father that he was a confirmed improviser, and while this was a most entertaining facility at a social gathering, it would not be suitable for a church service. Father would heed any score up to a certain point and then begin improvising, drifting away from the original and adding various asides and riffs all of his own devising. Eventually he might return to the piece he had initially sat down to play as composed, but then again, he might not. For an individual as stern and disciplined as he undoubtedly was, Father's whimsy surfaced whenever his attention turned to the piano.

Added to that were the funny noises he made. Why the truth is, Father pulled such crazy faces and rotated his body, humming and laughing, and more than giving Glenn Gould a run for his money when seated at the keyboard. Not saying for a moment that he could play as well as Gould but he imposed his personality on whatever he happened to be playing. The Fauré had been scored for an orchestra and a choir reasoned Mr. Montgomery, who had had advanced piano lessons as a boy and remained very interested in music, regularly attending concerts and recitals as far away as Chicago and New York. Father interjected claiming that he had heard an old recording of no less than Fauré himself on solo piano.

"That may well be so, but you sit yourself down and play as the muse hits you, William, and well that ole service could meander on for hours, the preacher will just up and walk . . . this here event is no concert, it's a burial for a most tragic . . ." the lawyer stopped speaking and sighed, shrugging with a stagey exasperation that nonetheless suggested suppressed traces of amusement just bubbling away and ready to run. There was something unexpectedly human about watching those two old friends, stiff and formal as they were, rubbing off each other. Mr. Montgomery did seem genuinely concerned about the funeral proceedings and mentioned that he had something else to tell us. But first he was anxious to finalize the music.

Father kept insisting that he should play at Susan's funeral. "Susan?" I must have started and without even looking at me, Father sensed my surprise. He glanced toward the window and cleared his throat, steadying himself, before telling me that "Susan" had been Mother's given name. "One she never much liked though; so when I met her first, I told her to just select another and she did exactly that." According to Father, she'd always wanted to be called Isabel. "Yes sir," said Father softly, "Isabel, Isabella. Who said I never indulged her? I did. I did. But that kind of thing can't go on forever and a day and . . ." he dropped his voice right down and he concentrated on aligning his desk blotter, muttering soft to himself, "and it didn't."

I'd never heard "Susan," although now that I think of it, I can't rightly recall Father addressing Mother by any name.

My concentration was drifting. Aware that my stomach felt gassy I nonetheless suspected I could be hungry. I was sickish, queasy, yet suddenly craved buttered toast with maple syrup of all things. Maybe I'd just walk out but decided to stay; my presence had been requested after all. The little, book-lined room was stuffy, heated by the bodies of the two men, their heavy suits, the dark fabric of which had that smell of dust and old sofas. There was also that distinctive scent of starch issuing forth from their laundered shirts. Little circles of steam sneaked out of the spout of the coffee pot and Mr. Montgomery was waving his smelly, damp-looking cigar in the air, like a band leader wary of losing the attention of his charges.

"How about Mozart 21? You know, the piano concerto?" Father suggested. "She seemed to like that," and he smiled confidently. But that came with an unpleasant story, one I had personally witnessed. My parents had been invited to a fancy supper by Mr. Dell Hutton, one of Father's clients, an old-money family with racehorses and much else besides, what Mother would refer to as "real class." This man had endowed various cultural projects including our school's senior orchestra, and he had finally achieved a minor victory on the racetrack. He wanted to celebrate by hosting an evening in a fine downtown restaurant famed for its bad-tempered, highly skilled Swiss chef. Father liked Mr. Dell Hutton. I had been invited because I had won a competition in which the man's son, Edmund Dell Hutton III—whom I liked and whose non-rider girlfriend (who favored Ralph Lauren clothing inspired by, but not intended for, horse riding) followed him everywhere . . . young Edmund, my secret fantasy love object—was a good rider but had not placed, although his horse had been shipped in from Germany and moved like a precision-built machine. My inclusion most likely was to prove that this family was far above the petty rivalries enacted on the field of sport.

Recorded music was being played at a discreet volume so as not to compete with the murmur of the diners' voices. After a while, something very familiar began. Mother's eyes lit up and she gave a start, mighty pleased crying out: "Oh that's *Elvira Madigan!*" Father shot back: "No, that's Mozart." But Mother was not to be corrected and insisted, "No, that's *Elvira Madigan*, I'd know it anywhere. William, you are quite wrong and this time I am corr-ect." She beat out the word in two halves, her certainty filling her with pleasure. But Father slammed home his advantage, announcing coldly, "Mr. Mozart wrote that about 170 odd years before a Swedish movie director whose name momentarily eludes me, came along and hijacked the second movement of that Concerto Number 21." He told her that the piece she thought she knew from the movie, was called the andante. He had announced this most pedantically and paused before continuing, "Meaning nice and slow, ideal for a suicide pact devised by doomed lovers, the pretty dancing girl cum circus acrobat and her deserter from the army." He smiled around the table, expecting amused appreciation of his casual knowledge, before resting his gaze, minus the smile, on Mother. Her face fell but she sat up straight, proclaiming, "Well, La Di Da, La Di Da" with a shaky laugh.

Her embarrassment filtered down the table toward me as if I would absorb it; Mother's faltering bravado was most painful to witness. Little gulping sounds accompanied her efforts. Even the "La Di Da" was delivered flat and lame. It had been very popular for a while after *Annie Hall* came out, and everyone seemed to have adopted it, along with the heroine's baggy shirts and ties and waistcoats and her easy country manner. But the movie reference had gotten pretty stale by then. "My dear wife knows nothing about music but she does enjoy a catchy tune." Father resumed eating, pleased with his cleverness, but all conversation had ceased. Our host was a gentleman and he was most affronted on Mother's behalf. He had unexpectedly—for him—discovered that Father had a mean side and so Mr. Dell Hutton II declared that he might just head on home. The evening had ended. His wife, prim and disapproving, was avoiding all eyes, and stood up, waiting for her husband to slide her jacket about her shoulders. They were polite people, the Dell Huttons, there was no scene. But their shared distaste for such unseemly behavior was obvious. They had in fact conducted themselves in much the way Father might have done in a different situation.

Fauré's Requiem was Father's next idea and he looked directly at Caleb Montgomery expecting agreement. He suggested asking Kathleen Battle, and said he recalled hearing that she had sung for the pope the previous year. "And she's an Ohio girl, just like Susan," he announced in triumph. The chances of getting an opera singer to perform at a private funeral were slight, countered our legal advisor, who again asked Father why he was so intent on selecting music that had nothing to do with Mother, reminding him that the program should reflect Mother's personality, not his. "Play 'Dixie' then, 'In Dixieland I'll live and die,' she saw herself as an adopted daughter of the South . . ." Mr. Montgomery directed a disgusted glance at Father before inclining his head sympathetically toward me, disassociating himself from the attempted joke. "That's a marching tune, William, entirely inappropriate," he said, in the tone of a disappointed teacher. Father realized silence was more prudent. That was when I made my contribution, mentioning that Mother had liked Simon and Garfunkel and said "Bridge Over Troubled Water" would be a good choice, describing it as a hymn, almost spiritual. And then I suggested "The Only Living Boy in New York": "It's about someone who has gone away . . . and there's another song . . ." I was speaking quickly, aware that I was making a case for Mother as a person who had lived her life in her own way. "There's a sweet little tune, 'April Come She Will,' it's almost prophetic, it sums up a life." What with Father and Mr. Montgomery giving me their full attention, I felt my face growing hot and I knew I was speaking faster and faster, intent on saying as much as I could before I lost my audience and Father did his usual thing—that habit of looking away with a disappointed sigh.

Don't quite know what came over me but one minute I was saying: "It's called 'April Come She Will'" and the next I was singing: "When streams are ripe and swelled with rain / May, she will stay / Resting in my arms again." Father stared full at me, I could sing well enough, just about, for alto in a school choir, a small solo now and again, and my voice that day in Father's airless study became flat if more strident, "June, she'll change her tune / In restless walks she'll prowl the night"— that got a reaction from Mr. Montgomery—"July, she will fly / And give no warning to her flight. / August, die she must / The autumn winds grow chilly and cold / September, I'll remember / A love once new has now grown old." They both stared at me, I stood firm and Father seemed thoughtful, conceding that it just about summed it all up—"'Die she must' and die she did." Caleb Montgomery smiled at me as if he was a benign uncle and I felt truly sickened by his presumptuous familiarity before recollecting that he was in fact my godfather. "Well, listen to you Miss Helen, aren't you an able songstress? My, where did that old brown eye come from? Your mother's were blue . . ." He stopped and had the grace to blush, recalling full well that my eyes were a taboo subject. But Father just waded on in and told him that

Mother had often suggested that I buy myself blue contact lenses. "Don't you heed either of us Miss Helen," Mr. Montgomery neatly countered, telling me that the man that would marry me would love me for both my eyes and all the rest of me as well. It was said with some gallantry and I had learned to live with my eyes, or at least, on that particular day, felt sure I had.

And that's how I came to sing at Mother's funeral. Singing for my dead Mother and dressed in one of her exclusive designer coats. Mrs. Faulkner must have been aware that I had nothing suitable to wear and she arrived up at my door, tap, tap, saying quietly in that concise manner of hers, "This might fit you Miss Helen, it's a dramatic garment, no denying." It was a long black evening coat, protected in a plastic covering and most likely never worn. The coat was cut like a man's tailcoat, very elegant. Black raw silk and lined in dark blue satin, a pinch tight across my shoulders, short in the sleeves, but it had a swishing urgency as I moved and made me feel like a figure of immense mystery and resolve. On the morning of the funeral Father scrutinized the coat and said I looked like a young Bismarck, about to address the Prussian court. I had been thinking along more imaginative lines, yet Father did react to the drama of my funeral apparel. It was not at all typical of Mother's taste in clothes. Its tailored simplicity must have impressed her; she probably felt obliged to buy it without really wanting to wear it. "My mother, your grandmother," Father began with the wistful low voice he adopted when referring to the past, "had a wardrobe of suitable attire specifically purchased for funerals and similarly solemn occasions. She was a practical woman, very organized . . ." His thoughts trailed off elsewhere and he forgot all about me. Always that distance between him and the world.

Yet I felt I had caught some insight into his tormented musings on that day as Mr. Montgomery spoke with us about the funeral. You see, aside from the music, there was the coming legal case hovering in the background and as Mr. Montgomery began saying his piece that's when we appreciated that Mother's little romance was far more complex, tragic, and a great deal more meaningful than either Father or I had up until then grasped. We, well me, and I guess Father was as bad, or as insensitive, even worse than me, we had, well at least I had sniggered about the "romance" deciding it was silly and desperate. I'd dismissed it as an attention-seeking device she had foolishly gambled on. Poor Mother, she was like those girls at school who spent lunchtime at the lavatory mirrors experimenting with eye makeup. Maybe it was my way of dealing with the embarrassment. But Mr. Montgomery told us, no—he warned us, that there was a lot of sympathy for the boy. "Boy!" Father finally exploded, and it was indeed fearful to behold. "Are you calling this crazy man a boy? A boy? At twenty-nine! Do I have to remind you, you of all people, Caleb Montgomery, you who should know better, you who does know better"—or words to that effect—that he, Father, had already been widowered—that's what he said—"widowered" for the first time when he was not much more than twenty-four years of age. "That damn fool killer fella," shouted Father louder than I'd ever heard his voice, "with his Gatsby nonsense and the flashy automobile, is a full-grown man, not a Romeo star-gazed, or some moon-crazed teenager." "Star-gazed and moon-crazed," those were indeed his exact words. Father made it more than clear that he didn't care if Walt Welter went to jail, was hung, drawn and quartered, yanked apart by mules, or ended his days in a lunatic asylum plaiting straw baskets. "Leave me out of all this melodrama," growled Father, "You hearing me?" He then began to collect himself, muttering with something like, "So hark at the sufferings of young Werther." Mr. Montgomery said that the accused went by the name of Welter, but then laughed as he got the reference, which I didn't but made a note of finding out what they'd meant.

Mr. Montgomery waited, hands behind his back. "You all right Helen? You shouldn't have to be hearing all this . . . We, or at least, I should have been more discreet." I insisted it was all fine; I would be honored to sing and I felt real sorry for Mother and I wished I'd known her better. What a thing to admit but I felt it would be wrong to accept pity and sympathy I didn't deserve. If only I was Jewish or Italian, a Catholic or belonged to people like Mitzi's who shouted and cried and hugged, swore like stevedores if they stubbed their toe or dropped a plate. I wasn't cold but didn't have normal emotions, only the same detachment that I so dreaded in Father and appeared to have inherited. We three had shared a fine house, but we were not a family. Not out of ill will, just ill timing, ill fitting. Three loners who just happened to coexist in our particular solar system without forming a unit; Mother had not understood what she was entering into when she married Father. And Mother's little ramshackle world of nervous smiles and sentiment and pretty clothes did not include being a wife or a mother, Father had noted that and did not forgive her for it.

There was a photograph, and it was about to be published. Mr. Montgomery had tried to dissuade the newspaper's editor. But it was going ahead. Father sighed, squared his shoulders and just said, "Yes?" He wanted to see it as did I. "This picture, it will have an effect. It is . . . beautiful," began Mr. Montgomery, preparing us; he spoke real slow, deliberate. "What we have here is a love story, William. Miss Helen. A genuine love story and this here killer is not going to be treated as a criminal madman. No sir, not at all." He paused and bowed as if it was his fault, which, of course, it wasn't. "I'd wager he'll be acquitted and you both have to accept the unfairness of it . . . None of this is going to be easy, not at all easy . . . isn't life so mighty damn peculiar?"

*

Checkmate. How to break the silence? Father appeared to be considering his options—outrage or plain indifference. Metaphorically speaking, he had been presented with a game of chess; I guess I should say poker, but he would never have played cards. So chess it must be and Father pondered his next move in a nightmare that kept on evolving, spinning in increasingly wider arcs over which, unusually for him, he had no control. Caleb Montgomery waited; his expression neutral. Father finally conceded that although detached by nature from the world in general and from personal relationships in particular, he was, through no choice of his own, fully enmeshed in Mother's tragedy. There would be people who would suggest that he had caused it to happen, and that was being said all around us by then, only we hadn't known. When people begin speculating about your motivations and actions, they seldom ask your opinion, never mind your permission. Father, who had been staring out the window, awoke from his reveries on hearing Mrs. Faulkner's footsteps coming up the hall. But she did not come in. Perhaps she had wanted his attention, only to think better of interrupting him? I'm not sure. Then Father cleared his throat, he had prepared a reply. Mr. Montgomery stood to attention. I felt that the world having slowed to a halt was now about to re-gather momentum. Father spoke, addressing us, Mr. Montgomery and me, as "Dear friends." I sensed I was about to hear something momentous that I'd never forget. He seemed to almost smile. I prepared to

remember his words for the rest of my life. But all Father said
was that he had to "make haste" for a dental appointment. This
was followed by a yelp of shrill laughter, more a strange class of
bark, and all coming from me.

"I'd doubt it very much if you are expected to attend, given
the present circumstances," remarked Caleb Montgomery in
his wry fashion, as he bent down with a noticeable creaking of
bones and joints accompanied by a rueful sigh and his mumbled
"Lord, I am a' getting old" to reach for something. It was a slim
leather folder, resting on the floor, it had, apparently, been leaning against the side of Father's desk. But I had been upstairs
when he arrived and had not seen Mr. Montgomery coming in,
I just knew that he would have entrusted Mrs. Faulkner as was
his custom with his hat and walking stick—his overcoat too if
he'd had one, but not then in that balmy late summer weather.
Inside the folder were a number of photographs, glossy, foolscap-
size and probably the last ones ever taken of Mother. "This is the
one that will be in tomorrow morning's paper, might even make
the television news," remarked Mr. Montgomery, lighting up
yet another cigar. He always ignited them very carefully, sucking
in the smoke as if it were spiraling out an opium pipe. Then he
would proceed to chew on each cigar for several minutes. They
quickly became wet and disgusting; he waved them around for
a while and then would just light up another, causing the same
ritual to begin all over again. The photograph looked professional
and had been taken in what appeared to be a formal rose garden.
Mother and Walt were posing for the camera; she smiling directly
at the photographer while Walt saw only her. They were holding
hands, like teenagers. "Love's young dream," muttered Father and
Mr. Montgomery sensing the moment, seized it fully and everything began to change, leastways for me. I've always felt I grew
up that afternoon, it was the moment I first acquired emotional

intelligence and began to understand something about how very difficult it is to live and that some mistakes, or perhaps I should say choices, do have enormous consequences.

Months later in attempting to explain this to Mitzi when I was telling her what had happened, about the killing and all, she cried and hugged me. I was surprised by her tears; I had felt a kind of release at having finally figured it out.

Mother looked lovely in the photograph, really young, no older than Walt. But more than that, she seemed so happy. Perhaps it was a trick of the light, but she was radiant and Walt smiled at her with such tenderness. He was very nice-looking in a weak, romantic, soppy sort of way; thin, not overly masculine, more like an artist, a tubercular composer, or so I reckoned, thinking of Chopin. There was nothing territorial about Walter's attitude, none of that "Look what I got me here." There was just his delight, he seemed grateful. His expression was soft and gentle. I had read that he called Mother "Izzie" and some other reporters had spelt it "Izzy" and I preferred the version with the "y," anyway it was a young name. I was taken with the idea of Mother being called Izzy or Izzie; either spelling conveyed such lightness. Anyone looking at that picture would have to agree that it was real sweet, affection come to life. Mother and Walt were the exact opposite of a pair of fugitives about to sneak off to the nearest hotel and hire a room for the afternoon. Father said little, aside from a half-heartedly irritated "And?" Maybe he had already sensed what Mr. Montgomery was about to explain.

Walter, began our Old World lawyer, carefully, really did love Mother and made no secret of it. He treated her with such respect and kindness, folk—that was the word he, Mr. Montgomery, used—stressing it, "folk may have smiled at" Walt's devotion but, "and here," he raised his voice, confirming that no one was laughing at Walter or at them. "This, um, joyful alliance," he said, had touched people. "We are cold; society has become hard and knowing, given to sneering," reasoned Mr. Montgomery, who was making a point that afternoon about people in general, not just Father and me. "We like to laugh at those movie stars and their weekend-long marriages and the big divorce cases, the division of the spoils . . ." Father cut him off, shouting, "God's sake, Caleb, quit smoking those tarnation cigars, how many more you got in your pocket? What in hell are you driving at?" He accused his friend of making it sound like he, Father, had pulled "that Goddamn trigger!" The reply was devastating, "You may as well have," mused Mr. Montgomery, continuing that "this boy, man, whatever" had treated his, Father's, wife with a "profoundly endearing" tenderness. It had been noticed, and greatly admired. "Even envied in some quarters." True emotion, love had, he argued, become "rare indeed." And Mr. Caleb Montgomery, lawyer and seasoned observer of his fellow man, as he stood in Father's den, was convinced that this genuine love was going to stand in Walter's favor.

Then we learned all about Walt's ailments; that he was on a bunch of experimental medications for his depression, that he had a weak heart, some congenital condition that should have killed him off at birth. Had poor circulation, really suffered in cold weather. Was prone to gout, a disease I knew about from reading nineteenth-century English novels and had associated primarily with aristocrats at the mercy of their own gluttony and heavy drinking. But it was less social class-conscious than I'd imagined and soon after that I read that Flannery O'Connor had suffered the same thing; though maybe that was lupus? On top of all that we discovered Walt had Type A diabetes and this fact was revealed as if it would prove his winning ticket to freedom. It was indeed something of a miracle that a person so poorly could get out and about at all, concluded Mr. Montgomery, who may as well have been making a case for the defense. He was supposed to be on our side and of course he was.

This had been a special friendship, Mr. Montgomery continued; Mother and Walt drove openly around in his fancy automobile, visiting public gardens and tea rooms, attending luncheon parties. And them just being "real happy together," nothing furtive, he said. Then to my enduring shame I heard my own voice, high and shrill, remarking "They probably never had intercourse. Walt wouldn't have been able, would he?" The two men were shocked, but not as deeply as I was. To hear myself shrieking "intercourse" was bad enough, although as an aspiring scientist I had no talent for coy euphemism, just direct, unadorned speech. Far worse than the actual word I'd used was the way in which I said it, it came out sounding irredeemably Southern, as well as mean and petty, prudish "innarcourse"—without the "t"— and I was triumphant with it. Untainted by illicit sex, suddenly Mother was exonerated. She had not corrupted a child; she was not in fact old enough to be his mother. No sex meant a love that was pure and ideal, mythic . . . Mother's romance was just that, romantic and beautiful and terribly sad. Now it was almost noble as far as I was concerned, not squalid. Father looked trapped, so many conflicting sensations, surprise and dread, confusion, all racing across his face and Caleb Montgomery just saying over and over: "He'll be acquitted; he'll be acquitted."

An impartial expert witness along with a number of psychiatrists who had treated Walt over the years had been approached and several of them, including two who had retired, were all willing to testify on his behalf. His family was intent on securing "a guilty but insane" verdict. Walt had never denied killing Mother, but he had kept saying over and over that he hadn't meant for it to happen in the street—"not there"—as if the choice of venue made the crime lesser or greater. The plan had been to drive out to the James River and have a picnic on the grassy bank, beneath the willow tree upon which he had carved their initials. It was a place they had enjoyed going to together. The female reporters always included that detail as proof of his romantic inclinations. It was there beneath the weeping willow that he would shoot her, and then kill himself. It was the only way. Fate had thus decreed it. Only it had not gone quite to plan . . .

"Such . . . balderdash . . ." rasped Father lamely, he seemed defeated and was looking at me, as if he now had cause to suspect that I knew more than he had thought. "Did your mother ever discuss this," pause, "friendship, with you?" he asked. Of course not, I replied, we had never really spoken about anything, I thought back to that day I had asked her to stop at the drug store. She had not even known about my periods beginning and that had upset her, it proved to her how unconnected to each other we were. It seemed to me that Walt was on his way to becoming a celebrity killer and whatever decision the jury arrived at would be shaped by the growing goodwill the public was developing toward him.

In such circumstances I wondered: could there even be a trial, had that prejudicial element already compromised it? Father was thinking the same way and he asked, "Caleb, you seriously think there is going to be a court case? You know how deluded the law is. This fella's not even in prison, he's been waited on hand and foot in a psychiatric unit, more like a hotel, most likely resting up some after all those interviews he's given with further to come, no doubt, just passing the time and watching his favorite TV shows." According to Father the thing was heading straight for Hollywood. "Pretty soon some enterprising people will start printing T-shirts with his face on them," he shouted in hot exasperation, suspecting that he was going to be presented as the real villain and this could only happen in America. Of course I laughed at that but Father glared at me and I stopped short real quick. His irony was usually funniest the angrier he got. He inquired again had Mother told me anything at all, even hinted? No she had never said anything but it was then I realized that had I been a normal daughter, interested in frills and makeup, borrowing her clothes, and enjoying going shopping, asking her to buy me things or dealing with boyfriend problems of my own—perhaps she would have spoken to me. I'm glad she didn't; what could I do save fall over with shock? But then again, perhaps I would have gotten to know her. You never know what you will do until it's all over and it's too late. The madness of it was making me sick, the room was stuffy, the cigar smoke which I had at first considered exotic and opulent was now adding to my nausea. I wanted air; I needed to go to the bathroom, I was about to have a bout of diarrhea, I could feel it churning around inside me, I felt a sudden cramp coming on, I dreaded the buildup of wind, the embarrassment . . . "You're upset, not surprising . . . Maybe go ask Mrs. Faulkner to make you a snack, get yourself some Fig Newtons and milk. Or try and eat a little soup or something? Tea with more sugar than you'd usually take . . ." Caleb Montgomery's suggestions confirmed that he had begun to fit into his role of the kindly comforter. I could see that he was more insightful than I had previously imagined, or maybe the extreme situation had just awakened his instincts and his natural protectiveness toward me added to that, I'd always suspected that he felt a little sorry for Mother.

We still had to get through her funeral and Walter's family sent a massive floral tribute and of course his parents and the rest of the immediate Welter family were present. It was an impressive attendance and I could not help noticing the number of mourners who made a point of commiserating with Walter's family. They would walk over to Father and then to me before moving on to Walter's camp. Aren't people just full of surprises? I had sung my song and then had to control myself as women came over, saying, "You're Isabel's girl," as if they felt the need to inform me of this fact. Then, some of them reminded me it was most fortunate that I was very clever and that "I'd get by." The relevance of this escaped me but later I reckoned they may have been telling me that although I didn't resemble Mother, at least my grades were good and if my looks failed to improve, I would still be able to get a job. I don't know, but there was the family of the killer all weeping fit to expire on the spot, while the victim's people did little excepting for my singing. Father had declined to speak in the church. So Mother's only relative, a sister I'd never met, gave a detailed account of Mother's career as a beauty contestant. I wanted to die about halfway through her rambling address. Then the woman, her name was Sally, now I had an Aunt, I smiled to myself, "Aunt Sally," spoke of them growing up together, just the two of them, in Toledo, Ohio, where their father had spent his life in the glass works. "Toledo's often called The Glass City," she had said, "on account of all the glass we manufacture up there." I knew Toledo was situated near the border with Michigan and when my new Aunt Sally mentioned Lake Erie, I did sit up and listened. Mother had told me about her girlhood vacations on the Great Lakes and how she had seen snow showers blowing across the frozen surface of Erie, the tenth largest lake in the world. Father always referred to her home place by another name; Frog Town—Toledo having been built on land reclaimed from the Great Black Swamp, the habitat of various species of frog.

Aunt Sally looked older than Mother, closer in age to Father. Her boxy beige jacket and dress would have filled Mother with a sublime horror. Sally was heavy, solid, not fat, and had a square-jawed, broad Swedish face, too big for her small, pale-blue eyes.

Her hair was light brown, possibly dyed, and her accent far closer to that of the Midwest than the fey Scarlett O'Hara warble Mother had fashioned so diligently. My aunt held her handbag across her stomach like the Queen of England does and referred to Mother as her baby sister, mentioning how pretty she had always been. "She'd wanted to be a ballet dancer and an air hostess, then for a while wondered about becoming a nurse but was . . . um . . . discouraged by the dirt and the smells. I think she dreamed about marrying a handsome doctor like in the movies but decided against it." Aunt Sally's reminiscence stuttered to a halt, as if she had suddenly realized that such anecdotes may not be entirely suitable for church. "Susan was so excited about getting married to William and moving to the South. She'd always loved *Gone with the Wind*; she expected that there would be far more flowers in the South than back home. We never had a garden, only a back yard . . ."

People must have been wondering who Susan was, most having known Mother as Isabel. Some of the assembled mourners may have suspected that Aunt Sally had wandered into the wrong funeral. Father didn't even seem to breathe and sat like a stone effigy with his hands on his lap, his knees rigidly aligned side by side. Aunt Sally stopped speaking and looked across at the Reverend and said that their father was ailing and sorry he couldn't be there. "Daddy asked me to say goodbye to Susan, so I'm here to say goodbye to Susan from Daddy and from me. I guess you've already met up with Mom," Aunt Sally had turned to address Mother's casket, assuring it that "Mom" would be waiting for her. I was watching a stranger speaking to and about Mother, recalling their shared world. I kept blinking, dependent on the tiny fluttering movement eyelids make, as if to confirm that I was awake and that all this was really happening.

My newly acquired aunt shrugged, bowed, thanked us all for listening and walked down to her pew, very carefully, nervous of tripping in shoes that, judging from the way she was walking, must have been higher than the ones she usually wore. She edged along, placing her feet as if she alone knew where the landmines had been positioned. I looked around the congregation, half expecting to discover that Walt had joined us. That was all the morning needed, him standing there, weeping, his boyish face worn from grief and remorse, not forgetting his assorted ailments. Walt appeared to be the kind of person who acted with abandon; he could be relied upon to throw himself into the grave, clinging to Mother's coffin, demanding to be let in. The reporters would love describing the spectacle, for them he had become a tragic hero.

By then he had already done something else staggeringly unexpected and that we only found out about later, in the evening of the day of the service. Aided by his family's wealth and local prominence, he had secured a ninety second slot on the evening news during which he spoke directly to Mother, addressing her as "My Darling Izzy" telling her that he loved her and wished her well; that they would be together for all eternity and that he was sorry, "so awfully sorry." He hadn't meant for her to die like that. The only way for him to have ended the item true to his style was to have blown his brains out there on camera, except he didn't. He smiled his hurt, bruised-eye smile, looking a little like that English actor who had played Sebastian in the TV version of *Brideshead Revisited*.

Yet Walt had not finished. Father had said days before he saw the little broadcast that night that we were dealing with "a man possessed of a decided sense of theater." And we were. There would be more drama; Father's response to Walt's scripted apology to Mother was one of spontaneous fury. But even earlier, at the graveside, there had been his terrifyingly sophisticated articulation of an acrimony that did, indeed, continue to fester deeper than I'd realized.

*

"They flee from me, that sometime did me seek,
With naked foot stalking in my chamber.
I have seen them, gentle, tame, and meek,
That now are wild, and do not remember . . ."

Father delivered the lines of Thomas Wyatt's famous sonnet with compelling deliberation, conveying its bitter eloquence, the underlying reproach. It was beautiful but also chilling:

"That sometime they put themselves in danger
To take bread at my hand, and now they range,
Busily seeking with a continual change . . ."

Standing by the grave on that still morning in Indian summer heat I realized it had taken the shooting and all the craziness that had followed for me to hear Father's voice as if for the first time. It was indeed splendid; he could have been a preacher except he didn't appear to believe in anything, or a Shakespearean actor. He was actually, in my opinion, a natural attorney. I always felt he had far more presence than Mr. Montgomery, although that venerable lawyer could certainly work a jury. Father was too aloof for that; his was the demeanor of a righteous, incorruptible judge.

Prior to his unexpected recital of the sonnet I had believed Father was more impressive in his silences than his speeches. He continued:

"It was no dream, I lay broad waking.
But all is turned, through my gentleness,
Into a strange fashion of forsaking;
And I have leave to go, of her goodness,
And she also to use newfangleness.
But since that I so kindely am served,
I fain would know what she hath deserved."

His tone conveyed puzzlement and he seemed deep in thought. Obviously the undercurrent of Elizabethan court intrigue, the many ambivalences of it, had not been lost on him. Wyatt, rumored to have had an affair with Anne Boleyn and for a time imprisoned for treason, had written lines that appeared to have struck Father deeply. He had never lost the habit of reading poetry along with his favorite nineteenth-century novels to which he often returned. He also loved history and enjoyed biographies of composers, painters, and military leaders. Although professing to despise him, Father was fascinated with Napoleon, and also admitted to admiring mad King Ludwig of Bavaria. Yet it was Jefferson, always Jefferson, who had been Father's absolute idol since boyhood and so he remained. Mother had never had a place in any of this.

Aunt Sally had been sobbing steadily long before we reached the cemetery. In fact she probably had not stopped since we left the church, causing her eyes to have become marshy red hollows. Mother would have been wearing sunglasses, having owned a collection of them which she wore, much to Father's disapproval, all year round, even indoors, at home and, I'm sorry to say, during meals. He'd say they made her look like a spy. Mother's sister didn't strike me as a devotee of dark glasses and had deep squint marks to prove it. She edged over to me, whispering, awed, "so gorgeous, so gorgeous," having begun to say "classy" but stopped and began again, blushing at her near miss. I felt ashamed both for noting her change of mind and also for being smugly aware that I felt culturally superior to a person who would use a word such as "classy." Aunt Sally had probably not gone to college, or was even moderately educated—Mother told me of her own "daring escape" in deciding to abandon high school in favor of modeling. Aunt Sally had most likely set the example that Mother had followed. But Sally was decent and sincere, no mistake about that; she had a simple dignity. Even a prig like me couldn't miss that. She may not have been overly educated yet she was sufficiently astute to refrain from saying "classy" while among the snooty company into which her hapless sister had married. It was obvious that the harsh ambiguity of Wyatt's poem and its irony had eluded Aunt Sally. She was instead responding to its silky rhythms and she saw it as Father's tribute to Mother. But there was far more to it. For the first time I grasped the depth of his hurt at the betrayal and most of all, his awareness of his emotional ineptitude.

A weak, flat voice had then begun singing "Nearer My God to Thee." There was no music in it, yet the singer was tenacious and persisted. Others joined in. Gradually the impromptu choir achieved a powerful resonance. We Southerners are good at singing and the regular churchgoers of whom there must have been a fair representation, lifted the sound, high, it seemed, toward the cloudless blue sky above us. I thought of the Titanic; I had seen that old black and white movie, *A Night to Remember*, and recalled the scene in which the leader of the little orchestra tells the musicians that they have done their duty. They turn to disperse but when he begins to play his violin, they again take up their instruments and join in. The sinking of the Titanic, a tale of human error, seemed an apt metaphor for the way things had ended up for Mother and Walt. I looked around for Father: he was already walking away, alone, through the cemetery.

Earlier though, after the church service, we had followed the hearse in the first vehicle; by we, I mean Father and Aunt Sally and me, the chief mourners. I was sitting in the back seat, and then noticed Mrs. Faulkner standing near the entrance with a couple I didn't know. I opened the car door and could feel Father tensing. Perhaps he had also seen Mrs. Faulkner, he had not invited Aunt Sally to join us; it had been the funeral director who had led her over to the black limousine in which we sat. Without uttering a word, the forthright undertaker had gripped her elbow and stuffed her into the automobile, pressing the flat of his hand down on her shapeless beige hat. Anyone watching might well have thought he was a plainclothes detective making an arrest. I could feel an inappropriate smirk threatening to ooze across my face, I knew I was heading toward one of my incapacitating spasms of bizarre glee, don't ask me why. It was the madness of it all, I felt I had fallen in with a group of actors and we were aimlessly trying to improvise a drama for an impresario who had lost any further interest in our antics.

Mrs. Faulkner looked up at me, I was suddenly taller than her and she had been so tall for such a long time, but now that too was over. The detached guardian of my childhood who had always seemed a silent giantess watching me from a bemused height was in reality no more than maybe five foot seven. How our illusions betray us. In the harsh noon light her smooth, dark copper skin looked thinly stretched over her high cheekbones and was grainy. She had more wrinkles than I had imagined and how dull her eyes were, in slightly yellowed whites. Close up I could also see that the pouches under them were purple and that there was a crack running the length of one of her front teeth. Perhaps it was a denture? I realized she too, as had Father, was beginning to age. Her heavy eyebrows were in reality gray. "Here, Miss Helen, you take this," she handed me a packet of Kleenex. I wasn't crying, maybe she was trying to bring this oversight to my attention? But my sorrow was still corralled by surprise, held within the closed fist of my fury, I was angry. None of this was fair. Why was Mother the one who had to pay? Because she was obsessed with clothes and not baroque music; did that make her life worth less? Why was all the sympathy directed at Walt? There was no pity left for her. She was the one that had died yet Walt was being hailed as the victim. Mother had been disregarded, dismissed as just a stupid wife who was bored and had strayed. Women, it appears, usually end up paying more in these situations. Later, when I attempted to discuss this with Mitzi, she had called me a feminist with the same degree of censure she would apply had I been a convicted terrorist. She is my best friend but she has never understood the rampaging ambivalence of it all. She is too orthodox in her opinions. How could she hope to comprehend any of it? After all, very little of it ever made much sense to me either.

Mrs. Faulkner declined my offer to join us in the mourning car, saying that she would follow us to the cemetery. The couple with her were her brother and his wife. He had tipped his hat and bowed to me as if I were the daughter of a plantation owner. I almost preferred the way his wife glared belligerently at me and pursed her lips indicating that I had offended her by simply existing. There was something exhilarating about her contempt; it made me smile at her, which I hope added to her annoyance. I ran back to the shiny limousine, enjoying the swishing sound Mother's coat made as I moved. "You should not have done that," observed Father, who had guessed at my invitation, "Mrs. Faulkner has her own way of doing things; she is a most impressive individual, resolute in her single-mindedness. But she is not family and this she knows." Aunt Sally laughed nervously, it was easy to tell that she was counting the minutes until she could make a break for the train back to Ohio.

In the time-honored manner of the lull before the storm, we had played our parts, Father and me. And it was all about to change with that evening's news. Walt's broadcast stunned Father, rendering him quite speechless, albeit briefly. Then every atom of rage that he had been suppressing exploded. He banged his fist down on the kitchen table; two cups, a saucer, and the drinking glass I had just fetched from the cupboard bounced with the impact, the vibration then caused them to topple. One of the fine china cups survived against the odds, but the other fallers shattered, the glass splintering abruptly. "Enough, enough," shouted Father, and he grabbed at the kitchen telephone. It rested in one of those wall fixture things and the first time he missed, the phone slipped and dangled by its cord. Father caught it and began dialing; I knew exactly who he would call. The phone on the other end just rang out and Father commenced yelling before the beeps of the message machine had sounded. "Caleb," he yelled, "you get on down here now, my patience has become fully exhausted," and he continued venting his exasperation along the silent line. "That little Gatsby man is not going to get away with this, I am issuing proceedings. He is a murderer, clear as day." Father had made up his mind. Walt had been playing all of us for fools and getting away with it. "Alas poor lunatic!" bellowed Father, "Ha!" proclaiming that Walt was more sane than he had ever been. His tirade continued after the message tape had clicked off. He then crammed the phone back onto its wall cradle with such black temper that the receiver kept falling off it. After the third or fourth attempt, Father, appearing slightly uncomfortable about his outburst, seemed to regain some composure and adjusted his tie. He nodded to me and just walked out of the kitchen, leaving the phone swinging by its cord. I replaced it and in keeping with the mood, unintentionally walked over the broken glass, which pierced the sole of my slipper before cutting sharply into my foot. I fetched another tumbler down from an overhead cupboard and taking it and an unopened carton of orange juice with me, headed for Mother's bathroom, in search of a Band-Aid. I smiled on acknowledging that, even in death, she remained the best source for such things. Not that she was practical, I doubt if she had ever applied one to my grazed knees. Her vanity over the years had encouraged her to buy shoes that were invariably a size too small for her, and she relied on Band-Aids to assuage and cushion her tormented feet. She minced along on her high heels, making me think of those Chinese women and that cruel and evil custom of foot-binding.

By the time Mr. Montgomery arrived Mrs. Faulkner had left for the evening. I opened the door and he was about to hand me his hat out of habit, but stopped, instead making a play of absentmindedly sliding the brim through his fingers. He looked tired and remarked that the day just didn't seem to want to end. "That you Caleb?" called Father and our visitor just walked wearily on into the study, prepared to absorb some much belated rhetoric. Soon after that, perhaps twenty minutes or so, the telephone began ringing. I decided not to answer it, Father didn't either. In the absence of Mrs. Faulkner I reckoned I should offer refreshments, I could hear Father's voice raised high, demanding that what he referred to as "this thing" be heard, "the entire sad and sorry saga of it" and, he insisted, before a jury. Mr. Montgomery did venture that it may well have gone beyond that stage, and he outlined the difficulty of finding impartial jurors, considering all the publicity. "Well just maybe there's some judge out there prepared to earn his money," was Father's response to that. I decided to go ahead and prepare coffee with a token snack. The Band-Aid had already parted company with my foot and had become a clumped up ball of plastic stuck to the inside of the slipper. I made instant coffee instead of fooling around with the specialist stuff Mrs. Faulkner always brewed so beautifully; there was lots of whipped cream and sugar to dress it up. Meanwhile in the refrigerator, lurked one of her incomparable maple and almond pies, which would easily compensate for the inferior coffee.

Just then I became aware of a siren's wail and was wondering where it was headed, what other outrage could possibly have been perpetrated on that day of days in an attempt to upstage our little drama? Then I realized the police car was hurtling up our drive, the gravel bouncing in sprays. Headlights were flashing across the darkness of the lawns, illuminating the front and side gardens in turn as no one had drawn the kitchen curtains.

The knocking at the door was urgent not polite, the thuds were signaling "Open up now" instead of the more customary Richmond—as it still was, even then—"Now you all just take your time." Father and Mr. Montgomery were already in the hall as I hurried from the kitchen. Father flung open the door with a stern, "What is going on here?" I didn't recognize either of the men. One of them said, "Evening Judge, Montgomery. Well Helen didn't you just spring up right tall! Must be riding that black son-of-a-bitch horse," turning smoothly to his colleague, he explained how Galileo had bitten someone called Jim when he photographed us at one of the county training shows at which we had competed. Intuition told me that these men were not police. The one who had spoken then introduced himself as the editor of *The Richmond Leader* and the other man as one of his "senior staff reporters." The editor explained that he felt that his readers needed to know what Father made of Walt's "little television appearance." It was a tense moment and the floor boards creaked accordingly. Father ordered the men to leave and shouted, "How dare you come here using that police siren as a means of gaining entry." The reporter leered revoltingly and bragged about its effectiveness. "Works every time, funny how folks are always ready to entertain the pol-ice." He appeared very much taken with the way in which he had drawled the word "police" making two long, slow syllables, snake-like and insinuating.

"Get out, you . . . get out now," hissed Father. "Evening Montgomery, evening Helen," sneered the editor, eager to say something face-saving. "Now you mind that black horse, he don't seem over friendly either. To be expected; considering his breeding. Bad blood runs real deep and all." The gentlemen of the press left, the door slamming nastily behind them. Father turned to Mr. Montgomery, a "now what?" expression on his face. The lawyer gazed back, saying quietly, "Better just wait and see what he prints in the morning's paper." He needed to go home to think out tactics for the case. Closing the door softly, he left. His steps moved slowly across the porch and down the path. I mentioned the coffee to Father and he turned toward the kitchen, me following.

We drank the lukewarm coffee. The pie was wonderful and became even better with cream heaped on it. "I have always liked whipped cream on cake and pieces of pie, more so than ice cream," Father declared solemnly and then, without any preamble, told me that his first wife had been called Helen. "Yes, Helen. That was her name." Then he said I had better get on to bed; it was late and already heading for the next day. Perhaps he wanted to tell me about the other Helen before I ended up reading about her in the newspaper.

*

It was a sickle moon that night; the merest sliver of white as if even it had been gnawed at by vermin intent on getting their pound of flesh. I imagined the reporters busy at their desks, yanking and pulling at the stuff of people's lives. Making up stories that exaggerated the wrung-out facts and then just ruthlessly leaving the truth for dead, along with the raw and tender feelings of those who had been left behind.

*

What would Father have named me had I been born a boy? My guess is "Thomas" after Jefferson. Up in my room I inspected my telescope, thinking that it was a night for exploring the heavens. But the sky had clouded over; the moon was in hiding, as were the stars. When I was small I used to listen to an old record called *Favorites for Children*. The man on the sleeve was wearing a big smile and a clownish straw hat. His face filled the cover and his name was Burl Ives. He was accompanied by a cute little terrier in a plaid collar. Burl Ives. A soothing tremor made his voice warm and he sang songs like "Lavender Blue" and "Big Rock Candy Mountain" and the famous Western ballad about cursed ghost riders "trying to catch the Devil's herd across these endless skies"—that one was meant for grown-ups, but I liked it. Even so, I wanted to hear a different song, a happy one—one that I used to sing out loud over and over, "Let's all go to the ball, to the ball, to the ball, to the ugly bug ball and a happy time we'll have there, one and all, at the ugly bug ball." The record began and I lifted the needle, skipping over a few tracks to get straight to "The Ugly Bug Ball." The familiar tune rang out, bright and cheerful and I sang along with Burl Ives, the next best thing to Santa Claus. Having known him as a singer from my earliest Disney days, it was surprising to discover that he was also an accomplished actor and had exercised imposing menace in movies such as *East of Eden*, *Cat on a Hot Tin Roof*, and *The Big Country* for which he won an Academy Award. I had sat on my bed and sang along, like a dog about to howl at the moon—which, for the moment, had gone into hiding.

Suddenly it was morning. The shower ran for maybe ten minutes or more. I had let the water thunder down on me as hot as I could bear it in steam so thick I couldn't see and pushed the glass door out blind, grabbing for the towel that must have moved or fallen from the rack. I felt my way to the bath tub as I knew there was always a fluffy towel hanging over the side, just for show. My hair squeaked clean and too hungry to dry it, or even bother finding a comb, I just headed on down for breakfast. Mr. Montgomery had already arrived and was in the process of telling Mrs. Faulkner that he had just eaten the finest breakfast of his "entire life." She nodded, as ever underwhelmed by the rest of us. Father was clutching a full cup of coffee in both hands and by way of greeting told me my hair looked like a bunch of wet rats. He may have meant rats' tails, but he was agitated, primed to explode.

Mrs. Faulkner motioned at me to sit, and she turned to the counter, coming back with a plate of hotcakes. A small jug of maple syrup was already on the table. She had also made me hot chocolate, all creamy in the large blue mug I most preferred to drink from. The smell of bacon was wafting through the kitchen, the stage was set. That was when I noticed the newspaper on the table. Although it was neatly folded, it was obvious that it had already been read. There just might be a connection between its contents and my luxury breakfast I detected. On non-school days—not that I had been there for more than a week by then—and on weekend mornings, I usually fended for myself because of hurrying to get riding. No, this breakfast carried weighty import. "Hotcakes good Helen? Of course they're good, Mrs. Faulkner makes the best"—Mr. Montgomery spoke to me as if I were out on a window ledge and about to jump, his tone of forced cheer was hiding something. Down went my fork and I reached for the paper.

"Don't," snapped Father, but then he shrugged causing Mr. Montgomery to nod, and suggest with a smile of defiance, why not. He virtually invited me to read it and pulled a jokey grimace, assuring me that it was all lies and stupid and that no one would take it seriously and that I knew the truth, we all knew the truth. He told me that I was "supremely" intelligent; known to be so, a scientist of the future . . . I had been curious, but now I was plain worried. Where was this prologue leading? What embarrassment had been published in the paper? Was there something new? Funnily, the first thing that came to my mind was that I'd be finding out Father had other children so I asked him outright if he had any sons or daughters I didn't know about. He said the only child he had was me. I began leafing through the newspaper and there I was—in a parade ring photograph on Galileo, no doubt taken the day he had bitten the photographer whose name I now knew to be Jim. It was a file shot and had appeared before. I looked shifty, my habitual expression for any camera, and the caption made me snigger, "Helem Stockton Defoe on a big black horse." That's what it said "a big black horse."

Was that all there was? I wondered, just a grim photograph of scowling old me with my name misspelt? Are they suggesting I just happened by chance to be sitting on "a big black horse"? It

read: "a big black horse" not "her big black horse." Why hadn't
they found out his name? He had won the damned event. Was
I too frightening to ask? Did they think that I too might bite?
Then I looked again, no, there was more. A little story and all
about me; I learned that I was "the true victim of this desperate love triangle." So much for the talents of the editor's "senior
reporter." I was described as "heartbroken," "devastated," "traumatized," and "forlorn." I apparently cried myself to sleep every
night and had in my "girlish bedroom," a large picture of Mother
before which I placed a single rose each day. I did? There was
more: I was reclusive, had a death wish that expressed itself
through the riding of dangerous horses and, oh yes, I remained
"sorely afflicted" by my glass eye that was sure to "dash her hopes
of becoming an astronaut."

All news to me; the article created a portrait of a lonely Bride
of Frankenstein figure; I was also referred to as "standing more
than six feet tall" with "a haunted pale face of incredible sadness." Even in winter my skin has always been sallow and if
I stood straight and stretched could just about make five foot
nine. Father was openly upset and not even pretending otherwise. I began laughing for real, not out of bravado. It was, most
definitely, a truly stupid riot of cliché. The reporter was lazy; he
had asked no questions and had not even resorted to the usual
"sources close to," the ones who always "refused to be named."

Mr. Montgomery told me I could sue, but what was the
point? Although I had been presented as a pathetic one-eyed
outcast who would not be able to become an astronaut, an ambi-
tion I'd never entertained, there was nothing offensive, no snide
comments about my being protected by Father's material com-
forts, the quality horses I had to hand, or my being indulged
by my school—which I was. My one fear as I read it was that I
would be presented as a variation of Alex, the appalling narrator

of *A Clockwork Orange.* How I had hated that vicious little yarn. Yet when our English teacher mentioned it in passing, it somehow became far more popular than any of the many books she'd recommended. "Horror Show" was a catch phrase for a while. Everyone liked that novel—except for me and when I admitted that in class, several of the girls were surprised and said that they'd expected me to love it, what with Alex being so partial to Beethoven.

In an effort to prove my staunch indifference to being inaccurately profiled by an idiotic reporter, I shrugged and remarked winningly to Father that it was unlikely now that my plans to win Miss America would progress any further.

Neither he nor Mr. Montgomery laughed. Yet we did all agree that the story was indeed trite, and ultimately harmless. "But them coming here, the small town audacity of it," fumed the lawyer. "They would never think of attempting a stunt like that in New York or Washington, Chicago . . ." Mr. Montgomery had always demonstrated an emphatic feel for language. "Small town audacity," I was taken with the phrase and vowed to remember it. He liked to see himself as a cosmopolitan and would refer yearningly to those big cities as if they were his natural terrain. He always felt he had to explain their subtleties to those of us who were destined to remain in Richmond. But this wasn't about inward-looking Richmond or how the stupid reporter had satirized me. The most disturbing aspect, maintained Father, was the obvious intention of the editor—that of keeping our story alive in his paper and through that, hoping to secure national syndication of every last ignominious detail. Next he said we would be reading a profile of Mrs. Faulkner. "She'd never agree to that," countered Mr. Montgomery, "she won't even speak to me." Father sighed and reached for the coffee pot, "That was me attempting irony Caleb, she barely speaks to me and I employ her."

Which of my eyes I wondered, had the newspaper hack decided was glass? I reckoned I'd finish eating and yet again examine myself in the downstairs cloakroom. But I had spent enough of my life studying my eyes. Had I been fat would he have written about it? If I had only one leg would he have made sure to describe that too? "Helen the grieving amputee puts a brave face on her suffering etc., etc." I realized that while my thoughts had been drifting Mrs. Faulkner had been on red alert. Sheriff Hodge appeared in the kitchen doorway, seeming to fill the room. I hadn't heard the door but obviously Mrs. Faulkner had. "Ignore the fools, Helen; they don't merit a second thought," said the sheriff. "Maybe you should hurry on down to the stables, I hear rain is heading this way."

Rain was about as likely that bright fall morning as snow. Jamie Hodge was attempting to protect me from further upset. However had he thought I had managed thus far? I made a move to leave; I still needed to comb my hair. But curiosity made me slow my steps across the hall and double back to the kitchen just as Father blurted "What?" Mr. Montgomery was too shocked to speak and the sheriff was leaning forward, resting his big paws on the kitchen table, crooning, "Maybe it's all for the better. Kinda brings an end to it and all." He seemed to be pleading for consensus. The telephone was ringing. "Do not answer it," commanded Father and Mrs. Faulkner stepped back as if she had been slapped. The three men seemed to hold their breath. There would be no trial; Walter Welter was dead. "Now I'm afraid I must insist Miss Helen, just go and ride your horses." Sheriff Hodge had sensed me standing behind him, he'd never spoken so sharply to me. I knew he meant well and still thought of me as ten years old with a mouth full of braces. Still I'd been privy to everything up until then and so stayed where I was, asking louder than I intended, "Did he kill himself?" I had a right to ask; he was the man who had murdered Mother. "Tell me, or I'll just be hearing it on the news soon enough or reading all about it in tomorrow's paper."

The sheriff dropped down into a chair, straining it and causing the table to lurch, pushed forwards by his enormous, quivering belly. I imagined the marks the legs of the table would be gouging into the wood but then remembered that the kitchen floor was one of the few that had tiles. There would only be scratches. A damaged floor—hardly a thing to be pondering on hearing that Mother's killer was dead.

Suicide seemed an appropriate finale. But no, the sheriff explained that it had been an accident. Welter had slipped in the shower and with his compromised balance and all, not eating much; he must have been weak, probably dizzy, and seemed to have hit his head. Quite a while had elapsed before he'd been found, someone had come into his room and saw it was empty, and heard the shower running, so they went in to turn it off, and "Lord," exclaimed Sheriff Hodge, "a dead man lying in a pool of water on the shower floor." He shivered at the image, he always was squeamish, an unusual lawman on every count. Father snorted before remarking caustically that it was such a shame; Walt had been denied the chance of slitting his wrists in the bathtub and then expiring in his own blood. "And what a touching photo opportunity that would have been." Sheriff Hodge was horrified and muttered a plaintive "hush now."

So Walt Welter the great romantic had slipped. Imagine that. "Just banged his head and died. That boy didn't have suicide in him," sighed Mr. Montgomery. "You could tell that. He is one . . . well . . . he was one of life's misfortunates; couldn't help himself causing trouble for all around him." The sympathetic tone irked Father yet he said nothing.

There would be no court case, the story had ended there. For Walt in the privacy of a shower; for Mother, as a public spectacle on a sidewalk. No justice for her in any of it, I thought as I looked closer at each of the men's faces, trying to read their feelings.

Mr. Montgomery stood up and fetched a cup for Jamie Hodge and poured him coffee without asking if he wanted any. He was aware that Father and Sheriff Hodge were very close; they shared the love of horses. Mr. Montgomery was a city man. For him horses just meant the races and dressing up for a social occasion. The sheriff raised the cup but stopped without drinking any, lowered it, looking around. Father just shoved the sugar bowl toward him and stuck the spoon he had been using in it. The sheriff smiled and began spooning in one, two, three heaped spoonfuls, announcing to no one in particular, "Yes sir, I take my coffee sweet and my tea bitter."

As I ran up the stairs toward my room, I heard Father telling his friends to take their time and have more coffee. "Help yourselves; just help yourselves," he said, explaining that he had to check on some lab results. I think he wanted to be alone.

Imagine being hauled out dead from a shower. You never know what is going to happen next. I was glad though, the circus was over and Walt had denied all those reporters a few more weeks of melodrama and speculation. There would be none of those impressionistic sketches of the accused in the courtroom, sitting, head bowed as his remorse was being studied from all possible angles. But the more I thought about it, the more it began to seem to me that Walt sure had had it easy, he hadn't even had to kill himself.

*

Galileo was relaxed that morning and we did about thirty minutes of flat work and a little jumping in the sand arena, most of it
overseen astutely by Billy Bob, whom I had taken to calling Mr.
Porter, which amused him no end. He had turned Monticello
out in the little paddock near the arena. It was coming up to
noon and Billy Bob had decided to let the horse have about an
hour or so of midday sun on his back. He had taken his rug off;
Monticello looked really well, still carrying impressive condition
and a beautiful shine from being groomed every day unless it
was cold, which it hadn't been, not for months. His big ears were
pricked and he seemed content, watching everything, he looked
directly at Billy Bob when he said, "You just sun yourself some,
Big Man and I'll be right back." Billy Bob then turned to run his
hands down over Galileo's legs. He loosened the girth and asked
me what I made of "this here black horse." Without thinking, not
that characteristic of me as I tend to weigh my words, I admitted
that my opinion seemed to change just about every five seconds,
keeping pace with the horse's moods. That time I laughed as the
session had gone well. Galileo's concentration had not lapsed
once and he had apparently decided against attempting to kill
me, at least for that day.

Billy Bob didn't refer to recent events, nor did I, although
I had almost been about to tell him that Walter was dead but
decided not to. I was real sick of it all and the yard was one place
free of court cases and killings and motives and reporters looking
for copy. On the way back to the stable, we passed the timber
loose boxes; they had just been freshly painted, green and white.
Then I remembered the stag and asked what had happened to
him. Billy Bob said he'd gotten the stag to walk on into the

loose box without any trouble. It hadn't hesitated. "Not once, just walked in like he lived in a stable, he was flat out with tiredness, no fight left in him at all." Billy Bob seemed pleased by my interest, and described getting hay for the deer as well as a little bucket of horse feed, "just to see if he'd eat it." When he looked back over the door the stag was lying down, looking, as Billy Bob put it, "like he'd gone to meet his maker." The next morning he had given him more food, and then just left the door closed but not bolted. "He was there and then, he was gone. But I got to look at him real close, mighty beautiful animal, one of those white tails, likely escaped from that little wild life reserve over in Caroline County . . . not that much taller than a pony, funny square body but a mighty pretty face. Big, soft eyes like a horse."

*

Death had conferred an ethereal quality upon the attractively gaunt features of Walt Welter, a face from which it was proving difficult to escape. And there he was again on the early evening news. I had been too hungry to wait until supper and was, discreetly I thought, making a few peanut butter sandwiches, despite being uneasily aware that Mrs. Faulkner's body language was signaling her curt disapproval of eating between meals. Of course she withheld comment yet I could feel her eyes burning holes in my back as I peered greedily into the refrigerator. The fit-to-bursting blueberry pie and bowl of fresh cream were obviously destined for that evening's dessert and not before. There was no orange juice. The groceries had not yet been delivered, although there were two pitchers of freshly made ice tea. I reached in for one and placed it on the table, but Mrs. Faulkner's jawline tightened somewhat so I quickly put the jug back, and instead took out a quart of milk. As I was preparing to convey my forbidden snack upstairs, having washed and dried the knife, diligently returning the jar of peanut butter to the cupboard, the jelly to the refrigerator, and wiping down the work space, the newscaster confirmed that the "tragic love victim"—why was it that he was never referred to as a killer?—Walter Welter had in fact died from a heart attack which was predictably described as "massive," heightened melodrama pursuing him to the very end. So he had not mundanely slipped and banged his head. Nature had rebelled, or at least his heart had. The body, looking long and narrow, draped in a green blanket, was shown being carried out on a stretcher from a Virginia creeper-clad red brick building, the psychiatric unit, and placed in a station wagon ambulance destined for the morgue.

The two-, maybe three-minute item gave a brief summary of his life and the fact that he had been very interested in natural history, particularly birds and flowers. Viewers learned that Walt's education at an exclusive boarding school in North Carolina had been frequently disrupted owing to his, by now famous, ill health. I was glad that Father had not been present to witness this unwarranted eulogy. Walt's distressed sire spoke of his son's "heroic struggle" against various illnesses and of course, his "chronic depression." He attributed the heart attack "to all the trauma poor Walt has had to endure." The reporter interviewing him even simpered sympathetically and meekly lowered his eyes when Mr. Welter matter-of-factly also accused the media of being partly to blame, "You folks never gave Walt any time to himself, yes sir, you did not." This said despite the Welter family having so outrageously manipulated the press throughout. There was no mention of Mother, she may as well have been drunk and disorderly and crashed her car before making a random rape allegation that no one could possibly have taken seriously.

Mrs. Faulkner glanced at me as if to say, there are ways of getting around things if you have the means and the money. As for the sheer nerve it had taken, old Father Welter was resourceful, give him that. Anyone new to the story would never have imagined there had been a murder involved. I gathered my guilty snack and retreated furtively upstairs.

Sitting on my bed, chewing the sandwiches—the bread was beautifully soft, the milk was creamy and chilled; I would have liked more of both—I wondered was Walt's story now finally over. My feet felt hot, damp in fact. Having removed my boots and socks, I was astonished at the length of my toenails, how had they gotten so long?

A blue jay landed on the windowsill. As I put two pieces of crust out the bird flew off, but that greedy jay returned soon enough and pecked at one, ate it, and then lifted the remaining piece in its beak to dart away. How much would a heart attack have hurt? I wondered. Was it instant? Or had it been painful? Was there fear? Had poor tragic Walter Welter screamed out for help at the last minute? Was he a lunatic or a coward or both? I hoped that he'd experienced terror and that he had sobbed and whimpered as his dying heart had raced and heaved, and he'd writhed helplessly, pitifully. And that he'd gasped for breath under the immense pressure that would have, hopefully, been crushing his chest and that he'd wept like a girl. I prayed he had suffered the scourges of hell for as long as it took. I liked to think of him encountering hellfire, excruciating, suffocating pain, true torment, for far longer than Mother had; it was only just and fair for him to have his taste of agony. God had at long last taken some small hand.

Walt's businessman father would later give a long interview to a medical journalist, outlining his reasons for insisting on an autopsy. He felt that it would be important for the Welter family to have the heart examined, in case preventive procedures could be used to help his siblings and of course, the old faker had added as an afterthought, "and for others; the wider community." But even more important, he stressed, was to have his son's brain studied in the hope of finding out more about mental illness. Mr. Welter acted as if he was a pioneering force in the battle against depression. He had slyly succeeded in transforming what should have been a criminal investigation into a soap opera culminating in a bogus humanitarian gesture with the promise of expensive psychiatric research to follow. It was a stupendous feat of public relations based on the blatant distortion of the truth. His triumph was short-lived though. Some insider, perhaps a member of the medical team, may have also had their suspicions about Walt, because further information about the condition of the dead man's heart began to filter through to journalists and it made several front pages, including that of Caleb Montgomery's beloved *Washington Post.* Walt's heart attack turned out not to be a random blow of fate; he had deliberately engineered it by injecting sufficient insulin to have quickly felled a man weighing about 300 lbs or more than twice his weight. So lax was the security in the luxury psychiatric unit masquerading as a secure facility where Walt appeared to have been treated as a guest not a patient, never mind a murder suspect, that no one had paid much heed to his thrice-daily insulin which he administered himself —without supervision. According to the report he was believed to have had injected about a ten days' supply, or a lethal dose, all at once—as his medication bottle was empty and it had been a new refill. The cellophane wrapping and carton were found on the floor, near the bed. Although his entire system must have gone into immediate shock as his blood sugar plunged he had managed to get into the shower seconds before sliding into the fatal, self-induced coma. His father was immediately on the attack, announcing that he would sue the psychiatric unit personnel for not "protecting my son from himself." How I gloated over the unintentional comedy of that statement. The cosseted hero had suddenly become a suicide and was being more severely castigated for killing himself than he had ever been for murdering Mother.

Our phone rang for hours. Father was downstairs in the small drawing room, subjecting that Bartok piano sonata I had never much cared for to playing of a sustained aggression. I lay in the dark, listening to the acoustically strident piece which Father may have selected specifically to drown out the persistent ringing of the phone. I thought of the esteemed members of the press all busily backtracking and looking at ways of suggesting that they had long detected that Walt—now being referred to as Welter—was obviously unstable and highly devious. His ill-deserved patina of romance appeared to have died with him.

Hours later after supper, I turned over on my bed, preparing to pull the blankets I had been lying on up over me, and noticed through the window a large yellow moon glowing mistily. It seemed to have a halo and that eerie, cursed moon shimmered with a bloated, diseased luminosity. It all seemed deeply symbolic. Although again hungry, I couldn't face going downstairs. Father might want to talk but could as easily nod and walk away, or just pass me in the hall without a word.

Morning arrived very quickly. It seemed that I had only been contemplating going back down to the kitchen and then it was time to get up. My throat was sore; it felt bruised as did my glands and it hurt to swallow. I had decided to stay home from school, a decision I often made, but that day I actually was ill or almost. I went to the bathroom, conscious that Mrs. Faulkner would make clear her opinion that I should be going back to school. In order to consolidate my position I remained in my pajamas and put on my robe, leaving it open, apathetically allowing it to drag on the floor behind me. I looked in the mirror, pleased to note my unwashed hair and felt that no one could possibly dispute my impaired well-being. Deep sleep often leaves me wan and exhausted and had obligingly done so that day.

While sitting on the toilet and preparing myself for the inevitable confrontation with Mrs. Faulker, my dream replayed itself; Father had been dressed in a tuxedo. I don't think I had ever seen him wearing one. His hair seemed more white than gray and there was a red carnation in his buttonhole. He had a long black cloak which he tossed back over his shoulders while reaching for a sword which had appeared suddenly from nowhere, a thin rapier or it could have been an épée, which he flexed like a piece of willow. Then he cried a crazed "En garde" in a throaty French accent and there in the middle of what looked like an immense stage stood Walter Welter in a pale-pink suit. Father ran toward him across the endless surface that turned out to be an ice rink and Walt, who was clutching an old-fashioned microphone—he seemed to have been singing or performing, it wasn't clear . . . , spotlights shone bright upon him—lifted the microphone and squealed like a pig when Father sliced his head off all the while shouting, "Die, knave, die." I laughed aloud at the image; my dream had been enacted at cartoon speed. Father then hooted, baring his teeth which glistened like a wolf's and swirled his cloak around him before running up the stage curtain, the reverse of the way Count Dracula scales down the castle wall in the book. I rocked back and forth on the toilet seat shaking with laughter and thought to myself that I really should write it all down. Clearly I was more disturbed than I had thought. I

imagined telling Mrs. Faulkner about it, I could see her neutral
expression, that noncommittal stare and her slight frisson of
impatience, her waiting for me to be done so that she could continue her endless daily battle of keeping our beleaguered household afloat. But of course I would never tell her. Conversation
with her was like physically trying to push a large rock up a very
steep hill. Yet her stern, always silently judgmental presence was
sufficiently supportive in its own way and it had been there for as
long as I could remember. She was part of my buttress, although
she would have denied it.

As I approached the kitchen I knew the importance of
appearing as weakened as possible. Tactics are vital when honor
is involved. I moved very slowly. Mrs. Faulkner would expect a
privileged child such as me to crawl to my fancy school, so mani-
fold were my advantages. Her brother's children had been working since they were fifteen she had once chillingly announced as
if to put my obsessive shampooing of Galileo's mane and tail into
perspective. She did not approve of the pampering of horses . . . I
never knew if she had any children herself. Now that I think of it,
I never even knew for certain if there was—or had ever been—a
Mr. Faulkner. She regarded me spoilt; and so I was in my quiet
way. No one ever told me what to do; I enjoyed an adult's freedom of action, without any of the responsibility.

A large rectangular parcel was propped up on one of the chairs
grouped around the breakfast table. I assumed it was another
painting or a print, Father often bought pictures as presents.
His secretary's birthday was approaching, it was possibly for her.
Probably a horse, another high-quality equine print wasted on a
woman with no interest in art; never mind horses.

"It's late," snapped Mrs. Faulkner flatly, glaring at the large
kitchen clock before appearing to assess me. I slumped weakly
into the nearest chair; the one Father usually sat in and informed

her I was too ill to attempt my return to school. When she asked me what was wrong I mumbled a comprehensive "Everything," hoping she would offer to make me some of her honeyed oatmeal along with her specialty: milky coffee. She sighed and stepped back to the stove. Aware that she was about to present me with an invalid's breakfast, intended to tempt, I concealed my pleasure. Victory was mine. Being ill wasn't all bad. "Here, you make a start with this," she said, placing a rack of toast on the table and with it the expected cup of sweet milky coffee with chocolate sprinkled on top. A victory easily won, it was difficult to sustain my subdued demeanor yet I did. "That's for you," she motioned at the package.

Instead of leaping up and ripping off the heavy wrapping paper with its series of red and black heraldic crests, I remained huddled in the chair, pretending to be too weak to move, and clutched the cup with both hands, consolidating my projection of debilitating illness. Mrs. Faulkner wanted to see what was in the package, but would never admit her interest. I decided to tease her by delaying. The minutes trickled by, I could sense her staring at me, at the parcel, willing me to open it, open it. I loved the power. I felt like a cat tormenting a mouse, the thought did cross my mind that I was, beneath my mild exterior, a deeply unpleasant individual. But then I smiled inwardly, there was good reason; I had grown up around adults intent on secrecy and it had affected me, causing me, no doubt, to develop mildly sadistic impulses.

Not until the cup was empty, did I stand up; I could feel Mrs. Faulkner's inquisitive tension. She said nothing, did not even respond to my remarking on the beautiful gift wrap, and thinking of the way she had salvaged all Mother's discarded tissue paper, I said that it was such a shame to disturb the package. But

she made no reply, intently watching, as curious as was I, about
the contents of the mystery present.

There it was, I gasped at its splendor. Despite her iron discipline Mrs. Faulkner gushed raptly, "My, it's so . . . clear and
real-looking, you would think it was a photograph, not a painting." I told her it was a photograph, one of the most historic ever
taken. I could sense she was angry with herself for being wrong.
But I continued, obliged to inform her that the glory before us
was an enlarged reproduction of *Earthrise*, the wonderful image
taken from Apollo 8 by William Anders on Christmas Eve in
1968. I did indeed feel like weeping. The mission had entered
lunar orbit and one of the other astronauts had taken two black
and white shots, but it was Anders, moments later, who took
the color picture, it was he who had said that they had come
240,000 miles to see the Moon, only to discover that Earth was
the important one. The framed photograph by which we were
transfixed, had, for once, also been reproduced at the exact angle
Anders had taken it, with the moon providing a vertical frame to
the right, its chill surface contrasting with the vibrant blue and
green of Earth. Usually Earth is shown as if floating above the
moon in the photograph. This version replicated the original;
it was as Anders had observed, and it set the scene. It made it
possible to feel what it was like, being inside the spacecraft, passing the moon and staring through the vast black ocean of space
toward our planet. Mrs. Faulkner softened and actually placed
her hand on my shoulder; we were both surprised at the gesture
but she smiled and thanked me for explaining "the story of the
picture." She said she could feel the Lord's hand in it all. That
made me pause; I'd never thought much about God in relation
to any of it. I had also quite forgotten my illness and just filled a
bowl with cornflakes and hot milk and studied the picture. How
pretty Earth looked, adrift in the darkness of Infinity.

I carried the frame sideways to get it upstairs. This was Father's way of saying that he was sorry for the upheaval, the endless hoops of fire which had followed Mother's death, all the pecking and prying; the indecency of it, the reporters, Walt's demented side show . . . Father had tried to ask my forgiveness with a gesture to express what he could not put into words. All he said when we met in the hall was something about Anders not being much younger than him, "But I never got to walk on the Moon." Then by way of countering my remarking that Anders hadn't either—the mission had been a lunar orbit, not a landing, Father replied, "I am of course speaking metaphorically. But no, I never did get to walk on the Moon."

*

Jamie Hodge looked like a boy, his vast face soft. He and Father were sitting in the kitchen, coffee cups long since pushed to the side in favor of a bottle of Irish whiskey and two squat tumblers. Also on the table was an apple pie that looked as if they had been slicing bits off it without bothering with plates, before they settled into just pulling pieces away from the crust, with no pretense at social nicety. Dollops of pulpy apple spotted the tablecloth. The sheriff was in mid-sentence as I came in, my eyes resting directly on the beaten remains of the pie. "Big Red was touched by God, no other explanation for it." Father laughed and said it was a bit more complex. In his opinion, "gods plural," all of them, had been involved. "Zeus touched him and then ordered the rest of them to do the same which also helps explain his color. He's not chestnut. No, he is bright red. It is a fact, a singular shade, exclusive to him." Father offered me some whiskey. He had never done so before. Recent weeks must have made me become something of a fellow survivor in his eyes. "Grab your good self a clean drinking vessel," he directed with a regal wave. Since the pie was no longer in any fit condition to share, Father had turned to the whiskey. His face was flushed and I realized with a start that he was on the way to becoming a little drunk. Sheriff Hodge was already far from sober, if not yet too intoxicated to fail to convey mild disapproval at Father's offering me hard liquor. Then he too smiled. "We're going a' visiting; it's time . . . time we checked up again on Big Red." The two men began laughing—the sheriff wheezing disturbingly—and then they raised their tumblers, shouting out in unison on the count of three, "Why did he run so fast? Because he could! Why was he so great? Because he was!" They both laughed and brought their glasses down together with a synchronized thud. I had never seen Father so animated and without any trace of his natural cynicism. He got along very well with Mr. Montgomery; they were two clever men who enjoyed their sharp, opinionated exchanges and frequent battles of wit. But Jamie Hodge brought out a different, kinder side to Father. They had real affection for each other. Whereas Mr. Montgomery enjoyed Father's disagreeable comments, unpleasantness genuinely upset Sheriff Hodge; he wanted the world to be better and mankind to be happier, more neighborly. Mr. Montgomery, I have always felt, liked thinking he was superior to the rabble, he reveled in the imperfections of others as did Father.

The whiskey was interesting, sweet, almost like the cough medicine in the main bathroom cabinet of which I often took secret swigs, when in the bathroom, and straight from the bottle. But the whiskey, hmmm, sweetish and it made my stomach glow as if a fire was burning deep inside me. Big Red was obviously a horse. "The heavens opened and behold, instead of rain and deluge," intoned Sheriff Hodge, "the Lord delivered unto us in all his glory, his younger son—Secretariat . . ." Father groaned and asked why he felt compelled to bring religion into everything and then smiled wildly over at me, explaining that the subject under discussion was the greatest racehorse of all time. "He is sublime, an athlete without equal. His feats more surreal than Mr. Beamon's excessively long, long jump at the Mexico Olympics. Think of Mercury, think of Jupiter, think of Mozart . . ." Jamie Hodge agreed, "Secretariat is an artist, all old Ronnie Turcotte had to do was stay on and shut up. Let the master get on with the job." The two men sniggered gleefully and poured each other more whiskey. Father reached into his jacket and pulled out two cigars, telling Sheriff Hodge to have both. "Caleb has a warehouse full of them . . . I think he ships them in from Spain or Cuba, some place hot . . . now there's two less for him to chew on and make a mess out of and all over my study, as ever . . ."

Something made me want to stay and become part of their little celebration, Secretariat was a magic presence; I'd heard his name so many times, always uttered with such reverence, and had been present at foalings when the comment most often made was, "Maybe this one will be another Secretariat," followed by "Yeah and pigs will fly," so I asked them to tell me about him. I looked at the sheriff and although he was drunk I hoped he would talk. I always loved listening to his rich, warm storyteller's voice. When I was small he had often told me tales of the Civil War in which his great-grandfather had fought, although for a long while I had believed it when the sheriff told me that he as a small boy had also taken part in it, "riding my little gray pony . . . I would have been about eleven or maybe twelve at the time . . ." he used to say, all bright-eyed and innocent-looking. He also claimed that he had met Abraham Lincoln who gave him a bugle. I had believed that story too.

So tell me all about Secretariat, I asked. "With pleasure, Miss Helen," and Sheriff Hodge began by explaining there's greatness and then there's greatness, and then you go some and there is even more greatness, "but no greatness known to man or horse," he had mused, "no, not even old Dancing Brave his good self and all—you attended him that time with the ligament thing as I recall, as well as treating his momma," he digressed looking over to Father who nodded, then the Sheriff continued "approaches that of Secretariat." The 1973 Triple Crown winner, first and only horse to win the Kentucky Derby in under two minutes, victory at the Preakness and for an all-conquering finale—the winner of the Belmont Stakes by thirty-one lengths, "and this I know because I was there and I saw it all." Father immediately disputed Sheriff Hodge's version, reminding him that he'd been "too busy weeping," and that he, Father, had been there holding Jamie Hodge's hand. "Passing the Kleenex, you cried your way through those races, you didn't see anything. I alone maintained full composure while pandemonium reigned elsewhere."

The sheriff laughed but before long he was half-crying and barely coherent, admitting that just thinking about Secretariat, never mind watching him, always made him tearful. "Just so glorious, so brave . . . such power, awesome . . . could have carried a house on his back . . ." Father kept providing details, facts, observations. Secretariat had been foaled just down the road from us, at Meadow Farm. His father was Bold Ruler, and he had won the Preakness in 1957 and finished third in the Belmont after placing fourth in the Kentucky Derby—the three Triple Crown races his greatest son would win sixteen years later—while his mother, who had only raced once, went by the name of Somethingroyal. "Something Special more like it," said Jamie Hodge. Father nodded, and then suggested, "How about Something Auspicious?" Father had always felt, he said, that the mother was vital, "Always is in breeding; you look to the mare, lots of people don't. Their mistake." Secretariat's dam had been eighteen when he was foaled. Somethingroyal was descended from a daughter of the great foundation stallion Eclipse, famed for passing on the X chromosome, or a large heart, on the female side. "And she lived to the age of thirty-one, only died a few years ago. Now there's genetics. Eclipse's heart weighed about fourteen pounds . . . I can but imagine the size of Secretariat's. He has a huge chest; he's a big horse, seventy-four-inch girth . . . even when he was racing looked more like a show jumper in there with the Thoroughbreds, mighty powerful animal, yes sir, mighty powerful indeed." Father spoke as if he too remained mesmerized by the wonder of this big red horse. I would enjoy the story, he told me, because there was so much history in it. "And you like history more than anything." I was to grasp the full relevance of that remark not long after that . . . But Father was in full flow and described how Seabiscuit had lifted the American people at the height of the Depression but what Secretariat had done was even more important. "Just when America had badly needed a hero in the squalid aftermath of Nixon and Watergate, the nation's abhorrence of Vietnam," Father was saying, "along comes a god, a mythic hero of old born anew, and a good-looking one at that . . ."

With passion heightened by whiskey, goodwill, and his emotional response to things, Sheriff Hodge interrupted dreamily and claimed that "without fear of contradiction" watching Secretariat was the greatest experience of his life. "I do worship at his feet, um, hooves. I thank God I was alive to witness such divine bounty." Father was more restrained: "Sublime, sublime, only word for him . . . Great horses, including Sham, who was ultimately devastated by Secretariat," and Father weighed our reactions as he said, "even my beloved Monticello, they all had their hearts and their spirits broken. None could comprehend the greatness, the majesty of Secretariat, the sheer grandeur . . . none of us can. He'll keep us trying to figure it all out forever. As I have said, he must have one hell of a heart . . . that has to be part of it . . . A huge engine . . . extraordinary lung capacity to stave off the inevitable effects of lactic acid that has to hit any athlete as soon as fatigue creeps in, which it does, or should, unless you happen to be Secretariat . . ." Father decided it was time I saw perfection. "Follow," he ordered, picking up the bottle as he, walking slightly unsteadily, led the way down the hall to his little study. Sheriff Hodge with me in tow, obeyed like the faithful at church. In the small office, still warm with the heat of the day, he reached up to a row of videotapes and selected three. "I never loan these to anyone," he announced, as if warning Sheriff Hodge not to dare ask to borrow them. Not only had Father recorded each of Secretariat's Triple Crown victories in full, he had detailed commentaries, slow-motion sequences and the individual split times. "Welcome to my archive," he announced, "the story of Secretariat, a considerable deal stranger than fiction."

Jamie Hodge burped in agreement and said that he needed to sit down. "I tend to get overcome, and I am not ashamed to admit it . . ."

It was as they said, Secretariat defied reason. He would suddenly emerge from the back as if he was bored and just wanted to hurry on home. The Belmont race was bizarre; he just ran on and on, getting faster and faster, causing the astonished race commentator to sound more like an awed fan uttering a bewildered, "And Secretariat moving like a tremendous machine," the word "tremendous" ringing out like a slow two-syllable chant. And Secretariat was galloping, no, surging, surging along courtesy of his powerful, bounding, supernatural stride. I'd never seen anything like it.

Tears slid down Jamie Hodge's fleshy cheeks. Father nodded happily; pleased I think that he had initiated me into the wonders of Secretariat. And me? My heart was pounding and I couldn't speak; the thrill of it and I just wanted to get to meet this astounding horse who treated a race like a saunter down the street. The drive to Claiborne in Paris, Kentucky was about seven and a half hours, maybe eight, a little under 500 miles from where we were. Alone with Father the journey would be an endurance test, his tape deck was still jammed and he refused to listen to the radio—"No one selects my music for me"—so we would be sitting in silence, unless Father chose to hum, which he could do, without pause, for hours. But with Jamie Hodge along, telling his stories and his needing to visit the men's room every time we stopped for gas, and then wanting snacks and something to drink, it would be some adventure. But first, there was the book, *Secretariat: The Making of a Champion* written by a sports journalist, William Nack, who had been assigned to follow Big Red throughout his Triple Crown campaign. I really had to read it. Father smiled and explained to the sheriff that I had always had to find out more about everything. I didn't mind him saying that, it was true; I wanted to read the book that night and I asked Father if he had a copy. "Yes sir, right over there; pay no heed to the purple prose, it's more than justified."

I had a sense of a new beginning awakening in me that evening. At first I felt a slight guilt, as if Mother had just been forgotten, but then I realized I'd shared a similar excitement with her over my discovery of Simon and Garfunkel. But no, the two did not compare. I began reading Nack's book, just got into bed still in my clothes, only took off my boots and didn't even clean my teeth. Within minutes I discovered that Secretariat shared his birthday, March 30th 1970, with me; omens don't come better than that. I too would be going to visit "God's younger, better-looking son."

*

Claiborne would have to wait though. Father was speaking at a conference in Munich on the treatment of joint disease and radical bone trauma. He would be away for four days and then he was hosting a breeding seminar in Richmond. There were a number of consultations as well and he had been appointed chief veterinary advisor to the United States equestrian squad. Despite his having four senior veterinarians working in the practice, he was always busy. Without fail Sheriff Hodge fretted about going away. He approached each absence as if the fate of Virginia County hung in the balance and postponed and rearranged his plans several times before he ever actually got around to going anywhere. His deputy was used to repeated briefings and being given long rambling notes that the sheriff would then quiz him on before changing the plans. Jamie Hodge, who had lived with his mother until her death at 103 while pouring a bourbon, also had six dogs to be cared for like children—although the eldest one, Citation, a beagle (named in honor of the 1948 Triple Crown victor, the last one before Secretariat) would be traveling with us to Claiborne. As for me, even I had a commitment, aside from school, there was a state science competition and I had been asked by my science teacher "to please, please enter a project." But more immediate was the offer of private lessons with a former German international eventer. He had been invited to give a series of workshops at various equestrian centers throughout the east, but was also coming to Virginia to stay with some friends.

I had been asked if I was interested, as he would be available for a week. It meant driving about thirty-five miles each way, every day, but it was a great chance to find out what a top class rider would make of Galileo and me. As well as that, the people with whom the coach was staying had their own private indoor arena. At 300 dollars a lesson it was expensive but I had savings; I rarely spent my generous allowance and, as we had a yard, I didn't have to pay livery charges or buy feed, and all my veterinary needs were there, at home. The tuition was a chance to figure out if Galileo was better jumping or on the flat; I had also considered eventing him but was only too aware that he would be tricky to control in the cross-country.

Dieter Bernhard had competed in the three-day event at four Olympics and had two team golds as well as, I think, an individual silver or bronze; he wore sunglasses all the time, which Father would have frowned upon, yet Herr Bernhard did have what Father would refer to as "a military bearing." Father often told me that had I been a boy he would have sent me to West Point, and yes Thomas Jefferson had been involved in its founding. Lucky escape for me, I would have hated it. Anyhow Herr Bernhard also spoke English with a stilted correctness that initially made me laugh, much to his annoyance. One of the first things he said was typical of his didactic style, "Your horse appears a most unpleasant personality, for this we may almost excuse him, he is very talented, perhaps excessively gifted. We shall see." This left me feeling like an onlooker who just happened to be riding him and I quickly discovered that Dieter Bernhard did not believe in either praise or encouragement. Whenever I did anything right he immediately announced, "Yes the nasty horse is very clever," or, "This horse he wants to work," and most frequently, "Yes it is blatantly evident to us (he seldom spoke in the singular) that he is intelligent." Well "blatantly evident," just imagine that for a turn of phrase. Herr Bernhard's blatant lack of charm didn't bother me, I knew the session had begun well and it would be important to find out if I could survive without having Billy Bob's encouragement and kindness there to help me. Herr Bernhard had also decided that my name was Halley, pronounced as in Halley's Comet, I didn't much mind that either; for me it was another good omen. I had never liked my stiff, formal name, something else I had in common with Mother—although I would have been happy with Susan. But "Helen" I had always disliked, and with a heightened rigor since discovering that it seemed it had been intended as a memorial to Father's first dead wife. "Halley, Halley," Dieter Bernhard would bark, with a sharp little clap of his hands, "attend to this horse he is waiting for your instruction. There can be no vagueness in the aids; he is not supposed to be a mind reader." Well, I disagree, when it is going right, the horse and rider do appear to read each other's minds. I said nothing.

Each day I drove back to the Willards' prosperous stud farm, always ensuring I arrived at least thirty minutes before the hour-long sessions began. On the fourth day, Mrs. Willard appeared in the yard as I was unloading Galileo. She told me that "Dieter" had said I was very good, a sensitive, intelligent rider able to deal with a difficult horse. I tried not to look astonished as my heart contracted with joy—it was not about ego, it was knowing that yes, I was managing, and I silently thanked Billy Bob over and over. Then about five minutes into that fourth lesson, the first one we had done in the outdoor arena, Galileo threw in about five bucks for no reason that either Dieter Bernhard or I could see—aside from maybe feeling good about being back outside in the sunshine. I rode it out and Herr Bernhard just nodded his head and said that there were some horses that one could never fully trust and that Galileo was "probably one of them."

No probably about it, I already knew and could confirm it in writing.

The jumping had been going well over the first three days and had progressed on to a little track of six jumps between three foot six and a little under four foot. But we also did a lot of flat work. It must have been about a half hour or so since the bucking episode and Herr Bernhard had said nothing aside from issue instructions. Then he motioned to me to ride into the center of the school, where he was standing. "We are thinking," he said, and I thought, "Here it comes; he is going to tell me that I am not able for this horse. And so . . ." But he was thinking along a more interesting track, "This horse is very fast, very strong, can jump, and moves well. So yes he is well-equipped for the three disciplines the sport of eventing requires . . ." He was for sure a dour, humorless man, with a pained expression; he gave the impression that teaching was a chore but that riding was more than a job, it was a matter of life or death. Even to me with my obsessive tendencies, Herr Bernhard's attitude seemed borderline crazy. I was beginning to think that I would give up competing and ride just for fun; I was serious by nature but his agonized fanaticism made me suspect that perhaps it was all a bit ridiculous. "Just so, a talented animal and you have very good balance and can jump him better than you should be able to . . ." I felt the sting of that. "But he is not good-natured. No. We feel this animal could go insane on a cross-country course. This is the problem with the Thoroughbred blood; it can be superb, designed as it is for supreme performance or then again, just too highly strung. His head, his mind, I think, may not be suited to jumping and cross-country and dressage over the three days, the cross-country will be a disaster . . . he will go out of control. Kill himself," he paused and added, "and possibly also yes, to kill you," but that was only said as an afterthought. "Yet we feel," he continued in that irritatingly ponderous manner as if he were imparting what really happened to the last dodo, "that he should specialize, concentrate on one thing. He could be a superb dressage competitor. Do you like dressage? We find Americans are cowboys and just want to gallop, too impatient to ride correctly. But you ride well on the flat, better than the others we have seen on this visit."

It was the most detailed exchange I'd had with this man who seemed far more interested in studying Galileo than he was in teaching me and I'd just nodded and smiled. But it was time to reply, to say anything at all, he was expecting an answer. I didn't want to sound as if I was whining. So, conscious that he had been a three-day event rider I said I had always liked the way the Australians called novice events "encouragers." He looked blank, and simply swatted away my cheerful non sequitur as if it were a fly not worth heeding. "Does this mean you have no interest in dressage?" he asked. "I do, I do," I insisted, saying that I enjoyed flat work and then just blurted out how much I love music. It was the first and only time he smiled, and even removed his sunglasses. I had expected him to have icy blue eyes or stone-washed gray pebbles, to match his graying blonde crew cut. But instead he had dull little brown ones, made even smaller by squinting in the strong light. There he stood under a blue, cloudless Virginia sky, looking older, more worn than he had in the dim natural lighting of the indoor school. He told me I had exemplary teeth—when I heard "exemplary" I thought that perhaps he was going to praise my riding but no—and he had looked so thoughtful suggesting that something profound had just struck him as he announced in full seriousness how all the Americans he had met were not afraid of smiling, "Because the teeth are so good. Big like horse teeth yet so white, unnatural this whiteness . . . In Europe people don't show their teeth so much.

When we smile we cover our mouths with our hands." His own were tiny, like baby teeth, only chipped-looking and beyond yellow, more like pale beige and almost transparent. I had a mental image of Europeans walking around with their hands up to their faces. It sounded more than weird. Perhaps it was a joke? Maybe it served me right for being so ambitious as to presume to have lessons with an Olympic rider. He probably thought I was spoilt and rich, harboring delusions of talent. I always seemed to try so hard. But I still had three more sessions with him and no one else knew about them, except for the Willards. I concentrated and imagined my mind being washed free of everything except the complicated, mean-minded but intelligent horse I was attempting to ride. Herr Bernhard's flat, mournful voice droned on, "We will now, by 'we' this time I refer of course to you and the horse, to please to try a dressage test, yes?"

*

After a week of being called 'Halley' and 'Hayley'—although admittedly only a few times, as Dieter Bernhard had demonstrated little interest in me, preferring to address his comments to Galileo; indeed he had often sought his opinion alone, "And so, Mr. Galileo, what do you think?" or "Now inform us, my dear sir, why did you do that?"—it was quite sobering to revert to being referred to as Helen. I wondered about how I would have felt about being named Anna, or Olivia, or better still Meredith, Alexandra or Cameron; I had a liking for Cameron; it made me think of Scotland, a green, mysterious land of damp and mossy glens which I hoped to visit someday and Edinburgh, where Mother's *Black Watch* pajamas had been made, funnily, by appointment to the Queen of England. Even Sarah or Louisa were acceptable; either would be an improvement on Helen. Yet, perhaps not Louisa, too close to Louisiana, and that also ruled out Virginia, Georgia, and even Caroline because of the Carolinas . . . Addison would confer authority, or how about the splendor of Ariadne, with its aura of mythic drama—now there was a name to encourage one to stand tall. An emphatic no to Margaret, a bank clerk's name, and I was most grateful not to have been burdened by Eunice, or Edwina or prissy old Lucinda . . . Why had I not been named Elizabeth? or Emily? Elizabeth, dignified without being stuffy and Lord knows I am stiff and stuffy, while Emily, genteel with a hint of fire, but maybe I only imagined that because of Dickinson and Brontë, haunted women, possessed of fearless genius . . . yes to Emily or maybe Flora but no, never, not Florence . . . Mrs. Faulkner had been named, aptly, Prudence . . . no, that's not quite right; her name was Prudentia. I forget how I found that out . . . and then there's Tiffany even worse than Sandy or Candy—the only Tiffany I knew of being that dreaded Ralph Lauren-wearing creature—she who had seized the heart of Edmund Dell Hutton III. None of us knew her because she was four—or was it five?—years older than he was; "a veritable lifetime" as Melanie Taylor who had had her hair straightened "all for him" had put it. I kept my romantic fantasies to myself acting politely interested when Melanie tearfully announced the sad news of the engagement. I wondered had he even noticed Melanie's hair. He had addressed me directly, once; and as he had approached me I had felt my face redden. Breathe in, breathe out. But he only inquired as to the bit I was using and was surprised, nay awestruck on hearing it was a standard hollow snaffle. He raised his hand to pat Galileo's neck, but true to his cantankerous disposition, the horse lifted his head, then his lips, and bared his teeth. Edmund swiftly backed off and smiled sympathetically; telling me that I had my hands full. And that was it, not exactly an encounter upon which to build a future together, although Melanie probably would have interpreted it as the first step toward a white wedding.

Life had settled down to be quieter, very quiet, library reading room-quiet without Mother. How she had filled the house with her moods, her essential chaos; the quick little footsteps, the sharp scents of perfume, the jangle of her bracelets and always, with a nervous twitch, the click of her purse continually opening and closing, "Now where is my check book" and, "What on earth did I do with the lipstick, the one in the silver thingy." Her movement and bustle, like that of a large, fractious child. Could she be described as mercurial? No, not quite—Mother was volatile, a natural hysteric, the kind of nervy woman Jung would have pretended to study, and hoped to seduce. I remember thinking when I had first seen that movie *Amadeus* that the actor's frenetic portrayal of Mozart could have been based on Mother's erratic mood shifts. She would drop things, declare to the household at large that she was late; scream if she thought she saw a mouse— yet had flatly refused to allow a cat into the house because of what she dubbed "the ensuing slaughter," and always insisted cats would drag dead birds and rodents indoors to display their kill. Cats, she announced, were insatiable hunters. Nor would she permit a dog and I had been offered so many puppies. I always wanted a dog that would be mine and mine alone.

Fear of appearing to have callously waited for her to die made me reluctant to belatedly ask for a pet. Did I miss her? I don't really know but I was aware of the new silence and it was my first experience of someone being there and then, not. An instant death such as hers leaves no time to prepare. Father appeared little changed, only older. Perhaps he looked the same to everyone else and only appeared older to me because I then knew he was old or older than I had thought. He continued to speak to himself; but then he always had done so, as indeed do I—an early sign of madness some may say. Yet it is simply a habit shared by loners and the lonely alike—and I think he may have been both, a loner and lonely, as I was, only it took me some time to realize that.

Days passed and the mornings grew darker. When I woke earlier to work on my science project, I soon needed the extra light cast by my desk lamp. I've always hated the end of summer and fall, two seasons that are pretty much as one for us, dry and balmy. But the winter, those drab gray daytime skies, the lack of light, the bleakness . . . I don't mind the cold, not that it ever becomes overly cold in Virginia; it can bring that quick, blinding winter sunlight, but I dread those dank, dark mornings. A touch peculiar that, when considering my love of the night skies, the theater of the stars. I almost enjoy not being able to see them by day, as they are there and I delight in knowing that they will reappear as if by magic in the incandescent (my favorite word) darkness of a clear, moonlit night.

The science teacher seemed even more excited than I was about the project; for her it amounted to a personal triumph, extracting something from a class not exactly aglow with scientific endeavor. Teaching science at our school was a challenge. Shortly after Mitzi had arrived, the teacher brought live frogs in for us to dissect and the girls screamed, a couple cried, one even vomited. The school chaplain became involved. Several of the parents protested, Richmond's like that. I liked our science teacher and saw her as a pioneer. For me the project was a pleasure; a chance to wallow with a purpose and to gather material I had already amassed. My subject was, not surprisingly, Galileo. I gave it a grandiose title: "Exploring the Heavens: The Life, Vision, and Cosmology of Galileo Galilei (1564–1642)"—he had been prickly, opinionated, opportunistic, resourceful, and real skilled at exploiting the egos of his patrons such as when naming the four new stars around Jupiter the Medicean stars to honor, more like flatter, the Medici family. He didn't invent the telescope as he claimed, although he had improved it. His geometric and military compass was very successful in its own right. Intent on standing up for his belief in the Copernican system he had played cat and mouse with the papal authorities for quite a while behind the veil of his wittily ambivalent writings. He never was martyr material though, and even while living under house arrest in his villa after the Inquisition, had been able to continue his work. He was wily; no saint and not a hero, a real human with lots of warts. It was possible to write a readable project and I'd had far more time than the official several weeks allocated to prepare, I had been preparing for years. All my hours of dreaming and wondering; imagining what it must have been like to have been there, more than three centuries earlier, caught up in the excitement of revelation. I did not regard the project as a task; it was my party piece, a labor of love. It was a privilege to be chosen as a knight of old representing the honor of the school. Anyhow no one else wanted to do one. My days, nights, and early mornings were dominated by Galileo the astronomer and the afternoons and weekend mornings, by Galileo the horse—two self-absorbed opportunists, or perhaps three which includes me too.

Ironically the project was virtually completed before I formally began it, but I admit that I exploited the generous free time I was given by my school, which was my haven, my club. I loved my school; I loved my school days, although I often took days off so as to think, I've always needed time to think.

We would be leaving for Claiborne in a few days—at long last. I was looking forward to it, the project was "in hand" as they say and I'd also finished reading the Secretariat biography and just wanted to touch his bright red coat and bask in his genius. He appeared to have a sense of humor, and enjoyed teasing humans; he even had a trick of grabbing the nearest yard brush in his teeth. At the sound of a camera, Secretariat was ready. Galileo the horse had the temperament of a debt collector whereas Secretariat was a prince, amused by his invincibility. I had decided that the Claiborne visit—we were staying overnight—would give me a brief vacation. Meanwhile I continued schooling grumpy old pain-in-the-neck Galileo, with a decided specialist objective, dressage. It seemed a good plan, Billy Bob did not appear overly surprised and as he battled another of his alarming coughing fits, managed to wheeze, "Dressage is just a fancy name for fine riding; you need, well, he needs discipline— might just help him settle himself, he attacks jumps as if they was the enemy . . . I think he has mental issues, know what I mean?" Yet again Billy Bob qualified his comments, conceding that Galileo had been bred for racing, "It's in his blood, those old Thoroughbred genes, edgy, spiky . . . We gotta make some allowances . . . Sure he's teaching you loads of stuff, but he also gotta learn him some manners real bad . . . He needs to be more polite."

Father was out for the evening, at some official dinner he didn't want to attend. They could prove ordeals for him when he wanted to be on his own, which was most of the time. Still, it meant I could again explore his little library. Had he been there he would have sighed and probably made no comment as to whatever book I took. On the rare occasion he would say "Yes, you should like that"—almost an order—or "Hmm, never finished it . . ." or "Lost all patience with that one!"—as he had with *The Rainbow*. But he wasn't there; I was free to make my own mistakes. *The Good Soldier* caught my eye but as I reached for it, another cover with pale-green letters on a tawny color known as buff with a black swirling design encasing the title on the spine in icing sugar-like flourishes, distracted me: *To the Lighthouse*. I thought of Robert Louis Stevenson, how I had loved *Treasure Island* and *Kidnapped*, and by chance had discovered that Stevenson's family built lighthouses. I took down the book and smiled when I saw the author's first name in white letters on the buff of the front cover—"Virginia." She obviously had not come from here. She was the daughter of a distinguished and overbearing English intellectual father, I could sure empathize with that. By then I had read my way through Father's collection of nineteenth-century British writers, but not so the more modern novelists and had made a tentative beginning with *Point Counter Point* by Huxley. I liked it so much I immediately read *Brave New World*, which is far more famous but I sure hated that book.

Time to try again, as I was too fond of the Victorians; I stood by the bookcase, holding the copy of *To the Lighthouse*, enjoying the texture of the dusty, chalky, paper jacket. It had a faded, sun-bleached look about it, as if it had been left out on the lawn during a long summer's afternoon—although it probably had looked much the same when it was new back in 1927, a year or two before Father had been born. I decided to read *To the Lighthouse*. There was an inscription on the flyleaf: "To William, love always, Helen, 1950." It was stylish handwriting, an expert probably would have said it conveyed confidence—the ink had paled with time—not sunlight. The book was also a first edition and valuable. Father would have been, I reckon, about twenty-two at the time, young but older than me. I had never thought of him as ever being young. All my life he'd had gray hair and spent his time putting his glasses on and then pulling them off, hastily thrusting them down into his jacket pocket as if they were sticky or hot to the touch. He had been very tall, or so it seemed to me when I was little, now he was merely tall as I was no longer small. I worried if only out of despair and embarrassment, not vanity, about my ill-matching eyes and my immense, if perfect teeth which appeared to dominate my face. I had, however, by then, begun to suspect that Father was vain and yes I had noticed that women became all fey and fluttery when around him, nauseating to watch and sort of calculating. But although being cynical about grown-up human motivations I sometimes settled on being semi-romantic, and could visualize standing at an open doorway, watching my beloved riding off to war . . .

When I noticed the handwriting, though, this faceless Helen proclaiming love eternal to Father and who, had she lived, would have been my mother, I almost put the book back; it seemed as if I was violating his privacy. Mother, as I knew her, would never have given Father any book, certainly not a novel and most definitely not a rare first edition.

I placed it down on Father's desk to better examine the cover for stains, all the while rubbing my hands up and down on my blue jeans, fearing there were residual traces of leather conditioning cream on them. It would have been a pity to mar the vintage dust jacket, but no, there were no marks. It was fortunate as I had been cleaning my tack and my hands were never overly respectable. I only seemed to wash them after I had been to the bathroom, and even then, I fear, not all the time. My hands were at their cleanest after a shower or a bath or having cleaned my teeth. As for the remainder of my waking hours, I bow my head—I would pat a horse, check his legs, lift his feet, and then eat a candy bar without a thought. Father was particular about his books and never broke the spine of a paperback, another habit I inherited. The house was empty, not a sound, except for the creaking of the floorboards as I crossed the hall. Her Woolf was spelt differently from the other Wolfe I had read. In common with most Southern teenagers I'd read *Look Homeward, Angel* and had thought of the tormented author, a Southerner adrift in New York, alone and prowling the moonlit sidewalks of Manhattan.

How come old hardbacks tend to smell slightly damp, musty, as if they're going to turn to dust? So I decided to read the book that a woman who had died before I was born, and otherwise could have been my mother, had presented to Father when he was young and very different from the stern, remote individual whom I barely knew. Would it help explain him to me? Unlikely, it had been the title, evoking the lonely image of a lighthouse, that had attracted me. As for the rest, it just happened to be his book.

That novel drew me into its ambiance of memory; an upper class family gathers on the Isle of Skye in the Hebrides at their vacation house. It is idyllic, an annual pilgrimage, home away from home. The story opens in 1910, four years before the Great War. Mrs. Ramsay, an alluring earth mother figure, getting older but still beautiful, is the center of the household, its life force. I wanted to be her, or like her, the peacemaker, the teller of stories, the heart of a lively clan, yet I feared I would most likely be a Lily Briscoe figure, the lone watcher, attempting to define the essence of life as lived by others. I heard the hour strike eleven on the grandfather clock that always seemed to lurk in the hall as if hoping to chide a body for wasting God's time on frivolous pursuits. I read on and forgot all about the minutes ticking away, and never heard midnight sounding. Nor had I noticed one o'clock strike. The death of Mrs. Ramsay shocked me, reported as it is in a terse single sentence, little more than an authorial aside, particularly as Mr. Ramsay reminded me of Father.

A postcard had been left in the book; it was worn, the edges tattered, dog-eared, and must have been kept for its attractive picture, a photograph of the window of the New Library, an eighteenth-century addition, in Christ College Oxford, where Lewis Carroll studied and spent most of his adult life. In the background, there's a view of the tower of another college, Merton, I think it's called. What appears to be late afternoon sunlight illuminates the old floorboards and two reading desks are seen in half shadow. It was an elegiac picture. Time captured in an image. There was no message written on it. Once upon a time it obviously had meant something to Father; I decided to use the postcard as a bookmark while reading the novel. Then I would return both to Father's bookcase.

It was late, judging by the number of pages I had read. Father hadn't returned, leastways not while I was awake. I slept for a while but woke early and continued reading. So much change during the course of ten sad, long years, so much death. By the time the surviving Ramsays finally set off for the lighthouse, it is no longer a quest, more a ritualized gesture. Again I was struck by Lily Briscoe, fated only to observe. Would that be me?

I had a quick shower, elated at having read such a thrillingly sad, profound narrative, and squeezed the water out of my hair. The kitchen was quiet, no sign of life—or food; no fresh bread, only rolls left over from supper and they too hard to interest me. But there was cereal and I was hungry and wishing for something sweet, cake or cookies, ate two bowlfuls of bland wheat flakes, supplemented by lots of sugar, then drained the residue milk from the dish after the cereal was gone. Halfway to the yard I remembered I'd left Galileo's new tendon boots in the washing machine in the laundry room. It would spark a major domestic incident. Mrs. Faulkner had made several objections to my washing saddle cloths, leg wraps and tail bandages, and had banned "all nonhuman items" from the house machine. There was a washing machine in the yard for such purposes, but I was lazy and certainly enjoyed breaking Prudentia's decrees—if only without her knowing—I can't deny it, I have a sneaky streak which I keep well concealed. Anyhow, I ran back to the house, into the kitchen and beyond it to the laundry. Not a sound. The ironing board already in position, a basket of sheets was awaiting action in the wake of the extensive wash done the previous day. The boots were still in the machine, I smirked happily. Yet again, I had gotten away with it, not that the boots were all that dirty. I wanted to soften them, the straps were stiff.

I hurried back out, still no one in the kitchen. No sign of life. Was it that early? From the far end of the stable yard Billy Bob lurched into sight, his lop-sided walk more exaggerated than usual. Although heading in my direction, it didn't look like he'd seen me. He was staggering. It was obvious that he was drunk, this must have been an extended binge. To be so drunk at that hour, he must have been drinking all night. I could not avoid him, so would make no comment, just "Good morning, rain held off." I rarely saw him like that although I had heard a yard-boy mention with some awe that "Mr. Porter" was about eighty percent drunk most of the time, only no one ever noticed. He seemed to be sobbing, and when he lifted his head his eyes had disappeared into mushy pockets. Tears had made tracks down the film of grease and hay dust that always coated his face, he was calling blindly, "Missy Helen, Missy Helen, the boss . . . the boss . . . he's gone and died. He dead . . ." That's why it's so quiet, I suddenly understood the unnatural stillness, and oh the guilt, how quickly it hit me—I would never have contemplated going to Claiborne until I realized how pleasant Sheriff Hodge would make the drive, how he would fill the silence in the car with his wonderful chatter and his frequent need for the men's room and snack breaks. I was finally truly alone; Father and Mother both gone, leaving me on my own.

Billy Bob was gagging and retching, snot coming out of his nose. He was sweating and so, so distraught. He fell to his knees, wheezing with grief; I dropped the tendon boots I had been kneading between my hands. It must have happened so fast, his heart, a stroke. I knew Father would never kill himself . . . and I'd always imagined him at eighty-five doing battle with a sly cancer but patrician-like refusing to die . . . rigid with determination, prepared to endure. But now . . . Billy Bob was old; he was seventy-three, fifteen years older than Father . . . my new knowledge, gained from the newspapers. Despite all his drinking he had managed to outlive Father. Had he been drunk before he heard the news, or had he gotten drunk because of it? Perhaps he was actually sober? He was an emotional man, that I knew and of course he had loved Father, I just hadn't realized how much . . . regrets such as these darted through my thoughts, competing with my numbing awareness of helpless shame, always the guilt that seemed destined to stalk me through life. Billy Bob had first come to the yard from Georgia as a boy of fifteen to work for my grandfather, when Father was two months old; they shared a history. He had been dismissed briefly, exiled for drinking, and returned to Georgia remaining there for a while. He may have had a child, or so the story went, it was never definite, just something, a comment . . . I am not certain, so what? Billy Bob eventually reappeared but had kept some token contact with his other life, not much, just hints, here and there. Now his world had crumbled. I think he usually slept in the stable yard, most likely in Monticello's roomy stall. Billy Bob may have been wondering about the future, he was old and would be homeless without Father. His future? What about mine? I was now fully alone. I had never given much attention to being their child, but I had an intense awareness of having become their orphan, destined for the next few years to have to answer to Caleb Montgomery. "It will be fine, Billy Bob, Billy Bob, listen to me . . . Mr. Montgomery, he's reasonable . . . we can keep the horses . . . it will be just the same, almost the same . . ." I didn't know what I was saying, Billy Bob howled and threw up some vile-smelling mess of alcohol and whatever it was he'd eaten. He was crouching, face looking downward on the ground, his hands splayed flat in the dust and splattered by his own vomit. I had never been confronted by another person's woe. Mother's depressions had been theatrical, impossible to take seriously. That day at the funeral when Aunt Sally had been crying, pretty much continuously, her weeping was under control, almost like background music. Billy Bob's was different, it was elemental. I knelt down beside him, dreading that he too might have a heart attack, and die in my arms. I tried to comfort him but felt as awkward as my words sounded, lame, bewildered. How I prayed that Mrs. Faulkner would appear and take charge of things. Billy Bob looked smaller, hunched over on the ground, his poor joints creaking and his arms wrapped tight around his sides, keening. He was swaying, his very body contracting. I kept patting his back, telling him we'd get by and was surprised that he felt so spongy as if beneath the layer of fat the rest of him was composed of heaving jelly. This little old man had given me his time and patience, his encouragement and kindness for years, I'd never actually thanked him, just took it as my due that he would concentrate on my riding.

When I was small he had told me to call him Billy Bob—his name was William Robert—William the same name as Father. William Robert Porter had made me a rider for sure, and all I could do was awkwardly pat his back as if he was someone else's dog. I do better easing a horse. Why was it that I didn't know the right words, the proper way to offer comfort? Was it because I had never seen one human tending another? Although I had—I had once been given a glimpse of true compassion. It had been that evening after Mother's killing when Jamie Hodge had held Father's hands in his own, and wept in his place for Father's loss, our loss.

Yet again I was shocked by my lack of response, Father was dead but I just felt myself floating, numb as if sedated by the dentist. Where did that fury of the bereaved come from? Why was I excluded from it? Maybe Father had been on heart tablets without my knowing; most old people take all kinds of pills and stuff. Had he been silently grieving and given up taking his medication? And then, just to collapse and die suddenly, a snap of the fingers and no more.

Thoughts race fast and confused at times like that. It was a cold morning; the sun was forcing its way through the cloud cover. How had Jamie Hodge's poor heart continued to pump blood along arteries that must have been clogged with fat as thick as churned butter, whereas Father's had stopped. When would my mind cease picking over the details and allow me some emotion? I had gone to see Mother, but couldn't bear the idea of looking at Father confined to a casket and finally passive when I had known his domineering ways. Billy Bob continued wailing and sobbing, clutching my arm so tightly it felt like the flesh had been pushed sideways off the bone. I would support him, stay at his side, be there; I owed him that much and more as he shed tears enough for both of us. My old life was over and I can remember thinking, cold sweat chilling my back as I bent down to pick up the tendon boots I had dropped, "So this is how my childhood ends."

*

Billy Bob was choking and not making much sense but then I wasn't listening that closely; what with my eyes burning from the heady fumes of the alcohol, the sweat, and the liniment seeping out through his pores, my mind was racing. Instead I concentrated on half-lifting, half-pushing the poor man toward the kitchen before the yardmen arrived in for work and saw him. Yet he struggled, apparently intent on going in the opposite direction, back round to the stables. Of course he wanted to check on Monticello. Billy Bob often put a heavier stable blanket on him last thing at night, depending on the season. Those rugs needed to be taken off early though to prevent Monticello from overheating. It required an exact balance, not too cold but not sweating up either. Billy Bob always fed him and I wondered how he'd managed that morning, considering the state he was in. If he hadn't been able to, I could feed Monticello, I knew all about the special mix and the supplements he got. Only it was impossible to imagine Billy Bob neglecting any of the many rituals, even in his dazed condition. I was surprised though to notice the stable door ajar. Now that was something you would never see. Billy Bob lived in fear of Monticello stepping on a nail or a stone and monitored the horse's every movement. Still it was early enough and the esteemed old gentleman was probably sleeping, or resting, unaware that Father had died.

Monticello was lying peacefully like a king, his two stable rugs, including the traditional Witney red, black, and yellow woolen blanket sent over from England, still on him. He was dead. There was no fear of his overheating now. Billy Bob sank down beside him, trying to contain him within his arms. I couldn't believe it; he'd always been there, all my life, the perfect horse, a prince. His noble head motionless, his eyes not quite closed as if he was sneaking a final glimpse at this world he had graced but most importantly of all, was looking one last time at the man who had tended him with such devotion. Monticello was the Boss, not Father, and he appeared to have slipped away; there was no sign of distress or a struggle. He must have just drifted and died in his sleep. I patted his long neck, admittedly thinner than it had been, the first traces of his winter coat coming through. I put my hand in under the rugs and he still felt warm but was so still. There would be no miracle. The rugs were sustaining an illusion of life. Billy Bob was shaking; I saw him kiss the horse's eye, his soft muzzle, the great flat cheek, and he gently rubbed the dramatic splash of white, the star with its trailing tail that ended midway down Monticello's face, all the while Billy Bob was crooning softly, "Best horse in the universe, best horse in the universe and then some, you is for sure . . . the best, the very best, my boy, my own boy . . ." his loving mantra repeated over and over. How often I had heard it. This time it was different, "I told you not to go anywhere without me, you was supposed to wait for me . . . You not supposed to leave me all alone without you . . . " Billy Bob rocked back and forth, whispering and sobbing, his denture slipped out and I saw him just pick it up and toss it to the back of the stable where it sank down through the straw . . . "He look so handsome, don't he Miss Helen, like he was young and ready to run and all." I listened as he explained that he had come in to him, "just to check him." But then Billy Bob half-smiled and shrugged and admitted that he was lying and he knew that I knew he was lying and that every night when the yard settled he'd come in and lay down beside Monticello or maybe just sit quiet if he was standing as he usually was, "I spent the night here with my old friend, every night. Gave up smoking and all; in case there'd be a fire, he's the love of my life. I never went anywhere, never wanted to. Once your Daddy say he was mine to care for, my charge, my horse, I never left him, never left my buddy," and as if he were talking in his sleep, the old man chanted dreamily that he had just liked walking in the sun with him; "just me and him together and him tasting the grass, me talking, him listening, like always, my best horse . . ."

He cried as he told me that he must have fallen asleep, but only for a little while, "and when I come to, he gone, gone and left me. Why would God do that? I done no wrong." He had never worried that he might get caught under him if the horse rolled. In fact Monticello didn't lie down that often latterly as he had encountered increasing difficulty getting up. I knew sometimes that it would take three of the yardmen to heave him to his feet and they were sworn to secrecy not to mention this to the other veterinarians in the practice. Not that any of them would have dared raise the subject of Monticello's situation with Father. There had been several crisis moments but Monticello was a great fighter, brave and dignified, incredibly intelligent and so determined to live, a very special horse. He would gaze with such tenderness at Billy Bob as the little man fussed over him, combing his mane and his tail, brushing him, rubbing that mint stuff into his legs, and holding intense conversations. There's no doubting but that Billy Bob had told the full story of his life to Monticello alone, and to no one else. Poor brokenhearted Billy Bob, helpless and distraught, looked around at me and asked where I thought Monticello's spirit had gone. It was as if this elderly man had suddenly changed places and he saw me as the grown-up with the answers. "He has gone to heaven," I said, "where all the great horses go; he is in paradise and his legs are free of pain and he is happy and he is saying how grateful he is to you, how lucky he was to have found you; that you were his dearest friend, his soul mate, the love of his life." I said all that and meant it. My words such as they were made Billy Bob smile and it reminded me of all the times he had said to me when I was little that the world was full of nice horses and if a body was lucky they'd meet a few. "But you only get one love, there's one horse that means more than all the rest of them, the horse of a lifetime, you all only get one shot at that. I have mine here. I don't own him, never even rode him but I love him and he loves me."

That morning was truly the close of a chapter. Billy Bob was paying the price of having been granted that rare, elusive, privileged great love. He turned away from me and lay so wearily back down across Monticello's body a merciful god would have allowed the old man to die then and there. I could hear movement, the yard staff was arriving. Monticello's ears looked pricked but they had become rigid. I looked out over the lower door and just closed the top shutter. No, Father had not died. I watched Billy Bob as he spoke to Monticello soothing him as he had for years, telling him that he loved him and that he would find him and that they would be together forever. I envied him the full agony of his grief just as I had always been jealous of the love he had shared with that kindly, gorgeous, wonderful horse. They had adored each other. I often pondered about what was going through Monticello's mind as he watched me battle Galileo—a very different manner of character and one devoid of any fellow feeling or natural empathy.

Among the tears and the endearments, his profound anguish, Billy Bob made one utterly coherent comment. He hunkered down on his heels, then thought better of it, long years too stiff for that kind of movement and began in a quiet, measured voice that he had often feared that he would die first and that there would be no one who would care for Monticello the way he had. Then he said that only a few days earlier he had decided that he'd ask me to look after the Boss, "But he beat us to it and all, gone off his self and now, well Missy Helen I don't got nothing left to live for, he gave me my . . ." his voice trailed away and he turned from me, back to Monticello. I offered to go fetch him some coffee and ran back toward the kitchen, conscious of the crunching sound my boots made on the gravel path.

*

Father wanted the grave dug in the rose garden on the side lawn; that way he would be able to see it from his study window. He was planning a grand memorial and a landscape artist had been engaged to design an inner garden around Monticello's resting place. Billy Bob kept vigil by the body and was no longer making a secret about sleeping in the stable. It's not easy moving a horse, we forget how heavy they are; the average Thoroughbred weighs about 1,000 lbs. It didn't take long to figure out that in order to move Monticello, by which I mean lift, not drag, the front wall of his stable needed to be taken down on both sides, the entrance extended. Father supervised this and the men didn't dare even scratch the wooden doors, much less mark Monticello's brass name plate that Billy Bob had always kept polished and shining bright. He had stopped crying, at least for the moment, and instead his expression was fixed, almost stern. Billy Bob had by then entered a state of shock, his eyes glazed and when I brought him down a tray of food from the kitchen, he smiled weakly but ignored it. The fish stew and vegetables had been elegantly prepared by Mrs. Faulkner, she may as well have been feeding a head of state, and all she said when she handed me the tray was to make sure he ate the food for its goodness and to tell the poor man how very sorry she was to hear the sad news about his horse.

*

When Monticello was lifted from his stable, Billy Bob walked
beside the machine which inched along at a snail's pace;
Monticello's great head dangled loosely, his red mane shimmering as it caught the light. The grave was a generous space. Father
had the entire surface area covered thick with flowers; his cher-
ished horse was laid to rest on a bed of roses and tulips and every
other out-of-season floral import from Holland. I had heard
Father on the phone to two of the big florists in Richmond,
"Just bring whatever flowers you have," he had said, an element
of uncharacteristic hysteria entering his voice, "and all your roses,
roses—red ones, yellow too, and enough to cover an area of
about ten by eight, I need a good bed of flowers for something
special, I will explain." The people taking the calls must have
reckoned he was planning a homecoming or a surprise party.
Billy Bob stood staring into the pit. Father had kept about two
dozen red roses separate, on the grass near the grave; he began
placing them on Monticello, still wearing his English stable rug,
its bright yellow and red stripes just about visible through all the
flowers. Then Father handed Billy Bob a rose, my sweet, generous mentor who had become ancient in the hours since the
death, began to sob, and climbed heavily and stiffly down into
the grave. He kissed Monticello's cheek and placed the rose in
under the blanket, on the horse's chest, as close as possible to
his great heart. Father looked away and then walked back to the
house, head down, shoulders rounded with sadness. Billy Bob
was helped up out of the grave by the two yardmen who had
waited. They then pulled a navy tarpaulin over Monticello for
fear of rain. Father had told everyone to leave the place quiet, and
that later in the evening Billy Bob's friend Nathan was coming

over with another machine, it was for moving the soil. Billy Bob would need some privacy for that. Father gave him $500 to pay the man. I heard Billy Bob thank him, and Father paused before saying, no that he thanked him for all he had done for his boy, "Our boy, our brave boy, our splendid, splendid boy."

I decided not to ride for a few days out of respect for Billy Bob and Monticello. Before I went to the yard the next morning I visited the grave. It had been filled in. Someone had placed more roses on it. The sky was overcast, as if daylight had been trapped like a nerve and I felt the cold air on my face and an emptiness inside me, deep in my very being.

There was no sign of Billy Bob around the stables, not in the tack room either when I went looking for him, although I knew I would be of no help to him in his grief. Back up in the kitchen Father was reading the newspaper and drinking coffee, a good deal of it, judging by the large pot on the table. I mentioned that I had not seen Billy Bob. Father sighed and said to leave him be, that he imagined that Billy Bob would need time to heal himself. "He will be drowning his sorrows, but he has to eat as well. I was planning on going down to him in a while." A couple of days passed and I began to feel uneasy. I never saw Billy Bob again; he vanished, as simple as that. Again I was left with guilt. I'd never thanked him near enough for all the encouragement he had given me, his belief in me, his help; his husky cries of, "You can ride that ol' black horse, you sure can." His disappearance was more starkly final than Mother's killing, which had seemed to linger on because of Walt's extended pageant. But Billy Bob and Monticello; they had been the heart of the yard and of me, and suddenly they were both gone.

*

From that time onward Father retreated into a morose humor. The first unexpected thing he did was to buy a large glass tank which he installed on a table in his study. It was a specialist's aquarium about four feet in length with lights and a pump that hummed steadily, like a refrigerator. He then purchased two odd-looking fish, it was hard to decide whether they were graceful, possessed as they were of a sinister beauty that took some getting used to, or were downright repulsive. I reckon they were both. Theirs was a menacing allure; they were angelfish, one was black and the other was white and they glided about like predatory demons on the lookout for souls. Father seemed fascinated, and sat staring into the tank, his face reflected in its greenish glow. "They are quite temperature-tolerant," he had said, I couldn't pretend to be interested. What on earth had tropical fish to offer Father? This was the beginning of madness or so I suspected and I prepared to observe closely. The previous day Jamie Hodge denounced this new hobby, correctly I felt, as "mighty surefired ridiculous" and said in a loud, jokey voice, "Gone and lost your mind William?" but stopped short and quickly raised the subject of their trip. My mood brightened; I was ready and told him that I'd read Secretariat's biography, but Sheriff Hodge shook his head and said he and Father would first be going to North Carolina to see a quarry. Why? Luckily Father was just then called to the phone and the sheriff quickly explained that Father wanted to order a special stone for Monticello's grave, and that the granite quarry at Mount Airy, in Surry County, was the biggest in the world. The rock there, he said, was "something special; very beautiful, a seamless granite, noble, the stuff they'd used to honor the Wright Brothers." He also added in a low urgent tone, not to mention Secretariat, "not just now, your daddy always blamed him for breaking old Monticello's heart—his heart along with the hearts of a whole bunch of other fine horses too . . . and there's Secretariat held up as some kind of bad boy for being so darn good, why he doesn't even know Monticello ever existed . . . poor Monticello, always was beautiful and kind, a lovely, lovely horse but lacking the black fury that makes a champion . . ." Then the sheriff glanced across at Father, still on the phone, and again whispered, bending in low to me, wanting to know had Billy Bob reappeared? I shook my head. Jamie Hodge said he was very worried and that it was time we went looking for him. He didn't find him either.

An eerie sense of loss stalked me and I believed that Billy Bob was dead; I'd seen him grieving and the way that he had looked the time he'd said that he had nothing left to live for. I knew it, I could feel it. There was no one to discuss it with. In time I told Mitzi and her reaction, yes well, I'll come to that too . . . But in a while; it's a slow, painful business, this act of remembering—so many images observed and words spoken, overheard, the slightest gesture. It all sticks in your mind and weighs you down, even if it ends up making sense.

Sheriff Hodge and Father had arranged their visit to the quarry. And it was a powerful tribute, Father personally selecting a memorial stone to honor his beloved horse. Just after Monticello's death when I was still searching for Billy Bob, I had looked into Father's study and he was standing by the window, staring out to where the grave was. He heard me before I addressed him; he had half-turned and said in a low, thoughtful way, "How I loved that horse, how I loved him." His sorrow made him sound young; Father was dejected, brokenhearted. All of a sudden he seemed so human, bereft. But what really struck me was that it was the first and the only time I had ever heard him utter the word "love." I still see Father, as if he is standing before me, caught in a frame, whispering, "How I loved that horse." Father simply did not say "love"; it was not a word he used. He would admit to being partial to something, or to have a liking, a preference, an inclination, "I am quite devoted to Mr. Handel's operas," but he did not say "love." He had never told me that he loved me. And the one time in my life I heard him utter those two words—"I loved"—it was in relation to a glorious, crippled, sweet-natured horse.

That day as he mourned Monticello, he told me that he had ridden him, only once, shortly after Monticello's retirement from racing. That Father had been hunting regularly at the time, and being aware that he was a good rider, and riding fit, must have given him the confidence . . . I listened intently, curious and a little bit shocked, even so, that he would attempt to ride a race-horse. He said he'd done some flat work in the sand arena on him, not something that many middle-aged race horse owners would ever consider, riding circles and figures of eight, at canter, on a recently retired race horse, even in an arena. Then, confident that he had a feel for him, Father went out on the gallops that Grandfather had redesigned on the basic one initially constructed almost a hundred years earlier by his father, Father's grandfather, my great-grandfather. I must have gasped, well it was a foolhardy feat to contemplate much less attempt; there is a world of difference between quality hunting horses and Thoroughbreds conditioned to race. Father agreed that it was crazy and decidedly out of character. "But I had bred him, foaled him, and had been there with him . . . I was very close to that horse." Father would have been in his mid-forties at the time and I would have been very young, about three years old or heading four, I guess. The lunatic wonder of it; Father had surprised me, again.

Had he done it to impress Mother? I'd wondered, but was shy of asking, for fear he would stop speaking and turn away from me, step back to his private thoughts and memories. Content with hearing only what he was prepared to tell me, without pressing him for more, I waited.

Monticello went well but as Father described it, it seemed to have become a dream, "Then he picked up speed, got faster and faster, he dropped his head and my word, began to gallop . . ." Father paused. It went real quiet for a minute. Then he spoke again, "No chance of me holding him, he just rocketed, big strides. I thought I'd end up dropping the reins. The terror, I have not forgotten it. It is a different kind of riding, the jockeys, they just perch, they have no nerves, you can't . . ." Father recalled the stupefying fear and mentioned how the scenery had become blurred, the trees just a continuous green line rushing by. The only sound the whoosh of the air caused by movement; the thudding of hooves, the heavy, synchronized breathing of the horse moving beneath him . . . Father paused as if reliving those moments and peered directly at me, and admitted that he realized that he had no control. It was a faster, flatter action than he had previously experienced and he knew that his panic only made Monticello— a young horse bred to race—suddenly aware his rider was terrified, falling forward and grabbing at his neck. Monticello did what came naturally; bolted and galloped even harder. I heard Dieter Bernhard's words replaying in my head, his voice saying that Galileo was unsuited to cross-country. There was that ever present threat of the often suspect Thoroughbred temperament and that he could kill himself, or minor detail, me . . . Father was still speaking, thinking aloud.

He mentioned that although he did not fall off it was not due to his horsemanship. Monticello had simply slowed and pulled up. "Yes sir, came to a halt and began to walk back down toward the yard." According to Father, Monticello had let out a great sigh and shook himself, the way horses do after they've rolled. Except he hadn't rolled, Father felt he was telling him, no, warning him, not to attempt such folly ever again. "I could have fallen, broken my neck . . . like . . ." I knew he meant his first wife, but he didn't know which would upset me more, to hear him say her name, Helen, or to hear him refer to her as his first wife, Mother's predecessor, the one he had really cared for. Father had, most unusually, deferred to my feelings. That had never happened before. I stared back at him, until he looked toward the window and its only point of interest, Monticello's grave.

He was withdrawing, ever further into that relentlessly sporadic yet distinct maze of memory. He had taken to sitting with his fish. A few mornings or so after Father had told me about his outing on Monticello, Sheriff Hodge had arrived, excited at the prospect of the expedition to the quarry. It was about a four-and-a-half-hour drive from Richmond to Mount Airy. How many miles would that be? I'd asked. The Sheriff was drinking a quick cup of coffee. "Little over 260, maybe 265 or so . . . could take some time though, you know my many requirements, I get hungry and thirsty, have to visit the men's room, frequently, some might say excessively often . . ." and he had laughed good-naturedly. Such a joy, that man. Mrs. Faulkner came into the kitchen, carrying a basket of tomatoes from the hothouse. According to her Father had already left for North Carolina, before she had arrived, "and that was more than two hours ago." Jamie Hodge was embarrassed and obviously too hurt to hide it. He absorbed it like a punch then looked at me and shrugged, trying to excuse Father, and said that he must have confused the time. He hadn't though. Sheriff Hodge was never late for anything, he was too eager for company. Father had just gone off without him, it being the kind of thing he did.

*

Then there was the supper, a most unhappy occasion. Father's behavior that night defied all reason. He gave a performance; I would say that he set out to shock, only he was far too out of control to have deliberately planned it and the evening had evolved with a grotesque spontaneity uniquely its own.

Mitzi was scared; Father may as well have worn makeup and an evening gown or danced naked on the table, balancing the soup tureen on his head. She looked at me with bewildered compassion, expecting me to react—I didn't. Instead I opted for polite indifference, the attitude of the stranger witnessing a couple preparing to fight to the death in a restaurant. Father asked Mitzi a question about her parents and then answered it for her by mentioning the bakery and began humming "The Blue Danube" before she could swallow her food and prepare a reply. Father, a verbally intimidating presence at the best of times, smiled sardonically at a Californian girl newly arrived into my world of increasingly Southern semi-Gothic. No wonder she was trembling. He had also insisted that we ate in a formal setting, which for us was the seldom-used dining room, with Grandfather's heavy Spanish silverware, white linen on the table, and the housemaid, Mrs. Faulkner's protégée—was she her niece?—in attendance, and wearing a frilly white apron, an idiotic affectation left over from the days of Mother's afternoon soirees.

Mitzi had probably reckoned on a snack in the kitchen. Our friendship was still new and I'd enjoyed showing her around the stable yard, it was a novelty to her, a city girl more accustomed to going to the beach at Malibu, that's where Californians go. It was clear she was not that taken with Galileo. She was a little nervous, well, actually, plain terrified and backed away from him as if he was a wild animal which could sense her fear and he moved in on her, like a cat spotting a mouse, or more like a snake getting ready to swallow it whole.

Father soon lost interest in Mitzi, preferring to introduce what would prove a lengthy discussion about my braces. They had been removed about a year earlier yet that night he decided they were still very much present, boldly encasing my teeth and in need of adjustment. I could see that Mitzi initially thought it was merely a not-so-funny family joke. When she realized it was more like a blood sport, she became uneasy. I refused to participate. Admittedly I had feared he would begin asking me about my riding or something to do with science—both subjects excluding Mitzi, but mention of my braces was unexpected. All in all Father enjoyed one-sided arguments and could pursue a line of insane reasoning without losing a beat. I had heard him playing such games with Caleb Montgomery for years, they were like varsity debates and highly competitive—really irritating for onlookers. It was the first time I had ever entertained anyone at home and Father's decision to transform the evening into a spectacle was destined to flounder badly as Mitzi was the wrong audience. His display was not clever, nor even amusing. I felt like telling him that he could do much better, but was determined to remain silent, and I did. It eventually ended if only because Mitzi, without warning, stood up, offered a curt thanks and insisted that she'd "better be going." Father asked her if she got up early to bake. Mitzi missed the irony or perhaps had chosen to ignore it, and in either case she looked coldly at him and paused briefly before announcing that her parents had a large staff, it was a big bakery and they had "lots of plans." She was impressive and said her parents were great people: "They really love life." Then she walked out of the room, I followed her, prepared for her to blame me. But all she said was that she would see me in school.

She seemed more drained than angry, and disappointed in me, that's for sure. But there was no point trading sarcasm with Father, he was very quick. When I returned to the dining room to eat my dessert and Mitzi's—she had left hers untouched—I felt Father's peevish umbrage at my apparent indifference and my silence. He was uncomfortable, aware of having conducted himself badly; and, attempting a false gaiety, noted that my friend had left "somewhat abruptly" and asked had she enjoyed the evening? I assured him that she was ecstatic, and overcome by our Southern hospitality. Father smiled his executioner's smile and remarked that this was "most gratifying" to hear.

*

The goodwill that had briefly flourished between us in the immediate aftermath of Mother's killing appeared to have waned. Father resumed his habit of walking past me as if I were invisible, humming to himself, reading while he ate and retreating into his study when not in the surgery or out on consultations.

Caleb Montgomery arrived at the house, within an hour of the delivery of the large bouquet of flowers he had sent on reading in the newspaper that my project had won the state science prize. He said that he wanted to personally congratulate me. I hoped he would not expect me to kiss his lined and withered cheek—and I didn't. I shook his hand. Father already knew that I had won, having also read it in the morning's paper. Yet all he said was that it was not exactly a science project, "More of a history essay." Mr. Montgomery pooh-poohed that, and insisted

of course it was a science project, "All about that fella Galileo,
always thought he was mighty in-arresting myself," he drawled
smugly as if he had personally supervised the damned assign-
ment. But Father disagreed. "No, I don't think so. Helen here
has written about the man's life and times, the world within
which he lived, his interest in the heavens beyond that world,
and she has chronicled all the conflict his views caused. Clearly
most compelling indeed, and elegantly presented Helen." There
followed one of his pauses. Father so enjoyed his pauses. "But
it is an historical narrative—history. I don't see any science in
it. And I did search for it, the science I mean, most assiduously.
If there is some science in it, tell me where?" He continued to
goad me, repeating I might well become, in time, a historian,
but I was not a scientist, and that nothing I had done to date
suggested that I would ever be.

And on he went, in circles. Mr. Montgomery informed him
he was acting "positively menopausal," and making light of it,
asked me to investigate the possibility of securing coffee, "or
whatever sustenance might be more convenient for the good
and gracious Mrs. Faulkner should she wish to appease a hungry
man." I left the two men to bicker and snipe at the deeply flawed
human race. Between them they could secure Mr. Montgomery's
snack. I hurried directly up to my room, my face molten and my
heart thumping at the injustice. My school was rejoicing, there
would be a presentation, more fuss; another ordeal for me. I had
won a handsome silver trophy that I could keep and generous
prize money, $10,000. Not bad for a history essay "masquerad-
ing as science."

Father had already begun to unravel any notion I'd entertained of myself as a scientist. Like a light switch I had forgotten
about in a dark attic through which I had stumbled, I recalled
with a start his comments the evening he and Sheriff Hodge were

discussing Secretariat. Father had made such a point of telling me that I would like the history, instead of the obvious—that I would be fascinated by a mercurial champion racehorse. Yet he had; the more I thought about that night of his Secretariat celebration, Father had pointedly emphasized history, almost laboring the bit about historical relevance. And I had begun to see why he had done so. He could be so calculating.

A couple of days after the scene that had been played out before Mr. Montgomery, Father again decided to inform me that my passion for science had little to do with science. "Your subject is the history of science, not quite the same as being a physicist." He asked me what research had I ever undertaken. And sneeringly remarked that I had a significant collection of telescopes up there in my room, but did I possess a microscope? Had I ever even looked into one? Then he pursued his argument in earnest, and said that he felt compelled to advise me that I should major in history. "You are interested in the history of science, not science," he reiterated. "What makes you think you are a scientist? Why I am more of a scientist than you are," he boomed exasperatedly, large hands aloft and went on to list out all his research into bone conditions and joint disease, his extensive, "and if I may say, my pioneering work on glucosamine absorption rates across the equine gastro-intestinal tract," as well as mentioning his "innovations in the levels" of blood-testing. Put bluntly, he reasoned, there was nothing to suggest that I was—or would ever be—a scientist. Frowning as if with great effort, he admitted that he could not recall any inventions of mine, or perhaps I had solved a major theoretical problem of which he was unaware? What theories had I challenged?

Then he described his father's disappointment when he had told him that he wanted to become a veterinarian. "I may as well have announced I wanted to run a casino, I do declare, my father wanted me to train supreme racehorses; breed them and then train them, like he had." That was part, if only part, of Father's bond with Monticello. It had apparently, at least for a while, seemed that Monticello might emulate Grandfather's champion Twist of Fate, who had won the Kentucky Derby. Father had never asked me if I wanted to be a veterinarian, and I had never considered it. Yet completely unexpectedly there he was lamenting how he had hoped I would have succeeded him. That he had built the practice and it was a fine one, among the best in the United States—and acquiring an international reputation. It grieved him, he claimed, to think that he would retire or die and that someone else would take over. That was why he had never made any of the practice veterinarians a partner. "I thought," he said theatrically, "no, I had hoped, prayed, assumed, I would be handing over to you. And I have waited, apparently in vain, for you to stop dreaming about star clusters and dead Italians and instead consider the rewards of equine science and this world which I created and into which you were born." More guilt for me to carry; that was the first time Father had ever raised the subject of my future plans. As you can see, I'd lived and dreamed within my own little kingdom. Billy Bob had prolonged my aspirations even after Mother's death—the same aspirations then being exposed as fantasies—but Billy Bob had vanished and his absence had begun the radical disintegration of my private universe, a process which Father appeared set on completing.

During the following weeks he continued to fence and parry on the subject of my career as a student of history, usually by asking had I decided to switch to the humanities, which he had taken to describing as my "natural and obvious home." Rather than get drawn into a debate that would speedily become an argument, or more likely yet another one-sided harangue, I decided to appear open to the idea without saying anything definite. It stung me, I had gotten used to being referred to as a future scientist. The school librarian even ordered in all the specialist science publications just for me. Science had become part of my identity. About this time, Mitzi became very excited; she told me that she'd heard an old song about a scientist and she had immediately thought of me. She had been waiting outside the language lab when I came out; I was trying to teach myself German. Mitzi smiled and eagerly grasped my arm—she was very tactile, it took me a while to get used to that. We walked down the hall and she said that she guessed that the song was about Copernicus or "that guy who looks like a wizard, the one you named the horse after." That took me by surprise, and I was about to ask her why she reckoned Galileo looked like a wizard, but I was pleased as well as very curious as to who could have written a song about an astronomer. Well, it didn't take long; she had the lyrics all printed out in a pink folder, together with the record, in her locker, and handed them to me, delight in her eyes. It turned out to be "Starry Starry Night," something Mother had apparently sung to me when I was very small. I didn't remember, but once when we were in a restaurant, probably at The Clock Tower, she had said "hush" and told me to listen; explaining that the tune the pianist was playing was one she had sung to me when I was little. Mitzi's face fell when I told her it was about Van Gogh. What was that? she had asked. Not a thing, a Dutch artist I explained. "Never heard of him," was her confident reply which managed to convey that he couldn't be all that important. By then I had realized that Mitzi was not really what I would call an Austrian, she couldn't speak German, none of her family could, her mother just knew some phrases and Mitzi had no interest in learning the language. Nor was she drawn to Austrian or German culture, and as I have said, she did not much like horses. But it was fun to have a friend, I liked listening to her chatter, she seemed so content with her life. She also had a mission; she wanted her brother Karl, a champion miler, to marry me. She thought we would get along, "you're both obsessives," she reasoned. I did not entirely agree but Karl was really nice, in spite of being so good-looking. He was sincere. I wondered if he had noticed my funny eyes, he didn't seem to have but then Mitzi had probably briefed him. Even so I tried not to look directly at him and was well practiced in standing side-on when in conversation. His teeth were slightly crooked, so he had a genuine, natural smile. He was also very quiet, and like me, not exactly scintillating company. We both needed to find ourselves an extrovert, someone like Mitzi. She had arrived unexpectedly in the yard one Saturday morning with him; he was mildly injured and so was "resting" or off training.

Mitzi climbed up on the railing around the arena, shouting my name and waving her long, multi-colored scarf. Galileo reared up and spun, it would have looked more threatening than it actually was—I knew that he was just letting me know that he didn't like spectators. Mitzi suggested I join a Wild West Show. By then I was so depressed with Father's orchestrated insults about my bogus self-image as an aspiring scientist I would gladly have run away to any circus in need of a trick rider and a card-carrying, proven bad-tempered horse, which I could certainly supply. Karl watched calmly. Later he followed me back into the stable asking if I needed any equipment fetched or buckets filled. Mitzi had run up to the house to use the bathroom, where as she told me later, Mrs. Faulkner had snapped, "There are facilities in the stable yard for visitors," and had slammed the door. Mitzi hadn't needed to go to the bathroom; she just wanted to allow Karl time enough to propose. I doubted that he wanted to invite me out, never mind marry me. Yet I did feel that he was about to ask me if he could sit up on Galileo glistening in the sunshine and I was silently rehearsing the friendliest way of leading him to an easier horse without sounding territorial or appearing boastful, implying that Galileo was too advanced for a beginner. Aside from that I knew the horse was dangerous. Karl cleared his throat, "Here it comes," I thought, and I hoped my riding helmet didn't smell and wasn't sweaty and disgusting. But all he said was that Galileo seemed incredibly vicious and asked if he was always that aggressive. I laughed stiltedly, and attempted a, "You don't want to know," which sounded so false and silly but though I felt my face turning red I didn't feel at all defensive. Galileo was not likeable yet he was fascinating; he had that mysterious dynamic that separates very good horses from potentially great ones. Mitzi's brother was a serious person; I could see that and it was not surprising that he was such a good athlete. His arms were beautiful, slightly tanned and his skin was perfect. I imagined it would smell of vanilla. He was the sort of person who would take anything apart, be it a clock or a poem, to try and figure out what made it work. He spoke slowly and with marked deliberation, because of a speech impediment which he managed. He also sighed a great deal, which was disconcert-ing as it wasn't clear if he was exhausted or bored or both. I tried to move the subject away from horses so I admired his Nikes. He was thrilled and thus held forth on running shoes. "So this was small talk," I thought, and could see that he was even more socially inept than me.

Over the next month or so I began riding a series of dres-sage tests; I would look toward the railing, expecting to see Billy Bob motioning me over to share his views. But he wasn't there; I tried to assess my riding the way he had done. Sometimes I would tack up a hunter and ride through the fields and on to the forestry and along the mountain stream trail. It was so easy, restful, out there riding along without having to second guess

Galileo's moods. If he was a man he would inevitably drive any woman involved with him to suicide or murder, causing me to feel guilty about Mother all over again, like always.

Well now, flash-forward to what seemed an unexceptional morning. I had come back to the kitchen, very happy at the session we had just had. Galileo must have decided I deserved a fleeting glimpse of what it would be like when I eventually climbed to the top of the mountain with him, providing I was still in one piece. I imagined us doing well as a way of paying tribute to Billy Bob's memory. Nothing could make me accept that he was still alive somewhere, not without Monticello.

Father grunted by way of a greeting and I decided to have a second breakfast. He snapped open the newspaper and folded it, asking had I read it? He is initiating a neutral conversation I had thought; at least one that might not revolve around my future as a history major. I feigned interest in the greater world and lied, pretending that I had of course planned on reading the paper after I had eaten. "No, no, I don't mean the news in general; I mean this, just this piece of it." He beamed and smacked the paper with the back of his hand, "Do cast your eye," he commanded. The headline was in heavy type: "Virginia Breeder Impresses French Olympic Buyers."

Strong sun was streaming in the window and I could barely see, I was not in the mood for Father and just wanted to eat in peace. But I knew from experience that were I to act interested, he would soon walk out of the kitchen without a glance. Whereas if I openly switched off, he would begin another heckle that could last an hour and would include more comments unpicking my science fantasies. I skimmed the top of the story; it said that French buyers had paid just over $700,000 for a young horse bred in Virginia by a major US veterinarian and consultant advisor to the US equestrian squad. The bay gelding had been spotted by chance by one of Europe's leading horsemen. He believed the horse, initially intended for racing, had the potential to challenge for Olympic eventing gold. I said offhandedly and with some perception that the point of the story was that the US Equestrian Federation should have stepped in and purchased the horse instead of allowing him to leave the country. Father agreed but insisted I read on. It said Mr. Judge. No, that was the reporter's mistake, he had gotten Father's name wrong. So Father had sold a horse. "Which horse?" I asked. He smiled before replying slowly as if he thought I would want to carefully transcribe each word of his answer, "Why the one you've been riding." Bad news they say, can at times feel like a physical blow to the chest. And I was actually winded. "But you can't sell Galileo," I shouted, panic rising through me, "why would you sell Galileo?" Father was affronted. "What? Why wouldn't I sell him? I did. He's my horse, not yours. Did I ever give him to you? I think not. No I did not. Did you think I had given you that horse? Who said you could call him Galileo? Did I? No I did not. I had been thinking of calling him The Raven, a little salute to Mr. Poe. I just hadn't gotten around to it. And now I don't have to." Mrs. Faulkner walked in, sensed the tension and retreated directly back out through the kitchen door. I heard the vacuum cleaner going up and down the Oriental rug in the hall. She spent a long time that morning cleaning a carpet which barely had a chance of getting dirty.

With two deft moves Father had deconstructed my life as it had been up to then. He had mocked my dreams of being a scientist and now he had reclaimed Galileo. Yet he demanded that I answer his question and confirm that no, he had never given me the horse. Or any horse for that matter. I merely rode "his" horses. His voice droned on, I fixed on the window, able to see the sky now as the sharp sunlight had eased from blinding to pleasant. A red and yellow hot air balloon drifted into view; I was on the verge of laughing uncontrollably. The balloon looked innocent, like a giant toy escaped from a nursery above the clouds. Who was aboard the balloon I wondered, and how would one set about going up in one? "Are you even heeding my words?" asked Father. I looked at him, then again toward the window, the balloon had disappeared. I realized that I had unintentionally facilitated the sale by having those lessons with Dieter Bernhard. Had his hosts, the smiling, ever friendly Willards, been aware of his talent scouting sideline? The irony of it, he was the European bounty hunter, on the lookout for any quality horses rich, indulged American teenagers such as me might just so happen to be riding. Herr Bernhard had been interested in Galileo, he could see he was the perfect machine, a competition horse that would either win a gold medal or die in the pursuit of one. It made sense; having ridden at all those Olympic Games he knew the rare, edgy kind of horse that reaches that level, if in the hands of an equally gifted rider—one capable of steering both of them safely over the cross-country course, the discipline in which he had suspected I would encounter trouble controlling Galileo. I heard my voice small and pleading telling Father that it would be such a shame for Galileo to compete for France when he could represent the United States. I wasn't asking for the horse for me, but for an American rider. "I don't care who he wins for, it is academic," Father retorted. "My daddy bred a Derby winner, I might end up having bred an Olympic champion, I don't care who he wins for . . . it's academic. The Europeans came here looking for American horses, not Irish horses, not English ones." They saw the best, he said, eyes shining, and it was American. He always felt that American bloodlines are not fully recognized in Europe. "Those close-minded Europeans fail to appreciate that the best stallions are from here. Look at Northern Dancer, well he is a Canadian, but it is still North America. That black horse I bred here at my home, my family's home, is an American Thoroughbred, bred for racing. I have his mother, bred her too. I find this . . . fulfilling." He made a steeple shape with his fingers, muttered something I didn't catch and then said he regretted having had him gelded. I sat on the kitchen chair, tensing my buttocks against the hard wooden seat, hating the grasping Dieter Bernhard who had been paid by me as well as by the French buyers.

Meanwhile Father was holding forth about his friend Bill Steinkraus, "from Ohio just like your mother," who had won the show jumping gold at the Mexico Olympics. It had been the first US show jumping gold and the horse he rode, Snowbound, was an ex-race horse. "That big-hearted horse never got credit for his considerable exploits, another Thoroughbred, makes you think, does it not?" I was thinking—but not about Snowbound just then, I had nothing to lose so I said in as calm a voice as possible that I had really enjoyed riding the black horse; that I had learned so much and that it was all due to Billy Bob and that I had wanted to do well with Galileo, I corrected myself, "your black horse," for Billy Bob. Father remained indifferent. "You never asked for him, I would have given him to you. Had you asked, but you never did. You presumed that he was yours, and that is wrong. Nothing in life is there for the taking; it must be earned, or at least sought, requested." He accused me of a lack of humility. I wanted to hit him, hard, in the face. I longed to smash his glasses and grind them into his eyeballs. I wanted to tell him how I loathed him and hated his cold, sneering smirk, his pompous voice, his self-righteousness. But all I said was, "I didn't think I needed to ask, I thought he was mine, after the client backed out of the deal." I turned away and tripped over the vacuum cleaner. Mrs. Faulkner was standing just inside the cloakroom door, listening no doubt. I asked her what she thought of that, spitting out the words. She pretended she thought I was referring to the vacuum and said she had not intended to leave it there but deflecting any blame from herself, remarked that it was always useful to take the time to look where you were going to avoid falling over things.

Later that day, after hours spent brooding in my room, hunger drove me back to the kitchen. I knew there was a newly iced chocolate cake; I planned on taking all of it upstairs, along with whatever else I could find in the refrigerator. Spoils of war. I would not be surfacing for supper. Father heard me in the hall and called my name; he was in his study, sitting in the shadows cast by the late afternoon sun. Staring at his damned fish, his face glowed green: he looked unhinged. His hands seemed huge, magnified against the glass of the tank. "They come from the Amazon, you know, angelfish are native to Amazonia, I have been reading about them . . ." Quick as a flash he looked back up at me, he had something else to say, "That horse is far too good to be wasted on a hobby rider. I'm not saying that you are not good, you are but he is a professional's horse with a killer's need to win and you managed him very well, up to a point. That German fella was most impressed and had said so to the French people. They would have had you ride him, had you been here when they came calling. But you see Helen, this is your problem; you are a dreamer. Herr, his name eludes me, was quite astute; he said you are talented but lack motivation, what he rather grimly referred to as 'the competitive edge.'" Father took a moment to laugh at the memory of the earnest, humorless Herr Bernhard. Even in my despair I almost smiled at imagining how Herr "his name eludes me" Bernhard would have articulated "competitive edge" with that demented fervor he had, implying that riding well was of monumental importance. Father continued his by now highly irritating spiel about my thinking I was a scientist because I knew about what he described as "those Renaissance lunatics," who, he claimed, were all crazy, deeply disturbed, at war with the popes and each other, confused about God and heresy. "And then," he concluded, "it all happened again, a few hundred years later with Darwin and the Victorians." He told me I would never ride to win, just like I would never work in a lab. He defined me as a dilettante, "Some class of amateur intellectual, not such a bad thing." But, and he kept emphasizing it, I was not focused, just drifting, and he said this was wrong as it wasn't as if I had not recently experienced what he referred to as "sufficient harsh reality" to have woken me up.

Galileo was not my Monticello. There was no love, he just about tolerated me. And I guess I didn't like him overmuch either and had never trusted him. Had I tried to hug him he would have bitten me for sure. But he had given me much more than an angry, bad-tempered, bully of a horse should have. I was more ambitious than Father suspected. I had been going to wait until my plans were realistic, and then I would have announced my intentions and sought Father's support. I stood in that room, watching those evil fish glide around amid the throb of the bubbles pulsing like a heart or a pair of lungs, and I thought of that painting of the man on the mountains, staring down in the mist, and identified with him, the *Wanderer Above The Sea of Fog* by my hero, Caspar David Friedrich, and felt, "Yes that's me." The mist is the future, the great beyond. Well that is the way I was thinking that day. Then I remembered another of his great paintings, far less romantic, but the one that best explained how I was feeling just then. It's called *The Sea of Ice* and it's about desolation. Huge sheets of ice dominate a bleak scene; a wrecked ship is barely visible. I was that ship, or at least the doomed vessel represented what was left of my hopes. My blood was probably moving very slowly through my body as I felt entirely on my own, defeated, in a room alone with Father, a man I realized I barely knew and didn't feel anything for, not a speck of regard. Had he dropped dead on the spot, I would have walked away, free as a bird and maybe even attempting to whistle.

The ticking of the ever-disapproving grandfather clock in the hall seemed louder than usual. Father laughed mirthlessly, his little victory cackle. I jumped at its harsh yapping sound. He was smiling indulgently at his fish and without looking up at me, remarked, as if passing on a fact that he had just read, "This is a mating pair, I may have mentioned. They are, apparently, given to eating their young. As for the veracity of that, well, we will just have to wait and see."

*

END OF PART ONE

PART TWO

Off went the first postcard to Mitzi: Raphael's *Saint George and the Dragon*; the horse was a pale baroque warrior and the dragon was black and snake-like. Knowing Mitzi she would probably decide that the dragon was Galileo, or perhaps Father, considering her views on him following the supper party. The painting is very small, and its box-like frame seems to contain it, surrounding it like a protective barrier. I liked the youthful look of St. George, and hoped he would inspire me to valiant deeds. As for a friendship-saving message I decided on something neutral: "Well I got here! By the time you read this I will have drunk at least one cup of very expensive hot chocolate in your honor. Au Revoir! Mon Amie." The truth is I had three large bowls and cake. There is only so much you can write on a postcard and I had several attempts before I managed to write one that did not look as if my hand was shaking, which it was, or that I was still annoyed with her—which I was.

At first when I phoned her at the bakery, her mother answered and I had to wait a few minutes before I could share my news with Mitzi. She sounded helpless, as if aware her power over me had been challenged. Then she was furious, convinced I had run off in crazed pursuit of Galileo, which I hadn't. She didn't believe me and that hurt. Only not as much as her obvious surprise at my choosing to do something—that truly irked me. "Helen considering you've pretty much sleepwalked through the first part of your life you then go and do something as stupid as this!" she'd shouted down the line. Who else was listening to her I wondered, before feeling that she'd no right to say I'd sleepwalked through my life, I was doing things with my time.

She had never viewed me as capable of taking independent action. My little rebellion was deliberate, not impulsive. It had been devised to show Father that I was not a complacent idiot. Whatever I had hoped to prove to him, what I did discover was that Mitzi credited me with the mental age of a six-year-old, and that stung. That and the fact she was convinced my sole motivation was arranging a reunion with Galileo. "Are you sure Helen, come on you can tell me . . . are you trying to track down that insane over-bred equine? You know you shouldn't. He's probably already killed somebody by now and is in police custody. May even be dead himself. Don't they execute killer horses?" Only the fact that I might end up on a highjacked airplane or get hit by a speeding car stopped me from yelling at her, or more true to my character, hanging up. It would be horrible if her last memory of me was of an abrupt final click from the phone. But she thought I was lying and nothing I said would change her mind as she kept repeating Karl's views on Galileo's intimidating attitude in the stable—which was hilarious as Karl had been terrified and stood staring at Galileo as if he might eat him.

What bothered her most was my not having trusted her, "your best friend, maybe your only friend," and I had been waiting for her to say that. And she did, pointing out in an arctic tone not like her normal one that I'd waited until I was safely at the airport before phoning her to reveal my daring escape, which to be fair to me was not at all furtive, it had been executed in style, along with a first-class ticket paid for with my prize money. Initially she reckoned I was kidding and she played along, informing me that the French didn't believe in showers and that the lack of personal hygiene common among Europeans would drive me crazy. Then she saw it was for real and hey presto had her rescue theory all worked out. The more she told me I wanted the horse back, the more I knew I didn't. Maybe the worst thing was when she said, "Your funny little black guy, the horse whisperer, should have known better." That really cut deep, hearing her refer to Billy Bob as if he was some kind of careless fanatic. She'd never even met him. For me though the whole thing with Galileo really ended when Billy Bob disappeared. Only it took a while for me to see that.

*

Paris it was—as it seemed a bit more imaginative than simply stomping off to New York. I felt the French might not be as inclined to mock my accent as readily as a streetwise toughie from the Bronx might. More seriously though, it looked less like running away and closer to a deliberate gesture of rebellion. Skulking around Lower Manhattan would have been too obvious, even to me. Not that I went in pursuit of Galileo, Mitzi was wrong: I had no desire to foil the dastardly Herr Bernhard. Galileo was gone; I couldn't afford to get him back even if I'd wanted to. With the signing of a check he had become very valuable and, anyway, as the French federation had purchased him, he was state-owned. For me, I wanted to show Father that I was not content with simply taking whatever I wanted as it had apparently seemed to him. No, it was vital to prove, to him and to me, that I was capable of rational thought and had revised my old notion of who I was, now that Father had destroyed all of that for me. I missed Billy Bob and continued to visualize him and Monticello walking slowly down the stable-yard paths, or standing together in the sun, both of them just enjoying being together.

Sometimes, without any warning, that freeze-frame of Mother being shot would flash across my mind's eye, as did the tiny flicker of relief with which I had begun to imagine she had greeted death. Paris was bound to present me with an entirely new set of images, or so I hoped, and it would be exciting seeing buildings and monuments familiar from books and the movies . . . Notre Dame and the Eiffel Tower, the Arc de Triomphe all in real life. For me New York was a giant running track congested by harassed commuters, whereas Parisians would amble about in muted sunshine and I'd get to see handsome men with liquid eyes carrying bunches of flowers and those long, thin loaves of bread. Everyone would look as if they were in love . . . I'm not sure if I really did see Paris as romantic, perhaps I was too aware of its history, the revolutions and unrest caused by bored kings in powdered wigs and I'd read a lot of Balzac and Zola. Life was harsh in nineteenth-century France, especially in Paris, where the angry citizens gathered in the streets. The Bastille was gone but it would be neat to stand on the site where it had once been.

History, yes, as ever, Father was right. For me, it always was history; a yearning to know what everything had looked like 200 or 400 or more years ago. Living in my head made me want to live in the past. I was also determined to see as many paintings as possible and to walk in the famous gardens. Some time ago our art teacher had given me a cutting from a magazine, *Time* or *Newsweek*, maybe *Life*. Or perhaps *The New Yorker*; it was about a Vermeer painting and she was sure the article would interest me. The painting was called *The Astronomer*; it showed a scientist in his study consulting a celestial globe. And it had a story, as do so many paintings. At some point during the centuries it had been acquired by the Rothschild family, who had then lost it when the Nazis invaded Paris. After the war it was returned to the family—except with a small swastika stamped on the back, a very sinister reminder of so much evil. Debt forced the family to part with it and by way of a donation to the state, it had arrived at the Louvre in 1983 . . . I wanted to see it . . . along with so many other paintings, particularly the Géricaults. I love his work, much of it suggests desperation, turmoil—that feeling that usually gripped me whenever I allowed my thoughts to wander, I always needed to be thinking, reading, riding, I could never drift freely, I knew that, it worried me. Géricault had killed himself; I lived in repressed panic and was interested in suicide as an act but had never considered it for me, except when, but that was later . . . There was only one Caspar David Friedrich in the Louvre, but it was a great one . . . the one with all those crows in it.

Americans, however, do choose Paris, as a rite of passage of sorts, particularly for Americans of a certain social class, so why not for me? Not that I saw myself as an Isabel Archer. But I was in need of a place in which I could begin figuring out who I was, or who I wanted to be, now that my familiar structures had been ridiculed. That was more or less my thinking at that time: confused, hopeful, apprehensive, defiant, and also right pleased with myself as I set off on my solo adventure, or as Mitzi referred to it, my "teenage rebellion". Rescuing Galileo had nothing to do with it.

I sat on the plane and attempted to recall a Maupassant story about a crippled beggar; his legs had been "écrasés par une voiture." I had kept saying the phrase over and over; I loved the sound of it. Maupassant lived a brief, unhappy life during which he had traveled widely and in an intense ten-year period had written almost 300 short stories and six novels as well as travel books. He had failed at suicide and spent time in a mental home where he died at forty-two. Before all of that though when he was about eighteen, my age, he'd saved the English poet Swinburne from drowning. My copy of Maupassant's stories had a Degas painting on it, a woman at her bath. I flicked open my passport and studied my face as it had been three years earlier when I had been going to visit London with my parents. Father knew people who were very friendly with the woman who had inherited the Whistlejacket painting along with her father's private collection; they were descendants of the Second Marquess of Rockingham, a flamboyant character, twice British prime minister, and the owner of Whistlejacket[1]. It was he who had commissioned Stubbs to paint the stallion when it was thirteen years old. Whistlejacket had tried to attack the painting, or so the story goes. Father reckoned "so seminal a picture" would eventually end up in the National Gallery in London, where everyone would be able to see it. But at the time of our proposed visit a viewing was still only possible through contacts and careful planning.

The trip had been canceled. But I had gotten the passport including a photograph in which I looked demented. My braces showed. They were so bulky I couldn't close my mouth and it gave my younger, more rounded face an apologetic expression. Now I felt tougher, already tested by life. When the airport official looked at me, she smiled and said it had been worthwhile. "Excuse me?" I said, my voice sounding shrill. "The braces," she said, knowingly as if she alone was privy to my secret. I just looked at her, resenting that she felt she could make such a personal comment about my teeth. Had I been a bit older she would have said nothing, but because I was young, she obviously felt I was not entitled to any privacy. My sharp retort had, in turn, irritated her; she reverted to cold technicalities, "Minors traveling alone abroad need to fill in that form." I had already completed the document; Mr. Montgomery had signed it for me and had asked no questions. I handed it to her, stating, stupidly, in a flat neutral tone, "I've never worked in a mine, leastways not so far," and walked by, waiting for her to tap me on the shoulder, but she didn't. I would have enjoyed an argument, I needed to shout and be involved in a scene having spent years watching them. As I boarded I'd wondered was I going to storm about Paris picking fights with strangers. It seemed unlikely, but then again, my anger had already begun surprising me . . .

For the first part of the flight I was excited, wondering what the meal would be like, anticipating working through the neatly presented little tray, dismantling the various packets. Eating the plastic meal was a diversion that would pass some of the time. I dreaded sitting still for so many hours, most of which would be spent passing over the ocean. I thought of all the water, a world of water, dark and cold, miles deep below us, a gigantic version of Father's fish tank. How long would it take to die should you fall in? And then I took to wondering would things have been any different if we had gotten to England that time. Would my parents have been any happier? Would Mother still be alive? What if she had never met Walt? Or more importantly, what if she had never felt she had needed him? What if? What if?

Who was riding Galileo? Did I care? Sort of. Was he confused by the different sounds? The new language? Did horses hear words? Or was the sound something that became associated with meaning? My mind was tired; I was sick of thinking. I felt I'd been programmed for processing facts and random details, no more. The air stewardess handed me a blanket in a plastic bag, asking what I'd like to drink. I was traveling in style, although the airline blanket was synthetic and had a cheap smell. I had lots of cash in the form of several books of traveler's checks, thanks to my generous allowance and my prize . . . I looked the part

of the child of oldish wealth which is what I was. The little tray
came with my orange juice in a glass, accompanied by a dish of
mint chocolate wafers. First class passengers did not drink from
plastic cups; we got served in a chunky little glass. I smiled at the
absurdity of the class system on an airplane. The stewardess must
have reckoned I was the offspring of a rock singer or a movie star
being flown to Paris for a brief visit. Perhaps she approved of my
not demanding an illicit gin and tonic?

My mystery tour was set to commence in a smart little hotel
on the Left Bank near the Sorbonne, the Fifth Arrondissement,
not far from the Musée de Cluny where *The Lady and the Unicorn*
tapestries are kept. This all makes me sound like a culture-driven
tourist, but that more or less much describes me.

Tearful farewells at railway stations are so much more heart-
rending than the ones at airports amid all the security and closed-
off areas. At least on a train, you may weep through a carriage
window and wave. But I had no one to cry for. No one to cry
for me either. On my return would Mitzi have Karl waiting for
me, our futures planned? How much brainwashing would that
take? I smiled; she was really intent on enjoining me with her
brother. She had even mentioned that it would be great; we could
go together to the Olympics, him to run, me to ride—well, I
wouldn't be going to the Olympics . . . Perhaps I would return
from France transformed? Worldly, sophisticated . . . Eager to
share my prodigious experiences . . .

It was like stepping onto a movie set; the light in Paris was
different, the competing smells of coffee and tobacco were everywhere, the width of the streets, no, the boulevards; the Seine with
its narrative presence, or so I saw it on account of reading the
nineteenth-century French writers. Life seemed more spontaneous than it did back in Richmond, more uninhibited. What was
my most abiding first impression? The Japanese tourists, many

with two or three expensive cameras suspended from necks that were tense from watching, taking pictures of everything. They reminded me of policemen, intent on recording it all; they even photographed the traffic.

The little hotel was more like a boarding house in that the guests stayed for weeks or months. But to me "boarding house" had begun to sound sordid, so I insisted on referring to it as a hotel until I discovered the word "pension." It was possible to have all of your meals there but I never had lunch, only the breakfast and often the supper, although I also liked eating at the cafés, even if it was only hot chocolate and cake, or pastry. Among the guests or lodgers was an Englishwoman and what I assumed to be her adult daughter or niece. They were a grim pair, sitting mostly in silence, and turned out to be employer and employee. The "adult daughter" was a companion, paid to listen to the older woman's complaints. I forget how I found that out.

There was a group of very good-looking Italians; three girls and two boys, all so beautiful as to be sexless. They shouted out their French which lacked the rhythmic roll of the Parisians, who appeared half in love with the sound of their beautiful language. The Italians were doing very well and were confident. I, on the other hand, had been quickly subdued—well actually, devastated. There was a canyon-wide gulf between speaking French at school in Richmond and reading out passages while your classmates listened with rapt admiration, compared with attempting to address it to natives who made a point of wincing with pain at the sound of my accent. My carefully constructed sentences complete with correct grammar sounded labored as I faltered and stumbled, my face ablaze with embarrassment, particularly as the person usually proceeded to reply in a torrent of impatience, all in French. My notion of returning home fluent evaporated in hours, I knew the words but was unable to summon them sufficiently quickly. I reverted to hand gestures and shrugging, lots of shrugging.

On the train in from the airport I remember sitting behind two young girls. They both had their hair pushed upwards in lop-sided buns resembling collapsed towers. The brown-haired girl was reading, without ever changing the page; her friend was pale and blonde, probably tentatively lightened by a home dye. She was standard prettyish pink-skinned and never stopped fumbling with her clumsy little hairdo. She spent the entire journey taking her hair down, combing through it with her short, little fingers. Her nail polish was red and chipped. Her busy fingers kept roll-ing her hair, resetting the elastic band, patting the messy hair, twisting it into a knob and shifting in her seat, glancing at her languid friend, who ignored her, pretending to be on her own, and who never once adjusted her bun of brown hair. The brown-haired girl was astonishing to behold; sultry and plump, quite tanned. Her clothes had a careless ease whereas the merely pretty girl had all the appearance of having changed and re-changed her clothes a hundred times before leaving for Paris. Nothing matched and she seemed disheveled and uncomfortable, anxious to be more like her friend. I identified with her awkwardness. My comfortable old pair of short riding boots had somehow become dusty as if I had walked for miles through a desert and I wondered why I didn't have ordinary shoes like other people, was I that weird?

The girls began to speak, not quite New Yorkers, perhaps Maryland. The blonde girl said she could hardly wait, but her friend just smiled condescendingly, too self-aware to admit to excitement. I guessed she had been to Paris before, and that she wanted to sustain her petty advantage over her friend for as long as possible. Why would I think that? I wondered, alarmed by my cynicism.

The days there quickly settled into a routine, just as they did at home. Instead of rushing to breakfast and on to the stables, or to school, I went to the Louvre. My first week in Paris consisted of walking to the Louvre, spending most of the day there, leaving only to eat in as many of the little cafés as I could. On one day alone I think I had about six hot chocolates at various places before finally ordering a café au lait; it was much too strong and required maybe ten spoonfuls of sugar before I could drink it, recalling how much better Mrs. Faulkner's was and I imagined her horror at the casual hygiene—I had sent a cup back, gesturing at the traces of lipstick still visible on the rim and left before the waiter, who acted as if the smudged red lipstick was all in my tortured imagination, returned.

So Mitzi viewed me as an idiot, yet I was touched by the way she tried to look after me, even to the point of marrying me to her very solemn brother. Deep down though I resented her certainty about everything—and naturally I felt guilty as Mitzi was the first person I had ever met who really made me feel that she cared about me, albeit to the point of bossing me about all the time. I disliked her telling me that I only rode to prove something to myself and to impress Father, which had made me laugh as he inhabited his own little astral plane. Because she could see no point in riding horses, Mitzi felt that no one else should.

The cafés with their rickety little tables appeared designed for watching people and for being watched, the food was almost secondary. I love looking at people . . . I saw small, thin women with skinny legs and wary eyes. Some of them minced along in high heels, self-conscious and aware, reminding me of Mother, only she never had that hard, knowing expression. Even when she smiled she looked as if she was waiting to be corrected—it must have come from living with Father. The women in Paris were mainly dark or had dyed-red hair, whereas Mother was blonde and so very eager, waiting for something wonderful. What would she have told me about Paris? She would have fretted about my clothes and warned me about the men. I could hear her voice, "Don't bother with poets and intellectuals, they're all depressives, find a rich, older man, they're so attentive." Not sure how Father fitted into that.

I enjoyed looking upwards, beyond the street level to the next floor and above that still, to the domestic lives going on within. Many of the buildings seemed to be six or seven stories high; most had balconies and shutters painted in faded blues and greens, red bled to pale pink. What would it be like to live in an apartment in Paris? I wondered, would I too be walking to work each day through a park and speaking in long, orchestrated sentences? The conversations all around me sounded so intense, philosophical, all the sighing and gesticulating . . . they could have been debating existence or planning murders or bank robberies, adultery. These were people who looked deep into each other's eyes but mostly they were probably complaining about ordinary things—the price of having a boiler repaired, the man whose car had broken down, again. The woman who had despairingly conceded that it was time to finally purchase a washing machine—at least I think that's what she was saying. They all spoke so emphatically. It was time to tease Mitzi long distance; I wrote her another Louvre postcard. The picture was of a calm gray horse with spots, *Le Cheval Pie*. It looked quite modern; I was surprised that the artist had lived in the seventeenth century. He was Dutch and called Paulus Potter, it sounded like a wood gnome's name. He had died at twenty-eight and was just about old enough to have fought in the Thirty Years' War. Later I discovered that he had died of tuberculosis. I studied the card, imagining how Mitzi would shriek on receiving another horse picture from me. What to write on the back, not history:

"Dear Mitzi, have fallen in love with a Russian count, he is in hiding, his fortune, diamonds, sewn into his long black coat. We are fleeing to Tahiti, it's the only way. Will see you again, somehow, much love, your friend Helen." No French, the message was too urgent.

The coffee tasted of boiled milk and the cake was dry, I decided to move elsewhere and try out another café, I was still hungry. I had seen *The Astronomer* and had sent a postcard of it to the art teacher. I didn't mention the Russian count, just described the painting and thanked her for telling me about it. I seemed to have gotten taller; the women were very short and most of the men appeared to have stopped growing at about five foot five or six . . . I missed riding and lamented waking each morning without all my reassuring posters of the night skies and galaxies . . . Saturn and its rings. The little hotel room was comfortable though and clean enough with a beautifully aged wooden floor and a cast-iron bath tub. It had a long green riverlike stain on the chipped enamel. The tarnished faucets were stiff and groaned when I turned them. Small, lead panes divided the view from the window into neat, slightly blurred squares. The glass must have been very old. That impressed me hugely, I really was in Europe.

I loved the galleries. For the Louvre alone I would stay for another couple of weeks or so. Paris was fine but I had no desire to live there. I noticed a church and crossed the street, Rue Jacob, I think, to look more closely at it. The church building was modest in size whereas the gargoyles were huge, crouching, outlined against the fading light. It was a bit odd sitting in a café contemplating malevolent gargoyles that appeared poised to leap down and pounce on the table. I selected a strategically positioned place to sit from which I could comfortably spy on my fellow diners and ordered a cheese and spinach omelet and a hot chocolate. The waiter looked disgusted "No wine?" he said in English, "Non," I replied in defiant French, causing him to make a clicking sound with his tongue. Unperturbed, I gazed back at the church, feeling autocratic, even intrepid, almost, and in control of my destiny. I was Father's daughter, in Paris, France. Someone nearby began playing a suitably evocative tune on an accordion.

The music was coming closer. A teenage boy, dark-skinned, perhaps a Romanian, knew exactly which pieces would suit the mood. He had taken up position on the sidewalk, and stood playing, gazing impassively at the customers, swaying with the movement of his bulky instrument. The café staff made no objection; it was good for business and irresistibly atmospheric. Little white candles began to cast deepening shadows on the red-and-white checkered tablecloths as well as the faces of customers. I had been watching a man sitting at a nearby table; he, in turn, had been consulting his watch, drumming his fingers, glancing toward the café entrance. His hair was black and quite long, lank, shining or greasy, I couldn't say, and flopping down over his face. He tossed it back with a quick movement of his head, never using his hands. There were hollows under his eyes and his face was thin. I reckoned he was about thirty, possibly a poet, who had lived carelessly; ravaged by wine, women, and song. I sniggered knowingly to myself, worldly-wise; the new me and better at reading people. He was waiting, and obviously, for a woman. It would be interesting to linger and have a look at her arrival. A single red rose lay on the table, he picked it up, fiddled with it; tapped his wineglass and then waved the rose at the waiter. Again he consulted his watch. He looked resigned to his vigil but good humored about it; and must have said something funny to the waiter as they both laughed. It appeared to have happened before, perhaps it was a regular occurrence and she was often late—or so it seemed. The waiter returned with the wine bottle and the man gestured for him to continue pouring. The wine reached the rim of the glass and the man downed most of it in a single swallow. I had never noticed how the human throat works, the amount of movement involved; it's a muscle, I guess, and his gulping reflex made me think of a snake eating its prey. He caught me staring and slowly tilted the glass toward me with a smile. Perhaps I smiled back, out of embarrassment though at being caught staring, usually I'm discreet. But not that time.

"Allemande?" the man was leaning over my table, bearing his rose and his wine glass. I had not noticed his moving across the room, not with the noise of the busy café, and I'd looked away once I had realized he had spotted me staring. I knew he was asking me if I was German, I shook my head, then he said something else, it may have been Hollandaise, again I indicated no. He made a point of holding his hand high, over his shoulder; he seemed to be telling me that I was tall, too tall to be French. No one would mistake me for French, not with my tailored tweed jacket and straight brown hair, not black, not red, not hennaed; just plain, ordinary Virginian brown. I could pass for English, not exotic and obviously from Blandland which I'd invented when Mitzi told me that her family were Austrian; Austrians with American accents who didn't speak German . . . but never mind; many Americans seem to want to be from someplace else—I guess it's from being culturally land-locked and who'd want to be Canadian? Before I could say "Américaine" in what I hoped would sound a flawless French accent, he was announcing it to the café in general, "Américaine, Américaine." He'd peered triumphantly into my face, "les dents, les dents," as if a new pope had just been elected. My perfect teeth had given me away. My non-matching eyes would be next up for comment. His were blue, not brown; they had looked darker from a distance. Close up he was older, a bit shook-looking from all that waiting, never mind the hard living. He told me that he would sit with me, he didn't ask, he told me. I was nervous, if attempting to appear at ease by means of my carefully carefree shrug. No one in that Parisian café took much notice. Back home in Richmond, the little episode would have caused a mild ripple of disapproval—the idea of a mature man suddenly sitting down beside a school-girl—although I did hope to be looking more like a college student. But in Paris, social behavior was certainly fluid. He seemed happy to have found a way of passing the time until his date arrived in a flurry of wide, tormented eyes. I wished my French was sufficient to decipher his girlfriend's excuse when she arrived. No doubt it would be a piece of theater. French people reminded me of Mother, in the way they declaimed the hardships of daily existence; the shrugs, the sighs, the little poufs, and especially that peculiar habit of seeming to kiss the air.

I had already decided he was almost good-looking in an exhausted way, weary, with the beginnings of hangdog folds running down each side of his mouth. His teeth were haphazard; he was missing a few. His smile amounted to a funny grimace, lips closed, with his cheeks bunched as the creases momentarily deepened. It was an amused smile which was certainly appealing I thought, less studied than so much of the stagy glamour Paris specialized in. As usual I was being an uptight kid from Virginia, as Mitzi often reminded me, at least once a day. Well, that's probably because I am an uptight child, girl, from Virginia, not a kid—a kid being a young goat as Mrs. Faulkner had endlessly repeated throughout my childhood. It had stayed with me; I never say "kid." Believing that my European trip had matured me I was certain that I had indeed become a connoisseur of human nature. My meal had ended; the dishes had been cleared, leaving only the empty cup and my longing for more hot chocolate. I was wary of ordering anything else for fear he would think I was expecting him to pay. I dreaded arguing over the bill, with my insisting, thrusting the francs into the waiter's hands, ignoring the funny little tray he held, causing the money to flutter to the floor leaving me looking stupid and clumsy. Aside from a second hot chocolate I was still hungry, having planned on sampling several desserts. But this new development had interfered with my investigations. Still, it would be worth waiting on a while to see his date.

Time passed. He asked me what I was doing in Paris. Mitzi's voice sounded loud in my head saying "she's in pursuit of her deranged horse." I gagged and said without thinking, I'd come to practice my French. "So practice on me," he pointed to his chest, laughing. He still had what was left of the rose and waved it at the waiter, who walked over—with a bottle of wine and another glass. The waiter's expression had become serious. He filled the clean one and placed it before me, and then poured more wine for my self-appointed host, who then tipped his glass off mine, intoning, "Welcome, welcome, welcome." Did I like Paris he asked—well what he actually said was "You are liking Paris, yes?" I didn't reply as he was already answering his question, assuring me that all Americans love Paris. I didn't, but it was interesting listening to his assumptions, the ideas people can have. Again, he drank greedily as if the wine was water and he close on emptied his glass with one loud gulp. He motioned at me to do the same. A sip was enough. I don't like wine. Aside from the whiskey I had had with Father and Sheriff Hodge, the only other liquor I enjoyed was the cough medicine I drank in secret. Now and then, I would buy a bottle, but only one at a time, as I knew I could easily drink a few at one sitting, I suppose I was addicted to its sweet syrupy flavor, but it was probably the codeine. And although I had yet to experience any side effects from drinking children's cough linctus, there was the sinful thrill of enjoying it, alone in my bedroom, on my own, swigging merrily away. I'd nod to Mrs. Faulkner, she would incline her head—no need for small talk, we had an understanding—and I would ease my way by her in the kitchen or the hall, an empty cough bottle stashed in my school bag, ready to toss it in a nearby trash can. What would she say if she knew I was addicted to cough medicine? My secret vice; it was similar to my pleasure in breaking her rules about putting tendon boots and tail bandages in the laundry room washing machine. The wine was sour, not sweet like the cough medicine. I had no interest in drinking it but my companion urged me on, I said I didn't want it. That irritated him and he stood up. I braced myself for his walking away before the watching eyes of the other diners—except they weren't taking any notice. Instead, he sighed and with mock exasperation, ordered, "Attendez, attendez, wait here, wait," he said. "A moment, a moment," and off he bustled to the bar counter, returning with two small goblets of water. I was glad to see them and reached for one; he stopped me and poured some of it into my wine, "Now, drink," he said.

It seemed to sweeten the taste, I thought, by diluting it. Whatever it was, it was not water. On we drank, clinking glasses, in increasingly giddy good humor, waiting for the girlfriend who never did arrive. I was feeling drowsy and hot. When I tried to take off my jacket, I couldn't free my arms. Removing them from the sleeves suddenly seemed to require an effort beyond me and then I recalled all the times I had watched as Sheriff Hodge strained to take off his jacket and regardless of the season, his shirts would invariably be stained by perspiration, great damp patches spreading out from his underarms, tracking inwards to meet across his wide, wide chest. Steam would surely be rising from me that night I thought and urgently needed to go to the bathroom but I didn't know where it was and the rest rooms in those cafés were always dimly lit and dubious; no soap, no hand towels, no bathroom paper. Toilet bowls mossy with slime and always, the smell of urine catching in your throat. I was an uptight Southerner, no doubt about it. Mrs. Faulkner had trained me well and I laughed to myself.

Again, there was Mitzi's voice in my head retorting that I should have gone to Zurich. The Swiss were more fastidious. I must have laughed. My companion assumed I was reacting to something he had said. He was pleased and said we should leave, we had waited long enough.

What about his girlfriend? I asked, my voice sounding muffled to me, as if it was coming from some great distance. She had disappointed him he said. What was she like? I asked, what was her name? Was she a student? No he said flatly, a model, very beautiful but stupid, "very stupid." Looks aren't everything I thought. Without my saying anything he said he did not wish to discuss her, shrugging with mock petulance, not until he had forgiven her. That sounded fair to me. Then his expression brightened, he laughed and said some musician friends were having a small party, we could perhaps join them? He looked quizzical, giving me time to process his suggestion. He gathered the remaining rose petals and dropped them slowly into my empty glass.

Sweat sneaked down my face, along my back, into my armpits. I could feel my hair wet behind my ears, my neck damp and clammy. My fringe was tangled; I actually felt drops of my sweat land on my hand. Most unpleasant. It seemed as if I had begun to melt. My legs were weak, perhaps from sitting for so long but no, it wasn't from sitting. The wooden chair under me felt sticky. Were my blue jeans wet like Jamie Hodge's shirts? Would anyone notice? Without having to look I knew my face would be all blotchy and disgusting. I really needed to go to the bathroom but more than that I wanted to escape into the chill night air. I had always been able to hold my pee for as long as required but this time I felt about ready to burst. There I was concentrating on not urinating in public, while Marc, that was his name, mimed dropping baskets. It seemed eccentric to want to play basketball late at night in Paris and he must have been expecting an American to leap high with joy at the prospect but I was way too shaky and had never played any sport. But he was only asking me if I played basketball, not if I wanted a game. I said I didn't know the rules, which sounded somewhat pathetic. He was surprised but then his face lit up with certainty, "You are a high jumper." I corrected him, "Show jumper, well, sort of . . ." My elation plummeted; I did not want to begin brooding about my riding. Marc's reaction made me laugh, he seemed to think that a show jumper was a high jumper who gave public demonstrations, "Displays," he said. I said no, that I rode horses over jumps. This excited him greatly, he took my arm and leaned into me. We were about the same height, "You are a female cowboy, fantastique. Not in the circus, you are for the rodeo . . . I like the horses, to watch them but, for me, not to ride, they are highly strung, no?" He wanted to show me Notre Dame; we could sit by the river, he said with a smile.

And all of a sudden we were walking through Paris and at night. Me, the girl most likely to win the Nobel Prize at least as far as my classmates were concerned, while equally being the girl most unlikely to be walking through Paris with a captivating older man. But who was, in fact, walking arm in arm with a captivating older man and through that very city. It was more friendly than romantic, and he wasn't all that captivating, but I didn't mind. Paris at last seemed about to come alive. Marc tucked my hand in under his arm, and beamed at me. I enjoyed the sensation of contact. Mitzi always touched me, took my arm, tapped her finger on it to make a point and held my hands when she had something to say. It made me uneasy, not being demonstrative. When Mrs. Faulkner had stood beside me, looking at the *Earthrise* photograph, we had both gazed at it in silence. She'd put her hand on my shoulder causing us both to jump as the repressed individuals we were. But there I was in Paris, walking as close to this laughing stranger as if we had been tied together, chance partners in a three-legged race. Not that I'd ever been in one of those either. I thrilled at the solid feel of my side against his, our strides keeping step. I liked the chance companionship, that's how I saw it; reassuring not sexual. His voice was just a sound, making words like water. I was only catching part of the meaning, too tired to make sense of the stream of French, recognizing parts of it. I was so tired, my feet were hitting the sidewalk hard because the rest of my body had become loose-jointed, as if the bones had fallen out and my head was so very heavy I was waiting for my neck to snap in two, leaving me with a body made of rubber about to collapse onto my boots. I laughed weakly and wanted to sleep.

At my side, Marc walked on. He appeared to have seen every Western ever made and was incredulous I had never met a Native American. "You mean redskin," I said. The archaic term thrilled him. "Redskin, redskin," he repeated happily, "redskin." He spoke about the years he spent watching a weekly TV show in which the white man wore a mask and the Indian was very clever. I knew he was referring to *The Lone Ranger*. All I said was "Tonto" and he hooted with glee, delighted and bellowed "Kemosabe." That made me laugh, so he said it again, and again. He asked me about riding through the concrete valleys. It took me a moment to realize that he meant canyons and it was easy to see that he was confused on hearing I'd never been to a desert and back where I

came from the landscape was green, like in England. The western United States, I explained, California, Arizona, Colorado,
New Mexico, Nevada, Wyoming, Utah, was arid, dry, more like
Spain. He interrupted with "How about Texas!" and I enjoyed
watching his face drop when I explained that Texas was in fact
considered part of the South . . . Marc ignored me and kept
on talking, shouting out in English, random statements about
Westerns, "the only type of movie Americans can make," naming actors and characters, he recited garbled plot summaries,
and repeatedly told me that I should wear a cowboy hat, and
that my boots were not quite right, "not Western." He began
walking bowlegged and shouted "John Wayne," saying he liked
bank robberies and train holdups in particular. He seemed to
think that Jesse James was the American equivalent of Robin
Hood. I disagreed and he seemed offended. We walked along
in silence, not as quickly as we had started out. We passed by
what looked like expensive stores. Most of the show windows
were in darkness. But then we approached one that was well-lit,
a jeweler's, the kind of store Mother would have loved and I
would ignore, its contents holding no appeal for me. Except that
the centerpiece of that Parisian show display happened to be a
fabulous orrery, complete with Earth and the sun, the planets,
all in gold and connected with thin silver rods. Although I was
dizzy and felt tired, my voice sounding high to me, my sentences
clumsy, spoken with intense effort, even in English, I exclaimed,
"Look, look," calling him back because he had walked on when
I'd stopped to stare in at the orrery.

Elated at seeing something that reminded me of my other life,
I began to explain it to Marc, but he only pointed out its lack of
stars. He dismissed the orrery as a dull piece of fake mechanical
cleverness. "A thing a bored clockmaker fabricates." He said "fab-
ricate" with a shrug, tossing it off, proud of his fluency which was

somewhat more sporadic than he realized, although far superior to my French. Then he began to laugh again and said the only thing worth talking about was the stars and it was his place to explain the stars to me. "The man shows the stars to the woman; the woman sighs, she listens and then submits as planned." I thought he was kidding and laughed on cue because I felt I was supposed to. But he wasn't really laughing; he wasn't interested in anything I had to say. I was a way of passing a few hours.

He was an artist, he said, but he was working at a friend's clothes store. Later he said his uncle owned the shop. But perhaps I had misheard, it didn't seem important.

At Notre Dame, we sat down. The riverbank walks were alive with people, sitting in groups, oblivious to the great cathedral—relegating it to a mere backdrop against the night sky. The tinny sound of tape recorders competed with the stronger tones of student types hunched over guitars. Snatches of various songs drifted around us, so many voices; English lyrics sung in rich foreign accents. "Heart of Gold," "Blowin' in the Wind," "Suzanne," "Both Sides Now," and through my foggy state, "The Boxer"—which I knew very well and could play on the guitar. "Here, have this," said Marc, handing me a cigarette from which he had already taken several deep puffs. I said I didn't smoke. He smiled, shaking his head. "This is different, it is herbal for clearing the head. Good for you to have it as I can see you don't drink." I didn't want to smoke. More than that, I hated the thought of putting something in my mouth that would probably be damp from his. "No, no, you must. I say this as your host and also so that you will not insult my friends when they offer you food and wine, which they will." It felt surprisingly small, the cigarette, which was in my fingers, like a tiny bomb, and I couldn't figure out how to hold it. "Smoke it," Marc shrieked, insistent. I tried to. There was an overwhelming taste of burning paper in my mouth, I breathed in and choked. My throat felt as if I was bleeding hot liquidized blood. There was an acrid, musky scent and my head spun, my eyes hurt and I felt I'd been punched in my heart, which in turn had begun to race as if I was running for my life. Then I sat forward, my arms folded around me, hot one minute, then shivering with cold the next, and steaming vomit plopped into my lap at about the same time that I'd finally gone to the bathroom, there, in my blue jeans, on the riverbank. And all with Notre Dame towering up above me; I could smell my warm urine seeping out and filling the air around us with its sharp tang. My controlled existence had ended, all the discipline, the books I had read, the facts I had accumulated, had all oozed away. I used to ride horses; I had had some authority as well as a bunch of telescopes. Now I was drenched in my own urine. "Serves me right," I thought, for having misunderstood Mother. My adventure had ended, I was paying for having belittled her catastrophic love affair and had found myself in the middle of something far more squalid.

Marc stood up, his hands in his pockets. It looked as if he was wondering which way to go, abandoning me to my shame, while I sat staring at my vomit, poised to retch again. I wanted to find a phone and call Mitzi and tell her everything. Only it was too shameful. I could never tell her . . . Where was my hotel? I wondered, not that any taxi driver would want to deal with anyone in the condition I was in, I'd have to walk. The smell was making me sick; my stomach was contracting, more of the burning mess was on the way. "Come, come," coaxed Marc in a resigned tone, sounding like a parent who had no choice but to take up his screaming child and leave the restaurant, allowing the other diners to eat in peace. He took charge and said I needed a bath; that he could wash out my blue jeans and dry them somehow, at the window perhaps. "There is a washing machine in the apartment,

we can use it. The drier, he is broke." He said, "he is broke" not
it is broken, and for some reason I took comfort from the way he
said it, I felt he knew exactly what we had to do, even if he said
it in a different way, the awareness, the meaning, was the same.

Standing was difficult, walking even worse. My teeth hurt; I
imagined the corrosive vomit eating its way through the enamel
and on into the bone further undermining my teeth. Marc
marched onwards, silent, gripping me as if he was assisting a
crash victim. Obligation had replaced companionship. I was
reduced to a chance responsibility. Suddenly he slowed, I thought
he would leave me there in the street, and rush off into the night.
"Kemosabe, take heart, help is at hand," he tittered shrilly and
I joined in, relieved at his change of mood. He stopped and
pressed a buzzer located in the wall, leaning into the button
as if the task required all his weight. After a minute or so, he
paused and then began again, finger held in position. That time
he waited for perhaps two minutes and then shrugged, thrust
ing his hand down into a pocket. Out came a key, he opened
the door. We stumbled along a narrow hall before he pushed me
forward into the darkness, explaining there were six flights of
stairs ahead of us. "Only the brave will survive," he announced,
imitating a general leading his men into battle, something else
he'd seen in a movie. "The weak will just have to die, here, on the
stairs," he cackled merrily. My heart thudded as we negotiated
those impossibly narrow steps. I wanted to stop but he urged
me on, dragging me until we reached another door. He pushed
it inward and we entered as one, together, into a small vestibule
which opened onto a larger room, all in darkness. There was no
one there. The room was empty, as was the rest of the apartment.
It had a deserted airlessness about it and seemed uninhabited;
a stale, forgotten void. Just the lingering, musty stink of smoke
and something foul; a dead mouse but more likely rotten food or

a dirty kitchen cloth floating in a sink of greasy, smeared dishes covered in scum. I wanted to close my eyes and be anywhere but there. If only I could sleep.

*

An antique sofa was the first thing I noticed; possibly because it was also almost the only thing in the room. Upholstered in a faded damask, it was most incongruous in such a drab setting and looked as if it was a stage prop, stolen from some theater. That thought made me laugh wildly. Even in my somewhat altered state, wet, drunk, reeking of urine and vomit, lingering traces of civilized behavior honed by Mrs. Faulkner's disapproval, told me not to sit down on it for fear of staining the fabric. Out of deference to the venerable sofa I squatted on the floor and then carefully eased my body completely flat, stretched out like a corpse. Uppermost in my thoughts was that my head might suddenly crack wide open. The room was moving, everything people say about being drunk is quite true—the world does spin and could even tilt if you're really unlucky, as I seem to have been, convinced no one else had ever gotten quite as sick from drinking wine and whatever. The floor was a ship's deck and solid ground was nowhere in sight. Marc's voice began to push its way into my thoughts. He was telling me that we must do the laundry and I asked if he often attended to his chores at such unusual hours. He was concerned about my clothes, and insisted they had to be washed. It made sense; of course he was trying to help me. Touched by his awareness of the mess, my mess, I got up slowly, off the floor, asking about the washing machine. "Direct me toute suite to la machine à laver, vite, vite," I commanded, delighted with my command of French. But he said I should lie down on the bed and that he would look after the clothes. I quizzed him about the sofa and he seemed bewildered, what sofa? He replied distractedly, appearing never to have noticed it but was only half-listening to me. He led me across the living room, into a small, very dark room and I lay down, aware of the loud noise of springs, a jangling sound. It was an ancient bed infused with a bad smell wafting off the pillow, and competing with the stink of new vomit, mine own; along with the tobacco stench apparently ingrained into every surface throughout the decrepit apartment and something else as well, too vile at which to even hazard a guess.

Marc had begun tugging at my boots; I alerted him to the zippers in the side. "Each boot has a zipper, well at least the two I happen to be wearing," although not for a moment suggesting that every boot has side zippers. "But these ones here most definitely do." I thought this very witty and howled gleefully at my brilliance. There was no reply. Instead I heard my boots thudding to the floor as he tossed them in turn over his shoulder and pulled off my socks which were damp and smelling of swimming pool changing rooms — exactly why, who knows? I didn't. My hot, sweaty, swollen feet were at last free but had been somehow transformed into bloated white sponges. Normally they look quite tanned and are decent-looking feet, one of my better features. Shame so few people have seen my more-than-decent-looking feet; what had happened?

Was I nervous? No, not at all. I was not even surprised at not being nervous because I was too busy enjoying a feeling of bizarre exhilaration. My sole aim was one of not wanting to spoil the elegant old ottoman. That in mind I then, quite unexpectedly, vomited over the side of the bed. A steaming torrent of goo splashed down in heavy plop-like drips upon the glossy cover of a magazine; I was struck by the fact that the magazine was in French and that even the most trivial of articles in it could prove beyond my comprehension. *Quel dommage* . . .

A voice summoned: Marc was requesting my blue jeans; he explained he wanted to rinse them out in the bath before putting them into the machine. He stood beside the bed miming a wringing action with his empty hands in case I had not understood. It was the right thing to do, a pre, pre-wash rinse, I was mightily impressed. Such housekeeperly diligence and from a man, who though living in squalor, clearly had standards and washed clothes before he put them into the machine. He fumbled with the button and the zipper, pulled my jeans down, efficiently, brisk in his attitude, brotherly, and stepped over to the bathroom. I heard them flop down on to the floor and he came back and said he would try to clean my jacket with a sponge but would not put it into the machine. "Not so good an idea," he said, advising me it would shrink. He mentioned he knew about clothes, from working in the store and that he had helped his sisters at home. I had thought he had already mentioned that he was an only child, just like me. But maybe I was confused, I was confused. My jacket seemed stuck to me, but that was because my arms had inflated. I imagined them swelling like sausages ready to burst on the pan, or was that what had happened to my fingers? I couldn't decide; thinking had become difficult. The bedroom was dark and I felt composed entirely of rubber, ready to lurch to one side and throw up more of the endless amount of liquid that had somehow accumulated inside me, along with the congealed omelet.

Never again would I eat an egg: I silently vowed to renounce them forever and realized I would never eat again. An underwater feeling had taken over my body; my head was contracting and expanding like a lung. No it was throbbing—as were my heart and my teeth. Why had Billy Bob, apparently by choice, lived in a state of semi-drunkenness? Had he been able to see straight? I couldn't; even my eyes had been affected. Inebriation—a Victorian, almost medical-sounding word to describe complete physical collapse—conveyed no sense of the agony. Perhaps there was a skill needed to arrive at the exact balance sober/drunk to achieve a pain-deflecting stupor? I wondered about that. I had read that people drink to forget, yet there I was remembering everything with an enormous clarity, each willfully obscene detail. Extraordinary what the mind does; where had Billy Bob gone? I was mumbling loud enough to be overheard. "Who is this person Billy Bob?" inquired Marc, "Is it your boyfriend?" The question was a wet slap and made me think straight. "He not it," Billy Bob was my friend, I said about to cry, "My very much older friend," older even than him, older than Father, but he'd gone away to die. This I knew for certain because that was my feeling. I did believe that, I had from the beginning, but when I told Mitzi what I really thought she had been horrified and said it would cause so much trouble I had better keep my "dark and dire" theories to myself. Mitzi could be real bossy.

My jacket would have to be dry-cleaned Marc was saying, although he would try and improve it, he said for me to give him my shirt as well. "Here," he said, and handed me something that smelled musty, a vile, pinkish, flesh-colored thing. It was an old tracksuit top, nylon and obviously contaminated like everything else in the hovel; truly disgusting, but dry. "I will do all of this," he said, taking my shirt as well, leaving me in my cotton singlet, holding the tracksuit top and he told me to go to sleep, assuring me I was safe, he only liked women, not skinny boy-girls, "not the toms," he said, meaning "tomboy" I suppose. I laughed to show I didn't mind, not the least, all I wanted was sleep, to stop the vast surging in my head, which seemed to be forcing my eyes out of my face. Earlier on, back in the restaurant he had told me that I was "android," I knew he meant androgynous. It didn't bother me. I was very clever and could pass any exam put before me and could also ride nasty, talented—even nastily talented—horses. Mother always maintained that my "gray matter" as she called it would compensate for my physical shortcomings, my peculiar eyes . . . I am sure she had never meant to hurt my feelings and instead had given me a kind of confidence; no, a resilience. That is what I had in abundance, resilience, very useful when balancing my standard-issue face and ill-matched eyes, and, hopefully, the dreams Father had belittled but which I would salvage. I thought of him back home in his office, watching his evil fish, counting the bubbles in their tank as they swam round and round in circles. Perhaps they had succeeded in finally eating each other. Well, good for them I thought.

My eyeballs had turned to cones, reaching out into sharp points as when a cartoon character suffers a shock or encounters a ghost. I was waiting for Marc to scream at the sight. But he remained very calm. Sensible, a good person to have on a battlefield, tending the wounded and the dying; he would be able to push my conical eyes back into their respective sockets. It would be fine. In time they would retract, subside. I informed him that I planned in future to drink only cough medicine; it agreed with me, unlike wine. He went back to the bathroom. Perhaps he had cough medicine stored in his bathroom cabinet and all for me? Our meeting had indeed been fated. Finally I could feel the drifting that would bring me sleep. The last sensation of which I was aware was a feeling of such warm gratitude. So many of the girls at school had already suffered dreadful experiences with supposedly civilized boys from good families, Virginia's finest . . . and all in the name of romance. Poor Mother—such disturbing images, relentlessly re-playing in my memory. Yet I had been fortunate to have been rescued by a struggling artist who was compelled to labor in a store by day selling clothes, perhaps even washing them, and whose home was this miserable apartment. There were no signs of it being his studio. Had he told me he was a painter? Perhaps he was a poet, or a novelist. His dreams unfulfilled, I thought, yet he was unselfishly caring for me as I lay in a disgusting state. Late as it was he was still up, washing my blue jeans and endeavoring to salvage my jacket. Lucky for me, I thought, that my first experience with a man had been a good one. The mishap was of my doing but he was busily rectifying it. Such luck, I smiled and found the energy to murmur, "Thank you, thank you." He made no reply. The room was tranquil, not a sound. I had gotten used to the filthy pillow, and its scent of consummate unwashedness and was waiting to hear the faucet judder and the running water groaning through the pipes but must have drifted off, in all that silence.

*

It was the sight of a horse's head staring at me from the foot of the bed. Somehow Galileo had been traced back to me. I had known he was dangerous and should have spoken out, exposed him as an evil force. Mitzi was right; he had killed someone and now I was being held responsible for his violent activities. His mane was shorter than I remembered. I could feel a sharp poking sensation in my backside, the barrel of a gun; I was going to be executed, ingloriously shot in the behind because Galileo had trampled his new rider to death; all that money paid for a murderous horse, or to borrow Mitzi's favorite phrase, "an insane, over-bred equine." It seemed unfair that I was being blamed but

I was not going to cry. The probing became more annoying, insistent; silly not menacing. I jumped and swung around, my elbow connected with something sharp, Marc's front teeth. He shouted as I did; only I was loud, louder than I thought I would ever shout. "What in hell you doing boy?" somehow very aware of sounding just like Father. Marc sat up, wiping one hand across his mouth, as shocked by my temper as by his split lip. "Hey," he said, recovering quickly and in a sneering manner for which I did not much care, said "Smell this!" He thrust his finger into my face, smirking like a jackrabbit and pushed me back, flat on the mattress and proceeded to kiss me, sticking his tongue into my mouth. I gagged on it, as sickened by his foul breath as by his sudden, very different attitude, and then he forced his hand into my panties, squeezing hard on my private parts, his nails catching in my pubic hair. It had been his finger not a gun that had poked my bottom. The horse's head was only some fool dream caused by residual thoughts of surly old Galileo still preying on my mind. Marc lay down on me and said it was time to play, or would I "prefer instead . . ." he said pausing, while making a disgusting gesture that made me feel cold with dread, unease, wondering how I had gotten into such a mess. He bragged that he watched girls like me masturbate all the time. "This I know," he said, "I can always tell, the girls who do the touching for themselves but act so pure, playing the innocence ('innocent' I muttered, even then correcting him), I can always see through the pretending," he made an ugly, licking sound and twisted my nipple so hard I thought it would snap off. I hated him with a sudden white anger and was plain furious. How dare he? I could see he was naked; skinny, hairless, and thin, with a slack, little pot belly and no muscle; his legs those of an older person, his penis hanging down, dead to the world. He was weak, what we in Virginia would describe as meager, undernourished. I cursed my safe, stupid, soft life that had not prepared me for such a turn of events. "I need to go," I said and pushed by him and he just laughed, he must have thought I was intending to rush out into the night wearing my torn underpants and his filthy tracksuit top. Cretin. "The bathroom," I mumbled, gesturing, "la salle de bain, la salle de bain."

The bathroom was all that one might expect of such a rancid habitation. I sat on the toilet in the dark, then stood up and ran my hands along the wall. The light switch was old-fashioned, a prime example of a premeditated fire hazard, placed in the center of a small, metal box that felt dangerously loose in the wall. I slumped back down on the toilet, aware that the seat was only balanced on the bowl and not secure. It shifted with my weight. Water dripped down on me from the cistern, one long obsolete in style, fixed several feet above my head; it leaked and gurgled. Cobwebs made the dim light from the bare bulb appear even weaker and cast dirty half shadows everywhere. I was trying to place the horse's head, what had triggered it? Then it struck me that the image must have come from that movie with the theme that Mother had liked so much, *The Godfather*, she used to hum it, it was a love song. The pianist at The Clock Tower often played it during our high teas there . . . That was where I had seen a horse's head mounted at the foot of a bed, in that old mafia movie I'd only half-watched. Then I remembered another horse's head, the one in *The Tin Drum*, but that had had eels living in it, Baltic eels from Danzig.

A wizened orange was on the floor, just one hole jabbed into its skin. It looked as if Marc or someone had stuck their thumb in it and then lost all interest in eating, too bored to continue peeling it, deciding instead to just drop it on the floor. What manner of individual would just abandon an orange down on the floor beside a toilet? Slovenly behavior . . . Then I spotted my clothes, left in a heap. The pockets of my blue jeans had been searched, the linings pulled out. The vomit was still visible; he had made no effort to rinse it off. It was the same with the jacket, splayed out on the floor, the pockets empty. My wallet gone, well it was just something too ridiculous for words, to have fallen prey to a grotty little lying son of a bitch . . . There had not been much in my wallet, I was careful with money and had only taken what I needed for the day, keeping the traveler's checks back at the little hotel, in the safe along with my passport and also had, as always, my emergency money, safe in my secret place. But I did fume and fester inwardly for being so fool stupid. Marc walked in; I glared up at him, black hatred in my heart, before glancing pointedly at my clothes. He noticed, casually announcing, "I need to piss." I stretched the tracksuit top down over my lap and waited for him to leave. Before I could stand, he slithered in closer, penis in hand, and urinated on me, a warm, feeble stream that trickled down my leg. Then he sniggered and said I should stay where I was, sitting there on toilet, maybe I wanted to lick him dry. He aimed his penis close to my face. I could smell it as he stroked it as if it were a blind baby possum, skinless, most likely dying or dead. I had seen so many stallions and geldings drop their penises that by contrast this first human one looked decidedly paltry. I moved my head away and he shrugged, faking a yawn, saying he was bored, "Too bored to fight you, a skinny girl, a nothing. I don't beg for sex, real women enjoy it," he declared haughtily, making a face at me, dismissing me, and then snarled he would much rather sleep. He indicated I was a disappointment. "Where is the washing machine?" I snapped, but he just laughed, "He must have run away, quel dommage . . ." There had never been a washing machine, that I had managed to deduce, finally, I should have realized nobody aside from Superman could have gotten it up all those narrow stairs. Stupid me, stupid me so many times that night. Stupid me. Marc's sad little posterior jiggled and sagged and again I thought how old he looked, this wretched little skunk, so devoid of honor yet how easily he had fooled me, the girl voted by my school as most likely to win the Nobel Prize, he had categorized me as an idiot and that stung me hard . . . I walked over to run the bath, too shocked and disgusted to begin protesting about his despicable behavior.

Something punctured my foot, a thumb tack tight in the ball of my heel. The bath was scummy and the water barely lukewarm. I didn't sit down in it, only stood, rinsing my legs and feet, and dried them on my jacket, draping it over the side of the bath, then shook out my jeans as well, and put them over the tub, hoping they would dry and I walked back out, planning to lie down on the sofa. But Marc was already huddled on it, his head tucked down into his shoulder, apparently asleep. He was a thief; more petty thief than serious rapist. No doubt he made extra cash by stealing from his guests. I decided to retreat to the bed and wait until first light. Confidence was important; the slightest hint of fear would give him an advantage. I could easily fight him. My head had cleared and I was stronger than he was, not as sneaky, but physically tougher, hardened from all the riding and a lot younger. More than that I was incandescent with rage—I so love saying "incandescent" —anyhow I knew my anger would help me. I could visualize Father's disgust and Sheriff Hodge's pain, he would be so distressed if he knew about this. But then, the strangest thought of all hit me, I could imagine how very intrigued Caleb Montgomery would be, him being such an astute observer of human nature. As long as I didn't manage to get myself killed and all, that is, he would be drawn to what he would no doubt describe as the "thrust and parry of it," a battle of wits of the most perverse variety. I could almost hear him say the words. It was late but morning, or at least light, was still some hours off and I knew it was better to remain in that vile little apartment, as the streets outside might be more threatening and I was still weary, slow on my feet, but sober, becoming more alert and had regained my interest in the business of eating; hunger would soon be adding to my problems.

What if he had an accomplice? It was an idea to see if I could lock the door from the inside, to allow me some time in case someone did arrive. "Where is the washing machine?" I demanded loudly, just to see if Marc was already sleeping. "There is no facility, I told you already," so Marc was still as wide awake as I was. "You said no such thing, you damn, sneaky, lying little bastard . . . you told me you had a washing machine." My voice sounded shrill, peevish, it irritated me to hear it. I made a point of turning to go back into the bedroom yet for some reason entirely unknown to me, in an attempt perhaps to deflect the degradation I was feeling, declared, "Mother died on television." Marc shifted on the sofa and asked if she was that bad an actress, I must have looked baffled. "Or she is a singer, no?" I asked what on earth he was talking about, Mother had been shot dead. He sat up and said too bad she had no talent and shrugged the way French people do, saying that in France the audience would simply turn away, ignore her, but not abuse her. No, there would be no real violence; perhaps someone might throw a wine glass or a shoe. "Americans," he hissed with open contempt, "everything, such a beeg deel"—big deal. This was indeed ironic, I thought, coming from a French person, a nation for which theatricality was second nature. "Shot dead," I repeated, "I mean killed." He was bored, too tired to pursue another energy sapping bilingual conversation, particularly after all that had happened; I could tell that as I felt much the same, caught in a standoff and yet some crazed part of me wanted to regain his attention, so I persisted,

"Mother was shot dead, in the street, by her lover." That got him listening. He looked directly at me, his eyes wide, and he explained to me, as if I needed him to define it for me, that it had been a crime of passion. He looked almost envious. What a bizarre little goblin he was. "If I was to kill a woman for a betrayal, I would stab her and watch as she bloods to death," he looked thoughtful and added that he would make a picture. So this was how an artist depicted violence, I thought, shocked but at the same time impressed, "You mean you would do a painting of it?" He looked at me, convinced of my stupidity. "No!" he shouted, before continuing in a conversational tone that he would take a photograph and send it to his victim's family.

"Mother didn't betray anyone, except Father. Mother's boyfriend loved her, but he was depressed . . ," I persisted. Marc raised his hands over his head, incredulity on his face, and spluttered that the lover should have taken a pill. "It's too disgusting, so stupid. Americans are horrible; they come here and shout at the waiters, I hate them. They make me sick, all of them, you." But then as if what I had said had finally penetrated his reasoning, he said he was sorry for my mother. People didn't think, they hurt each other all the time, he said, telling me that I should try to sleep. It was his way of offering comfort. I lay back on the bed, aware that however revolting and devious Marc was, he was intelligent, clearly deranged, but intelligent, I couldn't help feeling aware that so much of what he had said that evening had been filtered through what was for him a second language.

Not for the first time in my life I experienced unease on realizing that my responses were seriously askew. I would analyze anything, even an insult, always keeping the world at a distance. I was ashamed of having dishonored Mother's story in such a nightmare setting, and to such a lowlife individual. I slumped down on the bed, my back to the wall, my knees drawn up under

my chin, the dirty bedspread over me, reflecting on what I had
just done.

"Coffee, make some, now," Marc's yelling woke me, "come on
woman cowboy, now. Hey, you, skinny girl," and he snapped his
fingers. I must have slept, for a while at least. Everything looked
even worse in the cold morning light. Cobwebs made bridges
across the ceiling intersecting at the naked light bulb furry with
dust; the glass in the window was coated in a solid film of grime.
I could see that black paint made a scuffed border around the
floor of the room, it was like a frame, and that there was a gap
between it and the threadbare carpet. It was a room in which to
commit suicide; aside from the bed and a plain wooden chair,
it was empty. I needed to get my clothes. Marc, now seated on
the sofa which looked far more prosaic in the stark daylight,
was demanding coffee. Still naked, he was a sight to behold. I
walked over to him, by now certain that he was far closer to forty
or maybe fifty than I had first imagined and calmly asked him
where the coffee was, dreading the kitchen, it was the size of a
closet and certain to be filthy. "I don't know where he keeps it."
Who was he? I asked, and was told what I had been expecting
to hear—the mystery "he" was the owner of the apartment but
was rarely there. Marc only used the place when he needed it,
he had, he said, "an arrangement." For outings such as the one
I had shared I thought as I went into the bathroom, aware that
it would not be pleasant having to dress in my damp, stinking
clothes. "Make me coffee," repeated Marc, snapping his fingers
at me. "Check the cupboard for bread, crackers, olives—anything." There was nothing; no milk, nothing. "Then go, quick,"
he screeched. I thought I was being freed, but no—he told me
to fetch some coffee from the little grocery store on the corner,
and also to get him some cigarettes and matches. I had to stop
myself smiling at his confidence; he assumed that he could send

me back out into the world, and apparently believed that I would be fool enough to return.

Astounded, I played along, asking in my most earnest voice, what type of coffee, and also if there was a particular brand of cigarettes he preferred. He told me to buy a small jar of instant coffee and milk, which was amazing; I had thought no self-respecting French person would drink instant coffee. Yawning loudly, he acted as if I had already left, then he sneezed three times and asked what I was waiting for. "Go," he said, "hurry," and waved me away. "How about money," I said, "as you have stolen mine." Good old Marc, he smirked and said that I was very ungrateful, that he had entertained me and nursed me in my sickness. "Shame on me," I agreed, and then added that he may well be quite correct but despite his extraordinary hospitality, I would still require some of my money to buy him coffee. He reached under the cushion he was resting on, and handed me my francs from the previous night. "Here," he said with a kingly gesture contrasting with his ravaged physique, "Take this and hurry. Please not to lose your good person." He suggested I tidy my hair; he thought there was a comb in the bathroom, on the floor near the sink. He told me that I was ill-groomed; I muttered that he looked as if he should be attending a hospital. "Dépeche-toi," ordered Marc, assuring me that as soon as he had had some coffee he would accompany me back to my hotel, and I could get some money for our lunch. I had told him that Father had arrived in from Virginia and that he would give me my allowance. This delighted Marc, the thought of easy money and a chance perhaps of stealing my passport as it had not been in my ransacked pockets. I walked to the door, and then asked him again about his preferred choice of coffee and cigarettes. I repeated his instructions, promising to hurry.

I raced down those several flights far more quickly than I had gone up them so many degrading hours earlier. As soon as I reached the street, I paused shakily, trying to orient myself and took greedy gulps of cold, clean air. My teeth were chattering—yet I did feel victorious at having escaped so easily and snorted at the thought that he had actually expected me to return to the apartment. Back I went toward Notre Dame, the scene of my vomiting. Walking quickly, by the great cathedral, before breaking into a trot, I felt unwashed, my clothes had dried with surreal white high tide marks and were foul, but out in the air, where the smell was countered by gasoline fumes, might not seem worse than those of many a scruffy college student—well make that vagrant. I looked for a cab, I had money. I always kept $100 under the inside sole of whatever riding boots I happened to be wearing, an old habit and a useful one I picked up in a book. Marc had not reckoned on my boots; the bill was still in place. But no taxi appeared.

Paris is a big city. I had never mentioned where I was staying. Marc wouldn't find me. I felt sick to my stomach and realized that he had been the first person I had ever met who had made no comment about my eyes due to his never having actually looked at me. Thanks to a policeman who gave very clear directions I arrived back at the pension, hoping there would be enough hot water for me to wash away the previous night and Marc and all of it. The only person I met was the old Englishwoman's companion, her pale, anxious face bloodless in the morning light. She peered at me; I felt she could sense what I had been involved in, detect my enduring shame evidenced from my soiled clothes and overall patina of disgrace. But she only said good morning and that she felt it would rain. "It will help freshen up the streets, don't you think?" she said with a weary hopefulness, before sighing and remarking softly, "I do so love the rain."

*

Some things are beyond explanation, that's for sure. Why would I try so hard to steal a cup? Well, why indeed? Why indeed? I low to explain such a sudden and abnormal attachment to a large white cup? Delayed shock over Mother? Father deciding to sell Galileo? His comprehensive demeaning of my commitment to science? Billy Bob vanishing like that and without a word to me? The romantic Parisian interlude?—by which I refer to my mortifying fiasco with Marc. My fatalistic descent into disgrace? Do please take your pick.

My thoughts were chaotic yet peculiarly ordered; I was feeling cornered, fully deconstructed and in apparent free fall, wishing I was back in class; school was so easy and safe . . . Suddenly I was without hope; yet even so, another part of my mind was urging practical action. My clothes smelled, I needed a bath; there was no shower in the little hotel room, only the traditional tub . . . the water was warm, not hot, and I wanted it boiling like Vesuvius. I needed it to burst forth from the faucet, bubbling. I wanted to feel scalded, purged, fully decontaminated. I did sit in that chunky little tub with its splayed claw-feet and its icky, pitted surface, its tarnished faucets leaving a taint of tired, old metal on my hands. The bath was uninvitingly filled with lackluster suds and me shivering among them as I stared out through the net curtains toward the drab daylight, further dimmed by the shadow of the side of the building.

It was futile, wallowing in warmish, flat bubbles when I was hoping to be reborn. I stood up and reached for the largest towel, it was only medium-sized. Something to complain about I thought. Good. My room was at the back, overlooking a court-yard, I surveyed the scene. Down below I could see something moving, a cat I thought and yes so it was, and being pursued by a human, the old Englishwoman's sorrowful companion. What a grim existence she endured, making me recall Thoreau's famous quote about lives of quiet desperation. How quiet was my desperation? Well anyway . . . that lonely, middle-aged woman had taken to feeding the local gang of stray cats. She was doing some good, not like me. The cats hovered about like yollering ghosts in a churchyard, skinny and diseased-looking, crazed but defiant, intent on survival. Life was tough in Paris, there was a harshness. Behind all the glamour and the mannered sighs, it was hard and unyielding—what an expressive word, unyielding, most apt. Paris most certainly did not forgive. I felt that many an unfortunate lover in that city of illusions had been shot dead by an angry man or woman—the women did appear embittered, well some of them. Walt had been crazy; the French I reckoned would be more inclined to cold fury.

I had shed my unspeakable clothing and stuffed it into a white plastic bag intended for the hotel laundry not that I ever wanted to see any of those garments again. Within minutes I had put my boots back on—had to, as I didn't have another pair with me—over the clean socks by then on my aching feet before skulking down the stairs, to ask at reception if the boiler or the heating or whatever it was that controlled the water, could be put on high, to facilitate my having a "really hot" bath. I was prepared to be told that the morning's hot water had already been used by the other guests, and that I would have to wait until the evening. But one skill I had discovered was an ability to get my own way by sheer force of anarchic courtesy. I would claim a chill coming on, one of my heavy colds, and I did feel a chill but it was nothing to do with a physical illness. My sense of being had been obliterated and any effort to defy Father's authority had gone badly wrong. All I had was a sensation of feeling soiled and very ashamed.

Those few weeks in Paris had alerted me to the contrasting approaches of my countrymen and women. But Southerners are diffcrent: as a tribe we are either autocratic—like Father— or disarmingly civil, like me. As for the French response, well the Parisians appear to appreciate the fact that we speak a good deal slower than the New Yorkers who amass in Paris in force, or at least appeared to have done so during my stay. Marauding about in raucous droves, they shout and exclaim, being funny, loud, outrageous, regarding the *Mona Lisa* as merely a chore to be ticked off some kind of tourist inventory, along with the Eiffel Tower and a visit to the Folies Bergère.

Issues of nationality did not bother me—being American has never shaped my identity. I'm a Southerner, which counts for everything; what most preoccupied me were my strangled French and my apparent inability to master a language at which my teachers had considered me very good . . . And thanks to Marc, I also felt debased, diminished in my own eyes. I must have had far more of a sense of self than I had previously suspected and was painfully conscious of having relinquished whatever it was. The man at reception, however, was a new face; unaware of my recent humiliation. He seemed intent on serving the public with a clinical precision, "Of course, certainement . . . Yes, yes, I will attend," he exclaimed with a feminine flutter of his hands and he may even have clicked his heels. I looked closely; was he wearing eye liner? His hair plastered to his singularly flat head with old-fashioned brilliantine made me think of Mr. Caleb Montgomery, who would have been fascinated by my recent escapades. The desk clerk suggested that I go out and have a coffee, I could as easily have had one there, but he said I might enjoy "a leetle stroll" to the café, across the street. He spoke as if I were a poodle

waiting to be exercised . . . within the hour he could provide me
with a very hot bath. Steam, he said with a bow that was both
ingratiating and patronizing, would kill a cold before it established itself. "I blame central heating. Buildings are always too
warm. More open windows, less heat, but guests, your countrymen, they complain, they threaten to leave . . ." Do they indeed?
I mouthed to myself but smiled till my face hurt and I feared my
fabulous teeth would drop out, one by one, scattering across his
tidy hotel counter.

The Café Ganymède was decorated in pale grays and lavender,
with dainty pots of white flowers on the tables. Mother would
have loved it. To me it was all bijou surface and I preferred the
more rugged-looking traditional establishments with their take-
it-or-leave-it attitude, the exposed floor boards and the old cast-
iron fireplaces, usually with empty grates. I had been in a few
places though where bright flames reflected off the glass and the
dishes and that welcoming smell of a wood burning fire, much
more than the aroma of cooking smells, made me feel comfortable, if not quite at home, because I no longer knew what home
meant. Perhaps it amounted to Mrs. Faulkner's immaculate meals
and the scent of floor wax throughout the house; the stacks of
freshly ironed sheets, the starched shirts . . . I sat in that stage-set
café as if I were clinging to a raft, expecting the hot chocolate to
arrive in a modest little dish, as many of them in Paris had. The
Café Ganymède appeared to have marked pretensions; the sole
waitress on duty was fussy, and in contrast to the stock indifference apparently perfected by restaurant staff across Paris, she
kept asking me questions. Where was I from? Where exactly was
that? Did I like Paris? Was I studying? Was I an artist? Instead
of confessing to her that I was undergoing a complicated breakdown of some kind, which might have alarmed her, I responded
politely and mentioned my love of art in a subdued mutter.

The chocolate came in a large, white cup; almost bowl-like and big enough for me to hold in both hands. The rim was thick; I imagined biting it and smashing my perfect teeth. I suddenly decided I needed the cup; had to have it. I wanted it and could not leave it behind, it made me feel safe, that cup. Was I going insane? Perhaps I already had. I think I was slightly crazed, no disturbed, quietly disturbed. This is desperation I realized with a tremor. What if Marc had been bigger, stronger, more evil . . . what if I had been alluring, more provocative? What if I had liked him? Imagine if I had fallen in love with him and then he had turned on me like that . . .

The hot chocolate was good, approaching Mrs. Faulkner quality. I ordered another, I wanted the cup but the café was empty and I was the focus of the waitress's kindly attentions. Should I ask her if I could have it, I wondered, as a souvenir? What if I told her it was the best hot chocolate I had ever had. Send her off to make another while I escaped, clutching the cup to my black heart. Had I become so devious? Was I naturally corrupt? Mitzi would be speechless. Her family detested customers who left the tables looking as if a raid had taken place. What would she say of the theft of a cup? How would she react? I didn't want the saucer, which was like a small plate. I only wanted the cup; it was reassuring to hold. I felt it could heal me. The waitress glanced over and smiled, I wondered if I looked shifty, criminal or merely beaten, that was how I felt, well to be completely accurate, more like disemboweled. She waved cheerfully, asking if I would like another hot chocolate. "Please," I replied in my most creepily polite voice. Picking up the napkin I held it to my face. Then I slowly dropped the stiff cloth down over the cup. Exactly how rotten had I become? Could I stare directly back at her, brazenly, convincing her that I was the true and rightful owner of that particular cup. Not that one, this one. It was the only cup I wanted. I wondered what to do. Should I tell her about my ordeal, would it condone my actions?

A couple arrived at the café entrance; biggish man, tiny woman, the waitress greeted them, they knew each other. She was distracted; good. I seized my chance and scurried off to the restroom, taking my jacket and holding the cup, wrapped in the napkin. Inside the cubicle, I sank down on the closed lid of the toilet, my eyes burning and I peered at the cup. Why had I stolen it? What was wrong with me? I wondered if I was suffering from delayed shock. I shoved the cup down into my pocket, aware of its bulge. Strained and tight, my face looked back at me from the wall mirror, a trapped expression spreading across the blotchy skin; I had committed a theft. I looked . . . well, never mind, I looked mildly depraved, haggard, hungry, and forlorn, worse still, rejected. That's how I felt. How could I have spoken about Mother to that wretched little swine? Replaying her death as if it had happened in a movie I had once seen? It was shameful and even worse—it had been part of a craven attempt to regain his interest. I had dishonored her memory and also myself; it was disappointing that the mere thought of it all, that night with Marc, did not make me vomit again—there in that tiny cubicle. What would I say when the waitress inquired about the cup? Should I claim I had been raped, would that excuse my larceny?

I pushed my way out of the narrow restroom, catching my sleeve on a nail or a hook of some kind; I heard the sharp rip of material, the seam or the lining of the jacket gave way with a dry-sounding sigh. Count to ten, they say it helps, it doesn't, it didn't. "Let me out," I mouthed silently, sweat bubbling along my hairline leaving my bangs limp. The waitress and the couple were talking all at once, she jokingly handed menus to them, presenting them with a curtsy as if they were concert bouquets and led her friends to a window table, smiling back at me with a sunny "So."

Red-faced, I was clutching the large napkin, it had been too big to force into my pocket with the cup. She hurried toward me, grabbing several napkins in her haste, and thrust them into my hands, gesturing to me to take them all, nodding toward the bathroom. "Lentement," she urged gently. It meant slowly, a nice word, it was indeed soothing. Take my time; stop the world, slow motion, step backward and everything will improve. I took a deep breath as she encouraged me to return to the restroom, all the while smiling sympathetically. Guilt hit me, hating myself I slithered backward, this time taking with me the muscum shopping bag I had left on the floor beside my table, at last grasping that she must have thought that I had been caught without sanitary pads. That was why she had given me the napkins. I felt bad, touched by her empathy and intuition. I had stolen the cup and she was trying to help me. Shame made me want to scream. It would have been so much easier had she been as abrupt as were so many of the waiters. I could hear her speaking with her friends at top speed, but could not understand any of it, only a word here or there. What kind of French had I been learning at school? All those A's . . . It was not the moment to ponder what would happen if I attempted to converse using the German I had been teaching myself. Would a native speaker look bewildered? Mitzi's mother had said I was good, so Mitzi had told me. But Mitzi's pretend Austrian mother couldn't speak German either. I was supposed to be very good at French and there I was, paralyzed into incoherence each time I tried to speak it. Father would say it was all very disconcerting . . .

Inside the cubicle, again sitting on the creaking toilet seat, conscious of the smell of lavender air freshener, I pulled the cup out of my pocket and wrapped it in a napkin before sliding it

down into the bag. The deed was finally done. I did not want the
second hot chocolate. Without any logical reason I had become
a miserable thief. Perhaps this was shock, another person may
have wandered out into the street and straight under a car, or
would have run amok and stabbed their nearest fellow creature,
or climbed a steeple stark naked, but I was too inhibited to
do something that dangerous or memorable. My madness was
merely a token, the theft of a cup, how very non-heroic . . . I
decided to leave. The toilet didn't flush, I had not used it, but
I wanted to flush it, to make my stay in the rest room credible,
and had stuffed a wad of bathroom paper down the toilet, but
panicked when it failed to clear, so I pulled the wet paper out
and it fell apart, collapsing to the floor, leaving a suspicious mess.
Uncontrollable laughter caused me to hiccup and snort then hit
my elbow off the sink. The pain was little more than a pinging
sensation, very odd, fleeting, if sharp like a nerve vibrating; ah
the belated discovery of my funny bone . . . A voice was asking, "Are you okay? You would like me to help you?" It took a
moment to realize that it was the waitress standing outside; I
waited for her to mention the cup but she didn't. I said I was
almost ready and she said to come out and drink the hot chocolate, it would help me. Her concern made me feel even worse
about the cup and I considered taking it out of my bag and leaving it in the sink. But no, I wanted the cup and was determined
to bring it back to Virginia with me as a reminder, not a souvenir,
a formal reminder of how very badly wrong everything had gone.

What time was it? I wondered. Would the water be ready at
the hotel? The only place I wanted to be was the Louvre, staring at the paintings, frantic to imprint forevermore all those
images on my tired, beaten brain, so many resplendent pictures—a phrase I'd once used when I was small before I knew
what it meant, another of Father's words, as was incandescent

and so many others. My thoughts wished to be freed of strife. Just memorize the paintings I told myself, you won't get to see them again. Each day I made my disgraced way to the world's most famous gallery and bought more postcards, and true to my obsessive disposition had amassed quite a collection, dupli cates, triplicates of some, fours and fives of others. More horses with which to tease Mitzi, about ten of Caspar David Friedrich's *The Tree of Crows*, all for me, as bookmarks. How much self-loathing could I hope to squeeze on a postcard to Mitzi? Even in my smallest writing, could I begin to outline my dishonorable misadventures? Someone else might read the card; her mother; or the disciplined, judgmental, clean-living Karl, no. I wanted to die. Most of all I wanted to be eight years old again with all this atrocious, recently acquired experience, a cautionary tract to steer me toward a better path. I needed to phone Mitzi, to spit out some of it, clear my head . . . be absolved. Religion always gets you in the end. Had Mitzi believed I had run off to Tahiti with the Russian count? If only I had. How very different my evening with Marc had been, not like in the movies, leastways, not like in any movie I had seen. There was nothing romantic about my sojourn in Paris. I needed to return to America, to Mrs. Faulkner's calm, silent kitchen. I needed to resume riding horses, a horse, what horse? Any horse, please Father may I have a horse? Flight had proved pointless as well as embarrassing. Father's opinion of me as a complacent dreamer had been confirmed. How much more difficult it is to recover from stupidity when it is also squalid. It served me right. I'd responded to Mother's tragedy as if it were part of the natural course of things and yet there I was, trembling, like a rat, poised to face a firing squad, and all over a stolen cup.

*

"Too bad he got a wife"; the speaker had a low and rapacious growl, honed by years of hard liquor and tobacco. The kind of voice I imagined belonging to a rotund little man who had made his fortune by selling hardware in an intractable place such as Newark or Buffalo. Success had at last brought him to Paris on a trophy vacation and into the Louvre. Several people had paused to view Friedrich's tree with all those crows. It made me think of Edgar Allan Poe and it was an ideal postcard for Father, had I been of a mind to send him one—which I wasn't. I adored the picture, I had seen it in books and there I was, looking at it.

Caspar David Friedrich: my favorite artist. I even loved saying his name, the high priest of German Romanticism. His melancholy drew me. I had read that his younger brother drowned trying to pull Caspar from the ice when they were boys and skating on a frozen lake. The tragedy had left Caspar tormented by guilt for having survived. I could understand those feelings so well and admired him for having believed that paintings should be felt, not invented. His pictures tell stories and nature is his subject; he understands the way we humans stumble about, dwarfed within it.

Behind me the conversation, which had nothing to do with art, was continuing, "He's just using you, like I keep on saying, passing time, no vulture quite like a bored married man." But a squeaky female voice disagreed, "Naw, it's a lot better than being married. He keeps getting me stuff." Stuff, I wondered, was that slang for drugs? It seemed an odd topic of conversation for a hardware salesman to be having with a slightly younger woman. They were hardly lovers. What was the connection? "I'm telling ya when your looks go, he's gone too, bye bye blackbird."

I turned to discover that the hardware magnate was a tetchy-looking little old matron of at least seventy-five, leathery skin pulled tight over cheekbones that belonged to a discontented skull-like face out of which loomed huge white false teeth, so large her thin lips were unable to corral them. She wore a full-length mink coat; it hung off her frail tiny frame and reeked of that disgusting mothball smell. Her companion may have been forty or forty-five, bearing little evidence of ever having had any looks to lose and may have been the ancient gorgon's daughter or possibly her niece. Neither of them was looking at the paintings. The younger woman was saying that he—her male friend with the wife—had paid for her trip and that she had so much "dough" she had bought "tons of stuff, clothes." I eavesdropped, I mean listened; at least they were speaking a form of English. "I saw this dress, see, I just love it to bits and got it in all four colors it comes in, I'll wear one tonight." It made me think of Mother, if she saw a dress she liked, she would also buy it in every color. I wanted to miss her, I felt I should. Every so often something made her come into my mind, not with regret though, more by chance association. Then I would relive the way she had died, it always seemed to happen in slow motion as if she was falling for several minutes, her blood splashing down on the sidewalk and her eyes suddenly empty.

The old lady declared she needed to go to the bathroom "again" as if there was someone she could blame it on, and brought the discussion to a close. They walked away, slowly. The room was deserted, only me and the paintings. I wanted to stay and wondered had Friedrich really seen the tree, and had it looked just like that? Had there been so many crows?

*

The pompous little hotel clerk was as good as his word; the water was hot. I let the bath run while I rushed down the stairs to see if any food had been left in the dining room. There was usually something on the buffet table, the idea being that the guests might be hungry, and I was always ready to eat. I took a bunch of fat purple grapes and several small Danish pastries, as well as a fancy cheese wrapped in waxy parchment. No one saw me retreating back upstairs with my supplies. I had collected several bottles of an orange-juice-like drink, arranged in a group on the little bureau by the bed. I liked looking at them; they added some color to the room.

When I opened the bathroom door, I couldn't see for the steam, thick as a curtain, billowing forth like a genie escaped from a bottle. Even the bath was invisible, which is why I walked into it bruising both shins.

Encased in the scalding water up to my neck, an unbroken layer of bubbles, thinking about horses and that the only man to have seen me almost naked, was of the opinion that I looked like a boy, I thought yet again of Billy Bob. I knew where he had gone; Mitzi had been shocked and warned me against telling any-one. But I knew, I felt it deep in my heart. He had climbed into the grave that night after everyone had gone, down in under the tarpaulin, to be with Monticello. Billy Bob had been lying there, with a bottle of whatever it took to make him feel comfortable; ready to take his leave of life, before that friend of his, Nathan I think was his name, had come along, as agreed, to finish off the burial mound. There was no doubt, clear as day, my mentor had already made his decision as he stood in the stable, I had felt it. He would never be parted from his beloved horse. That was the end he had wanted, to be with his horse forever. How wonderful to be so certain of the thing you love. I've always envied him that profound bond, although it seems that when you find love, it sure has a mean way of disappearing.

It was time to leave Paris, but not quite the moment to head for Virginia and I considered flying to London, to finally see *Whistlejacket*, down in the old abbey in Exeter.

The owner's rich husband had made a special room for it. I dreamed of seeing the painting, it is life-sized, a chestnut stallion rearing, defiant, wild-eyed, but also a bit scared— it turns out he was. When the real Whistlejacket saw his likeness, he reared in alarm at what he thought was a rival and, apparently, Stubbs had to protect the picture, for fear the stallion would kick it to pieces.

Visiting the great galleries and the churches of Paris—I had even been to Église Saint-Jacques du Haut-Pas, where the Italian astronomer and mathematician Giovanni Domenico Cassini, who discovered the four satellites of Saturn, is buried—it had been the best part of my trip and compensated for the other disappointments; my infirm French, the lack of enjoyment and yes, had even almost, not quite, erased that night of humiliation.

Some of the residents at the little hotel had already left, the Italian students in triumph speaking better French than the French, to be replaced by new faces, including a honeymoon couple intent on making sure that all present were aware of the stupendous activities taking place nightly as well as frequently throughout the day in their room. The old English dowager was disgusted and stared through them, ignoring their greetings. Her companion though, the cat woman, sighed and smiled, delighting in their ardor. She passed plates and dishes to them, would they like more bread? the salt? and kept re-filling their glasses, so rapt that the water poured over the rims and soaked the table cloth. Her instincts were endearing, making me think of Aunt

Sally and if I'd ever see her again. She had that same goodness about her, you'd just know she was a good person without her having to prove it by anything she said or did.

I needed a nudge; I was drifting, as if waiting for a cut to heal. I sought a miracle. Perhaps I had hoped that I might fall in love. Time was passing, time was standing still; the staff in the Louvre shop had begun to notice my frequent visits. "You must know many people, or perhaps you do have a large family?" one of them asked me with false concern, "Do you spend your days and nights in Paris writing postcards . . ." she probed deeper as her colleague turned away and sniggered into her hand. "Are you sure you are not sending the same card twice?" They were mocking me. It was embarrassing, I may as well have been accused of shoplifting, the cup episode still burning in my thoughts, and I dropped some of the change on the floor. I heard it roll away. But I just smiled my coward's smile, incapable of summoning a sharp retort, and hurried out.

Those famous bookstalls along the Left Bank that you hear people talking about, and which often feature in movies and novels, were intimidating, or least they were to me. I felt too awkward to inch my way in and have a look. People stood so close to each other as if at a department store sale, all appearing to look at the same book, which of course, they weren't. It only seemed that way to me with my post-Marc renewed fear of human contact. Yet it is more pleasant browsing out in the fresh air than in some dark pokey little warren in which the shopkeeper stands so close you can't help but smell his breath. It would be good for me, I thought, if I could steel myself and have a look. How exciting it would be to find an old book I could bring back to Virginia with me, particularly if it was in French. I could try and tackle Maupassant stories or a Dumas classic. I seemed to be able to read French and increasingly understood more of the stray comments and snatches of overheard conversations. Yet when it came to speaking it, I froze in the way I had noticed nervous riders lean forward and grab at the mane before falling off.

Rows and rows of old paperbacks, stiff and faded, looking as if they had been set out to dry under the desert sun. Nothing caught my eye, then I realized the stall I had selected appeared to be dedicated to crime novels judging by the amount of half-dressed, terrified blonde sirens staring out of the jackets. Some of the books had silhouettes of men wearing 1940s hats and I recognized what looked like a yarn about mobsters in Chicago. I moved on down the row of stalls. "Bonjour," said a male voice and I looked up at an older man, gray-haired and friendly, somebody's father. He asked me what I was looking for and I said "Rien, je veux seulement regarder"—he seemed to understand, at least he did not cringe at my abuse of the French language. Perhaps he reckoned I had exhausted my lexicon so he smiled and stretched out his arms as if to invite me to continue perusing. I did and found a battered hardback copy of *L'Étranger*—I knew that novel, having read it a few times in English. I opened it up, the pages were dry, and I wondered if perhaps I was cheating because I remembered the narrative, its tangible sense of apathy and inertia. Was I making this little exercise a bit too easy? I didn't care, my French had failed me so often I deserved some relief. The strangest thing about finding that book though, as I opened it, flicking through the pages, trying to reassure myself by translating a sentence here and there, a postcard fell out. The writing on the back was faded to pale gray, it was impossible to decipher and anyways, it was all in French, but the picture? Well, that was interesting. It was a photograph of a man in a suit, staring back at the camera, a coat over his arm; one foot already on the streetcar he was about to board. A famous Southern writer, his face reflected in the carriage window and he was very tall, judging by the size of the passersby, appearing to barely reach his shoulder. Thomas Wolfe—and he had indeed stood six foot six—and had taken to using the top of his refrigerator as a writing table and all. I knew he had been in Germany during the 1930s and was full sure that the picture had been taken in Berlin. There was a church steeple in the background but it was only a detail. He had such a nice face and was to die only a few years later, in 1938. The man in the picture didn't know that his life was almost over. Mother had lived a few years longer than him. That thought sent a chill through me and I was grateful for even that small response. The card was another of my omens, a touch uncanny. I put it back in the book and as I watched the book dealer placing the novel into a little white paper bag, I felt that photograph of Wolfe was a sign, him being a Southerner and all. I had no idea what I was doing in Paris, and Wolfe had also been wandering through Europe in search of something he could not quite define either, I took finding that postcard as a talisman. And my hunch about it was right, the photograph had been taken in Berlin, in 1935, three years before Wolfe's death at thirty-eight, all his dreams and anger ended so soon.

Pleased with my book, made even more special with the discovery of the postcard, I walked back down the line of stalls, the dealers speaking at one hundred miles an hour. And I paused to study the busy scene, the river behind it, sun reflecting off the water, and as usual attempted to imprint it forever on my memory. Then something from my other life caught my eye and made me smile. It was a large portfolio, *The Solar System*, with a striking image on the cover, the sun as a bright green ball. I knew the image was a NASA shot, created by extreme ultraviolet radiation. Paging through it I came across a picture of Venus, looking like a platter of beaten bronze. Most of the material was familiar, but I decided to buy the book and looked forward to bringing it back to the hotel room and remind myself of my bedroom at home with my telescopes and the privacy that kept me contented in my way. The next image caused me to sigh with pleasure; the *Rings of Saturn*. Their surreal beauty more haunting than any artist could invent and I recalled the simple stone plaque honoring Cassini in the church with its majestic organ, the oldest in Paris. The tablet was on the wall, just his name and the word astronomer, written in French, "Astronome." Cassini died in 1712—he had been eighty-seven, a great age at any time, remarkable for his day. How the world had changed since his remains were placed in the walls of a church that had withstood such violence down through the centuries. Father was right; history was a passion of mine. Perhaps it would be my future, a curious realization . . . a future spent looking at the past.

My thoughts drifted back to the present and the image of Saturn. The man tending the stall was youngish and good-looking; he was speaking to two girls, a few years older than me. They looked like students; the smaller one was alarmingly busty and had a pert, almost wizened face, like a clever monkey. She kept licking her lips and tossing her hair as if to alert the man to her interest in him. I realized they were speaking English. He admitted he didn't know how much the solar system booklet cost. "I didn't even know it was there," he said, explaining that it wasn't his stall; he was only doing a favor. He sounded Australian and shrugged. "Tell you what," he said, smiling at the girls, showing his white, uneven teeth, "Simon's rich, it's his stall. Here, you take the folder thing. He probably thought it was a coloring book . . . serves him right. Tough mate, you've lost this one. Anyone smart enough to show an interest in something serious like outer space should be congratulated." There was no price marked on it. "Well, then," he decided, "that makes it free." He put it in an old plastic Monoprix bag and winked at me. "It's yours, darling and the bag too." The girls smiled at me as if I was twelve years old and eager to be relieved of my allowance. I didn't care and recalling Mrs. Faulkner's definitive grilled cheese sandwiches, wondered where I could eat.

The Jardin des Plantes was on the way back to the hotel and I walked through it. There were a few joggers shuffling by on the loose sandy surface and it seemed such a nice place to ride a horse. The sun felt hotter than it had for days and I just wanted to feel it, warming my tired face. There was an empty bench and I hurried over to it, and laid the plastic bag with my solar system in it down flat, placing my jacket over it. I sat back, stretched my legs out in front of me, closed my eyes and just wanted to feel as if all the tension would somehow flow out of me, and drain deep down into the earth and far away. I thought of the way I used to love listening to the crickets on a warm summer's night back home, I had missed that sound in Paris. The heat was so good though, sitting on a bench and reclining in the sunshine was not something that I ever did much, but that day, I just wanted to doze like an old hound content to dream. Although the bench was hard, I must have fallen asleep and woke with a start. There was a slight pressure against my legs; a small gray dog, with a pug-like squashed face and not much of a tail. It just sat there, as if keeping guard over me.

The dog was very quiet; a little male with a band of black across its eyes like a raccoon's mask. There was only a jogger running toward the gates, about to leave the park. The dog was far too old to go running with anyone. I waited for any sign of an owner and spoke to the little guy, no reaction. I wondered what would happen if I patted his head. Nothing, just the merest shiver of pleasure and he sort of juddered his rump. I stood up and began gathering my things, I needed to eat but was unable to just walk off and leave him. He was very old; his

eyes already beginning to cloud. He stood on my left foot and
I sensed he was asking me not to abandon him. He had been
somebody's dog, but now he was lost. I imagined what it would
be like for him, wandering through Paris, a deaf old dog with his
sight failing. He'd be hit by a car or a cyclist. Would the police
take him in? How long would he be kept in a pound? I lifted
him up and placed him on the bench, he was very quiet, happy
to be touched. I sat down beside him and he shifted his squat
little body, close into me, and sighed, prepared to share a vigil.
Greyfriars Bobby, whatever brought that into my head? Perhaps
his master or mistress had also died, or was lying dead and yet to
be discovered in some chilly, forgotten garret? Twenty minutes
went by; no one rushed into the garden, calling a name. There
was no collar. I don't know what made me say, "Well now, Mr
Hector Berlioz, and what are you doing here?" but I did, and
that's how it began, me and Hector. I reached for the plastic
bag with one hand and then lifted him up. He was no weight at
all, just a little old dog who had gotten lost but had found me.
Hector was a good name for him; surprising that I didn't call him
Cassini, him being fresh in my mind, what with the picture of
Saturn, and having seen Cassini's memorial a few hours earlier.
The warmth had ebbed out of the sun and it was chilly, nearly
suppertime. I also knew I would need to buy food for Hector
and some type of carrier for him. I didn't want to draw attention
back at the hotel, for fear of objections. But I was sure he'd be
quiet; his days of barking and fooling around were long gone.
He made me think of Monticello, wise and serene, aware of his
need of a human and there I was.

I was to buy a few bags before finally finding a sturdy leather
case, one of those expensive designer carryall things intended for
a lady's cosmetics, a bag Mother would have admired. I saw it
in a select shoe store. But Hector's first sedan chair was a simple

straw shoulder bag bought in a corner grocery store near the
hotel—I loved the smell of the straw; it made me think of horses,
my other life. I missed riding so much and felt that even more
intensely on so luckily happening upon the solar system folder.
I had barely glanced at it and yet it was already making me feel
less directionless. Now I had a real purpose though, to protect
the little dog. Staying on at the hotel would be unfeasible. My
room was a few floors up from the street. He would not be able
to relieve himself at short notice and would have to stay in the
bathroom. It was cold in there. I would get both of us out of
Paris. It really was time to skedaddle and I had no regrets.

Most of the customers in the crowded adventure sports store
looked serious, a few seemed obsessive. There was no idle browsing; those people knew what they wanted. That mild fanaticism
similar to the one you can sense in tack shops made the store
seem more like a library. There was a difference though, instead
of the common denominator, horses, adventure sports involve a
range of people from enthusiasts to lunatics, as well as the veteran
practitioners conveying that world-weary expertise.

Within feet of a man sternly examining a heavy climbing
boot as if he believed that it alone would enable him to conquer Everest, stood another zealot, equally lost in thought and
standing between two feather-light racing bikes, assessing their
respective suitability for an endurance cycle event that the store
was sponsoring. Ski jackets were being tried on by individuals
too driven to even bother looking in any of the several mirrors.
A woman with a shaved head inquired about a newly developed
specialist belt with lights for exploring caves; "caving" is popular
in France.

Could kite-flying possibly be considered a competitive sport?
I wondered, looking at a large display. A couple approached
the cash register, they carried matching bright orange flippers,

snorkels, and elite wet suits and were heading for the Great
Barrier Reef as part of a tour party. It was a wedding present,
explained the new husband to the salesman who smiled encour-
agingly. Three middle-aged men bound for a safari in South
Africa waited beside a locked cabinet containing shotguns. They
were relaxed, joking among themselves until a fourth man, hard,
grizzled-looking, joined them and the laughter stopped as he
glared challengingly, wondering if they were made of whatever it
takes to destroy wild animals in their natural habitat. He turned
out to be a professional game hunter and was to be their guide.

Customers were requested to move aside as a yellow kayak,
hoisted aloft, was carried up through the store and out into the
street, and on to white water somewhere.

Activity all around me and all I wanted was an inflatable mattress. The friendly salesman looked directly at me before doing
a double take. He had noticed my eyes and glanced away for a
second as if to absorb what he had seen. It was a familiar reaction,
that slight shiver, fascination mixed with revulsion and then,
not always, sympathy. But having curbed his initial surprise the
salesman smiled and gazed calmly into my eyes. His own were
blue, ordinary eyes, lucky him. A large selection of inflatable
mattresses awaited, he announced brightly, as if they were mar-
vels worth studying. I pointed to a dark green one. He nodded
in approval before suggesting a slightly more expensive one—as
the price included a foot pump. It was a better deal than buying
a cheaper mattress and then having to pay extra for the pump.
He was not to know that money was not important. The mattress
was very good, he said, and also came in a similar shade of green.
In concluding his sales pitch he said it was made in Germany as
proof of its quality. Why hadn't I gone there? I asked myself not
for the first time. The poor man was waiting for me to make up

my mind about the mattress, yet all I could think about was why I had chosen Paris instead of Germany.

His attitude was not at all Parisian, and he didn't sound like a French person speaking English. Was he German? He flushed bright red at that and laughed, asking was I teasing him for praising the mattress because I had assumed it had come from his homeland. It wasn't that, I just suspected he was from somewhere else. "I am Dutch, from the Hague," he said and when I declared in reply that I didn't much like Paris he laughed and said no one really does, except the French. It may be because, he said, we are all expected to fall in love with the place but it's just another big city. His logic made good sense, particularly to me still sickened by recurring images of the night with Marc. But also I was used to the countryside. Well, I was mostly in the stable yard and arena, but we lived on 500 acres. Even my school was situated in a parkland setting, overlooking a man-made lake. The salesman's excuse for being in France was that his girlfriend was on a music scholarship, the last year of it would bring her to Vienna and he was looking forward to moving there with her. I was finally having a real conversation and it was very satisfying, after being cross-examined by Mitzi on the phone.

All she wanted to know was had I been raped and how quickly I'd gotten to a doctor and had I told the medical people that I'd been abducted by a pervert. Mitzi reckoned that Paris was full of crazies and that I was "a sitting duck" because of my giving the impression I was usually in a trance. I'd told her that I had not sought medical advice, that I was suffering from incapacitating humiliation and that I had figured that out all by myself. Then I mentioned my Hector dog. That set her off; she said he had rabies as if she had already tested him and was looking at the blood results. She never even referred to all the fascinating postcards I had sent her, aside from complaining about the prevalence of horse paintings. Had I never looked at a portrait, she asked. "You do know about humans?" Very funny; our call was merely an extended reprimand causing me to regret having phoned her and of course she'd asked about Galileo and did I have him in my hotel room. So speaking with the salesman made me feel less stupid and he'd whispered to me that he'd rather the three businessmen abandoned their "big game safari" and had some fun that did not include killing wildlife. He then held up his finger; requesting that I remain "exactly" where I was and darted away, disappearing behind a tall container filled with huge nets, the type used on ambitious deep-sea fishing trips, by wealthy pseudo-sportsmen hunting marlin, sharks, and such like so as to be photographed grinning beside a butchered corpse.

Within a moment or two the salesman returned, having checked something. There had been a special offer, another special offer I smiled. But this one, he assured me, was "fantastique;" if I purchased a four-man tent, the mattress that came with the pump would be free. I did not need a four-man tent, although for a moment, it seemed an inspired suggestion. I would be leaving Paris; Hector could not live in a hotel and I was worried for fear the bathroom was already ruined as the grouting between the floor tiles had become stained by his urine. Heavily perfumed bath salts were quite effective in masking the strong odor. Only I didn't like the chemical fragrance and the doggy smell was holding its own. I also left scented candles burning in the sink where he couldn't knock them over. The combined scents were overpowering, not that Hector seemed to mind, but the bathroom would eventually be beyond saving and I'd end up in jail. He and I were looking toward a future on the run. If Mitzi was correct about the quarantine restrictions, we would be traveling through Europe by bus and train, for the remainder of Hector's life, without hope of ever entering the US, whatever about Canada. I was still convinced that Father could get us back home; his clients were always moving international competition horses around. Stallions and brood mares were constantly being transported between Europe and America, and also back and forth to and from Australia. I doubted if many of them spent six months in quarantine. It was shortsighted, never mind real mean of me, not to have sent him a postcard, particularly as I had sent two to Mrs. Faulkner, one of them was of the *Mona Lisa* whose smile so reminded me of our housekeeper's enigmatic grimace.

In another life perhaps it would have been just dandy to be planning a camping trip. I told the man that the tent was too big for one person. The display model was a variation of a Bedouin's desert palace; it looked like a small house. "But you could live in that," I blurted out. He was delighted, "And why not? If you find the right place, the right person . . . so romantic."

He would have been a lovely boyfriend, or *beau* to use Mother's phrase, and seemed sincere and imaginative with a playful demeanor. He was not cynical and revolting like Marc. Instead he'd arranged his life to suit his girlfriend's music studies, whereas I was destined to attract depraved villains and petty con men—characters referred to by Mitzi as low-life vermin. How wonderful to have a well-intentioned, attentive boyfriend. Only I was boyish, walked too quickly, and was generally described as "serious." Most of the time I was adrift—daydreaming about horses or space and just living in my head; I wanted to be back in my bedroom with my books and telescopes, it would be a comfortable place in which for Hector to end his days, with me there to love him and Mrs. Faulkner to feed us. Oh yes, Mrs. Faulkner, now, that would be interesting.

How Hector's life had changed, what kind of human had he had? He'd chosen me and I wondered what the friendly sales-man from the Hague would say if he heard for what purpose the mattress was intended. I promised to think about the tent and he said that I would miss out on the offer, but if I came back, he would reduce the price. Such a fabulous tent he had enthused, adding that it came in a few colors, "the purple and green one is very um," and he had reached for the word, "stately." In his eyes I was a girl who liked green and would favor a stately tent. He waved and said, "Have a nice day. Americans always say that, don't they? I think it is so cute." "Cute" sounded odd spoken by a sturdy-looking Dutchman—it is such a feminine word. But he was generous by nature, helpful, and proud of his girlfriend the cellist. He was happy in his life. And I did hope, that afternoon in a Paris street, that some person one day might say the same about me, not that it was looking that way.

The mattress offered a temporary solution; it was still in the wrapping and I hurried back to the hotel, stiff from the uncomfortable night I had had. Some part of the pump, probably the connection, made a clicking sound with each stride I took. Ear to the hotel room door, I listened, not a murmur. The Do Not Disturb sign, in French as it happened, was still hanging from the handle. I tip-toed across the bedroom and opened the bathroom door and Hector gazed up at me. The paper plate had been chewed ragged, all the dog food eaten. That was a good sign. Even better was that there was still a little bit of water left in the white cup, my stolen white cup. He was not excessively thirsty. I had given him the cup, aware that my act of theft had been justified and rendered almost symbolic—at least to me. I could monitor the amounts he was drinking. Funny, why I had never considered veterinary, what with my obsession for detail and so on . . . In order to prevent Hector from breaking the cup and cutting himself on the shards, I had placed it on a wet towel, keeping it stable. I could be practical, on occasion.

But we would journey on; both fugitives together as soon as I had figured out what to do. The mattress inflated with the creaking sound of a ship's rigging. It seemed it might burst, heaving and groaning with the pressure of the air within it, then it suddenly sighed and went quiet. The previous night, our first together, had revealed that Hector was not quite as stoical as I had initially assumed. I had settled him in the bathroom on a pile of dry towels and as soon as I'd gotten into bed, he began to wail like a Confederate widow woman. I couldn't put him in the bed as he might wet the hotel mattress and there was also the risk that he would tumble and fall. So I had slept on the bathroom floor with him. The hours crawled like years. That ordeal had sent me looking for a sporting goods store. The airbed was an improvement; I pushed it up against the wall of the bedroom though because the bathroom floor was very cold, and erected a makeshift fence around the inflatable, using three straight-backed chairs, including one I had taken from the corridor outside, to keep Hector on the mattress beside me.

By morning there were a few damp patches on the mattress. Yet the wetting was minimal, perhaps caused by his licking himself while grooming and after all, he had been confined for hours. It was normal, I hoped. Some of the puddles on the floor, near the bath and at the base of the sink, might only have been him marking territory. He seemed physically tough and healthy; self-contained and trusting. Most of all he really liked me. We needed a plan, but first I dampened a facecloth under the faucet and wiped the airbed down, then stood it in the corner of the bathroom to dry. There it lurked, behind the door, like an assassin. I hoped the cleaning staff wouldn't notice and wonder what I was doing with an airbed miles from a beach, but luckily they were very casual about their duties, which suited me as the smell in the bathroom was worsening. Most mornings the maids would smile and hand me some fresh towels, say a few quick sentences which I could just about decipher, and then leave. Mrs. Faulkner would have had them arrested on charges of criminal slovenliness. I had kept the *Ne Pas Déranger* sign on the door. Then settled Hector back in the bathroom with more food while I rushed down for breakfast, wondering where to head for in mainland Europe with my elderly bed-wetter.

All I needed was a map and to find a village somewhere. I thought of Bavaria, and liked the idea of living in the Black Forest. Perhaps it made sense after all to hightail back to the Dutchman and buy the tent? The one thing I wanted to do before leaving Paris was visit Longchamp, the famous racecourse, and more cunningly, I could perhaps buy Father a souvenir from there, a pennant for his study or a Prix de l'Arc race poster. He had been very pleased when one of his clients, Dancing Brave, had won the previous year—Father had also treated his dam, Navajo Princess a few times. First thing though, I'd send him a postcard and decided on writing a cheerful, "Paris is so interesting, am trying to sort out my future, probably do history, hope you are well" (but declined to mention his fish), all on the back of a postcard reproduction of Van Dyck's famous study of Charles I out hunting, striking a kingly pose reminiscent of Father. Yes indeed, it all sounds deplorably calculating and it was—but I needed to re-establish contact before seeking Father's assistance in getting Hector home to Richmond.

My last foray from the hotel would be to the Bois de Boulogne district, to the west, just outside the main city center, yet still within Paris. "Hippodrome" means racecourse yet I kept imagining herds of hippos grazing while sneaky white hunters lurked. I had had to wait for a race day; the calendar is much smaller than back home. No wonder the place looks so well, it is tended like a prize garden. With all my love of history, seeing Longchamp meant far more to me than a visit to the Eiffel Tower. The race-course is in a park area which had once been an ancient oak forest used for hunting wild boar by the medieval kings of France. More slaughter.

Joggers and bike riders merged among the racing fans. The damn French can be such poseurs; there were women on parade who acted as if convinced by divine right they should be photographed. They were far snootier than the race day ladies back home. The thing that surprised me most was the ease with which the public could just saunter about and look in at the horses waiting in the stables. Father would have objected. He always maintained that Nijinsky's racing career had ended so abruptly because he was far too high-strung to settle in an atmosphere as carnival-like as that of Longchamp on Arc day.

Ladies wearing afternoon dresses and high heels, little hats, some with veils, salon hairdos, and lipsticked smiles set me thinking yet again about Mother. Because she loved dressing up and being part of things, she delighted in special occasions and managed to go to the big racing events without ever once looking at a horse. Then I became aware of my dusty old riding boots and that, along with my tweed jacket, I could as easily have belonged to a trainer's stable team, on hand to lead a horse around before a race. The walking ring really set the scene, shaded by big trees. I wondered did horses often spook should the wind rustle the branches in blustery conditions. The stables were just off behind the short passageway that led to the walking ring. Some of the jockeys were getting legged up there before they entered the parade area. It was a beautiful sight, always is, eight, ten, twelve horses preparing to push themselves, oblivious of the humans so intent on making money that they miss out on the sheer grandeur of observing horses bred, as Father loved intoning, "For greatness, on bloodlines sustained through the centuries . . ."

Curiously, artists such as Degas and Manet painted the races, but had they ever ventured behind the scenes? I was in dreamland and shivered with that familiar anticipation even though I knew nothing about the horses about to race.

But well, it all happened as quickly as china plates being shattered on a stone floor. One horse eased past me, the jockey adjusting his stirrups and the next, why the fella slumped forward and just toppled off. His horse near jumped out of its skin, and spun and reared, dropped his head and reared again. Don't know what possessed me, but I ran forward and caught the reins and got that horse clear away before he stomped his jockey into the sand. "Hey boy, hey boy, whatchya doing? Whatchya doing? Where ya going? Hey boy, hey boy. Nice and slow, hey boy, hey boy, we're doing good, nice and slow," sing song, sing song, over and over, my shoulder into his. He wasn't angry, the horse was plain terrified. The jockey had been legged up and then seemed to have a seizure, it looked like an epileptic fit, I had seen one happen at a concert once, a man fell from his chair, foaming at the mouth. It transpired later that the jockey, who was very well-known, was a cocaine user and had suffered an immediate convulsion. His nose was spouting blood bubbles before he had even hit the ground, and on his way to ride a race. Can you imagine? There was a lot of shouting in the background and movement too, other horses panicked, another few riders were thrown. It was a blur going on around me but all my concentration and strength went into soothing that one colt. I saw a gap and got him out of the walking ring, back up the path toward the stabling area and kept him moving, all the while chanting and leaning in to him; his hot breath on my neck. His head was shaking and spit was spotting my face. Three men approached and one of them, the trainer, said, "Merci, merci," informing me that I was very brave. The owner was an Englishman plainly nervous of his own horse—they often are, owners I mean—and I heard him tell the trainer to give me some money. The trainer laughed and shouted back, in English, that he should really give me a job. I saw it as the solution to my predicament. "Give me a job, give me a job. I can ride, I'm a competition rider." The Frenchman, suave-looking and smiley, with slicked back hair and a nifty-looking brown corduroy trilby hat, continued to bare his teeth but remained wary and seemed even colder. He informed me in careful English that riding show ponies was not quite the same as dealing with real horses. I didn't let my chance slip, and I bragged in a way I never would and told him I was good enough to have been coached by a German Olympic three-day event medalist and the young show jumper I'd been riding back home had been recently purchased by the French federation with a view to eventing him. "I'm good, real good; I could ride this here individual easy peasy." I shouted all this back at him, still holding the horse, and repeated, "Give me a job; give me a job." He spoke low, tauntingly, into my face, "You've run away," and I just snapped back sharp, standing tall, well at least taller than him, and with a pert quickness more Mitzi than me, snarled, "Don't be an idiot, I'm a research scientist, not a delinquent. How dare you. Where is your yard? I'll ride for you for a few weeks; you are so very lucky, Mr. Trainer sir, that this small incident should coincide with my visit here today. Why, it appears fated. Would you not agree, sir?" Mitzi had told me that when I get angry I sound really Southern and being so riled, turned into a caricature. I can't believe that stuff I said and the obnoxious way in which I said it, but did and more—I so wanted to help Hector. Never before had I anything living of my very own to love, not even a horse. Galileo was impossible; I had loved Monticello. But he was never mine, Hector was. He had found me, picked me, and I wasn't going to hand him over to the quarantine people.

He only needed a little time; I'd get it for him. A place involved with horses would suit both of us very well and I realized I'd a skill to sell.

The colt had settled and I asked which stall was his, the owner followed at a safe distance and told me that I was American to which I replied as unctuous as only I can be, "Yes sir, you are quite right. I am from Virginia, major horse country and home of the American Thoroughbred. I am the daughter of one of the most respected veterinarians in the world and I will be delighted to assist your friend for a while." I turned to the trainer, Monsieur Gallay, we had all been by then introduced. The Englishman seemed convinced I was very capable. I asked the trainer, who seemed to have begun regarding me with slightly less irritation, where his yard was and he said, not overly helpfully, the Loire Valley. I knew that was quite a large area and persisted, "Where exactly?" "Near Amboise." Not much, yet it meant something special to me and I just shouted out like it was a quiz answer, "That's where Leonardo da Vinci lived, he's buried there." The trainer smiled at his owner and the two men appeared most amused. "What train do I take? Which station?" I had hooked my fish and I was not letting go. "Austerlitz," was all he said and true to my peculiar feel for facts and dates, I breathed, "Napoleon's greatest victory." The Englishman laughed, saying yes but also the beginning of the end, while the trainer shrugged, warily. "Peut-être. Perhaps. Maybe. I don't know. I train horses."

*

END OF PART TWO

PART THREE

SUCH A BEAUTIFUL PLACE—it was like something out of a fairy tale. And yes, there was a castle, or rather, a château, too gorgeous for words. The somewhat unpredictable Monsieur Gallay presided over his own enchanted kingdom. The château had been there for close on 300 years; the farmhouse was almost as old. Admittedly it was the castle that first caught the eye. Turrets, not something you see in Richmond, but I knew what they were. There was a working moat with water and carp, lily pads so perfect you'd think they'd been painted. The gates were massive and made of timber and iron, while the drawbridge seemed to be just waiting for a knight to come galloping up on a white charger, colored banners flickering like tongues in a line behind him . . . The trainer's parents lived in the château but were rarely seen; they came and went in a black Mercedes. It had tinted windows, adding to the mystery. I decided Monsieur Gallay must belong to minor royalty and wondered if he had taken up training horses on a whim. He had the airs of a lord but the thick hairy wrists and stubby hands of a peasant, all the more obvious were these defects as he strutted about, puffed up with smugness and ego, cracking jokes I couldn't understand, his fine boots always polished to military standard. Not even one bone in his body could be described as elegant; he didn't have the refinement of Father, who was naturally distinguished and apparently if the reactions of the matrons in Richmond were to be believed, handsome.

People really seemed to like Monsieur Gallay, I noticed that straight off. He was about my height, no a bit shorter. He was always taking your measure and usually without saying much, if anything at all. Sometimes he would just shrug, or mumble something in French, bestowing his irritating little smirk or even worse—his bland, wide-eyed indifference. He acted like an amused overseer. It did not bother me; I felt safe and my head slowed down, all that confusion of thoughts and images had eased on being surrounded by beauty and back among horses. At long last I was able to sleep again. There was a reason for that . . . Once I had gotten over the surreal novelty of staring at it, I lost interest in the château but the farmhouse—well, if ever there was a house that I would have loved to have owned, it was that one.

Often comes to mind, that farmhouse, even when I'm wide-awake, no better place to be . . . It was stone and wide-fronted, in villa-style, covered with creepers that made it appear drowsy and benign. Most of the deep window sills had boxes filled with plants, some of which were still flowering at the time I had first seen it, in the early fall. The shutters were faded green, everything secure in an allure which was absolute through having been there for so long, washed by the rain and dried by the sun and allowed to evolve without any interference. Set in the middle of the French equivalent of about 2,000 acres, unusually big for France, the entire complex had the feel of a medieval lord's estate largely because that's what it was; with the sand arenas and gallops, the little offices, the chalets for the staff and the various modern buildings, the canteen, the video room with a full-size screen—many of the riding sessions were recorded because the horses were studied from every angle—conjured up as if by magic. All the working facilities, including a large indoor arena, had been discreetly added. Father would have been impressed, and it got me thinking about elements that could be introduced back home . . . But as for Monsieur Gallay's domain, it was magnificent. To any French person the château was just one of the 300 or so still standing throughout the Loire Valley region. For me, though, it was a fantasy come alive. Thomas Jefferson had left his mark on our local architecture in Richmond, but it was formal; a classical influence that had been closely studied, then replicated. Monsieur Gallay's marvelous Eden of orchards and romance-tinged buildings, benches and giant stone urns and flower planters, the tangled gardens, connected by iron gates, mossy steps, the many terraces, old oaks and chestnut trees, had coalesced over time and exuded cohesion, life lived over centuries. No wonder he was reluctant to share it.

But I was wrong about that, it had nothing to do with sharing. It was my desperation that had alarmed Monsieur Gallay; he already had sufficient disturbed females with which to contend. He later told me that he had feared I would jump up on the poor racehorse—"the property of that nice English owner"—and gallop away had he refused to employ me. He said that I had spat at him like a crazed wood demon and that all he could see were my huge American teeth, "a most terrifying sight," and he smiled his knowing smirk. Very funny I thought. He was an original with a flamboyant turn of phrase—at least when he was speaking English—and he reminded me of Mr. Montgomery. Monsieur Gallay often declared that English was a very dull language, or at least the way we spoke it was "so drab, drab, drab" that it needed some life, which he certainly gave it. In truth he was an actor. But not in the remote, brooding way of Father. Monsieur Gallay was aware of having a great deal to hide; he possessed an ability to survive whereas Father simply did not wish to discuss personal matters and was far more circumspect. The trainer had mastered a different form of secrecy. Father was merely reserved; he was lonely, unhappy, and baffled at the way life had bequeathed him two dead wives. Monsieur Gallay had, by contrast, set out with a plan and had been able to follow it, improvise, shimmy, deflect, yet through it all, manage to stay on course. I must have been there for almost two months, I can't rightly recall, before grasping that he was not the heir, he had married into all of it. His wife's people were fantastically rich and owned land, forestry, herds of heritage cattle and shares in several businesses as well as being connected to one of the largest art dealers in France. The enigmatic couple living in the château were his in-laws. There was so much wealth it would have taken an individual as laconic as Monsieur Gallay to remain underwhelmed by it all. He had married into money, taken it as his due and was making even more through his very clever reading of what humans wanted from horses.

My arrival was about as awkward as anybody who knows me would predict. By the time I reached the yard, my face was sore from beaming at my good fortune. Convinced we'd arrived in heaven, I kept telling Hector that he was mighty clever to have chosen me. I lifted him out of his carrying case and he walked along beside me, sniffing the air, excited by the new delicious, rural scents. I was like Maria in *The Sound of Music* when she arrives at the Von Trapp residence, primed to burst into song. "This is more like it; now I know why I came to France," I said aloud, sensing it was a place in which to relax. And that was what I wanted; freedom from thinking; I had not mentioned Hector, yet sensed the château people were unlikely to banish me because of my stoic little old companion. All I had to prove was that my riding matched my bragging. The drive was long and the stud railing was impeccable. I was surprised to see so many mares and foals in the three large paddocks on the way to the main entrance up near the château. Not what you'd expect from a racing yard, it was a very different setup as I would soon discover; Monsieur Gallay was running a most unusual operation, with an original approach; innovative and geared to understanding horses. Father would approve, I imagined reporting back to him.

The first encounter with a human caused me some panic. With Hector back in his sedan chair I walked around, skirting the main château entrance then bypassing the farmhouse, and went in search of a yard office. When I found it, a young man wearing a baseball cap and those eerie reflecting aviator sunglasses, opened the door just as I was about to knock. He stepped forward and let the outer door bang shut behind him. I jumped. It was on a spring and snapped like a trap. I felt I was about to be expelled without a chance to explain my presence and not even saying hello, blurted out that I had come to ride. The man just shrugged and replied that there were no lessons, it was not a riding school but that there were several in the area as well as a trekking center. I became flustered and could feel my face reddening. The man had already walked away and I hurried after him, trying to catch his attention. Hector had begun to wail as soon as I put his case down on the ground and I could hear him howling but I caught up with the man and told him that I had come to ride for Monsieur Gallay, that I had met him at Longchamp and he'd offered me a job. "Why?" was all the man in the sunglasses said, before mentioning he already had a full staff. Hector was yapping and I turned to go back and fetch my things, aware of the need to appear confident, as unflustered as possible, and explained that the English owner had suggested it and that Monsieur Gallay had agreed. "Here I am," I said, asking to see the stables in a business-like tone. The man made a clicking sound that implied it was all news to him and turned back to the office, the outer door slapping shut in my face. He pushed the door back open. "There is a hook for to hold this," he said, leaving me to pull the screen door aside. The office was like a set designer's idea of a den for business meetings. Photographs of horses covered the walls. An impressive, possibly antique desk had been recruited to hold a computer and two thick ledger-type books, paper clips, two staplers, an unused roll of scotch tape, a holder full of colored markers. It was a desk that someone wanted to look far more used than it probably was. The low coffee table under the double windows with a view out on to paddocks had several easy chairs grouped around it and a tray with the remains of fancy sandwiches, a plate of pastries, and a large pot of coffee. "So you have brought your dog. He is your advisor?" Suddenly I was very hungry and glad when the man half-heartedly gestured to the food, saying to have a sandwich, some cakes, the coffee was long cold but there were cans of coke in the refrigerator. He said he didn't know where he—meaning the trainer—was, but directed me toward the guest chalet and the club house where the meals were eaten and stood up to leave, then remembered to tell me that the other girl had gone into town. I hadn't realized that there was another girl. How good a rider was she I wondered and was she French, more pressure. Then the man addressed me quite sharply, asking about my riding hat.

In hindsight it would have been so easy to lie and say I left it on the train. But I wasn't smart enough, causing him to assume that I was a very sloppy breed of a rider indeed, which he made clear with another click of his tongue. It was uncomfortable, I couldn't see his eyes. He was still wearing his reflecting sunglasses, the style of which I particularly dislike; they make me think of flies, and I already felt foolish, intimidated. He told me that he had no idea of what to do with me. "You may as well just have a look around and try not to get yourself kicked or bitten," he said in a snooty sort of way. Then he marched out, leaving me with a mouth full of sandwich.

*

Red cowboy boots, not fashion ones, but authentic, made of tooled leather with well-worn heels. She was very tall, skinny, and bug-eyed, like a giant embryo. All she did was flop down on a chair at the long wooden table, pushed away the cat that was walking over the generous platter of bread and inquired in a bored voice, before even asking my name, "Where you from?" As soon as I said Virginia she just gave a loud fake yawn and sniggered, "So daddy must own a plantation. Cotton huh? How many niggers you got?" I said we didn't have any, but she ignored that and gaped rudely at me and then said, "Bennington, I can smell preppy liberal shit a mile off." Stupid old me volunteered I planned on attending the University of Virginia, and to that she just drawled, "Jesus," before pursing her lips and looking around, asking where had old Belmondo gotten to. I presumed she meant the cat and said nothing. She began pounding her fists on the table, asking about supper. Did she have to rustle up something herself? Two men came in speaking French; she announced she was about to "expire real fast." They ignored her. She didn't like that and turned back to me, saying her name was Lone Star. I swallowed my snigger, even without the alias I had already guessed she was from Texas but asked her anyway and she looked surprised, "How'd you figure that out? You mustn't be as dumb as you look." I told her it was the boots. She laughed long and loud about that, saying that she had several times already "almost been killed by guys trying to git them." A small, pleasant-looking woman looked in from what I realized must be the kitchen and said something in French. One of the men answered her. He nodded at us and spoke in English, saying that we were all ready, "time to eat." Then I noticed that he was the person who had spoken to me earlier. He had removed the baseball cap and his sunglasses exposing his left eye which was badly swollen, almost closed. "Still sore, poor Belmondo, told you I'd make it better if you'd let me," teased the girl.

He looked very different; younger, softer, and was nice looking with curly light brown hair and one very open bright amber-colored eye in contrast to the injured one. He had unusually good teeth for a French person, unlike the other man who had come in with him and was missing a few. Lone Star sure liked Belmondo. It was embarrassing to behold. I felt as if I had walked in on a play after the interval and had missed too much to begin to follow it. I guessed she must be a very good rider as the men made it obvious that they didn't like her. Not having ridden for weeks and weeks I was worried; there she was, probably very capable and saddle-fit. She would be effective, not stylish, that was my assessment; a Texan accustomed to dealing with the unexpected in open spaces, not like pampered, privileged me, used to riding in the controlled environment of arenas. All I could do was sit quietly, hungry as usual and already uneasy about being found out the next morning. I needed to prove myself as I really wanted to stay, only would have preferred if Lone Star was elsewhere, preferably back in Texas.

Another man arrived, also young, and then two others, older and small, not riders—yard hands, I smiled to myself. They were stooped and tired from monotonous physical labor. I could recognize the type. Lone Star asked me if I could speak what she referred to as the "local lingo." I groaned, just when I had begun to understand what people were saying I was going to be faced with a dialect. I asked her if it was difficult to follow, "Jeez, don't look so surprised, it's called French, how come you haven't noticed? Did you reckon they were just speaking English with a funny accent? These guys have a completely separate language. Why they're like the wetbacks back home gibbering away in Mexican, Spanish, whatever—they revert to it when we're around, you'll see. They do it to keep us in the dark. Not exactly neighborly huh?" She jutted her chin, defiant. It was plain she would wrong-step me every chance she got. Inwardly I was already crying. It was exhausting; everything she said was a challenge, constantly goading me, making me feel stupid. She was not very bright yet she was sharp, quicker than I was, what you'd call streetwise, like Mitzi only brash. Then, leaning in close, she whispered not to say anything but that Belmondo was "really into me" only she said he had to keep it quiet when the others were around. She kept staring at him, desperate for his attention. I felt like informing her she was wrong but she probably would have screamed and accused me of lying about Father's slaves. She said she had some potato chips upstairs and she would get them while we were waiting. Fleetingly I remembered how much I had missed potato chips. Mrs. Faulkner usually kept a supply of them in a kitchen cupboard. I'd had a very easy life in Richmond, that's for sure. Lone Star made the most of her exit upstairs, she was not wearing a bra. Her slack little breasts jiggled about and I was uncomfortable and dreaded what it would be like when she rode, with them bouncing about. The men would be looking and even with my Iron Maiden sports bras which I had lazily lapsed into wearing all the time, I would be so self-conscious; while she wanted to make sure everyone got a good look.

Lone Star patted Belmondo's head as she undulated by. It was such an unnatural way of moving, her frizzy hair like spirals uncoiling with the heat of the room. I just laughed out loud, one of my sharp, sudden bark-like yelps. No one reacted. Belmondo was sitting with the other men and a hard scowl passed across his face as his hand shot up to swat away hers. She had provoked him yet he said nothing and she flounced out. Perhaps they'd had a relationship that had ended badly; even that seemed unlikely but you never can tell with people. Mitzi came to my mind again and I smiled, yes sir, she would have figured it all out in seconds. Mitzi could be earthy in her opinions because she was Santa Monica smart, my Virginia diffidence often exasperated her. But Lone Star was vulgar, plain uncouth and even stupid me could appreciate the difference.

*

Lying becomes easier when there is a good reason and Hector was mine. Lone Star lied all the time; for her it was an instant reflex. She didn't even think, just said the first outrageous thing that came into her mouth; her mind never appeared to be remotely involved. After she had reeled off the names of a few rock bands and I admitted to never having heard of any of them, she just shook her head and muttered, "Tragic, real tragic," and renounced all further interest in me. She was not the kind of person who'd want to make friends. Hector's needs were my priority and I was happy with that. He was very responsive and I loved his trust. It was as if he expected me to be able to improvise, the more complicated the lie, the better, as I believed detailed explanations were consistent with what Mitzi had referred to as my earnest approach to life.

When the young man named Belmondo showed me the sweet little room up in the eaves of the old stone chalet, I could only sigh with longing. It was so much prettier than the modern accommodations that were allocated to the staff, and it also had a balcony similar to mine back home. That Amboise room delighted me and it was obvious that it had been someone's private chamber at one time, in the same way my bedroom was exclusive to me and me only. The walls of the chalet room were decorated with botanical watercolors; serious period prints, arranged neatly in groups suggesting they had been collected with care. Father had three original works by Maria Sibylla Merian, a pioneering lady naturalist who predated Darwin and Gilbert White, and he also had books, historical studies, and monographs on botanical art; it was another of his many interests that I'd also acquired. The genteel calm of the chalet room was enticing and made me want to settle in there and make us a temporary home. There was nothing Spartan and functional about it; it had been lived in, and I could tell. "You might stand out here and sing to the birds," announced Belmondo, sweeping his arms across the spellbinding vista as he stepped out on the balcony.

Yet it wouldn't suit Hector and with deep reluctance I insisted on being downstairs as I was inclined to sleepwalk. Sleepwalk! It was the first thing that came to me. I stared at Belmondo as surprised as he was by what I had said. Within seconds he had regained his usual expression that seemed to suggest, "What next?" He must have been forming a strange opinion of Americans, what with Lone Star's predatory nonsense and my emerging neurosis. I thanked him when he led me back downstairs, to a far less atmospheric room that did, however, open out onto a stone patio, enclosed by high beech hedges. The door leading on to it also had a screen, similar to the office one, only more ornate. He said the patio was very pleasant in the summer and then added that it would be useful for my dog. I liked the fact that he had noticed Hector and thanked him. He smiled, adding that his name was not Belmondo. "They call me Mathieu; that is to say my name is Mathieu." Then he shrugged, stressing he had no idea why "that girl" thought otherwise. I watched his face as he said "that girl" scrutinizing his expression for clues. Mitzi would have been able to detect something, some sexual frisson if there was one, but I wasn't sure.

Mathieu said he hoped my sleepwalking would be enjoyable as there was nothing to fall off and, speaking of falling off, that I could try some riding in the morning. I was none too happy with that "try some riding" but I smiled back and listened to his steps as he walked away, thinking that he seemed nicer than I'd first suspected with a slowly ironic sense of humor, sitting on the kinder side of Father's. I guessed he was about twenty-four or so, but later heard that he was thirty-one. Anyhow, rosy satisfaction caused me to hug Hector, proclaiming that we had done very well and that I must go and find the horse that had spooked at Longchamp and formally thank him. True to my fretful nature, I then set to pondering as to exactly how good a rider was Lone Star, reasoning that she must be very good, indispensable, if she could act the way she did and not get herself murdered never mind fired. The thought struck me that perhaps she was autistic which might have explained her inability to sense atmosphere or react to the moods of others. But there was something else, she had a hunger that I had read about without really knowing what it was, it was an explicit sexual need that I couldn't fully grasp being more interested in romance. She was only eight months older than me, when I'd reckoned on several years. All her innocence had been used up; she had a wanton staleness about her and regarded me as a child still in grade school. It struck me that she was undermining me much in the same way as Marc had, which was disturbing, but all of a sudden I felt too sleepy to care and kicked off my old boots—the only things I had with me that still made me feel a rider—as well as of course my sports bras not that they counted. Bras made me reflect again on Lone Star. Only the hope that I had not completely forgotten how to ride remained. Having not ridden for weeks I was apprehensive, if it went badly wrong I would be curtly dismissed. Even worse, they would think I was a bragger and I would have hated that, blushing with shame at my bravado back at Longchamp.

Hector wanted to wander around but I knew it would be impossible for me to concentrate if he was loose—and to my surprise he assumed a somewhat martyred attitude when I cut short our early morning outing and carried him back into our new quarters, putting the T-shirt I had slept in down on the floor for him, before pulling the screen door across. The sun was already shining into the room and at least he could smell the air. Which was busy with bees; fat black and yellow bumble bees, the largest ones I have ever seen, and made sure that Hector did not get stung. By chance while walking him I discovered the swimming pool. From the outside it resembled a huge Victorian-style greenhouse and reminded me of the pictures I had seen of Kew Gardens in London, England. The water in the pool was seductively tepid and there were large troughs and stone planters filled with ferns and other greenery, some of which were vines, thriving in the humidity. I reached up and touched the grapes and imagined floating in the water on my back, lulled by the gentle heat and gazing up at the blue sky through the glass roof. Even if they decided that I was the worst rider this world had yet seen, I was determined to swim at least once in that pool so that I could remember the experience for ever and ever. Then it was time to eat and I hurried toward the main chalet where we'd had supper the previous night.

Breakfast began badly. Lone Star was wearing a tiny black singlet that was so cut away under the arms as to be barely covering her. When the straps slipped down, her puny chest was revealed for all to behold. It was embarrassing and I stared fixedly at the various cats congregating on the table. A couple of them began intense grooming of their genital areas, slurping and moaning, not really what you wish to contemplate during a meal. No one seemed to mind; I had never seen anything like it but was to become used to it. There were a lot of these languid, fat cats, at least three generations, and they prowled over the table, haughtily drinking from the milk jug in turns and walking on the food, grabbing bits of bread. Never knew cats ate rolls. The dogs were more subtle, they begged as if they felt they were obliged to look for scraps.

Having informed me, several times, the previous evening that "Belmondo" was "so into" her that she felt "real sorry" for him, Lone Star ignored me. Then she just blurted out loud, "God, your eyes are so weird, like mega yuck . . . is the green one a fake or something?" Mathieu immediately cut across and said that my eyes were wonderful and that his sister also shared this, "It is a sign of great fortune and also intelligence, perhaps future genius. My sister is going to be a doctor, hers are one blue and the other gray, not quite as," he paused, "superb . . . as Helen's, but nice also, very nice." I was speechless. Lone Star grunted, failing to conceal her irritation, annoyed to hear me being complimented instead of teased like she'd planned.

Up she rose and undulated out, dropping her slice of toast onto the table, half a cup of coffee still steaming beside her plate. I checked, she was again wearing the cowboy boots. Would she wear a regulation riding hat I wondered, but of course, no she would defy the safety rules and produce a sweat-stained Stetson. Funny, she was, as I've said, tall and skinny but stiff and not at all athletic. In fact for someone riding racehorses the skin around her waist was surprisingly pudgy. I hated her but was amazed that Mathieu had defended me, or at least, my eyes. Lone Star had no muscle, so where did her strength come from? Was she unusually subtle? Was she a horse whisperer? I'd never met one and had been bewildered when Mitzi had expressed shock at Billy Bob allowing me to ride Galileo. "Why," she'd declared during one of her many anti-horse tirades, "couldn't that little old black guy, your mentor Billy Joe," she always referred to him wrongly, never once managed to remember that his name was Billy Bob, "If that guy was such a horse whisperer how come he couldn't fix Galileo?" That was when I first heard the phrase "horse whisperer" and there I was wondering if Lone Star was one.

When I looked over at Mathieu, I noticed he had washed his hair and it looked fluffy. More golden . . . he was busily eating, attending to his breakfast, his thoughts already elsewhere. The man with the missing teeth and another fellow, very dark skinned, more Spanish-looking than French, were drinking coffee and studying what appeared to be a sales program. I asked them was Lone Star a good rider. They both glanced over at Mathieu, he did not react, but the one who had lost some teeth said, "Fantastique, fantastique," and the Spaniard applauded, adding, "Magnificent" in English as if he reckoned the French equivalent would be beyond my comprehension. I tensed, upset that she would be better than me at something at which I had always worked so hard. They both smiled at me, but in a friendly way, as if they could read my thoughts. Those men were never unpleasant or offhand to me, not even at the beginning.

Down in the stable yard, Mathieu pointed out the tack room and suggested I find a hat and then gestured for me to follow him on over to the indoor arena. I was very impressed, I had already seen the outdoor arena; the indoor was in behind what looked like a grove of birch trees. There was a path, like the one that led from the kitchen back home in Richmond to the yard. We didn't have an indoor. The one at Amboise was a full-size competition space with seating, and billboard-sized advertisements from various local sponsors; feed stores, restaurants, car dealerships, and all adding color and atmosphere. There was an announcer's box, a giant scoreboard, a large clock, even a warm up area. Small competitions, on a similar level to the training shows I had gone to, were held there, all very serious, the facilities were good enough for regional championships. It did not take much to imagine horse trailers and trucks driving up, from all over, to compete there. It was a most unusual establishment, a dream facility catering for a range of disciplines. Monsieur Gallay was as interested in show jumping and dressage as he was in racing, which is very unusual. While I was looking around, awaiting the next surprise, Mathieu walked in leading a bay mare, tacked up in a quality Swiss riding saddle, not a racing one. That pleased me. "Here, I give you a leg up. This is Marie Antoinette, she is seven and only raced four times, placed twice, before we decided to try her at a one-day event, she is a good jumper and very fast at cross-country, a bit sharp, nice dressage, a talented horse with a brain—we bred her. The dam was fourth in the Arc, quite talented. Marie Antoinette is going to one of the German sales next month and she hates men but not me." Mathieu didn't waste words. She seemed mild and well-mannered and we walked off, me aware that the stirrups were too short but I wanted a feel of her first before I began fidgeting with the lengths. Behind me was the sound of the double doors opening, and electric lights came on, transforming the space into a stage even though they were not necessary, there was sufficient natural light. And I heard voices, all speaking French.

The mare had a fluid, active walk and she was also aware of the people coming in. Monsieur Gallay had decided to call my bluff and wanted to watch. Stay calm, stay calm, over and over; I played my little games, the survival tactics I'd used on Galileo. I asked for trot and we did a series of circles. She was very fit and well-schooled, engaged. I began to feel more confident and took my feet out of the stirrups at sitting trot, taking a chance I know, but it was more to convey my confidence to the watching Monsieur Gallay. After several circuits of the full school, it was easy to see that she was a good horse, with a big action. I brought her back to walk and lengthened the stirrups, before heading back out on the track and trotted a few circles, then straight into a collected canter. She was easy or perhaps seemed so because she was very unlike Galileo. Here was a talented horse holding no grudge against mankind. She was enjoying herself as much as I was. For me, it was perfect, reminding me of why I love riding.

Mathieu and one of the men set up a few jumps, I thought that was a bit early but I acted as if I barely noticed and contin ued schooling, the mare held a beautiful shape and had a fine, developed neck. I wondered to what sale she was intended. Then Mathieu called me over and said that Monsieur Gallay wanted me to take her over a few jumps and he asked was I okay with that, I wondered if he was trying to tell me something. Was she expected to catapult me off and was that why she was heading for the German sale? I said I would try, that I had done a little jumping. Mathieu had taken off his sweater and tied it around his waist; he had beautiful arms, young man's arms, like Mitzi's brother; perfect skin and slender muscles. Any normal person would have laughed. There I was, perhaps about to be bucked off by a strange horse, yet was being distracted by the sight of a pair of arms . . . My thoughts returned to the horse.

I walked her around the jumps; there were three of them. A little course and all for us, I let her have a good look and it settled both of us. The distances between the fences were accurate, that was impressive too. These men knew what they were doing, if exactly what was going on was not all that clear, aside from it being a multi-disciplinary approach by all accounts, seemingly centered mainly on Thoroughbreds who had been sidestepped out of racing and given the chance to test their potential elsewhere.

So Monsieur Gallay was asking for a small course on what appeared to be my trial ride. I decided to take my time and have a few practice jumps over the most obvious barrier, the one with the straightest approach. It was about two and a half feet high. They knew the horse's ability but not mine, it was a bit ambitious on their part, or perhaps they just wanted a reaction from me by testing my nerve. I would call their bluff, and I circled her and asked for canter, steadied her and then we went straight toward the middle and over, she had no problem and was perfectly balanced. It was fine for me as well and we did it again and then changed rein and came down the other side of the arena, steady thud, thud of her hooves on the sand surface, her breathing that bit louder and again, no problem. We went over the three jumps; one, two, three. Nice and clean. I glanced over at Monsieur Gallay, no expression. He motioned to Mathieu, who looked around at me and said just keep her moving. It was obvious that the little discussion would result in the jumps being raised—which they were, to, I guess, three foot—or just over, the standard European meter height. A further two jumps were then added, to make a double. We went around as if we were an established partnership; she was a good, good horse. "Thank you, thank you," I whispered to her, patting her neck and trying not to smile, not wanting to look too relieved or show that I was tired. It had gone very well. Billy Bob was watching over me.

Monsieur Gallay stood up, pushed his hands down deep in his trouser pockets and looked away, seeming to sigh. He spoke with Mathieu and another man I had not seen before and walked over to the seating. Lone Star appeared, she had been sitting on the far side of the arena and I hadn't noticed her. Interesting, she had bothered coming in to have a look. I wondered would she ride next, as she went over to the entrance, glanced back and then was gone. Mathieu waved me over and the mare walked calmly on a loose rein as I eased my feet out of the stirrups and let my legs hang down. "No smiling," I told myself, trying to look as if I was used to being able to ride any new horse without feeling the need to celebrate. I did expect the trainer to say something to me. I was not cocky, not at all, just awfully pleased and relieved. It was my first riding in weeks, my first ever session in France. Mathieu asked me what I thought of the horse and I said she was good, very generous. He agreed and said he felt certain she would sell and it would be good to show buyers the level of horse they were producing here. Monsieur Gallay told him to get me to cool her down. Mathieu then asked him what he thought of my riding and the trainer just muttered, "Assez bien, assez bien." Well, I knew what that meant, "good enough," and he was letting me know that he was underwhelmed to say the least.

My face flared red and I was angry and glowered down at Mathieu, protesting heatedly, "Hey that's not fair, that was better than just 'good enough,' a lot better. How good is Lone Star?" Mathieu attempted to placate me and said I had ridden very well and that the boss had in fact pointed out that they were looking at a competition rider, "and a very good one." That appeased my silly little ego until he added that Monsieur Gallay had said I was not to work with the racehorses. My fury returned and I snapped, "So he reckons on me being incapable of riding in a straight line? Doesn't he trust me with his precious racehorses? I've ridden lots of Thoroughbreds. That's exactly what the horse that was sold to France was, and I'd been riding him." Was I only permitted to ride the mare because she was being sold? Mathieu surprised me. Instead of telling me to grow up, he said that the boss was thrilled and wanted me to concentrate on schooling show jumpers and possible three-day event horses that were being prepared for private buyers and for competition use, and also for clients who wanted good horses schooled for them. He asked me had I done any dressage.

Mathieu smiled at me for the first time, I mean really smiled and he said he was so happy to have finally found a good rider who was also sympathetic to horses, because so many of the better riders were aggressive "and a bit crazy," with, he paused, "power or anger or I don't know." Like Lone Star, I silently thought as he continued speaking. We would work well together he said. I must have relaxed; maybe I smiled too because he then said that I would have so much fun riding that perhaps I would give up sleepwalking. He laughed at his little joke and told me to ride on out of the arena and walk her back to the stable yard. It looked like I'd miss seeing Lone Star ride, but excited and eager to please, aware I would be staying on, did as I was told.

*

Monuments aren't always churches and statues of generals on horseback. There are plenty of modest houses in Richmond that are heritage buildings. The old stone barn at Monsieur Gallay's, simple and majestic, entranced me with my grand notions of the past as living history. The barn was one of several fine farm buildings and outhouses on the property, most of which had been converted into stabling, whereas the racing block was a bland, modern complex about 500 yards away and thankfully, out of view. The old barn was certainly alive as it housed thirty horses in stables of a quality usually seen in magazine features. Which stall in the old barn was Marie Antoinette's was not clear because all the doors were closed, and I was in a hurry, anxious to see what was so damn special about the annoying Lone Star with her stupid drawl; the insolent face, the endless babble of asinine comments, her sleazy walk, and just about everything else about her. A scalding wave of resentment directed at her self-belief and arrogance and the rest of it coursed through me, all that rage as well as the dread that she would ruin my adventure.

One of the older yardmen appeared. Pushing a wheelbarrow and with shovel in hand, he nodded to me, then at a box, implying some connection. I moved toward it, and opened the door, led the mare through and began untacking her. She was very sweaty. A decorated iron hook for the bridle was screwed into the wall directly outside the stable; someone had once taken care to craft that lovely hook, all the bridles that it must have held over the years . . . there were others, similar hooks, and each neatly positioned outside the various stalls. It was a fine detail, discreet yet telling. Such touches were evident throughout the yard, a rare sensitivity had gone into Monsieur Gallay's establishment, as if he was trying to match the splendor of his wife's family. I bent down to remove the mare's tendon boots and was surprised to see she wasn't wearing any. Force of habit, removing tendon boots, and I made a note of looking around for a pair. First though I had to hose her down and went out to locate a washing station, which was there along with everything you could possibly need. It didn't take long and I brought her back to the stable which was dirty. I checked some of the other ones and they all contained varying amounts of soiled bedding. The stable hand walked over to me and picked up the shovel he had left against the wall, and with a hint of increased insistence handed it to me. "No," I said firmly, in English, "I don't clean stables; I ride the horses but cleaning out is not my job." I turned away and patted the mare, assuring her I would be back and strode out of the barn, leaving the man to figure out my meaning. As soon as I was clear of his view I ran hard back to the indoor and eased the doors gently, hoping to get a good look before she noticed. "Let's see how good you are Olive Oyl," I muttered, and then laughed on having subconsciously realized that was of who, or perhaps I should say "what," Lone Star had reminded me—Popeye's skinny girlfriend.

Maybe Lone Star was special, I conceded, preparing to be impressed and jealous, maybe even learn something. The arena was empty. There was no sign of anyone waiting. The lights had been turned off; the small gate at the arena entrance was also shut, with the latch on. So she must be out on the gallops, with Monsieur Gallay delightedly overseeing from his jeep. No enclosed little sand arena for Lone Star, she required the wide open spaces—typical Texan big shot, big mouth. I trudged back to the mare, intending to groom her. Mathieu was there, waiting. He asked me why I had refused to clean the stable. Did I not know how? Of course I knew, I just didn't do it. Why not? I felt like saying because I'd never needed to clean stables in return for riding a horse. But I wanted to assert myself and said slowly with a calm resolve no doubt inherited from Father that I directed my energies into riding. He asked me how many horses I planned to ride each day and I shrugged casually with what I hoped was a sophisticated confidence, "About three or four." But he shot back, in a tone that may have been intended to sound challenging, and was, that he was thinking more like seven or eight. Touché, he was attempting to intimidate me. Father had trained me well; I was becoming less easily chastened and snapped briskly, "Sure thing" hoping that no tremor could be heard as I said it, and, picking up a body brush went in to the mare, aware that the most I had ever ridden in a day was two horses and very rarely three. That gave me something to think about.

Mathieu puffed out his cheeks but said nothing only walked on out of the barn. Well he could not have been watching Lone Star if he had been in the barn monitoring me. I began brushing the mare and noticed that she was bigger than she'd seemed when I was riding her. Then went to look around for a cooler sheet to put on her and found one hanging over the side wall of an even dirtier stable than the one I'd put her in. Ideally she needed a size bigger, but there was nothing else. The yardman was studying me; he had shiny black eyes, more like those of a forest creature than a human, and I guessed that he would clean out the stall once I left. I attempted to look important, beyond mucking out—me at my most Richmond. Although unnerved by Mathieu's annoyance, and it coming directly after he had seemed so pleased with me, I had bigger things on my mind, namely Lone Star's ability and how much better she was than me. It looked like I would have to wait, or so I thought. First stop though, Hector.

On the way to our little house, I stopped at the chalet we ate in, thinking that there might be something left out that I could take to my room for us.

"Hey Bennington, you done good on old Toots there; I do declare she is, positively, the biggest pony I ever did see." Lone Star's raucous comments sounded rehearsed, while her creepily disembodied voice was embellished with a fake Southern accent and all for my benefit. I heard her before I saw her. She had been sitting in the sun; it was bright although the day was chilly and her pipe-cleaner arms were covered in goose bumps. Instead of falling into a trap and begin tying myself up in knots by earnestly explaining that the mare was named Marie Antoinette, that she was a good 16.2, and no pony, I ignored her greeting and asked had she been riding out on the gallops. Lone Star's reply took some time in coming as she was laughing so hard that she then began to choke and cough, then wheeze. Finally she spoke. "Horseback riding? Moi? You must be nuts? Jeez, that's the last thing, very last thing you will ever see . . . horses and me, yuck and double yuck." Lone Star peered into my face and assured me that although she was "unpredictable and exciting"—her words not mine—that she was full terrified of horses. "Scared shitless . . . I hate those critters, the way they bounce and squirm. They always look as if they are about to throw a fit or something . . . they're . . . I don't rightly know, kinda nervy, sort of insane . . . inbreeding does it every time same as people and you should know." Unbounded relief must have flooded my face, although Lone Star misread it for amusement. "Old Belmondo looked real happy too, like he was watching Jesus walking on water. Did my little heart good to see the boy so . . . Joy-ous." She then told me that it was different for girls like her, she was attractive and outgoing, whereas I was a freak "sort of homely and inverted." She might mean "introverted" I suggested, sheer relief allowing my superiority some space to surface. "Yeah, whatever," she said, informing me that my backside would become deformed and that "horseback riding," as she put it, was a refuge for weirdos and that Belmondo obviously felt "real sorry" for me, she could see that. Then she looked around before adding, "what with your weird eyes and you being an orphan and all." I told her I was not an orphan and reminded her that she had made jokes about Father owning a slave plantation. She laughed, "Shucks, I forgot," with a nasty twinkle, thrilled to have offended me. But I did not care two Arabian figs for what she said, I had by then become immune—or so I thought—to her mindless insults and was delighted to observe, at such close quarters, that her skin was bad, crusted here and there with old acne scars and patches of permanent sunburn. More than anything I had wanted to ask her why she was called Lone Star. My chance had come. No one else could hear her if she decided to ridicule me. Did her father own a Texan cattle ranch, a spread? Again she laughed herself into a gagging seizure. Her father's company made reinforced cardboard packing cartons. They lived in a huge house which was, "come to think of it, ranch-style, real home-on-the-range," with a swimming pool and a sun room and "loads of other stuff," but it was in Austin, with no animals, not even a hamster. "No horse poop, not for one hundred miles," she said, asking me how I could bear the smell. I assured her that I loved it. She sighed, "Yeah, figures." Surprising myself I pressed on, why she was there? She mentioned something about her father being the king of cardboard packaging. Pleased at my interest she continued speaking, prepared to stay on a topic instead of making a whole mess of stupid random remarks as she usually did, so I pounced, asking her to explain the reason for "Lone Star." An expression of what Sherlock Holmes would call mildly intelligent cunning slid across her face and she prepared to confide something she clearly considered fascinating.

On her arrival at Monsieur Gallay's she had planned on assuming a more exotic name than her own, "Like, just for fun . . ." her voice going higher with pleasure and had decided on Celeste as it sounded "sort of French." There was a problem though, she narrowed her eyes, as if expecting me to have anticipated what she was about to say. But I'd no idea. My face must have looked blank. Lone Star was ecstatic, pausing to glance around, before mentioning the hog and had I seen it? I was bewildered. It turned out that there was a gigantic pig being fattened for Christmas and the ill-fated animal apparently was already glorying in the name of Celeste. "Yes sir, beat me to it," she said, as if the pig had selected the name. Looking back it was really funny and for a moment, if only a mere fleeting second, Lone Star seemed momentarily likeable and a lot younger as she told me she was so lucky that she had, what's this she said, "sussed" the existence of the pig and "averted like a real crisis." Could I imagine? she asked, her tone approaching wonderment, what life would have become had she pretended that her name was Celeste. "Like, I mean," she said, "what would Belmondo do?" Nothing, I said to myself, he wouldn't even notice. I guess underneath all the brashness and bravado Lone Star was as lonely and as uncertain of herself as I was.

By then Hector would be looking for food and guilty at having left him alone, I turned to raid the chalet kitchen, but paused further, still intent on finding out why she had come to a specialist training and breeding facility, instead of say, a beachside leisure center on the Riviera, or better still, hadn't simply headed for downtown Miami or Hollywood with all the other messed up people. Reluctant to waste her good mood I pounced, and asked her real name. "Joan, simple plain Joan—'Joanie baby' as Mom says—crap huh? I plan on changing it when I get older to something cool like Britney or Naomi, Bethany . . . I'm gonna be a model and probably end up in the movies," she shrugged wearily, affecting boredom.

Just as I was asking what she was doing in Amboise, Monsieur Gallay drove into the large yard, at the wheel of his dark-green Porsche. Without knowing for exactly what reason, I didn't want him to see me speaking with Lone Star. Our conversation collapsed as if we had been caught stealing. Lone Star looked startled as I just walked away. Rude, I know. With a shivering chill as if an evil spirit was passing close by I sensed that there was some squalid connection between the trainer and Lone Star. Could they be involved with each other? I gasped and could hear Mitzi saying "real creepy." But my disapproval was immediately countered as unedited images of my night with Marc, my vomiting . . . the incident in the bathroom and the rest of it replayed on that endlessly repeating TV screen lodged in my brain . . . well, who was I to feel so righteous? I too had fallen badly which made me feel pretty humble. Finally I hurried to Hector, only to detour back around to the dining chalet, aware that I still had to find us something to eat.

My miniature galaxy was holding tightly together, just about. In some strange way Lone Star's, that is Joanie's, professed fear of horses had empowered me. I also wondered if I would begin to feel warmer toward her, but knew it would be a false friendliness based on her not being any threat as a rider. I missed Mitzi and wanted to speak to her, but not yet. Not until I had established a routine. There was also my need to contact Father. Further deliberation and plotting was required in figuring all that out while somehow salvaging some token crumbs of honor.

A platter of ham, not Celeste, had been left on the table, along with a basket of bread rolls, butter, and various stoneware pots with three different jams and the usual honey. There was always honey with every meal; I had taken to pouring it in my tea. Just as I was about to gather together a little snack for Hector and myself, thoughts of the omnipresent cats swarming over the table discouraged me. They had probably been sitting on those very bread rolls and grooming themselves on the ham, slurping and sucking, hair and fur—oh God, the germs . . . the paw prints. I put everything back and went into the kitchen proper; the refrigerator was like Aladdin's cave, so well stocked as to make Mrs. Faulkner's appear almost frugal by comparison, which it certainly was not. There was cheese, but mainly those soft, runny varieties the French appeared to prefer—some of it was really smelly with mold, blue mold, as well as salad, beetroot, a vegetable pie. Best of all, a can of tuna on the counter and just waiting for Hector; I had amassed enough food to prefer not to be seen on the way out with it. And behold three remaining

slices of chocolate cake—or gâteau as they called it—on a fancy
scalloped-edged china plate protected by a glass cover, similar
to the ones Mrs. Faulkner used. I took two pieces, then put one
back. It would have been more difficult had I been fat—people
may have more openly studied my appetite yet because I was
quite thin nobody ever mentioned my eating which had often
alarmed Mother. It seemed I could eat what I liked, ask for second helpings, and order three desserts at one sitting without
being cautioned. There was no obvious risk of a skinny person
like me exploding. I was always hungry but dreaded being identified as greedy—which I was. Only no one ever said it. No matter
how much I ate, I always seemed ready for more . . .

Sneaking out the door, the way was clear to my chalet; I held
my supplies close to my chest, placing a full pitcher of milk
on the stone steps, intending to come back for it. "You could
have tapeworms you know. Bet'cha picked them up from the
horses, they seem to live in shit; it just falls out of them kinda
like nonstop, plop, splatter . . ." Lone Star had again ambushed
me, she had remained outside, lurking in the shadows, and she
informed me that I was like one of those starving street children
in Calcutta, always stealing food. I was shocked that she was
so observant, even, apparently, down to monitoring my colos-
sal food intake. Monsieur Gallay had left. Had they spoken or
perhaps planned an assignation? What in hell did I care? Then I
guessed that she was probably waiting for Belmondo. I asked her
why she called him that. Her face softened, "Jeez . . . well Mom's
always had a thing for this French actor guy." I was not sure if by
"a thing" she meant a relationship, or was it merely a liking for
and asked her to explain. Lone Star howled like a wolf, more guf-
fawing and choking, the usual spluttering—she found laughing
quite strenuous—and said I reminded her of a science teacher
she had back home. "Define, explain, clarify. You're so fucking

logical . . ." It felt like a slap, particularly as it was true, I was "fucking" logical. She wasn't sure about her mother's interest in the actor, and seemed to think before replying, "Maybe, maybe not." Oh well, but it was my chance, and I had to ask her what she was doing at Monsieur Gallay's. Lone Star announced with a grandiose flutter that made her look completely idiotic, that she had been "exiled." Pause. She told me that her father believed that she had gone to France to learn French, but the truth was "I got me busted." By busted, she began to explain, convinced that I would not know what busted meant, I said it was okay. So she spoke about how she'd crashed her mother's car, drunk and had been taking drugs, cocaine, and all while fully naked. "Fully naked." No doubt I looked bemused by the contradiction, and that pleased her. While I had been busy "horseback riding" and "playing with your chemistry set"—as she put it and she was, again, surprisingly accurate—it had actually been my telescopes and maps of the solar system—she had been, as she told me with a lofty smile, "Real busy living." Inside my head I could hear Caleb Montgomery's voice predict that Lone Star would come to a very bad end. Inwardly I was smirking, thinking that Lone Star was like a slightly older version of the character in *Taxi Driver*, a movie I'd never seen but which I could recall Mother once describing as "a modern tragedy," an assessment that Father had laughed at, asking how she had arrived at such a verdict. My mind was reeling; Lone Star was a cliché, leaving me to wonder at it all, in fact wondering to such an extent that I almost missed her telling me that she had also been in trouble. Trouble, bad end, I could imagine Mitzi keeling over with laughter, while her mother, dear, dear Mutti, would have been simply tearing her hair out—as I felt like doing . . . Lone Star looked closely at me, inquiring had I not understood. Understand what? Liquor and drugs, yes I understood. But there was more; she stood even taller to reveal that she'd also gotten pregnant and had to have an abortion before she left for France.

My problems had been reduced to tiny pebbles. I felt sick. Why was I even listening and messing up my mind when I had better things to contemplate; asteroids and the mysteries of the solar system or on a more urgent level, finding a store which stocked jodhpurs, I only had blue jeans with me. Girls such as Lone Star/Joanie actually did exist. I asked her was her boyfriend upset. I had meant to say was she very distressed and had her boyfriend been supportive and well, what do you say to someone for whom you've nursed an instant aversion and who then proceeds to regale you with a barrage of personal disaster. But she was buoyant, pop-eyes aglitter, "Oh the guy, it didn't mean anything, he's like older, he's mom's personal trainer, well, sort of . . . no, he's not my boyfriend . . . he's just a guy." The pitcher slipped from my hand, milk everywhere. I had not realized that I had even lifted it up, but I must have, perhaps I had intended to drink from it? I began to kick the broken glass in against the wall; it disappeared into the ground cover, an entire jug smashed and concealed forevermore in the undergrowth . . . I said I had to go to the bathroom and Lone Star, Joan, Joanie, in fairness to her, suddenly seemed befuddled, with her endless arms coiled around her narrow tube of a body and looked at me with wary concern saying that she hadn't meant to dump all that on me. "Dump all that," where on earth had she learned to speak in such an ugly way, I wondered, I felt like getting sick, yet she didn't cry and instead appeared proud of her revolting adventures.

Had she wept or showed despair, a hint of remorse, I might have, I don't know, tried to show empathy, attempt to offer a comforting word. But what could I say? We may have come from the same country but it was obvious we'd inhabited very different planets.

*

Hector's fur smelled of fresh-baked cookies. It was warm and helped me gather my thoughts as we sat on the mattress, me holding him close, on my lap, his paws in my hands, my knees drawn up as if forming a protective buffer around him. Us alone; us together. He gazed into my face. I wondered what he could see of me, was I just a blurred image as that was more or less how I felt, a blurred image, barely an outline and waiting to be filled in. How would my parents have dealt with Lone Star? Mother would have fluttered and fretted, blaming herself; she was always so uncertain, excepting about clothes and lipstick, the most flattering hairdo. Father would have remained silent, a silence far worse than words, staring out to sea as if he was the commander of a doomed ship. Lone Star was beyond wayward; already burnt out. Her emotions apparently flattened into a sneering reflex. Most of her shock tactics had been exhausted. All that remained for her was full-scale crime. Perhaps she would someday knife a lover. If she did kill, it would not be in the madness of a moment as with crazy old Walt, whom I felt I should hate far more than I did. Lone Star would delay dispatching her victim until she had applied about five layers of smudgy eye shadow, all harsh blues and greens.

Was her extreme behavior a plea for help? How could anyone help her? She wasn't seeking assistance, nor did she seem obviously insane, although she must have been. Imagine if she'd had that poor baby? Hector shifted in my arms, reminding me that he was hungry. Aside from some rye bread, none of the food and cake raided from the kitchen was suitable for him and I'd forgotten a can opener for the tuna. I would have to go back and risk another heart-to-heart with Lone Star. Had she anything left to divulge? Her reasons for coming to stay at Monsieur Gallay's were still unclear. And then it hit me—thud, right between my eyes. There it was: he was her father. Was Lone Star really that conniving and apparently immune to remorse? Was she even colder than I had guessed? Her mother had probably been inclined to flash-flood love affairs. It suddenly made sickening sense; particularly given Monsieur Gallay's initial aversion to my coming to Amboise.

The mattress was very thick and old-fashioned, covered in robust stuff called ticking. Up till then I had only known about it from mentions in novels, but there I was looking at it, aware of what it was, an unbleached-looking fabric with faded blue stripes. Having fully converted to sleeping on the floor by then, I had also forgotten that Hector might wet the mattress, or more like had relaxed my vigilance, confident that unlike the little hotel in Paris, no one would notice if it became yet another stained old mattress with stories to tell. Anyhow the various chalets around the property were probably full of discarded objects; I had noticed broken furniture, stately old cabinets and a few chests of drawers, each missing at least one handle, and a pair of heavy curtains abandoned on a chair beside the window for which they must have once been destined. Unlike the stable yard much of the accommodation reflected an unfinished, work-in-progress feeling. Despite my increasingly relaxed attitude toward Hector's bed wetting I intended to buy a rubber sheet as soon as I could get to the nearest big town. And I did, following a most stressful episode in a modest department store in Tours, miming puddles and catastrophe until a small crowd of staff and random customers reached a communal agreement as to my chronic incontinence. I still had the inflatable but had managed to break the German-made pump.

Thinking back to the Dutch man in the sporting goods store and the ease of just speaking with him, I imagined what it would be like if he was my boyfriend and we were living in one of his nomadic tents. If life were a novel or a movie, we'd have gotten married after his girlfriend had died of something quick.

On heaving the mattress off the bed, I had pushed the frame out into the hall and on into one of the other rooms, a kind of lounge or living space that was empty save for a table and a bookcase with no books. No one ever said anything about the relocated bed frame. In many ways it was very easy living at Monsieur Gallay's—an informal sanctuary that appeared to have attracted its share of misfits: Lone Star, me, and even Mathieu to some extent, who was preoccupied, moody, and given to humming and puffing out his cheeks, staring off into the middle distance, almost identical to Father, who also engaged in brooding trances. Sometimes Mathieu just didn't respond, as if he didn't hear, so like Father. Mathieu's suppressed turmoil was private, aside from sporadic displays of temper. He only became animated when something went well with the horses. During the first few weeks, he would barely acknowledge my presence, then suddenly become very friendly deferring to me as if I were an expert, causing me to think we would be friends and allies, only to retreat or more like retract, and ignore me all over again. It was like watching a porcupine assume human form; you would reckon that a man like that would be right pleased with himself; good-looking, happy in his occupation, drawing pleasure from his love of horses. He was able to conduct himself. Monsieur Gallay kept him close, his right-hand man; no mistake about it. Mathieu seemed to be more than an employee—beyond even being a manager; I had spotted that right off. He was a confidant; the golden prince to Monsieur Gallay's ongoing impersonation of a dark and swarthy dwarf, not that the trainer was all that small for a Frenchman, a little bit shorter than me but he seemed more squat than he actually was. No doubt he was a ring master in control and apparently enjoying it all, although he could also become angry very quickly yet calm down within minutes as if nothing had happened. In time I was to spy him embracing the wife of one of the owners, pressing her up against a wall down in the training yard, his hand on her breast. It was furtive; the woman's sunglasses fell off yet he had managed to pick them up and neatly reposition them on her nose, his other hand still rummaging inside her jacket.

Monsieur Gallay was always looking at women, assessing them, the same way he did with horses. Mathieu was not like that. Lone Star was right; he was chaste, his eyes on your eyes and never running his glance up and down your body. I had already discovered that good-looking people, if they were any-ways bright at all, tended to be cold-water miserable. Exceptional beauty seems more curse than blessing. Why even Mother for all her enthusiasm and busy charm was never really fully happy, except for briefly, at the end with Walt and look how that had ended. Her frequent depressions could bring our household to a bewildered pause, lowered voices and tiptoe quietly . . . But that was all over and finished, in the past, and there I was in France where people had an entirely different way of looking at things.

By then I had also had my first glimpse of another girl up at the main house; she was, as Mother would have said, a beauty, and, confirming my theory, glum with it. She seemed a most unlikely housemaid; the Gallay residence was staffed by mostly older women, local wives, and mothers with homes of their own and children to look after when their working day ended. The help had probably been handpicked by Madame Gallay, a thin little woman with her hair always in a tight, tight bun, pulling the skin of her face back into a strained expression. She had a gracious way of speaking, a lady no doubt, and she wore dark red blusher on her cheek bones along with a fixed smile and well-tailored, subtle, good quality clothes. She was elegant; and favored blues and stone colors, grays, never patterns, a small scarf at her neck. Handsome clothes, which were simple, effective, and discreet; I thought I would like to dress like her when I was an adult out in the world. One look at her was enough to suspect that life with her consort was not as easy as it could have been.

The cook's son drove up each evening to bring his mother home and I could imagine her leaving one kitchen and one set of people, having fed us all, to go back and resume working in another kitchen, her own, devising another meal, one for her family. She was a cheerful soul, motherly, careful not to step on the cats as she carried dishes out to the table; she referred to those squalling parasites as "mes enfants" and never lost patience with the way, for all their stateliness, they'd grab at everything. The skin on her face made me think of wizened apples, lined and soft, flushed pink on sallow. But the sullen housemaid, well I had never actually witnessed her doing anything, aside from drinking coffee, and moving about, very slowly, as if she doubted her balance. I swear she was never without a cup in her hand. Maybe she had gin in the cup but no, I guess it was coffee, always coffee. Her hair was black and very thick, swinging loose down beyond her shoulders, and she would sit and braid it and then shake it all out before just braiding it all over again. I gave up saying hello to her as she always looked straight through me. She had those smoky blue-gray eyes that create the impression of being very dark brown yet aren't that color at all and she had delicate black eyebrows, slightly quizzical. Could be she'd have made a delectable spy, what with her fatalistic air of mystery and angry sorrow, her essential resentment. But real-life spies are nondescript and anonymous, blending with the wallpaper along with the

rest of us. She was a femme fatale, primed to leave devastation
in her wake. No one in Richmond would have tolerated such an
attitude from a domestic, but then she would hardly be working as one back home, where she'd be posing for photographers,
her face her fortune. Well, well, I'd thought to myself, instead
there she was in rural France and still waiting for something to
happen, some agent or a photographer to take the impromptu
shot that would change her life. The servant thing in France was
completely different, far more relaxed, some of them acted as if
they were doing you a favor. Mrs. Faulkner was so correct with
her perfected variation of an English butler's haughty reserve, yet
she was always deferential.

From what I had seen in Monsieur Gallay's realm the help
was like family retainers, even the yardmen wandered about as
if they were hobby gardeners who just happened to sweep the
paths and clean out the stables, but only for keeping busy not
on account of being paid to work. None of the maids at any
Richmond home would have been as insolent to me as that girl.
Everything in France was different and for the first time in my
life I was not a guest, the grumpy Cinderella probably classified
me as low-grade yard staff, and yes, that did amuse me some.
Mother would have studied her carefully. Being a connoisseur of
female beauty, she was always generous in her praise and equally
regretful if a girl or woman were to have some slight defect, a
nose that bit too big, a small mouth, thin lips, poor carriage,
a weak chin or a heavy jaw . . . There was no point in provoking the girl and as she appeared to have nothing to do with the
horses we would have no contact and that suited me just fine.
Some weeks later when I was settled into a riding routine and
enjoying it, Monsieur Gallay had sent me up to the farmhouse
in search of a horse passport he had reckoned on having left on
the kitchen table. Running an errand was my reward for riding

well and I was only too pleased to scoot up for the book, always eager for a chance to snoop around, I mean, to just have a look, it was such a lovely house with an ease of style which was new to me. Well there sat the girl, with her inevitable cup of coffee and one of those plunger coffee pot things, a French press, there on the table along with the remains of her breakfast. It must have been heading for noon. She was reading a glossy magazine, no doubt glowering at the fashion models that had already been discovered, and as usual, she ignored me.

One of the other women was busy at the big stove, tending to three large pots bubbling away. Why, that lady cooking made me think of an orchestral conductor, head bobbing here and there, coordinating all the cauldrons which together had created a heavy steam. My face felt damp in the condensation, hers looked positively wet. It turned out she was making jam.

There was no sign of the passport so I began making gestures, the cook smiled apologetically, she didn't understand me. The girl stood up and made clear she was resenting the effort it required and she walked over to a large dresser. It was the first time I had seen her move, she had her back to me and was wearing a short robe and she waddled most unbecomingly, earthbound I'd call it, although she was not exactly overweight, more generously shapely—Mother's phrase. Almost noon and not even dressed for the day, what kind of maid was she? Perhaps she wasn't feeling well and I do recall being disappointed on noticing that she had thick, heavy ankles. No ankles at all as Mother would have lamented, searing regret in her voice. The kitchen beauty was maybe about average height for what I had seen of French women, which was short. Yet she had big, flat feet just like a hobbit, with squashed little cocktail sausage toes. Big, ugly flat feet, slapping along the kitchen floor. Bamm-Bamm from *The Flintstones* would be a good comparison. You would think that a girl like that, Mother would have ventured, blessed with "such a face," but legs so bad, would wear long romantic dresses and "work on her posture." Mother took the idea of making the most of whatever God had given a body very seriously indeed. Smack, the passport landed on the table and the girl flopped down, picked up her magazine, and resumed reading without even a nod to me. "Thank you kindly," I heard my voice ring out, a well brought up Richmond girl learning all about how the French choose to conduct themselves.

*

The cake was very good, moist and drenched in a mix of chocolate icing and honey syrup. It had been the only thing I ate before preparing to sneak back for the can opener so as to open Hector's tuna. What time was it, I wondered. Off I set, back to the kitchen; first I stared down deep into his clouded eyes and told him I would hurry. A body would think I was about to race into the jungle, braving enemy lines and a succession of wild animals, all sent to test me on my way to fetch a can opener. Again, I braced myself before laughing at my mental image of bending down to smear mud on my face, hoping the whites of my eyes would not give me away. "Courage mon ami," I said in my D'Artagnan voice, aware that poor Hector could not hear a word, I held his adorable little face in my hands, and was about to trot out in my stocking feet, but thought better of it, all that gravel, and forced my hot and tired feet back into my boots.

No sign of Lone Star; I just about reached the door of the little house that had become home to me and Hector, and was ready to commence breathing normally again, when I heard movement behind me. It was Mathieu. He said we would have a meeting down at the stables and draw up a plan with the young horses and the ones sent in for re-schooling; we needed a schedule he said, a routine, it sounded like "routan." He looked very serious, I felt like laughing. Then he mentioned that Monsieur Gallay wanted to discuss terms with me. For a minute I wondered what the trainer intended to charge me for riding his horses, him being such a wealthy man scarcely in need of more money. But he would be paying me. Mathieu was so solemn, more laughter began bubbling up my throat. I coughed instead and wondered if he had a girlfriend or was he really as priest like as Lone Star claimed. "I declare to Jesus," she had sighed in one of her more mellow moments, "Belmondo's devoted his life to horses the way some folks think about God and holy stuff. Ain't it a full crying shame?"

The boss, as Mathieu referred to Monsieur Gallay, paid well and also favored special bonuses; some horses required more work, there were some, he said, who were like mysteries waiting to be solved. "You could earn much money," he intimated. All very interesting I thought, aware that I had a considerable amount with me and had never viewed riding as employment, more like an instinctive passion. My stay at Amboise was to facilitate Hector, not determine my future. Commerce did not interest me. Science was different, it was cerebral, a different class of love. The real work would begin tomorrow, proclaimed Mathieu, his eyes shining and he said he knew I would be marvelous. He pronounced it in the French and it sounded very alluring indeed, I felt happy. I always found it embarrassing being praised yet I love it, praise I mean; it meant more than stacks of fancy gifts tied up with ribbon. Mother always gave me things; they never meant much. I would have preferred something else entirely, a kinship.

Just as he was walking away, advising me to take it easy for the rest of the day, he'd stared intently at the can opener and advised me not to get drunk, we had work to do. Well I'd never even tasted beer, I assured him, explaining I'd borrowed it to open a can of tuna for Hector and asked him if there was a car I could use to drive off to a store to get some dog food. Just as I was regretting not having pretended I was an alcoholic so as to shock him, he said I could use one of the jeeps, before nodding over at a gray station wagon that I must have walked by more than a dozen times even at that early stage without noticing. It was parked over by the kitchen chalet. Perhaps it was a staff car? It suited me as I reckoned that the engine would be less powerful than any of the jeeps. Not having driven for a long time, and to be honest, not that often, I knew my driving to be a little shaky, in fact I wasn't much good and didn't even have a license. My asking if it had a gear stick must have caused him to tell me to hurry and that he would drive me to the village for my pet food. He said to hurry; he had to be back for a phone call. I was about to get my wallet, but he said he had money and we needed to go, he had to be back for the call. From his girlfriend perhaps? I wondered.

Never before in my life had I had such an awareness of being watched. My face was burning as I fumbled with the passenger door handle, an image of Lone Star, standing tall, unwinding like a serpent, her hard bulging eyes, like gray-green marbles, narrowing in concentration as she hexed me. I tensed, expecting the car to burst into flames as her precious Belmondo innocently drove off with me beside him and all just to buy some dog food, elopement a million miles from our minds. Perhaps I laughed or made some little sound, a gulp. "Okay?" he inquired, asking if I suffered from car sickness. I reminded him I was American. He laughed at that. "You people drive everywhere," he said. Not me,

I thought, as I reached for the safety belt, he pointed out there weren't any, we were in France not the United States. It was an automatic; I wouldn't have been able to drive it and could just about manage a gear stick. I stared straight ahead, my eyes watering with the strain of trying not to look at him, in case I laughed, burped, vomited. Silence. Just like being with Father. Mathieu pushed a cassette into the slot on the deck and this really horrible pop music blared forth. It reminded me of an old 1960s group called The Monkees, four men who made an awful racket. A couple of women were singing on Mathieu's tape, there was a high, clear voice, more pure than the other. The thought struck me that maybe one of them was his girlfriend. He was singing along, and seemed to know every word. As I was sitting there mesmerized by the bouncy raucousness, the jingle-badness of it, he turned and asked my opinion. It was probably a homemade tape, I decided. Perhaps he was one of the performers. Anxious not to hurt his feelings I gushed that it was great and asked was he singing on it, was that his band—me sounding all sincere and interested. No, no he replied and said "ABBA" as if it were a sacred word and so, well, all that caterwauling turned out to belong to an internationally famous Swedish pop group. I was surprised by two things; the success of such trite noise—trite, another of Father's words. So many words I'd first heard him say. And then quick, consult a dictionary. Memorize the word, Father's word, and make it mine. A thief in the night. Snap and it's mine, my word. Now where was I? Oh yes the music, trite, trivial . . . And then there was also the stretching sensation of my fake smile. It actually hurt. I imagined that were I to touch my face, the smile would peel away in my fingers like a Halloween mask. Mathieu continued singing, as toneless as a deaf man but he seemed happy. Just for a moment I pretended that he was my boyfriend and we were driving along to the grocery store before going home together to cook supper. But boys like him would never think that way about someone like me. I felt he regarded me as an able younger brother and I sat there, conscious Mathieu could be real mean, having seen him ignore Lone Star's persistent comments, but then reasoned maybe he was just being protective and he did despise the way she conducted herself, goading him all the time.

The tape droned on, complete with that disco thud masquerading as beat, all the way back to Monsieur Gallay's and Mathieu had droned on along with it, me just sitting there. As we pulled up, he asked me if I'd had Hector since he was a puppy, and I told Mathieu about him finding me in the park back in Paris and all. He smiled and said I was good to have saved a little old dog. I wanted to say that Hector had saved me and was just about to tell him that Hector was the reason I had fought so hard for the job, but Mathieu had become preoccupied again, and was no longer listening. His thoughts had moved off elsewhere, so like Father; small, small world. The first shopping bag burst, causing cans of dog food to scatter across the gravel. Mathieu did not appear to notice and hurried on over to the office for his call.

Lone Star was suddenly standing at the front of the car, her hands flat on the bonnet, her voice quivered and rasped as she asked had he taken me out for a drink. "Or something, you guys just have a date? Did he, you know . . . ?" I told her I'd needed dog food and that Mathieu had sung loudly all the way there and back, and I had nothing to report, aside from the picturesque countryside, some lovely houses, more of those fairy tale castles, other estates involved in winemaking and vineyards . . . and by the way had she ever heard of ABBA. But she had already high-stepped away, still wearing her red cowboy boots, without even offering to carry some of the grocery bags and there were at least five or six of them in the back clearly visible, with the tailgate still wide open. I had bought all the dog food in stock, along with some sacks of the dry mix and Mathieu explained that the man at the counter had asked if we ran a boarding kennel. Mathieu told him that we had horses. That must have set the salesperson thinking that we fed them dog food. My arms full of loose cans I hurried to Hector, he was always glad of my company. My Hector dog, we were an uncomplicated couple.

Relief must have made Lone Star feel more benevolent toward me. At supper that evening by way of greeting she said had she known I was going to the grocery store she would have come along as she was "clean out" of potato chips. Then she lowered her voice and whispered that she reckoned that she would soon "be needing" some Tampax. "I guess I am getting back to normal down there, know what I mean?" I smiled curtly, hoping to discourage further intimacies. She must have misinterpreted it as a sign of interest and she was off, tossing back her hair as a prelude to peering deep into my eyes and prefacing it all with she "had been thinking some" and that she felt real bad about shocking me. "On account of you being so sheltered from the world and all, like you know, protected, like, I mean, from all human experience . . ."

Everyone has a limit, even me. It was very strange, I had endured far worse from her, insults without even reacting, but that time I simply turned, shouting back at her what in hell did she think she knew of my life? Mother had been shot dead by her lover in a street full of people and all while a goddamn TV commercial was being made . . . my beloved mentor had gone and had himself buried alive, or drunken alive, what's the difference? . . . Father had sold my horse . . . He had decided I should do history, not science . . . and don't get me started on the subject of my eyes . . . Who in hell was she to assume anything about my life, I hissed. Lone Star's marble gaze widened and she muttered,

"What a son of a bitch." Again, I pounced. "Father is not a son of a bitch, he is a great man," I had hollered, shrieking like a five-year-old. I told her that he had made fantastic advances in the treatment of equine bone and joint conditions, that he was cultured, civilized, neither of which she would understand; that he was "betrayed and bereaved . . ." I repeated over and over that he was a great man, must have sounded as if I was a real daddy's girl before standing up so suddenly that she drew back, fear in her eyes, alarm. Did she seriously think that I was about to strike her? But slow, quiet, uncool me was shaking with fury, declaring Father's work was global and far more important than making stupid cardboard boxes. Lone Star's expression froze in bewilderment. "Jesus," she said, "I wasn't talking about your dad, I meant the guy who killed your mom; I meant that he was a real son of a bitch. Wow, so your mom, Jesus, blasted just like in the movies . . . fucking awesome. No wonder you're so weird . . . I mean . . ."

For once she was not trying to taunt me; even in my rage I could see that. Lone Star was completely shocked; it was as if she had been simply astounded by my revelations, my vile and unsavory disclosures, which she was attempting to assimilate. The yardmen began trooping in to eat and I glared at her, warning her silently, with a tight, mean stare intended to convey true menace, she'd better keep her peace or else . . . She remained quiet throughout the meal, ate very little, picked at the food, and went out without her usual attempt at banter. No one took any notice.

*

Lone Star's change of attitude was comic; on occasion—spectacularly funny. And also touching, she was displaying abject atonement. I wanted to like this new person, although certain we would never be friends. For a few days she was to circle carefully around me, hovering, as if she was a nurse attending a patient in remission, before finally asking me if it, meaning my messed up, pointless little life, still hurt.

She was subdued and it made me think that she had been practicing solemnity before the mirror in her bedroom much as I would have done in her position, me always being so careful, so earnest. I could imagine her busily rehearsing expressions of heartfelt concern, sincerity being an entirely new sensation for her as she seemed to have been living an ongoing soap opera, although at least it was one of her own making. I was merely an onlooker in mine and yet again images of that night spent with Marc slithered into my mind, infiltrating my thoughts, making me feel dirty and stained, unclean and befouled. It's a lot easier being small, make a wish and there I was seven all over again, with a fairy princess on my birthday cake and happily dreaming of becoming a ballerina, before I discovered horses, Father's art books, and science all of which helped turn me into a different kind of dreamer, gazing at the stars, seduced by the night skies . . . and reading about those astronomers, the ghosts that became my heroes.

The next morning I was down early for breakfast, feeling helpless and fated; wondering how many of his future champions Mathieu would have selected for me to try. What kind of horses, how difficult, what expectations, and would there be anyone watching how I got along with them, would I even be able to ride a succession of very different horses? Who was I fooling? Over and over again, what had I gotten myself into? Me, a privileged and admittedly spoiled girl from Richmond, Virginia, who was quietly angry at everything; for sure, I was nervous, but also excited. Again Hector wanted to stay outside after I had fed him, I knew he was eager to explore, do dog things, mark territory and he seemed very well, alert and confident. Coming to Amboise had renewed him. The little old city dog had taken to life in the countryside, albeit a restricted one. But I couldn't leave him mooching on his own; he would have to wait for my return at lunchtime. Again I had set him up before the screen door, with his famous white cup filled with fresh water and my T-shirt for comfort. At least he could sniff the breeze coming in through the mesh and enjoy the sun until I got back.

Before anyone else had appeared at the table I had eaten two helpings of some kind of hot oatmeal cereal, and was working through several pieces of toast, a nutty brown bread with honey dripping from each delicious slice. Mrs. Faulkner's hotcakes came to mind. The ones they made in France were very thin, flimsy, like paper, real bland. Two of the cats were busy fighting over my empty oatmeal dish when the cook bustled in, smiling as always, with a bowl of hot chocolate. She removed the squalling banshees and walked back to the kitchen, an outraged bundle under each arm. It was the first time I had seen anyone other than Lone Star attempting to deal with them, she would hiss, "Scat cat, or I'll skin you to the bare, bare bone," and they'd ignore her, accustomed as they were to full liberty, walking in and on and over the food without fear of correction. I'd gotten into the habit of huddling over my plate as if I was a prison inmate, blocking their access to it and trying to fend off the hairs that seemed to affix to anything I ate.

Her boots, heels hitting the floor, announced she was on her way, if walking with purpose instead of the customary undulating slink. "Here you take this," she said, without even a good morning or her usual, "How ya doing." I glanced up and there she stood, handing over a little figurine made of fired clay. It had a ragged cap of black hair glued to its head. It looked as if it was Mexican, a souvenir manufactured with serious symbolic aspirations. She told me it was for discouraging evil spirits. "Like, yeah I know it's too late for that, but it might help you some, from now on, maybe with those horses they've got lined up for you and all." She seemed to think I was on my way to the lion's den. Perhaps I was. But she was intent, deadly serious, and I thanked her, seeing her perhaps for what she actually was, just another miserable human, eager to belong, to mean something to someone. I knew the feeling; having lived with it all the time. I asked her where she had gotten the little doll and had she had it long and she should really keep it. It transpired that she had bought it in Paris during one of the day trips she had taken there with Madame Gallay. Mention of those outings made me recall being with Mother and our afternoon high teas at The Clock Tower. When Lone Star had first arrived, the owner's wife had apparently made a real effort at welcoming her before Lone Star had thrown a tantrum about something, causing Madame Gallay to withdraw and subsequently avoid her unpredictable guest, leaving her needs to the boss, who in turn completely ignored Lone Star. Yet his attitude made me wonder if it was all an act, me beginning to believe in my new powers of deduction and all; did they have a private relationship? Had they been involved? That kept me on my toes for a while, trying to solve the baffling little mystery. Again I had my chance to ask why Lone Star had come to the Gallay estate and at last, seized it.

It had all happened through her mother as I had suspected. It was she who'd met Monsieur Gallay at Cannes years earlier, he had been there with a party of trainers and horse owners—actors do love horses—attending the famous movie festival. Lone Star's mother was also there in the south of France, going to all the parties along with other aspiring young starlets. "Mom was in the movies you know, like usually playing the beautiful girl who goes and gets herself shot or something . . . Jesus, sorry, ooops . . . fuck it . . . I didn't mean that . . . shit . . ."

Mathieu arrived in to eat. He had gotten a haircut, a real close one, it made him look younger. I hadn't noticed until then that his ears stuck out slightly. Nor had Lone Star, and seeing them so newly exposed, pounced, "Hey Belmondo you look like one of the seven dwarfs," and she suggested he'd better get himself a hat until his hair grew back. He did not react but she battled on, desperate for his attention and she just blurted out that he should ask Guy—Guy was Monsieur Gallay's first name—to give Helen a horse as her daddy had sold hers and that as Guy had about a million of the overgrown ponies, he would never miss one. Again, Mathieu ignored her causing Lone Star to sigh loud and long, before saying to me, that she would "personally" ask Guy to give me a new horse.

Perhaps five minutes passed, very slowly. Peacetime conditions prevailed at the table, but not for long. No one was breathing, or so it had seemed, tension filled the space as if it was a dangerous gas seeping up from under the floor, working its way over our heads. Then Mathieu turned to me and asked how many horses I had back home in America. I loved the way he said "America," as if it was a strange and exotic place. Father owned several, I said, well many, horses and I'd always had a few to ride, "but I've never really owned one." That was all I said. I could remember too clearly the day Father had reminded me of that, along with my being a dilettante and an amateur intellectual lacking in motivation and "the competitive edge." Obviously I didn't say that bit out loud. Mathieu seemed surprised by my not having had a horse of my own and he was very interested in the story, I certainly had his attention. Lone

Star's as well as she stared at me, wearing that stricken expression that could appear and completely transform her face whenever she feared I had engaged Mathieu's curiosity. He already knew something; I could tell. Monsieur Gallay must have mentioned my having bragged at Longchamp about riding a horse that the French federation had subsequently purchased. "That must have been good, no?" Good that he sold it? I asked, but knew that he meant that the horse was obviously good before he had even explained his remark. I was not entirely sure that I wanted to go back over the whole mess but it was something to talk about and it made a change from enduring Lone Star's efforts at attracting Mathieu, and having to witness his subsequent rebuffs. I told him that the German Olympic rider I'd mentioned had talent-scouted the horse and that the French buyers had paid a lot of money. He looked thoughtful, sifting through the information. I excused myself and went out to the bathroom, but not because I needed to go. An unexpected tightness had come from nowhere and caught my throat as well as my chest and I felt I would gag. Never knew why, it was the oddest sensation of a pressure and I also wanted to be alone, to gather myself before the session. I was going to have to prove myself, be tested. I wanted to do well. Sitting on the toilet lid and taking deep breaths reminded me of how sick I was of humans and that I had no intention of allowing Mathieu to play me off against Lone Star. On top of that neither her newfound sympathy or the horse she was planning to secure for me were going to be a way for her to ingratiate herself with Mathieu. I was learning how to protect myself from the games people play, or so I thought.

By the third horse on that first morning my blue jeans had split. They were the loosest of the four pairs I had with me and I needed to buy some riding britches. I was just feeling my way and trying to assess my new charges with light flat work, no jumping for the moment. The indoor had several advantages, aside from reducing the chances of a low-flying airplane, such as a crop sprayer. I had had a few scares with horses spooking on account of those noisy machines back home, or a bird or anything that might scare a horse. I remembered Billy Bob's mystery stag and its effect on Galileo. There was also the bonus of privacy and a moment to figure out exactly what was going on. Mathieu had told me that he would be working with me and that Monsieur Gallay would continue to concentrate on the racehorses now that Mathieu had me working for them. A yard-man had appeared leading a fourth horse, a young chestnut mare that was already competing but had been sent back for urgent re-schooling as she had some dangerous habits, including rolling with a rider on her back. Great, I thought, so I can expect to get squashed. She went fine on the flat. So far so good I smirked. Mathieu said to cool her down and that we would have lunch.

On the way back up to the stable yard he asked me if I had come to France to try and get my horse back. "What horse?" Mathieu looked blank, and paused before explaining that he meant the horse that the federation had bought. I replied, more sharply than I had intended that Galileo was never mine; he'd never even had a name. I had just been calling him Galileo. "But you followed him here to France," persisted Mathieu, saying he found it very touching. He looked up at me, I was still sitting on the mare and he had been walking along beside us. There he stood, Mathieu, his funny ears sticking out, and his eyes reduced to slits, squinting into the sun, and no, he was not kidding. He told me that I was brave and that he could see that I was determined to get the horse back. All of this I denied, telling him that he was quite wrong, I didn't even know what Galileo was being called. By then he had probably been given a name as the French federation would have registered him. "But you loved that horse," declared Mathieu. No I did not, he was a bully. He had taught me a lot, I said, and I saw the very real surprise that came over Mathieu's face as I told him that I had been frightened of Galileo, that I had hated him, hated him with a passion, and I was glad he was gone. It surprised me too. I had ridden him for Billy Bob because he wanted me to become good—and so had I. What had hurt me was the sneaky way Father had sold him, without even telling me. It was the first time that I had put all of that into words and it was Mathieu that I'd told. Never even to Mitzi had I admitted being scared of Galileo; I guess I liked her thinking I was a serious rider and far too cool to be nervous. I didn't mind Mathieu knowing I wasn't that heroic, or insane. That was when I knew that I wanted him to like me.

*

It was not to last, Lone Star's transformation or whatever it was. When Mathieu and I went back up to the dining chalet for lunch, she was there, as if waiting for an explanation from us. She was doing her nails, a task she appeared to perform almost every other day, and from what I could tell, always in public. She was proud of her hands which were long and thin, very white, as were her fingers—reminding me of an evil witch in a fairy tale. Never having been interested in fingernails, I did not pay much heed. The smell of nail polish and the remover stuff was overpowering, I hated it, and always had since I was small and had first encountered it in Mother's slipstream as she prepared to venture forth and meet the world. When I had mentioned my phobia to Mitzi she had laughed, saying that she loved the smell of nail polish and the remover. Most normal girls do, she'd pointed out, but it was yet another of the many cosmetic smells that made my eyes water, along with the tang of strong perfume, whereas floor wax, fresh laundry, new-mowed grass, and best of all, the beautiful smell of horses, always made me confident that all was well in God's universe. Lone Star sat, full of purpose, an array of little bottles lined up before her. She put at least three colors on each nail, ceremoniously applying the polish as carefully as if she was putting the finishing touches to miniscule works of art. Watching her always reminded me of the time Sheriff Hodge had spent an entire year making a huge model of the battlefield at Gettysburg: he had hand-painted all the soldiers, tiny little figures, along with their horses, the fallen as well as the ragged survivors. It was a spectacular panorama, including burnt-out homesteads and trees, canons, wagons, bandages red with blood wound around heads smaller than a garden pea, all executed with exact detail and such patience. He also collected vintage train sets, beautiful things, he used to say the finest gift outside of a horse anyone could give to man or boy was a model train.

Lone Star's face, taut with anxiety, was pale; she glanced up, wary and alert. Her eyes only seemed big because they were so prominent, had they been set flat into her head they would have been smaller than average I concluded, meanly. Mathieu went on into the kitchen; he'd asked for sandwiches and some salad to be left out for us and re-emerged carrying a large pot of coffee and two cups. Lone Star stiffened and immediately asked what about her. Mathieu didn't react and turned to go back into the kitchen. There was going to be a showdown of sorts I sensed and hurried in to fetch a cup for her and a saucer as well as a plate and some napkins, a nicety I had acquired from Mrs. Faulkner, no meal too small not to have a napkin. Mathieu was already taking a plate of sandwiches off a tray and said that the lunch was only a snack and that it was for us, as we were working and

Lone Star could prepare her own. He asked me to bring in the bowl of salad. Lone Star's face again wore that familiar aggrieved expression. Then he said that he would drive me into Tours to buy some riding gear, I'd mentioned needing jodhpurs.

Before I could thank him, Lone Star dived in, remarking that the horses did not overly care about my wardrobe and then said she'd come along. "No," snapped Mathieu. Just a single, flinty "no" and well, she stood up, tears welling, and swept the coffee pot and most of the sandwiches and the other things clear off the table. He responded by sending her little bottles scattering to the floor and they both yelled at each other; he in French, she in English with plenty of swear words shared out between them. Well it was downright hideous to watch. I went back into the kitchen and poured some milk into a saucepan and put it on the stove. I made myself hot chocolate and grilled a couple of cheese sandwiches using the only cheddar I could find among all the soft, smelly cheeses, and remained in the kitchen, eating standing up. The walls were thick yet her screaming penetrated them. The door slammed as someone barged out. But I stayed put and heated more milk; I had no interest in taking sides and wanted to eat. Mother had had her tantrums from time to time, but her frustration had been different, never as aggressive as Lone Star's. It was more plaintive; yes plaintive, that was the word.

There was another chocolate cake, moist sponge, thick, thick icing, beckoning "eat me, eat me." I obeyed and contented myself with taking a greedy slice although I could have easily had a second. Then I cleared up my little mess and went out. Mathieu glanced up at me. At least he looked embarassed and asked what I had made of the outburst. All I said was something about needing to check on Hector before we went back to the horses. He suggested bringing him along to Tours with us. Hector would love the outing and it pleased me not having to ask if he could come. I was not about to make a case for Lone Star coming too.

That afternoon, I rode another three horses, short little introductory sessions and then Mathieu said we would finish early so that we could get to Tours before the saddlers closed. He gave me some money. I must have looked surprised but did remember to thank him. The last thing I needed was money; I had quite an amount of it, not counting intact books of traveler's checks I hadn't gotten round to using. Mathieu had asked Monsieur Gallay for an advance on my pay as he knew I would need it for my new riding hat, they were expensive. It was thoughtful of him. The drive there seemed about to be a repeat of the previous one as he put on the ABBA tape and the racket again filled the car, with him singing along, flat as a burst tire. The windows were closed and I realized that Hector had a stronger doggy odor than I'd previously noticed, maybe because I was usually on my own with him. So I asked Mathieu if he minded my opening the window. It was as if I had indicated an interest in conversation. Mathieu turned down the music and asked me about Galileo, what had happened, he wanted to know, and I began at the beginning; from the client that having asked Father for a horse, then backed out of the deal, which angered Father on account of his having bred the horse from one of his special mares. I told him about how Billy Bob had gotten me riding him and all the other stuff, about me bringing him over for those sessions with Herr Bernhard, me making plans, and then it all ending so disappointingly with the sale. It seemed such a long time ago. Then just out of the blue, he asked me why Galileo, it was an Italian name and I told him about my interest in science, the heavens, my collection of telescopes. He laughed and said he could just about remember the moon landing and that he had never met a girl with an interest in "outer space." How to answer that . . .

We reached Tours in time and I bought two pairs of English jodhpurs like the ones I had back home and a German pair with suede insets, all the French britches in my size were way too small. I also bought gloves although I never wore them outside of competition but I guess I wanted to appear professional and organized. Finding a hat to fit took about an hour, always tends to, I have a small head, and there was a extensive selection to work my way through. It didn't matter, Mathieu was busy. He had ordered several saddles to be made for specific horses and he and the two saddle-makers were all very serious, it seemed as if it was all a matter of life and death. Herr Bernhard would have understood. Mathieu shared his intensity. It made me begin to question the obsessive way I looked at things. Watching him, it seemed, would teach me a great deal about myself and yes, I did want to change, and become more like Mitzi, open and relaxed about living.

The men helped him load the new saddles. The smell of fresh leather filled the car, masking Hector's pungent scent. My little dog was happy to see us and we drove down the street to a grocery store. I got more dog food and carried it out to the station wagon beside which Mathieu was already standing, holding two large, bowl-like paper cartons of ice cream, plastic spoons standing to attention in them, like flag poles. He said he hoped that the ice cream would give me strength. It was prophetic. The next day's riding was tough and it was the first time I had ever experienced exhaustion. After supper Mathieu had begun to sing, and a few of the stable staff who had also eaten with us sang along with him. It took me a minute to recognize that the song they were murdering was John Denver's "Rocky Mountain High." Lone Star knew the song and well, she certainly surprised

everyone, Mathieu included. As clear as a bell and very tuneful
with that warm throaty resonance really good singers have. It
reminded me of Father once mentioning to Caleb Montgomery
that he had been shocked on meeting two very fine American
sopranos who had truly horrific speaking voices, sharp and grat-
ing, "Most disconcerting discovery oh me oh my, gifted singers
sounding like feuding fish wives." So good was Lone Star's voice
that even Mathieu stopped trying to sing, and she continued
alone, summoning another Denver song, that one about country
roads taking her home to the place she adores. The yardmen were
impressed. She was awfully good. All I wanted to do was go to
bed but I forced myself to stay awake, it would have been almost
cruel to leave just as she was finally getting attention and there
she was, the irony of it, ready to sing all night. But without warning the men stood as one and left to watch a TV documentary
about the life and times of a famous Belgian cyclist who had won
the Tour de France five times. I told her that she was really good,
but she stopped singing as soon as Mathieu left. She wanted to
hear about the shopping trip. Nothing to report I assured her; I
was too tired to speak.

Yet there had been something; Mathieu had mentioned that
when he outgrew his first pony, his parents had given it to his
cousin, a little girl. But he had loved the pony and went on
hunger strike to get her back. "I ate no food, only apples I took
secretly from the orchard. For maybe four days my parents had
to watch me push away my plate, and worried I would starve
myself so I win—I got my pony back." That must have been
very hard on the little girl, I thought, it was not as if the pony
was being sold off to a stranger. It made me think that Mathieu
was no saint after all and underneath his otherworldly exterior
he could be as selfish as the rest of us.

For the first few weeks, I would go to bed soon after supper; out like a light. Sometimes I slept in my clothes. Why once I woke with my toothbrush still in my hand. I've never slept as heavily. Hector just curled up beside me and the two of us would sleep through the night. And I did sleep, too tired to dream and glad to be free of the nightmares in which Mrs. Faulkner often walked into a dank and filthy cave that was festooned with cobwebs, to find me sitting on a bed wearing Marc's stomach-churning pink tracksuit top, him standing naked, leering at her, his little penis, which appeared to be detachable, held firmly in his hand. There had been other nightmares, that final image of Mother, but with far more blood; blood gushing from her mouth, her eyes, her heart. There were times when Walt's face would appear in the sky and replace the moon or I would see myself being caught stealing what had become Hector's white cup, and be shamed by the disappointment in the eyes of the obliging waitress who'd tried to help me. Then there had been the one in which I was swimming for my life, being pursued by Father's wraith-like fish and him wearing his Count Dracula cape, all the while waving my science project above his head. So many demons and all swarming revoltingly around in my head.

Throughout that period of bone-tiredness my brain just seemed to shut down at night and I went into a coma. Nothing would wake me until I had slept for close on ten or eleven hours, recharging like a battery. Then morning, rise from the mattress, have a shower, food, more horses; then food, more horses. Hector was my support, urging me on for another day. I love riding yet recognized that had I been schooling horses for a serious job, month in, year out, I would have soured pretty quickly. But this was for Hector, being in Amboise was ideal for him and I was loving it too and was not ready to talk to Father or even Mitzi. My mind needed to heal; I wanted to forget. As I became more confident with Mathieu I suggested that we move some of the sessions in the outdoor arena, just for variety for the horses—if also for me. He agreed. He sat well on a horse, but he was happiest just walking one and giving orders, his balance was surprisingly poor and eventually he told me he hated jumping.

My legs were strengthening up again. But I still got tired and would become drowsy at the supper table. Lone Star said that I didn't have to worry about falling off the horses, "all that fresh air is gonna kill you." We often ended one of the afternoon sessions with a little walk out along the perimeter of the estate; it was beautiful, through woodland and past some little lakes. If the horses even spooked the slightest twitch Mathieu would tense up and lean forward, grabbing at the mane. He was awful nervous and after a few of these little cool down walks he told me that he had had a bad fall and his nerve was gone. I was glad that he felt he could tell me, most people would never admit that to another rider. I told him about Galileo dumping me off onto the jump and then stomping on me, not forgetting the kick to the ribs. We went back and I rode another couple of horses in the indoor until it was dark. It was getting late in the year and it could be very cold in the mornings with heavy frost. Lone Star finally took to wearing more clothes and sometimes she would sit quietly in the indoor arena watching the sessions and then later ask me how come I didn't go crazy with boredom.

It became easier, I was not so tired. One evening at supper Mathieu asked me had I seen *The Mission* and that it was on at the local movie house. Would I come with him, he asked, he wanted to see it. Lone Star said she would "grace you with my presence" but Mathieu said no, he was inviting me. Lone Star reared up and said that just about everybody in the Western world, including "Outer Mongolia and probably most of the aliens on Mars and stuff" had already seen "the fucking thing" and she shouted that it figured that it had finally arrived in the middle of nowhere. "It's a crappy movie; I just wouldn't mind looking at that cute skinny English guy playing the big whistle thing. Shit, why can't I come too?" She whined and wheedled, suddenly upset and was about to cry, pounding her fists on the table. He refused to reconsider and she barged out. I was about to say I didn't want to see it. But then Monsieur Gallay came in, remarking that he had seen Lone Star leaving, "shouting and complaining, such a miserable person, never content. She should be tied to a stake, ah yes . . . Joanie of Arc." Delighted with his joke, he smiled over at Mathieu and winked, probably still unaware I knew her name was Joan, he said to me that he had told her mother that he would teach the girl to ride and that all Annette had said was, "I wish you luck." Monsieur Gallay shrugged and said that she had been right, "No human could help that girl, she is defective, no?" Then he mentioned *The Mission* and he also asked had I seen it. I said no. "Then go. Why not? It would be good for you to relax, do something not involved with horses." He put some cash on the table as if he was at a church service and said for us to have a good time. The lord of the manor, I wasn't sure whether to be grateful or just feel insulted as if he felt I needed either his permission or his money or both. There was something slightly unwholesome about him what with all his secrets, yet ever the polite young girl I thanked him. Mathieu was pleased. "Good, we go, we leave in fifteen minutes." I hurried over to Hector. It would be the first evening that I had not just collapsed into bed with him. I walked out onto the little patio and he lifted his leg against all three of the large planters, one by one. "Such a great little man," I said and assured him with a hug that I would be back—but felt guilty about leaving him there on the mattress when he had gotten so used to me just collapsing down beside him.

Was I rejoicing? Well yes and no. Pathetic and all as it sounds it was my first ever date and of course as soon as I had realized that, I was wondering if the fiasco with Marc would count as the first but no that was a setup, he had seen me as a stupid tourist ripe for being hoodwinked. I brushed my hair and noticed that it was very long, my bangs were falling into my eyes. Messy for sure, but at least my hair was clean. I wondered about putting it into a pony tail, but no, why give Mathieu the impression I was trying to look different. Yet he had changed his clothes and doused himself in a sharp, lemony aftershave, causing me to gag in the car. He smiled, settled in the seat, and reached for the tape. I suggested putting it on at full volume and opening the windows as we drove through the darkness. He thought that was a great idea, having his music fill the night. The evening breeze quickly dealt with the aftershave.

The movie house was a cute little place; it looked like a Quaker Meeting House and turned out to have been a lace-making factory. Mathieu collected the tickets, there were only a few left. *The Mission* had been nominated for seven Academy Awards and there it was, about to be screened for a capacity crowd in a small town in the Loire Valley. I felt I was being privy to a special event. Mathieu told me to wait; I thought he was going to the men's room. He came back with chocolates and two large bags of candy, some kind of pink soda in old-fashioned glass bottles and a greasy paper sack of popcorn. Maybe he felt that unless we had extensive supplies, our date would be a failure. The lights dimmed and all the chatter hushed. It was like sitting on an airplane about to take off. Of course never having been to the movies in France I was surprised that it was dubbed. The audience had settled and the opening sequence, panning over lush rainforest scenery was spectacular. There was a waterfall and a missionary, no doubt a Jesuit, had been murdered, his body left to drift slowly down the Amazon. That is all I recall because I woke with a start when the lights came on as the final credits were still rolling. I looked at Mathieu conscious of having failed him but he was sympathetic and said my working days were long and the next time we went to the movies we would go on a Sunday, the only day I didn't ride. He had said "the next time"; there would be a next time. Mitzi would have been dissecting everything he said, girls replay conversations she had once told me, she was right about that. There I was assessing tone and nuance, I felt I was moving on to the next stage in my life and about time too she would have said to that.

Driving back Mathieu told me a bit more about himself. Suddenly I was wide awake as the night air was clean and cold after the heat of the movie house. He thanked me for coming and told me to get some rest then he went off. The moon was shining and I decided to take Hector for a quick walk. We had not moved more than fifty yards from my little chalet when Lone Star was beside me, whispering what was it like? The movie? I asked, aware she was referring to the date but I gushed enthusiastically, describing *The Mission* as dramatic, a true epic, "such powerful images of a waterfall and a dead priest." Then I just laughed, saying that I had only seen the opening minutes. "That hot huh?" she sounded so bitter and I wasn't sufficiently sadistic to add to her humiliation. I admitted to falling asleep and, "Well, wouldn't you know? Woke up to see the credits, anyhow it was all dubbed. Knowing how sick you are of hearing French all the time, you would have hated it." Then I realized that I must have come to during it as I could also recall a scene with a man trying to climb up a mountain hauling armor on his back. What had that sequence got to do with the story I asked her, as she had seen it. But she ignored the question, too busy being hurt and outraged. She only wanted to discuss why Mathieu was so

frightened of her. He wasn't, he just plainly detested her. Lone
Star reasoned that she knew she had a powerful sexuality and that
it "was inclined" to unnerve younger men, by which she meant
any male under about forty years of age. I wanted to walk on
and accidently stepped on Hector's paw. He gave a little yelp that
sounded far louder in the still night. My tiredness had returned.
It was cowardly of me, but I wanted to look after Hector and
get us both to bed, so I told Lone Star that Mathieu had suffered
a very bad experience, something in his life had gone awfully
wrong and he was trying to fix it. I felt uneasy about mentioning something that he had told me, but thought it might make
her stand back and stop pushing herself on him. Instead of saying that she was sorry or express sympathy for her fellow man,
Lone Star was triumphant, vindicated, "I knew it, I knew it,"
she shouted. As far as she was concerned it was finally obvious;
he had had a disastrous relationship and this was the only reason
he had been able to resist her. Her reaction showed how different we were. I had been thinking that perhaps he'd had a spell in
the Foreign Legion and was still traumatized; Mathieu struck me
as the kind of impulsive boy who had done some crazy things,
like running away. His behavior over the pony had certainly
been extreme. But Lone Star seemed to think of life only in the
context of catastrophic sexual involvements, not emotions. She
grabbed my arm, I jumped and she explained that she had been
"real mixed-up" as usually she had to "beat guys off." I had to
stop myself laughing in her face when she declared that she had
what she described as a dangerous allure. "Always have, it's kind
of an animal magnetism, can be real tricky, lots of my friends
get so pissed off by it. Their boyfriends just can't stop looking at
me." That was probably because she was so funny-looking; Olive
Oyl as large as life and loud with it. Yet she was convinced that
she was beautiful. Beyond delusional, she was in prompt need

of professional help and wanted to believe that Mathieu was in love with her. It was as imbecilic as that. I could imagine Father saying, "utterly ludicrous."

As for Mathieu, he seemed quietly disturbed and working really hard at being disciplined; the horses were filling some deep need, and he had a real passion despite being nervous of them. Hector and I did a complete circle of the smaller walled garden, the one near the dining chalet. Dark shapes were outlined in the moonlight, and I felt I would sleep well and did; Hector pressed up against me, me tired out but feeling as if my life was about to improve.

My plan was simple and gutless; avoid taking sides. Mathieu was moody and Lone Star was unhinged. As for me I was managing. But I was curious about Mathieu and pursued my hunch about the Foreign Legion—which was wrong. He wondered if I was interested in joining, I said no but could see that he knew nothing about it either. Something else had upset him; perhaps a death or he had made a mistake, an error; killed someone by accident and was being tormented by guilt. He drove very slowly, as if he was an elderly reverend, peering at the road. Maybe he had previously been reckless and had run over a child or a dog. That could be it, no younger person, no man, drove the way he did unless there was a reason. It was none of my business, yet I couldn't help notice.

The next eruption was partly my fault, if entirely unintentional. One Sunday during lunch, it was a Sunday because I had not been riding that day, I'd asked to borrow the station wagon to drive over to Clos Lucé, the famous manor house in which Leonardo da Vinci had once lived. Lone Star butted in saying that her mother had known him, he was "big in the movies" and that she had to come with us. "A lot of those guys would know Mom, she was real hot. Like daughter like mother. Get it?" She

must have misheard me I thought, all I said was that I meant the
artist and inventor. Yet Lone Star insisted that she knew exactly
who I was talking about and that he was also involved in the
movies. "One of the big players in France, most likely I met him
too. He's sure to remember me, men like that love nymphets, we
fuel their fantasies. I've met a lot of big shots you know. Let me
come, he's bound to speak English." Her certainty was nothing
less than absolute. "Some of these French guys actually do know
how to throw a party, not like the horse bores around here. You're
practically Amish, all living like Mormons doing some kind of
pony penance thing." Mathieu said da Vinci was Italian; he was
smiling, a tiger poised for the kill. A couple of the real cats were
patrolling, slinking down the table, stretching and shaking their
feet as if they were wet. They were being even more indulged
than usual as one of the young males had been accidently run
over by Monsieur Gallay who had buried him with some cer-
emony, outlining the grave with white stones from one of the
ornamental alpine rockeries in the farmhouse garden. As for da
Vinci though, I was already regretting having said anything. Lone
Star had begun screeching like a child, Mathieu told her to shut
up, that the man had been dead for about 400 years and that her
mother could only have met him if she had a time machine. It
was sharply said, but funny and I noticed that Mathieu's sense
of the timescale was close, just seventy years out. But then it all
turned really vicious and he shouted at Lone Star, telling her she
was ignorant and that she should go back to school, or no that
she should go to school and she was stupid as well as ugly. The
poor girl just broke down and cried; her head on the table, her
hair in her food. The cook came in holding an icing pipe and
she pointed it at me, gesturing for my help and I was pleased to
escape into the kitchen.

Afterwards I avoided the others and went up to my room. Hector was happy to sit with me as I tried to read a book I had bought in Tours, a volume of Poe, all in French. It opened at the beginning of "Le Corbeau," I knew it was "The Raven" and thought of Galileo and of that day in the study when my plans had collapsed. While Father, who had inflicted all the damage, didn't care and mentioned that he had once considered naming him that, in honor of his literary hero.

A few days passed, I did my job, determined to speak as little as possible and only respond to questions put directly to me. One morning in the stable yard, I was checking the new list; three of the re-schooled show jumpers were ready for their riders to try them out in their new saddles. Mathieu was discussing a horse that was coming in for me and that it was very excitable. Then he apologized for having shouted at Lone Star, he knew that it had embarrassed me. He put out his hand and asked "Friends?" I shook it and smiled or something. Then he reached for my hand again and held it tight. He said he liked me and he walked down the stable, still holding my hand and me having to walk along with him. His hand felt surprisingly big to me, a lot bigger than mine, and it felt very different from Mother's frail little bird's wing of thin bones and sharp rings. He said he wanted to bring me to a restaurant that night for a proper French meal and that he was asking me in the stable. I could see that he'd asked me there to avoid a scene and thanked him, but also pointed out that I didn't want to see Lone Star getting upset. He groaned and made a face.

Our supper date was fun. We just finished up at the stables and I went to walk Hector, feed him, and change from my riding gear to clean jeans and a blue and gray cable knit sweater I had bought in Paris. It was my first time to wear it and it became my Mathieu sweater. He put on the ABBA tape and I wondered if it was a kind of reflex ritual with him as he sang along for a few minutes. Then he switched it off and began asking me questions. Did I have brothers and sisters and did they also ride. For as long as I can remember I have always been able to avoid speaking about things I would rather keep concealed or better still, completely forget—or at least try to. I would be a challenge for any interrogator—so aside from saying there was only me, I just began telling him about my friend Mitzi from sunny California and how she had come into my life on account of her mother being left a mansion on its own grounds. He said it was like *Gone with the Wind*, I didn't follow the connection but it was a movie I had seen and obviously knew the history so we began speaking about that. I wondered how much worse a blind date would be, but then it all got a lot better and he made me laugh as he told me stories about the people he had met through working for Monsieur Gallay. I wanted to find out what he knew about Lone Star's arrival there and finally asked him if Lone Star was Monsieur Gallay's daughter. Well, he clear forgot to drive and the car just stopped. "Is she?" he gasped, horror in his eyes as well as real confusion. So much for that theory.

Before we had even ordered at the restaurant, two men came over and joined us. They rode out for a big syndicate trainer who had a string of more than one hundred Thoroughbreds in training. It was easy listening to the three men; it all seemed relaxed and good-natured, not as competitive as Father and Mr. Montgomery, more like when Sheriff Hodge came around. That's how it began; Mathieu bringing me with him to meals or to see horses, sometimes the movies, the saddlers, or to browse in the big bookstore in Tours. We did eventually get to Clos Lucé on a bright morning when the skylarks were out in force and he thanked me for bringing him there. He would hold my hand and kiss my cheek, give me a hug and seem really happy to be with me. He kept saying he trusted me. If it was old-fashioned and courtly, genteel, it suited me just fine and maybe it was the beginning of me trying to understand Mother. Lone Star always seemed about to ask me some probing question but mostly she would just sigh and rationalize if for her own benefit, "You guys get along, but then it's just horse stuff, nothing sexual. That's so much easier, you being a kid and all—you're no threat. Know what I mean?" All said like taking a half-hearted swipe at a wing-less fly. But I didn't care, as I was beginning to know better.

*

Trust, affection, loyalty, faith, support, dependability, solidar-ity—they were all words that described Mathieu's requirements when it came to people. And trust was by far the most vital; Mathieu needed someone he could trust and trust in. He was not a loner by inclination, whereas I had been one, almost without noticing it, but had begun to change. More than that; I wanted to be in love. It had nothing to do with Lone Star's endless taunting. I had become indifferent to her telling me that I was like a boy. I wanted to experience emotion when it becomes so immense that it takes over your every waking moment and had not in my wildest imaginings dared dream that Mathieu would like me in that way. Somehow I'd become his special person by just being myself, the miracle of it, even if my liking horses had helped, or to be honest had probably made it happen. It was thrilling and unexpected but also slightly terrifying as I never wanted it to end, despite not knowing exactly what it was or where it was headed or why he had become so loving.

Perhaps he would weary of being nice to me? That set me to blind panic. I'm very boring, always off in one of my trances, daydreaming about the solar system or Kepler, and barely alert to the real world. If I dissected Mathieu's feelings overmuch though, as I did most things, a jinx was sure to come along and it would be unbearable to revert to the way it had been before when he used to hum and forget I was there about a minute after he had spoken to me. All those days and weeks when he switched his attention on and off were branded in my memory.

What makes someone decide to suddenly fall in love? I wanted to ask him but I knew it could all come crashing down; it was not a math problem to be solved. I liked being with him, I had enjoyed the approval, the respectful way he approached me as a rider, he had taken that seriously almost from the beginning. But it had moved on to so much more; little flashes of posses-sion, a gesture, his reaching for my hand, or sometimes when he'd put his arm around my shoulder or stand and look directly at me to listen to what I had to say as if it was awfully important. He was a bit taller than me and he had such lovely shining eyes, honey-colored. Amber; amber was the color. His eyebrows were brown, not black like mine.

Delightful as it all was, a part of me still felt wary. It's in my nature, always was; the doubts along with my stupid habit of putting everything said or done of any significance under the imaginary microscope in my mind. Lone Star had been right about that.

Aside from her manic displays on account of Mathieu I had heard snatches of lurid stories at school; witnessed tears at the lockers, lunches left uneaten, girls rushing out of class to go to the bathroom and being gone so long that search parties were dispatched to find them. Julie Ellen Parker had been already "blooded" three times—or so she'd claim to whoever was there.

She had even stuck both legs of her geometry set compass into her arm and hacked her hair, and had used the Bunsen burner in the science lab to make sure we would all be able to smell her pain. What made the odor so acrid? I speculated as her hair singed and crackled. Was it because it was bleached? Naturally in the interest of science I immediately burnt a thumb-sized sample of mine and it did smell different. Yet I'd moved on from putting my hair to a Bunsen burner; now I was in France and maybe in love and about to become normal, just another girl with a boyfriend. Finally.

*

Julie Ellen's flamboyant liaisons had always ended in lamentation. She was like a Queen Bee, fated for suffering and was invariably surrounded by a set of romance-starved drones who fed off her woe. They would surround her as she slowly walked from class to class, broken, head down, her tear-and-mascara-blotched face confirming that teen love was indeed a merciless business. Our English teacher had gotten very irritated by the chorus of sniggering that had disrupted our classroom reading of *Romeo and Juliet*. Love seemed to be both gruesome and hilarious, all depending on whether you were a victim or an observer.

When Edmund Dell Hutton III, the one boy that I had semi-liked, walked over to me at that training show, my heart did start to beat faster as he approached and I had screamed inwardly, "Relax, don't blush." Even so my face ignited as I watched his mouth open, hoping I would remain composed as he declared his undying passion for me. All he'd wanted to know was the type of bit I was using on Galileo. Perhaps Mathieu was only paying attention to me in order to discourage Lone Star; that thought did strike me. But he would seize my hand and smile, and took to singing a stupid little song from his tape: "Take a chance on me; take a chance on me . . ." I saw it as a kind of code intended for my understanding alone as he sang sporadic bursts of that same tune all day: "When you're all alone and you're feeling blue, take a chance on me; take a chance on me . . ." The yard staff had always been polite, but now they were friendlier, encouraging, watched me riding and made a point of trying to speak English when I was there. It was as if they approved; they all liked Mathieu and seemed happy for him. He kept saying how much he trusted me and having been singing loudly, oblivious to how dreadful it sounded, he walked over and whispered that it was good to get to know a person before everything else. The "everything else" raised my hopes.

"Everything else," there was more to come. I tried to stay calm, and just made sure he knew how glad I was. If he was to discover that I had never had a boyfriend he might think there was something wrong with me, an unspeakable flaw, far worse even than my funny eyes. "Boys hate first-timers," Mitzi had said, explaining with her worldly wisdom that it made them really nervous because above all, boys hate tears.

Mathieu would suddenly hand me a 7 Up or a bowl of milky coffee, a candy bar, some sickening Turkish delight—which I hated but would eat anyway and thank him—or soft toffee fudge, the best I'd ever had. He could arrive at the stable and suddenly produce a pear, some figs, hot chocolate in a ceramic flask. He was affectionate to Hector and surprised me with a really good weatherproof riding jacket.

One Saturday evening having carried a tray into the screening room, he then summoned me in a business-like tone, putting Lone Star at complete ease that nothing romantic could possibly be going on, and proceeded to play several videos of the equestrian events at the Los Angeles Olympics.

My days were happy, as were my evenings once I got used to riding so many horses and he was less rude to Lone Star. She became subdued and would ask me to watch TV with her or meekly inquire if I wanted to share the taxi she was taking into Tours. How about heading to Paris for the day? She often looked hopeful, desperate; less sneering, suddenly vulnerable. She even offered to do my nails for me, I knew I would never be able to sit and inhale the polish fumes but as soon as she took my hands in hers, she sighed and released them, exclaiming that they felt just like sandpaper and seemed to recall that people who rode horses always had warts. I said I didn't have any but she frowned, "You will." Close my eyes and I could be listening to Mother.

On a bright Friday morning Monsieur Gallay confirmed he was traveling to England to see one of his horses, a sharp gelding he had bred and trained, race at Kempton Park, as a practice for a run in the King George VI, a very famous race that would be run a few weeks later. He reckoned the colt was exceptional and that it would be a valuable experience for him as he was unusually well-developed for his age. Even more to the point, he explained, his finger in the air, that he wanted what he called "a preview" look at Kempton; he had not been there for a while and would be returning with some of the more seasoned horses for the King George. He would also be taking the drug-addict jockey who had fallen off that day at Longchamp, giving him yet another last chance. Monsieur Gallay was like that—and he did consider the man a genius, believing that the jockey would reform. The trainer could be tricky but his mad enthusiasm and that zealot fervor of his, which I had come to admire, had won me over. Mathieu disagreed about the choice of jockey but Monsieur Gallay smirked with friendly defiance. The horse was being sent by air, no expense spared, and Mathieu had been going as well, but then decided not to. Was it because of the jockey? I'd wondered but hoped that perhaps he wanted to stay with me.

That evening he announced in a formal tone that he "wished" to bring me to a jazz club in Paris. It wasn't Bach yet it was an improvement on ABBA. After being charmed to accept, a fear like black glue washed into my mind. Marc would be there and he would seize me by the throat before urinating on me again. But of course that couldn't happen. Besides, Paris is not a village.

Mathieu knew my views on provoking Lone Star and he had taken to discretion. We were conspirators before we were actually, well, everything . . . He'd said that he was going to drive us to Paris in Monsieur Gallay's Porsche. It would be interesting to see what the other drivers would make of seeing a powerful sports car like that being driven so slowly along the highway—they might suspect a Bible salesman was behind the wheel. Snazzy automobiles did not interest me much and I was not that eager about traveling in the boss's personal car. When we were about to leave for the jazz session Mathieu couldn't find the keys, so we went in the station wagon instead.

There I was, again walking through the streets of Paris, only this time hand in hand with a gentle person who seemed to really like me. It wasn't fun, the way it had been in the beginning with Marc, striding along, linking arms, with him shouting about Westerns. Instead it was very romantic, slow motion in a kind of a dream-like waltz step. What would Mitzi have thought? The club had a seductive buzz and was really grown-up but it was relaxed, not at all pretentious, more what Mitzi would call "cool to double-cool." There was a lot of drinking going on. Food was also being served, even café au lait, all night long. It was casual, really comfortable and friendly and revealed a different side to Paris, at least to me. The trio consisted of three middle-aged men, apparently revered in jazz circles and very famous, two of them German and the third, a heavyset American from Seattle. Mathieu kept turning from them to smile at me, gauging my reaction to the music. I felt very happy and so aware that had I not met Hector that day in the park, none of this would have happened. My Hector dog had given me a life; he'd saved me as much as I'd helped him.

As we drove back to Amboise, I felt that I had been with Mathieu for a long time and was contented, at ease though still excited. He asked would I be interested in competing. I could have my pick of the horses and then he asked would I like to stay at Amboise, with him, that he would love that and as it was his home, it could also be mine. Was I dreaming? All my plans of going to university no longer seemed to matter, as if they'd been erased. Never once had Mathieu spoken about America, aside from his wanting to visit the Grand Canyon and of course Claiborne—reminding me of how I had once almost gone there with Father and Sheriff Hodge—and I told him all about that. Anybody I met in France who mentioned America always said they dreamed of going there, but not Mathieu. As for me getting a horse, I said I had always wanted a special one, my horse, my horse of a lifetime, and I explained all about Monticello and Billy Bob. Then I remembered something that I had loved thinking about since I was small, Robert E. Lee's great horse Traveller—Traveller with two l's, spelt the English way—a horse he had ridden in the Civil War, the same horse who would walk after his funeral cortege and who was eventually buried beside him after years of his bones being moved around, on account of being stolen by generations of college pranksters.

That was something I wanted, my horse of a lifetime, my Traveller, my own horse. I wanted to spend my life working with horses and with Mathieu, speaking French, enjoying each day. There was a clean Spartan purity about it.

We arrived back very late and he parked the car, which still held a trace of the cigarette smoke from the club, seeping off our clothes and suddenly more noticeable in the clear cold air of the countryside. What would happen next, I wondered, half-afraid. He told me to get some sleep, "This will be wonderful for us, Helen," he said, and I've never felt happier or more alive as he repeated that we would be content together and he kissed me, a real, intense kiss, him holding my face between his hands; he was nervous—just like me. I went in to Hector, my feet suspended a couple of inches above the ground, and we walked two laps of the nearest garden, with me wondering where Mathieu had gotten to. No sign of Lone Star, just as well; I would have hated to blurt out anything to her and yet I wanted to sing. I wanted to tell Mitzi; I wanted to be like the girls at school when they felt they were about to have all their dreams come true.

Little more than an hour had passed, I was tired yet couldn't sleep, the smallest sound made me start. My muscles were tense and my heart was pounding loud enough to hear it, a deafening thump fit to explode. The door handle was moving; should I act outraged or pleased, scared, terrified of ruining everything. I supposed it was what happened next, after a kiss like that. The door slapped open, and about six of the cats came storming in and jumped all over the mattress, in a flurry of wild eyes and claws, as if it was a dare and they got Hector frenzied because he couldn't see them. My face got scratched; a paw had become tangled in my hair, very painful. Someone's claw sliced my finger. The outer door of the chalet had not closed tight behind me. I yelpt and felt an idiot, so much for Romeo arriving on cue. I was relieved though, and delighted to be still at the holding hands and tender-glance stage, aware of not being ready for anything more grown-up. Lone Star was right; I was backward, inept. Mathieu had told me that he'd had a relationship that had gone very badly wrong and he was still "remorseful about that business." More disgruntled than brokenhearted was the impression he gave me. It left me feeling even more close to him.

So Lone Star had been right about Mathieu having been, as she put it, "emotionally out of commission, like a wrecked engine." The cats stampeded around the room, amazing the noise they made, and they ripped and pulled at the little basket of bread and cakes I had, my stash in case I got hungry, before breakfast, as oftened happened. Three of them were fighting over a soft roll. I chased them all out and pushed the outer door, till it clicked tight like it should have the first time. For a brief few moments I felt really awake and calmed Hector, then must have fallen asleep soon after, feelings secure in that Mathieu was as shy as me; or maybe just more patient and experienced than I was, or possibly, even more damaged.

While we were in Paris Lone Star had taken the keys of the green Porsche and she'd had an accident, a head-on collision. By a miracle she was uninjured but the old man who had been driving the car into which she had crashed was dead and his wife was in a coma with little hope of recovery. The couple were local people and their daughter, Madame Perec, managed the stable yard accounts at the Gallay estate. Lone Star had breezed in at breakfast, bragging about what she referred to as her "fucking near-death escape." Perhaps she was unaware of what had happened to her victims and having been cut out of the sports car was too relieved to think beyond herself, not that she was given to introspection. Madame Gallay appeared; it was the first time she had ever come in during breakfast. Her strained face carefully made-up as always, her dark-gray suit jacket and skirt making her appear taller, a double row of pearls balancing the elegant

severity she favored. She greeted us and then quietly addressed
Lone Star as "Joan" and informed her that she would be driven
to Paris, to a hotel. "Be ready, soon," she said and told Lone Star
that her mother would be arriving from Texas that evening to
join her on the flight back to the States. "Goodbye Joan," she
had said, coldly, and as she turned to leave, Madame Gallay
smiled at me and then glanced over at Lone Star, adding, "You
have been a most interesting guest, but enough, enough." Lone
Star was indignant, and shouted that she was recovering from an
accident, and protested, "I'm Guy's guest. Slow down some, you
got no friggin right to boss me." But Madame Gallay responded
icily without raising her voice, "Oh, but I do. You have killed
my neighbor, Monsieur Hubert Perec, a dear, dear man I have
known since I was a child. You probably have also, by now, killed
his wife who is expected to die. I have told Guy many times to
send you away. Now I am telling you, ordering you, you will
leave my home, today." Mathieu looked down at his plate. The
room was so quiet, the only sounds were the blackbird that sang
most mornings, the scraping of a knife as I spread butter on
toast, and a loud gulping coming from Lone Star who had begun
to hyperventilate. That was that. I felt like sighing with relief,
but it would have been insensitive, unfair, or perhaps not given
the circumstances. That poor elderly couple, their life together
had ended just like that because of Lone Star having a tantrum
and stealing a car out of spite. Then I realized she would be gone
before Thanksgiving and I had planned on cooking us a turkey,
a proper Thanksgiving dinner for us all. It would have been
easier making a fuss when there were two Americans. I was too
awkward to attempt it on my own. But that plan had become
incredibly irrelevant. The cook was crying and Mathieu tried to
comfort her. More grief.

That strange interlude had not yet ended. It had begun to drizzle and we were in the indoor arena. Lone Star swaggered in and beckoned to us. "Hey guys, I gotta go. Hell, I'm being thrown out, that dumb bitch, she never did like me. Guess it's a generation thing, age versus beauty. . . Envy and all." She was determined to let us think that she couldn't care less. I marveled at Lone Star's bravado as she began, "Aw shucks Belmondo relax, it was never to be. I need a man and you're, well, just a boy and once I saw those fucking pixie ears . . . you were, like, so over for me." He half-laughed and looked at me, as always, checking my reaction. Then she walked over to me, closer than I had thought she would risk as I was sitting on a horse, "Bennington," she said, with a wink, it was the first time in weeks that she had called me that, "Well Bennington, see you around kid, I'll send the 7th Cavalry to get you outta here before these freaks turn you into a horse or talk you into marrying one. You get me?" What could be going through her mind I had wondered; was she distressed about having caused the deaths of one, probably two people, or did she not have a basic conscience. She must have been worried. Yet her parting shot was only about her failure to master French. "My old man's gonna go nuts. Might mail me off somewhere to a finishing school or something. Well, so long as there's a beach and some decent-looking guys." Mention of a finishing school made Mathieu smirk like a teenager.

And then she was gone. And with her went all the tension and drama, and as far as I thought, the secrecy. Mathieu took to sitting beside me at all the meals and spoke freely with me. Aware that I no longer cringed and held on to my plate quite as tightly whatever about shielding it from the cats, I smiled at Mathieu. When Lone Star became distressed she would grab whatever object was nearest her to fling at him. She sure liked throwing things to prove a point. Everything had become possible and

I was wondering about flying home for a few days to collect my telescopes but instantly decided against it for fear of leaving Hector on his own. Even Mathieu seemed a bit too casual about any animal that was not a horse and I hadn't forgotten the cat that had been run over. My list of horses was full, if I wanted to begin preparing one for myself to compete, it would add to the existing pressure of time already dictating each day. There were only so many hours. Mathieu was more openly demonstrative to me but when we were working we still had to keep an eye on the clock. Lunch remained a strict thirty-minute snack break, no idle chatter or watching the clouds drift by . . . I kept my eyes open for a suitable horse from Monsieur Gallay's stock; he was delighted by my interest in competing. "Maybe you could have a show jumper and also another horse specializing in dressage, so very good for illustrating my multidisciplinary approach." His eyes glittered with ideas such as getting some saddles made for me and he offered me one of his horse trailers; they all carried the Gallay insignia, the silhouette of a horse at full gallop in dark green on a pale-gray background.

The beginning of a romance is like nothing else. In the evenings we rarely went directly to Mathieu's stone chalet, or if we did, he would have a little dessert ready and when we lay together in his bed, I loved just being there, listening to his stories. While in turn he wanted to hear about my love of science.

After his father had died while having his tonsils removed, his mother had contacted several of her old boyfriends and went out a few times with each of them before deciding which to marry. She'd settled down again, very quickly, "Mama is very practical and married the man who could do everything—fix the car, do plumbing, and know about electrical things. He is also a clever gardener. He is not so friendly to me but her new home is very lovely." He said that she had a tactical mind—I think he meant calculating—and although his younger sister was studying medicine, his mother had never read a book in her life. Perhaps there was some sense in that? It gave me pause for thought, recalling Mitzi saying so much reading was bad for me, almost as bad as riding was. Ha. But I could tell by the way he spoke about her that Mathieu was close to his mother.

Mathieu's skin was very white, much paler than mine. His legs were thick, strong but not athletic, he said I should have been a miler and mentioned a famous French Olympic runner named Michel Jazy. I laughed thinking of Mitzi's brother. Yes, I had phoned her and she was happy for me and had said that I had been lucky finding the perfect boyfriend—a twentieth-century human male who did not smoke or drink, liked horses, and lived in a castle not to mention drove with the abandon of a Sunday schoolteacher. She wasn't teasing me and never mentioned Karl. I didn't correct her about the château.

It might be time to get my hair cut, I decided, just to shoulder length and grow my bangs out. I should make an effort. Mathieu was good-looking and girls would study him and then assess me. Well at least my teeth were better than his. We were down at the stable yard and he was singing his stupid: "Take a chance on me. Take a chance on me" ditty, it had become his theme song. We had to unload some horses; one of them was a Belgian mare coming back from injury. She had competed at the European championships and had been third in the individual, placing ahead of all three German horses and had also been one of only three horses clear in the team final in which the Belgians had finished sixth, and all thanks to her. Mathieu told me that he suspected she was unsuitable for the new owner and if so, would be a good horse for me—he was sure he could persuade Monsieur Gallay to buy her. "Wow," was all I could muster and he laughed, "So very American; so very American."

As soon as they were unloaded Mathieu was leaving to go to the dentist and I would ride that afternoon on my own, leaving the Belgian mare until he returned, by four o'clock. I didn't mind waiting. He said if the mare seemed promising we would celebrate with a meal in Tours that evening. I was no longer tired after so many daily hours of intense riding, and was eager to compete. Monsieur Gallay paid me so well I had amassed a disturbing amount of money, more than enough to purchase a top class horse if I had to pay for one myself but that was unlikely. Monsieur Gallay could be very generous. What would Father say, me riding a European horse? The only problem I had was feeling caught between my new life in France and the fact that a sizeable part of me ached to return to Virginia, maybe more than sizeable. Hector had been keeping me in France and suddenly it had become Hector and Mathieu together versus home. The Belgian mare was princess-stunning with a lovely head except for her wild eyes; too much white showing was something Billy Bob always considered a sure sign of trouble.

There it was again; Mathieu's raggedy, tuneless singing voice booming out: "Take a chance on me, take a chance on me . . . When you're feeling blue, la la la la la . . . la la la la la . . ." on and on, he had also subjected me to his guitar playing which was beyond abysmal but when you're in love and all that, it was possible to listen with a glaze of brainwashed pleasure on your face—and I did. He was in a giddy mood, croaking away in a variety of funny voices. I shouted that he was scaring the horses and that the Belgian mare would get a bad impression of French singing. He didn't reply and the mare came running by me. She had a loose shoe, I could hear it. I caught her and saw she was a lot easier to handle than Galileo, not as paranoid or as violent, slightly taller, maybe a fraction heavier, well-muscled, already a proven international and a terrific challenge for me.

I remembered how I would sing to Galileo to calm my nerves, whatever about his—I doubt he had any.

My French was getting better; I was more confident speaking it but was eager to master that casual, native syntax. I was wondering how to say: "You will frighten the horses," or "Your singing is so awful the horses will protest," or that they would insist on a no-singing clause. Too ambitious. What was the French for "no-singing clause"? For once I wanted not to speak in that stiltedly correct schoolgirl French that sounded so flat and labored. I kept trying out various formulations in my head. I walked her back around the truck, and Mathieu was lying on the ramp, arms outstretched. "Get up, that's so stupid, horses running loose. Lucky I caught her," I said as I passed him. "Just get on up, that's not funny." I sounded like a schoolmarm, haranguing him about careless behavior, setting a bad example in the yard and so on.

*

Something made me look around; a shiver caused by a cold gust of air. Why had my hands begun to shake? Church bells began to toll in the distance, a forlorn, surreal touch. I was about to vomit, hot bile gathered at the back of my throat, a burning sensation. Mathieu was still on the ramp. I shouted at him. Quickly ran the mare into the nearest stall and hurried back to him. He looked at me, through me, far away beyond me . . . I straddled him and began to pound his chest, one of the workers appeared, a grin on his face that turned to horror as he could tell that we weren't fooling around and that poor yardman's eyes immediately became round circles, his mouth wide open, no voice coming out. "Hurry! Hurry! Vite! Vite!" I shrieked. He saw what had happened and ran off to fetch help. But I already knew that Mathieu was dead. His gaze had turned to glass. Not a mark on him, a fly landed on his face, near his eye, paused a beat and flew off. Mathieu must have slipped or maybe the mare had kicked him in the head, it can happen that fast. And it had . . . I hadn't heard a sound. It all happened as quick as that. Everything had changed.

Monsieur Gallay came running, sobbing and choking; he stared at me as if I had killed Mathieu. "Explique," he shouted, "Explique." I couldn't reply. He tried to resuscitate him, his lips on Mathieu's mouth, Monsieur Gallay seemed to know what he was doing, but was speaking so fast I couldn't understand. Then he sank down beside Mathieu and said he was like his son, more his son than his real son. He had a son; I knew that, he was called Anton. I'd never met him. "Mathieu is more my son than Anton could ever be," Monsieur Gallay repeated that five or six times, wiping his eyes with the back of his hand as he cradled Mathieu's head in his lap and him rocking back and forth. The doctor from the village arrived about thirty minutes later and just shook his head. He squatted down beside Monsieur Gallay and sighed softly, then said, "Another cruel blow for poor Sophie," that's what it sounded like. I assumed that he was referring to Mathieu's mother—whom I never did get to meet—and I offered to phone her. Neither of them answered, so I repeated my offer and Monsieur Gallay stopped his sobbing. He looked up at me, the dazed expression on his face clearing away a little, and he said Sophie was not Mathieu's mother. "Sa femme, ma fille; sa femme, ma fille." His wife, my daughter; his wife, my daughter. The words vibrated inside my head. Monsieur Gallay also had a grown daughter; I'd never met her either. Mathieu had been married to the boss's daughter. He had been married. My mouth felt as if I was trying to swallow cobwebs. All the times he had told me how he trusted me. Trusted me, trusted me but just not enough to tell me that he was married, married, whatever about to the boss's daughter, he had been married. My heart had become a little stone sliding around inside a box and I was the box. I felt like a prizefighter being beaten to death, my arms too heavy to ward off the punches that kept coming fast and relentless.

What other secrets had Mathieu kept from me? Had Lone Star known anything? Well served me right if she did, I had kept secrets from her. And there was more. What would this mystery Sophie be like. Would she be soft and feminine, a child bride who did not much like being married or would she be tough and elegant, a sophisticated Parisian who detested the countryside and completely hated horses? The answer turned out to have been there all along; Mathieu's estranged wife was the sullen beauty up in the main house. The idle kitchen maid with the lovely face, the ugly, thick ankles; those blunt Bamm-Bamm feet and the caveman's waddle. Mathieu's wife, too depressed to comb her hair or get herself dressed, still sitting at noon in her pajamas, drinking cold coffee and staring at magazines. She had good reason for dragging herself through the hours. Their baby daughter had died; she had been born with her heart outside her body and barely beating. It had been a short, harrowing life with three operations and she had only survived for about five months. Mathieu and Sophie had had a baby and they'd remained tied together by their dead little girl. No wonder he had hated Lone Star's banter. I now understood his rage toward her but why had he pulled me into all of it? I was a fool; I had been his comfort, which left me nowhere.

On the day of the funeral Monsieur Gallay instructed me just to ride the horses and added that the yardmen would clean up and put the tack away afterwards when they returned from church. "Take your time," he said, "do as you like." That I could eat and relax, "Just do as much as you like, or less." He smiled weakly, his teeth looked brittle in the sunlight and stained brownish for all his money. Speaking as much to himself as to me he commented that he and Mathieu were very alike, and that they had both even married the daughters of the Big House. He laughed at that. I insisted that I wanted to attend the service and was trying really hard not to cry, my words tentative, in harsh staccato bursts of sound. He repeated that I did not have to go, it was not necessary for me to come and that I'd hardly known Mathieu, but the men did, they had worked together for years and they all loved him. I had not been able to cry for Mother when my tears had been expected and there I was crying for a man I had loved more than anyone yet was being told that I had barely known him. The irony of all that was that Monsieur Gallay, knowing and secretive and very clever beneath all the affectation, contrived eccentricity, and the indolent ease that wealth confers, was quite correct. I did not really know Mathieu, I had touched every part of him as he had of me and yet I did not know his real blood-self, his essential being. He trusted me—he had said that so often, along with so many declarations of love: "my darling," "my beloved." He had called me his "special love," often looking near ready to cry but he did not trust me with the essential facts of his life, and had only shared his fantasies.

Conceding that this trust he had kept speaking about was meaningless hurt like a knife cutting into the center of me. There I was pleading for permission to attend his funeral service. Just as I was about to tell the trainer that Mathieu had told me that he loved me and wanted us to get married and that he had asked me to live there with him, a puff of smoke and Madame Gallay appeared as she tended to, suddenly, silently, as if she could float through the very walls of her ancestral home.

Although she always wore high heels, I never seemed to hear her footsteps. She looked composed; and after smiling her familiar labored smile, resumed her customary neutral expression. Sophie was with her; slightly shorter, lower heels and very beautiful, cold and detached, more observer than bereaved spouse. She was wearing a dark purple dress and a long navy coat. Her blue-gray eyes were clear, well-defined by subtle eye liner and without any sign of redness unlike Monsieur Gallay's whose were bloodshot by then. He was shaking and far more distressed than either of the women. Sophie, Mathieu's widow, held a fine woolen scarf in her left hand; it was navy and probably cashmere. Shaking it out to wind loosely around her throat, before slowly tossing the ends over her shoulders, she pursed her lips and glanced at each of us in turn as if we were her vaguely unruly subjects. Riffraff. I gulped and panicked. Why was I about to laugh? Then she said, in English, that she had often told Mathieu that he would eventually get killed by one of his stupid horses. "Only I had thought that there would be more drama, that he would fall off and break his neck."

*

END OF PART THREE

PART FOUR

SOUND, A REGULAR RHYTHM, marching feet, an army on the way to war, it was relentless and had begun to push its way into my head, interfering with the ongoing sensation of having been forced into a glass bottle. Reduced to a mere pump my heart was no longer an organic form, only a mechanical object. The sound turned out to be a downpour; and it had been falling for hours but I had forgotten about rain. It hadn't rained much that fall and early winter; Amboise was cold and dry or, at least that's how it seemed to me, a long sequence of chill, brisk days with the papery snap of leaves underfoot, colder than home for sure and rarely damp. That night in the room it had been bright, in the fading light of early evening. As the hours, so many hours, went by, it had gotten dark and I just sat there, Hector on my lap, me praying, begging God to make it not to have happened. The doorway opening onto the patio was black, then purple, then gray and then it was the next day. That terrible day was over and gone but it could not be undone. I was wearing Mathieu's sweatshirt and I clutched the stupid ABBA cassette in my hand. Off I'd scurried after the doctor arrived and Monsieur Gallay had begun shivering, he was in shock and sobbing in endless choking shudders as if he would vomit up his heart and lungs right there on the spot. It seemed disrespectful to stay and watch, although I would often see him cry, as he would me, in the weeks and months that followed and each time with a little bit more understanding, a dawning clarity.

Slowly but surely, he would piece it all together. I had been on the verge of telling him the entire story when his wife appeared, still distressed about her neighbors. What she would have made of it all, my irrelevant romance only a small part of yet another tragedy adding to the loss of her grandchild and of her daughter's husband. Eager to flee, I had rushed away to retrieve Mathieu's homemade tape which he had so patiently put together by recording the songs in his order of preference. He'd say it was the only tape like it.

One minute he'd been alive and singing away while I was making some fool attempt at saying something funny in French. We'd planned on me riding the Belgian mare when he got back from the dentist, only Mathieu never did get to the dentist. Monsieur Gallay was weeping and the old doctor made me think of the way that Sheriff Hodge had tried to comfort Father. So much death and it seemed to be following me. I had run to the station wagon assuring Mathieu's spirit that I would protect his music and keep it safe. I felt that if I continued speaking to him that he would stay with me, inside my heart and my mind; we'd get along, we would manage. If you really love, you don't leave, you hover at the shoulder, like a guardian angel. He wouldn't have to go away. How long had it been since he had held Sophie and had he ever told her that he had trusted her? How long had they been married and what had happened to them? Did they move apart because of their baby or had it been going wrong anyway? Her not liking horses and all . . . Who could tell me? There was no one I could ask. My French did not have those subtle nuances that you can draw upon in your own language, the shimmy and shift, the precise testing of the mood, interpreting facial expressions which often reveal so much more than words. The French I spoke came filtered through a polite grammatical barrier like tinted glass. The cook was sweet to me—I could have asked her—but she didn't speak English and it would be excruciating to stand there while other people discussed what it was they thought I was asking about. Imagine how badly wrong that could go. The cassette made a faint crackle like a gasp, I was squeezing it as if it was the sacred key to something, I don't know what, just didn't want to break it. Would the heat of my hands erase the singing? Those songs which I had mocked but now needed to preserve so that I could keep Mathieu close to me. By then I had already sneaked into his chalet and taken his sweatshirts and three of his sweaters, and all of his socks and his funny little woolen hat as well as his baseball cap. I would wear them in my room, on my own. I pulled about five of his tops on over my cotton shirt and hoped that no one would see me running off with his clothes like some mean-minded scavenger sifting through the debris on a battlefield. Even ran back and took his khaki jacket, it was one of those old uniform-style combat ones, British, I reckon.

A horse had been left tacked up for me in the stable. A man I had never seen before was mucking out. He looked African and squinted up at me, wide smile, big teeth, perfect like mine, only as nature had made them without the help of a fancy orthodontist. "Hey, hello, not heading to the funeral?" He sounded American but turned out to be from Senegal and had been living in Amsterdam, where he had learned his English with a Yankee accent. Where had Monsieur Gallay found him in the middle of such devastation? Ruben, that was his name, turned out to have been visiting friends and had offered to help out. "Word gets out, and here I am, free to step in for the day. Easy money. I really like horses, they're so cool, to touch, I mean, not to climb up on, though . . . A few of these guys tried to bite me, until I did my voodoo witch face thing—that scared them good. Ha-ha." He beamed, happy in his skin and had a booming laugh, a small earring, and was smoking as he worked, even though it was not allowed. Everyone had gone to Mathieu's service and I was expected to carry on as if I had not a care in the world, reciting the periodic table as I rode around in circles, schooling each horse in turn. His funeral was being held in a small church in the next village, Mathieu had once taken me there. It had a beautiful churchyard. There was a First World War plot dedicated to three sons of one of the large manor houses. Only six years separated the youngest from the eldest in age and they had all died on the same day, sometime during the Battle of the Somme. It was a story that would have sent Father off into one of his thoughtful silences; he was fascinated by war and admitted that he tended to romanticize it because he had never fought in one. And to think that he had said that he would have sent me to West Point—had I been a boy.

The war memorial was not at all military and consisted of three elegant, life-sized stone angels standing guard over the trio of brothers in a plot that looked more like a small garden in which there was a stone bench and a birdbath. Such a tranquil spot, even the birds seemed to sing more softly. Mathieu had recalled that there was some confusion; rumors about there being only one body buried there, that two of the brothers had never been found. No one knew the truth now; it had all happened a long time ago. The facts were lost, dead like the brothers as were all the people who would have known the story. We had stood together inside the little church and I had thought it would be a lovely place for our wedding. Without Mother there would be no need for an extravaganza. My wedding. What a thought; everything had been destroyed and in a matter of a few weeks it would be as if it had never happened. It was just a dream after all and it had been doomed. Mitzi never heard any of the wedding plans. Instead she would be hearing about a funeral I was unable to attend. I lifted the saddle off the horse and Ruben glanced over at me and asked me if I had changed my mind. I mumbled about needing to go to the funeral and he registered mild surprise and said, "So you knew the guy," as if he was making a formal declaration and did not expect a reply. I offered none and took the station wagon, it was never locked. Mathieu always left the keys under the passenger seat and I fetched Hector. I wanted him to be with me.

It was a stone church, very old and dating from the nineteenth or possibly even the eighteenth century, very brightly lit with an organist playing, hidden from view in the loft, up above the congregation. Somewhere among the mourners were Mathieu's mother and sister, only I never met them. So many lilies standing in tall containers, just like the ones at Mother's funeral back in Richmond with that same waxy scent which had been so much stronger probably on account of the central heating in St Paul's. The reverend in the little French church was businesslike, not at all personable. He had wild white hair which was standing on end and he mumbled at speed slightly slurring his words, as if eager to be done with the proceedings. I stood near the back, the secret lover reduced to feeling I had pushed my way into a theater without having bought a ticket. Monsieur Gallay then appeared on the altar and walked across to the lectern. He raised his hands as if he would lead a communal prayer but then began weeping, his arms falling hopelessly at his sides, unable to speak, his fists balled and he hung his head, sadly in a sorrow which was profound. I felt so sorry for him and shared his desolation. But I was only an outsider and walked on out of the church.

Back to the yard, it was as if I'd never left, no one had seen me. Leaving Hector in the car, I went to look at the Belgian mare. She was eating hay, a mild, faraway expression in her eyes;

she looked to be daydreaming. Had she killed Mathieu? If she
had, did she even know? It would have been an accident. Or
maybe he just slipped and hit his head? What would it feel like
to ride the horse that had caused Mathieu's death?

How would Monsieur Gallay react if I told him? Would he
just shrug and say the horse did not plan it? Or would he have
ordered her to be shot, like Father had done to the hunting horse
when his first wife died. How could I approach my employer,
a man I barely knew but who was the one person with whom I
could talk about Mathieu, and tell him about our love and the
hopes we'd had? Yet I would have had his wife not appeared and I
stopped myself. I always had mixed feelings about that mare. But
then it could have been any horse; all it took was a slip. Maybe it
was nothing to do with her? Mathieu might have lost his balance
on the ramp and hit his head on the side of the truck . . . or had
suffered a freak blackout? Maybe we were never supposed to be
together? I don't know.

Everything had been reduced to sitting on a horse and it was
time to concentrate. I had ridden the Belgian mare a few times,
over days that had merged into a blur, before Monsieur Gallay
appeared, unexpectedly, in the indoor arena, asking me what she
was like. Actually, it had been his voice, shouting out the question, without even first announcing his presence and to be fair,
Monsieur Gallay was not rude. He was an unusual person, not
quite an enigma like Father, Monsieur Gallay sure took some getting used to and certainly seemed intent on appearing eccentric,
the moody rich man with a vision, yet he was not impolite as
such. When I heard him, I must have been startled as the horse
began a series of little skitters across the school. Monsieur Gallay
had shouted, "Wonderful, wonderful," I can't imagine why, it
may have looked dramatic or something, she was a beautiful
horse and moved very well in a bouncy, extravagant action.

He had great ambitions for the mare, he explained as if he reckoned I knew nothing of the plans for her. It was important, no, vital, he emphasized, that she was good because it would be in honor of Mathieu as he had believed the horse would do well. That all seemed pretty obvious to me, she already was a proven international, not a raw youngster to be developed. Still I managed an enthusiastic nod, always ready to agree but pointed out that she was only getting back as she had been injured for months. Monsieur Gallay said, "Bien, bien." Off he slouched; his hands thrust deeper than ever in his pockets, thoughts elsewhere, head down as if facing into a nonexistent gale.

The horse was sharp and very strong, even when unfit. Yet there was no malice in her and I knew all about malice thanks to Galileo's repertoire of dirty tricks. Maybe it is a pointless occupation, riding around in circles on big animals that would rather be running wild in a herd, but it helped me get through the hours, the days, the weeks. I'd become a shell, and while I was alone in the indoor, the only sound was the thud of the hooves in the sand, the creaking of the saddle, the breathing of the mare and sometimes her abrupt little whinny.

There was a poem I'd remembered, one written by a German poet, Gottfried Benn, who was a surgeon. It was a dark little meditation; he had been performing an autopsy on a drowned man who had been brought into the morgue with a flower stuck between his teeth. A callous joke or a commemorative gesture of sorts gone badly wrong, it was difficult to tell, but the speaker, the poet/doctor, decided to put the flower, a lavender aster, into the corpse's chest cavity. I felt as if a decaying weed had been sewn into mine and I continued to ride round and round until somehow I noticed that the mare's breathing had become labored. She was running sweat, far more tired than I had intended. I'd become a sleepwalker, bewildered as to how

I would manage to get through the days and again considered heading off to Bavaria with Hector. I would have to call Mitzi and I dreaded doing that, it would be like failing her. She had sounded so pleased that I had managed to get myself a job, and after having made my crazy stand by going to Paris and all, that thing with Marc . . . It was she who had told me that I would never smuggle Hector into America, so that's why I'd bragged so hard to get to Amboise, and then I had met Mathieu. She had dubbed him the perfect man and she'd never even got to meet him. It had all ended. No matter how many times I replayed it over in my mind I knew that it wasn't my fault but that did not make it any easier and by then it had struck me that I was paying for my disconnected reaction to Mother's death. Mitzi's theory about karma proven right for sure and all.

*

Monsieur Gallay would watch the mare and ask some questions, half-listen, mutter something and then give me a vague wave of his hand and off he would go, without his former sense of purpose. His emphatic stride had become slow, unsure. He had lost weight and seemed older all of a sudden, far less dynamic and no longer dapper. Sometimes he looked as if he had been sleeping in his clothes and would go days without shaving. He missed Mathieu and had genuinely loved him. How close was Monsieur Gallay to his children? Sophie seemed a bored ice queen, restless if apathetic, and I had never met Anton who Mathieu had said was an art historian, interested only in Paris. None of it mattered to me. Just did my work and the biggest thing that happened in a week would be if buyers were due. That would make me tidy myself up, put on a clean shirt, polish my boots, and ride as if I was doing a dressage test. And that's how I tried to get by, eat my supper and go to bed, me and Hector, and it was during those sad, silent evenings that I read *Walden*. It was easy to imagine going off to live in a cabin in the woods, just me and Hector, alone together, surrounded by trees, well away from humankind and all the grief that it generated as it certainly had done in my experience.

Had Mrs. Faulkner been working for Monsieur Gallay in an aftermath of loss as she had with us in Richmond, she would have simply continued preparing the meals and serving them, beautifully and correctly, stoic with no expression on her face aside from concentration, always attending to the work at hand. The little Amboise cook was different; she was so warmhearted and generous. Her smile which would light up her ruddy features, making her lively eyes dance before disappearing in a web of fine wrinkles, had vanished.

Everyone called her Maman, even polite, formal me. I never did get to know her name. Her sturdy eldest son, who had four children by four different local women, came along each evening in his battered old truck to bring her home and they greeted each other as if they'd been parted for years. Throughout the day she was there, working in the kitchen and always ready to look after us all as if we were helpless and tiny. It was easy to imagine her on the alert with a box of Band-Aids and a jar of candy, ready for all level of emergency. But she'd become subdued, as bereft as the rest of us.

Everything changed; it was never the same after Mathieu died, the men only ate because it was necessary. The old enjoyment was gone; they would take mugs of coffee and thick slabs of bread, pieces of chicken straight into their hands or reach down deep into the basket, gathering two or three buttery croissants at once. No one wanted to sit down anymore. Maman took to deep-frying drumsticks and offering buffet-style menus, plates of sandwiches and onion or beetroot soup from a huge blue and white tureen, to be drunk not eaten in large mug-like bowls, making it easier to ingest standing up. The dining chalet had become a fast-food counter or more like a hospital kitchen on a battlefield enabling Maman to deal with us, the wounded; the ones who had gotten left behind. It was sad how different it had become from the days when we'd all watched Lone Star taunt Mathieu, waiting to see whether or not he would react, how much bread would be thrown, how many plates broken, with most of her displays ending in those wailing exits.

As for Monsieur Gallay, he'd descend among us to survey the scene, extend his arms and offer his encouraging smile, although he knew the situation was hopeless and that we, his troops, were staring at certain defeat. If no one else was there, he would pat me on the shoulder, sigh, and inquire if I was well, if I needed a new riding hat. I kept saying no, the one I had was fine, I'd only had it a little while. I remembered the day I had bought it with Mathieu, an afternoon of new saddles and ice cream and excitement. Even so, over the course of several weeks, Monsieur Gallay would continually ask if I wanted to go buy a new hat. Two owners had come to see how their horses were doing and I had brushed my hair, changed my shirt, and pretended to myself I was in an Olympic final. My fantasy made me focus. Monsieur Gallay seemed pleased and he made sure I was involved, everyone spoke English. Then one of the owners asked to ride his horse and it was passable on the flat excepting for him pulling at the young gelding's mouth, causing it to jerk its head high and up at an ugly angle. When he tried to take a little jump, well, it went badly. The man lurched forward, fell off, and lost his temper, blaming the horse, me, the gods, but no, never his own self. He got to his feet and retrieved the whip he had been using and thrashed the horse hard across the face. Monsieur Gallay grabbed that riding crop, shouted at him to stop and rasped, "Please to leave my property. If you would like to take your horse, very well. Better still, I buy it." Either way he said there was no charge, "Not for all the work that Helen has done. But never come to me again, I will not deal with you." Subject closed. Monsieur Gallay strode away and the man asked me how much the horse was worth. I'd no idea. But something made me look directly at him, not usual for me, and say something like, to try and ride a horse, you need to be patient and honorable and fair, and told him he rode really badly. The man called me something in French that sounded decidedly unflattering and turned his back on me, before swinging around only to roar that Monsieur Gallay could purchase the horse and to get him to phone with an offer. With that he left and I just laughed at how much ego was tied up with humans riding horses.

※

Christmas had come and gone and poor old Celeste had duly perished, no doubt served up with an apple in her mouth. I declined my invitation to the festivities. What would Lone Star have had to say? She probably didn't know about Mathieu. If she had she would have blamed it on bad karma as she did most things, just like Mitzi always did. I had tacked up a big former eventer that was on his way to England as a hunting horse for one of Monsieur Gallay's friends, a Member of Parliament— about equal to being in our Senate—and I had gone riding across the estate on Christmas morning. There was an extensive area of forestry, obviously a commercial plantation, in addition to all the old woodland and the wide open park as well as meadow and tilled fields you could skirt around near the ditches, avoiding the heavy soil. But aside from not liking pork even if I had not been acquainted with the donor, I didn't much care for the idea of sitting down at the meal, staring at Sophie and agonizing about how much Mathieu had loved her and whether she had ever loved him for real. I retreated early to my room; it was very cold outside and the yardmen had predicted snow, but it never did come. My plan was just to get through the days. It was time to phone Mitzi but I couldn't, and I needed to call Father, but was unable to manage that either. Monsieur Gallay was being very kind; he had purchased the horse from the boorish bad rider and said he was sorry for me having to be in the presence of such an unpleasant character. Soon after that he began asking me if I missed Mathieu, I said I did and after putting that same question to me maybe five or six times, over several weeks, one afternoon he announced that he had suspected that I had been, "Maybe, perhaps, a little bit in love with Mathieu." It didn't take much, only that and I began to cry and sort of crouched tight against the wall of the stable I had been standing in and then sank down on my knees, my hands pressed over my ears, wailing and sobbing. Monsieur Gallay placed his hand on my head and asked me if Mathieu had known how I felt. That was when I told him all about our plans; Mathieu's hopes and dreams for us and about us vowing to be together always. I braced myself, expecting Monsieur Gallay to order me to leave.

But he didn't. All he said was that Mathieu was married to Sophie and had I not known that. When I said no, not at all, and that Mathieu had never mentioned it, he swallowed, blew slowly through his teeth, and absorbed the information. He then tossed me a curry comb and pointed to the horse in the stall. "Good," he said, and seemed about to leave but stopped and asked me if I was close to Father. Well, how to answer that. I said not really because he was a quiet man but then I just felt it was time to be honest and I told this Frenchman, whom I barely knew but who had paid me a great deal of money for the pleasure of riding his horses, had in fact given me and my dog sanctuary, and with whose son-in-law I had been planning on settling down, that actually Father and I were two of a kind; repressed, miserable, lost and lonely, plain terrified of living in the real world and that in common with Father I shared a distorted notion of romance and had read far too many books to be good for me, while I, for my part, unlike Father, actually knew very little about anything. That gave Monsieur Gallay something to ponder. He then gazed closely at me, and after all the months of me being there day after day, confessed that he had never noticed before that my eyes were two different colors and asked if the world looked exactly the same through each of them. It was a most perceptive observation and made me suspect that he was, after all I'd wrongly surmised about him, someone that I could speak with; an adult who'd always heeded his fabulous imagination and had lived and lied and experimented and made plenty of mistakes, all the while learning a lot about himself and about other people. Above all, he had loved Mathieu for almost as long as I'd even been alive.

*

Sophie, conceded Monsieur Gallay with sincere regret, was a cold-hearted creature, "Very beautiful, a work of art, quite unexpected when you look at her parents, but not very warm, in fact—not nice. Empty. She informs me I am a peasant. What a

thing to say to your father." Then he asked me would I say such
a thing to Father. That made me smile. Then after that, still pursuing personal themes, he suggested that I should marry Anton.
It was not exactly sensitive considering that he knew about my
feelings for Mathieu. But Monsieur Gallay explained that by
marrying his son I could stay on at Amboise, that all I had to
do was marry him; Anton would want to live in Paris. Madame
Gallay was anxious to at least try to have her line continued, he
said, "But me, as for mine, my line, I could not care a shit." It
sounded funny the way he said it, like an indignant cartoon character, reminding me of that skunk, Pepé Le Pew . . . I had often
watched Monsieur Gallay being charming with women, and as
I have said, there was that incident with the wife of one of his
owners . . . I'd never met Anton. All I could say was that I envied
his having become an art historian. But Monsieur Gallay corrected that. "No, that's wrong, not so. That boy, he never studied
a thing. He works in one of the art galleries owned by my wife's
family, he has never studied art. Does he look at the pictures he
tries to sell? I think not . . . He likes Paris. My son and my daughter are not interested in anything; they have no passion, not like
Mathieu." Then he laughed halfheartedly, more like a wince and
admitted that he would not want to marry Anton either.

Time was passing, I was drifting again, like before, like
always. It was easier to stay where I was, riding horses by day
and spending my evenings with Hector, trying to read and to
sleep; not even sleeping, just lying in bed until it was time to
get up and eat and ride all over again. Each day I would plan on
phoning Mitzi but failed to because I couldn't tell her about what
had happened to Mathieu. One night while I was eating supper,
Monsieur Gallay came in and sat down beside me. I thought that
perhaps he was about to ask how much longer I was intending
to stay. But he wanted me to go with him to Belgium to see a

horse, a full brother of the mare I was riding, the one Monsieur Gallay insisted on calling Mathieu's mare. More like Mathieu's murderer. He had also given her a name: "Pirate Lady," that's what it sounded like but he was actually saying "Prairie Lady," an odd choice of name for a European horse, but I didn't much care what he called her.

Then he inquired if I was happy, ridiculous in the circumstances and I shot back without thinking, out of character for cautious, careful me, the big question: was he Lone Star's father. Monsieur Gallay shrugged and calmly shook his head but did add quite candidly that he could have been had she been about ten years older as he had had what he called "a very small interlude" with Lone Star's mother, "Just for three days in a hotel room in Cannes, wine and love, well sex, and television, room service, laughter." He liked Annette and said that she had been charming and fun then and was always very nice—"not like her horrible bitch brat daughter."

The trip to Belgium was enjoyable; we drove so as I could take Hector. It was flat countryside but Bruges was really interesting and the Belgian breeding programs were impressive. Although the full brother was not quite as developed as our mare, the deal was done and he too was bound for Amboise. All the while I kept sensing that Monsieur Gallay and I had become not exactly friends, more like war veterans sharing memories and feeding off each other's pain. Even so, we also had horses in common and I remember one night telling him about Father's friend, Bill Steinkraus, who had won the Olympic gold medal for show jumping, the first American to do that. The point of my story for Monsieur Gallay was that Mr. Steinkraus's horse, Snowbound, had been seriously unsuccessful on the race track, but having gotten a second chance he came through with his big heart and generosity as well as his courage to become a great show jumper in spite of suffering from chronic tendon trouble. Monsieur Gallay loved hearing about Snowbound, another Thoroughbred that had successfully switched disciplines, and it set him off on a long, rambling, and often quite comical account of the many wonderful horses he had known in his life. As did most conversations between us, it soon came back to Mathieu.

"I met him at a Thoroughbred yearling sale in Saumur in the grounds of the castle and he was just a boy, fifteen years old," and he sighed, describing Mathieu as very engaging, innocent, full of hope, "with those big eyes and the funny ears, like a garden gnome." The memory made him smile while I did too, because for me it was funny hearing a Frenchman say "gnome" pronouncing the "g" the way some Americans do—as in "g-nome." "His father had died, maybe two months before, I think, very stupidly, when having his tonsils out. It is a children's operation, no? Yet it often kills adults . . . and that bad luck had left Mathieu and his mother and a very young sister, only a little thing then, now she is training to become a doctor." They were all alone, Mathieu and his family, and with little money. Monsieur Gallay seemed happier than I had seen him since the day . . . well, you know, that day when it had happened . . . He told me that he had dropped his sales program and his pen and when he bent down to pick them up had banged his head off Mathieu's. "That is how we met, banging our heads together at a yearling sale. Prophetic, non?" He'd asked him was he buying, because he looked so young. "Are you rich?" he had said to Mathieu. "And this boy answers that he had come to look at the horses because they were so very beautiful." Monsieur Gallay sighed and I could imagine Mathieu saying "so very beautiful" in that wistful way that he had. Monsieur Gallay must have read my mind and said that it was so like Mathieu. "I showed him the ones I was interested in looking at," and he recalled having marked the numbers in the catalog and that he'd invited Mathieu to eat with him before looking together at the horses he was considering buying. "Maybe five minutes later before our food even arrived, I said, 'Here, you come work for me,' and he did." That would have been sixteen, almost seventeen years earlier on my reckoning and it was easy to see that Monsieur Gallay had enjoyed having a protégé. He was very aware of having been seen as the opportunist who'd married into wealth. "Mathieu was a worker but with visions of how things could be . . ." said Monsieur Gallay and he admitted that he also would have had that type of life, always seeking the impossible except that he had married his rich wife when they were very young. "And do you know? I had forgotten what it was like to be poor until I met Mathieu . . . he helped me to stay in touch with the real world." A long silence followed that, he seemed to be waiting for me to say something, but I just sat there not entirely understanding Monsieur Gallay's perception of the real world, but more importantly, again I was struck by how very little Mathieu had told me about his life. I had heard all about the dreams, but not about the facts, and none of the history.

The short days and the darkness made me feel half-alive; my mind was closing, shutting down. I had begun to find thinking an effort beyond me, and reverted to reciting the periodic table to stop myself going completely mad. Easter was a long way off and the winter, which had been slow in coming, proved even slower at retreating. Most days I just rode in the indoor, usually on my own, with a yardman bringing in horses at forty-minute intervals. It was not ideal, I actually like untacking a horse after I have ridden; it's part of the ritual of riding. But there was so little time and the men were anxious to wash the horses and rub them down, I did my part. Hector was content. I monitored his weight and made sure he did not exert himself; he could get very excited and had taken well to wearing the little coat, a kind of sweater thing that I had bought for him. Most of all he loved being stretched out beside me on the mattress.

Winter only began in earnest after Christmas and it became bitterly cold. It made me remember one of the running gags Father had had with Caleb Montgomery. When it was cold, one of them would declare, "My, my, it's as cold as Arlington Cemetery, which, as we know, is always colder than the North and South Poles." Or they might say, "My, my, it's even colder than Arlington Cemetery, which, as we know, is always colder than the North and South Poles." And they'd cackle like a pair of witches. Their context being that when they had attended the reburial of John F. Kennedy in 1967, it had been below zero. I'm not sure if they were at the actual reburial or if they had decided to pay their respects privately, but it was usually freezing at Arlington. Some years later I went there too on a school trip and I thought I'd gotten frostbite, my hands and feet stung so badly from the cold, I'd expected to find my toes all broken off and stuck to my socks. A chill breeze always seems to gust in hard from the Potomac or so people say and I guess it's true. After the school trip anytime Father and Mr. Montgomery performed their little routine, I could laugh along as well because I knew what they were talking about.

From when I was little there were always allusions made to Mother's depression, she used to refer to her "mope days." I never paid much heed. As I became older I lost patience with her. But suddenly it was my turn and there in France I'd entered my own twilight zone, maintaining a vigil, wearing Mathieu's clothes as I huddled on the mattress desperate for sleep. Only for Hector and those horses I don't know how I could have negotiated the days. Sometimes I felt Monsieur Gallay was suffocating me with his memories and his awareness of our shared secret.

Yet at other times I wanted to be with him, just hearing how he and Mathieu had practiced their English together, agreeing not to speak French, and sometimes they'd play English-language tapes and repeat it all, together. Simply visualizing them correcting each other—they were both so pedantic by nature—made me smile and it helped keep Mathieu alive.

Truth has a habit of making its way to the surface like so many bull frogs lurching forth from the swamp. It took several visits to Mathieu's grave for it to finally dawn on me that he had not been buried with his little daughter. Although it was not easy for me to put such an intimate question to Monsieur Gallay, I did. My only excuse I suppose was that in all the grief he had shown for Mathieu there had been none for the baby girl. I had not even heard her name mentioned and she was his first grandchild.

It had been early, the sun just about breaking through, so bright I knew it would not last. A heavy frost had settled during the night and the way walking over to the dining chalet looked even more pretty than usual. Everything was held fast in a powdery frozen layer as if someone had gone crazy with icing sugar. Maman was busy, talking to the cats that were all present and accounted for in the heat of the kitchen, it was way too cold for them to venture out and they seemed to be holding humankind entirely responsible for the weather. I ambled in and greeted the cook. Back she smiled and gave me my hot chocolate, motioning to the stove with a gesture that clearly meant, just another minute. I sat at the table, my thoughts nowhere and my hands wrapped around the large bowl of hot chocolate. Then she emerged out of the kitchen carrying a big dish of porridge, the honey was already on the table, as always. Well that was the finest porridge I had ever had outside of Virginia. Mrs. Faulkner made the very best, but that morning's was indeed approaching hers and reminded me yet again that I should really contact Mitzi for sure. But far more overdue was a call to Father. I had not even sent any postcards, and I thought of all the horse images I had dispatched from Paris to the singularly ungrateful Mitzi with only one to Father. There I had been an idle tourist; here I was a worker, that was the difference. About halfway through the porridge, enjoying it and feeling that it was the first time in a few months I had even tasted food—prior to that I had been merely shoveling it in like it was gas in a car to stoke an engine—Monsieur Gallay arrived, smiled at me, and went into the kitchen. I could hear a quick-fire conversation between him and Maman. For some reason they always seemed to shout good-naturedly at each other and I liked listening to them, missing the meaning of most of what they were saying, but I always noticed how it contrasted with the diplomatic exchanges Father conducted with Mrs. Faulkner.

Monsieur Gallay had decided to breakfast with me; he came out holding a cup in one hand and the large coffee pot in the other announcing, "I will become an American and eat like you." Maman followed with toast and then went back in, to fetch a plate of bacon and eggs which she placed on the table before him, fussing and polishing silverware in her apron. He asked me if I was ready for the day and then took a large gulp of coffee before making a face, discovering that he had forgotten to add sugar, which he then did. That's when I just asked him where the baby was buried. "What's that?" he looked surprised and frowned. Awkward with embarrassment flooding my face I persisted. I needed to know, "Mathieu's baby, his baby with Sophie, Sophie's baby." I needed to know, I needed to know. He told me that she was buried in the Quignard family vault. Her name had been Delphine. "Little Delphine who lived and died and never had a life. Tell me the fairness, the justice of that."

But why wasn't Mathieu buried there? Monsieur Gallay's blunt reply was followed by a shrug of his shoulders. His wife—"the mistress-in-waiting of all we survey," I'd begun to refer to her as—refused to have Mathieu placed in the vault, because he was not family. Monsieur Gallay almost smiled while telling me that and I could see he was weighing the potential impact of revealing something else. He looked at me and his expression softened. I knew by then that he had begun to regard me as a friend; he could tell that I was maybe a bit more than a dopey teenager with only horses on her mind and perhaps he had guessed that I was even more messed up than he was. And oh yes, for sure, he was thinking quick and intently, but first he ate some of his breakfast—he always ate with his mouth open, noisily, chomping dogmatically—and he poured another cup of coffee, asking if I wanted some. I had finished my hot chocolate and he just poured some coffee straight into my empty bowl. He had more to tell me.

A few years earlier Sophie had set off to conquer Paris and had had a portfolio of professional photographs taken of her face from all possible angles, smiling, pouting and all the rest. I felt my attention waning; indifferent to Sophie's modeling aspirations, I could have said her very existence had burnt into my grieving soul. Of course I was jealous. Anyhow her stupendous face did not compensate for her stocky figure and those pillar-like legs or the Stone Age feet. There would for sure and certain be no future for flat-footed old her as a catwalk model whatever about the other stuff. Monsieur Gallay winked at me as he conceded with clear amusement that she'd inherited her peasant's body from him. "And for this she does not forgive me," and yes her hands too, were also his. When I studied her close up, I had noticed her blunt little paws ending in thick, stumpy fingers. Blood usually does out, as Father always said.

Monsieur Gallay then became solemn, slightly apprehensive, and watched for my reaction. It seemed that Sophie had gotten in with a wild set when she was in Paris, very different from the finishing school she had attended in Geneva—no wonder Lone Star's mention of finishing school had caused Mathieu to snigger. Sophie had had a few relationships, which Monsieur Gallay described as "skirmishes." He said that he always felt that she had been pregnant before she had returned home. The mistress of one of Sophie's boyfriends had phoned Madame Gallay with all the details and his wife, ever a woman of discretion and tolerance as well as deceptive determination, had summoned Sophie home.

Once restored to Amboise she had suddenly become interested in Mathieu, even deciding to briefly profess a new fascination with horses, and Mathieu had been very flattered. "He was smitted"—he meant "smitten"—and Monsieur Gallay, with that wayward amorality that had helped him get through life, admitted to having encouraged what he referred to as their "arrangement." I was glad he did not say romance; it would have hurt me even more.

Several weeks before the baby was due Sophie took to her bed and then there was a crisis and she'd been rushed into hospital in Tours. About ten days after that, Delphine had been born. "And then it all began, trying to fix her . . ." Monsieur Gallay spoke in little more than a murmur although I knew that Maman would never be able to follow, she knew no English and, as I finally figured out, was also slightly deaf hence all the shouting. It was not clear if there was more to be told, but just then two men arrived at the door. Monsieur Gallay greeted them and gestured toward the coffee. He looked at me, and nodded. I knew that meant time to go and I went back to check Hector. When I got to our room, I was so very tired and decided everyone, humans and horses, could wait. Slowly, feeling shaky on my feet, overwhelmed by my pathetic joy at having a morsel of Mathieu released back to me, I picked up Hector and although I had already had a shower, went into the bathroom and locked the door. There was no bath oil left, so instead I poured in some shampoo to make bubbles, opened the hot water faucet and got into the bath as it was filling. Hector sat on my clothes and I gasped as the boiling water transformed my feet into two scarlet lobsters. The bathroom steamed up. Hector dozed and I just waited, my legs turning red to redder as the water thundered onto the old enamel. Soon I could slide down like a submarine, immersing my head under the layer of hot foam, and I held my breath until my lungs hurt and realized that, somehow, I was still alive.

*

Hector died. Suddenly, during the night while I was asleep. He must have died in my arms; I was holding him, unaware that he was dying. He had gone quietly. Perhaps he had been dreaming? It helps me to believe that. He looked so peaceful. All I could hope was that it had been as easy as that for him, just falling into a deep, deep sleep and never to wake again; my sweet, courageous little dog. It was morning, heavy with exhaustion I reached to pat him, and said, as I had so often, "Come on little guy, we must go and greet the day." And I moved carefully, as always, unfolding myself from him, allowing him the space to get up and follow me over to the patio door to relieve himself against one of the large stone pots before going on into the bathroom with me. But he never moved, and he would always get up, no matter how comfortable he was because he was my loyal shadow, my dog. And then there was that familiar chill of unease, and me thinking he had gotten sick, me getting ready to panic. "Hey Buddy Boy, come on with me," I coaxed and urged, wondering how quickly I could get him into the veterinarian in Tours. But Hector didn't move, I held him close, then tried to open his mouth but his jaws were clenched tight, even though he still felt warm in spite of the cool morning air. I lay down beside him and drew him in close, against me, that small, compact size of him, pulling the blankets up over my head and tried to think, tasting the tears that were blinding me. My chest heaved, it hurt to breathe. I felt dizzy and so very alone. It was all over, the little life we had made together dead and gone.

Only the previous afternoon after finishing up in the yard, earlier than usual, I had hurried over to the churchyard, Hector with me, in the old station wagon. I'd gotten better at driving it, more confident. There we had knelt in the fading light beside Mathieu's grave, still a tidy mound of earth, hidden beneath wreaths, me reporting to Mathieu how the horses were going, mentioning the lame one and that I had been thinking of setting off for England by ferry, me and Hector, to finally have a look at the Whistlejacket portrait that I had told him about. And that I had planned on hiding Hector in my shoulder bag, I knew he would deal just fine with the train ride. Better still, I could just drive the whole way, take the ferry and then drive to Exeter, it was near London. I could manage that, having finally figured out the automatic. Planning a weekend trip would make it seem that I was trying to live normally and that because I was keeping such close contact with Mathieu he would never leave me. It was the talking, all those words, me discussing things with him, putting questions to him that I could imagine him answering, I felt it would work. We just had to preserve our connection and I knew I could do that. But Hector, my Hector, he had been the defining presence. He was such a brave little dog, could barely see, couldn't hear a thing, yet his courage was anchoring both of us.

Pretty soon after first meeting him and addressing him as "Mr. Hector Berlioz," I knew that he was really Homer's Hector from the *Iliad*, a true hero, noble like a lion. He had made everything good happen. My little dog, his trusting clouded eyes gazing at me through his black raccoon's mask. I had always suspected that I was just a blurred shape to him but how he had loved me, as I loved him and there was no Billy Bob around to comprehend my despair. It was time to leave Amboise, I recognized that. But I couldn't leave Hector; I knew I could not bury him and walk away. I had had no role in Mathieu's burial, been denied the right to mourn; had not even met Mathieu's mother. Monsieur Gallay had apologized for having told me not to go to the funeral. He didn't know that I had been there, standing at the back of the church like the outsider I was and I never did tell him. But with Hector, it was urgent and it had to be private, just me and him, I did not want any kindly offers for help in digging a grave. Hector was coming back to America with me. The vicious irony of it all; Hector alive would face so many difficulties, that long separation of quarantine. Mitzi had made it sound like a death sentence, which I suppose it was for an old dog running out of time. Yet Hector dead could come home with me, I'd just have to organize it.

A rogue tremor was causing my teeth to chatter fit to break; I was in shock and needed to go to the bathroom. My hands were shaking as I pulled at my pajama bottoms; I was sobbing and gagging, but needed to get to Tours. Without even taking a shower I dressed and hurried over to the dining chalet and into the kitchen. There was Maman, happy to see me even in those now sadder days. In another life she would have been the kind of mother I would have run to and cried in her arms, telling her about my dog. Miming pain I held my throat and my glands, acting real sad for being unable to face breakfast. She had had enough children to reckon on my having inflamed tonsils and I shuddered at the memory of Mathieu's father dying while having his out. Turning to go, I knew that she would alert the yardmen that I would not be riding that morning. I didn't eat anything, just ran back and lifted Hector so gently, his little weight, the small bundle I knew so well, wrapping my blue and gray Mathieu sweater around him, and hurried to the car as if we had been in an accident but there was still hope, which there wasn't. The drive to Tours required such effort; I leaned in over the steering wheel, elbows locked against my ribs, peering at the road ahead, my vision blurred from crying. Somehow I got us into the town and looked out for the gas station. The people in there could direct me to a funeral parlor; I needed one that provided cremation services. What was the French for that? Hector was not going to be buried in France. Bad enough that I could do nothing about Mathieu, but I was going to bring Hector home. I had lots of money.

By the time I had been asked to vacate the premises by the man in the third undertaking firm I had approached—the people in the first two places had threatened to summon the police—I was hysterical and felt fully beaten. No one wanted to help. The French are most peculiar; no matter how far you get outside Paris they still consider any foreigner as an alien from outer space. But a woman typing away in the office in that third firm as I begged the man to please cremate Hector so as he could come home to America, had been listening. Somehow she'd misunderstood or I'd given the impression that Hector had traveled with me to Europe, so I had stuck to that story hoping someone would take pity on us. I was full sick of hearing that it was a hygiene issue. Hell's name how on earth could any dead person possibly object to a dog being cremated in the same facility; it did not make one atom particle of sense. But luck finally intervened. The typist had understood and wanted to help. She said she was sorry and suggested I try a crematorium in Orleans because the undertaker there owned the place and had his own views on how people looked after their dearly departed. I did not much like the phrase "dearly departed" but was encouraged when she told me that the undertaker had cremated her uncle with two of his cats, one of them had already died and was buried in the garden, and the second cat was put to sleep so as it could be cremated with its owner. Bit drastic, she said, but maybe the cat would have pined away. I got the address and then asked where Orleans was and how far? She told me it was 117 kilometers away, which meant about seventy-two or seventy-three miles to me. It would take me some time. The people back in the yard must have reckoned I was consulting a doctor in Vienna, I'd been gone so long, but I knew by then that I would be leaving. Without Hector there was no reason left to stay on at Amboise. It was time to return to Virginia, and become a veterinarian as Father wanted. I could do it, forget the planets; forget studying history. He had hoped to pass his practice on to me and I would manage, my life having been demolished, of course I could treat horses and still ride, the new me, a zombie. I'd had two great loves and had lost both of them but at least I'd had them, if only for a little while. Now it was time to pay the price, and I would.

Tears just kept tracking down my face and my eyes were burning but once I got out of Tours, the route was direct and I concentrated on getting to Orleans, wondering what year it had been that Joan of Arc rode in, wearing armor, misguidedly intent on helping an ungrateful king. That was all I could muster in connection to Orleans, a saint who had been burnt at the stake and there I was, trying to arrange a cremation. Fire. How could Hector have gone without any warning, no goodbye. It was unbelievable, my thoughts kept returning to that afternoon in Paris when he had found me in the park, the Jardin des Plantes. He had been a gift from the gods; I knew that, a life-giver. It seemed such a long time ago although it was only months. "It's the only way Hector, we must do this. I can't go home and leave you behind. You will be like a Greek hero, like the other Hector, the flames of immortality carrying you up to Heaven, you wait there with Mathieu for me. People used to burn their heroes, it is an honor and I want to honor you. This way I can take you with me and then you will be buried with me and we will be together for always and always." I drove faster than usual, sweating and shivering, calling out to Billy Bob, my eyes stinging from all the crying.

*

The undertaker in Orleans refused to get involved, feigning horror. "Non, non, non." But I pushed and pleaded and tossed a fistful of francs on his desk and then more, and then another wad, neat-bound with a rubber band. It bounced off the desk and hit the floor; I fetched it up and slapped it back down with the flat of my hand. He began to get interested. His face was disgusting. How his mean squinty little brown eyes had glittered then moistened at the sight of so much money. I showed him Hector, stressed how little he was and asked the man if he had a dog. He had had several in his life and I seized on that and cajoled and pestered, said I would wait and take Hector away with me. No one need ever know that he had helped us. I was leaving

France to go home and Father was alone, waiting for me and our dog . . . that Mother was dead and that Hector was everything to us; Father and me. How I lied. Father did not even know of Hector's existence. Had I contacted him at the very beginning, Hector would have died at home and I could have buried him in Monticello's garden. No one would ever know, I promised that mercenary French undertaker, it would be a secret. His hands were full of money, yet still he had not agreed. I repeated that I would never tell anyone. He looked at the money and then up at me. He said that he would like to help, but that it cost a lot of money to heat up the furnace, a lot of money. "Beaucoup, beaucoup," and the grasping charlatan faked helplessness, as if he had to answer to a superior but I knew he was in charge. "Here, have some more," I said, and I pulled further notes out of my jacket pocket, so much money concealed about my person, including the usual stash in my boot. I was like a deranged magician pulling rabbits out of a top hat, although I hadn't removed the hidden cash from under my heel. He didn't know I also had about four books of traveler's checks with me. He looked suddenly crazed, as if he had happened upon a phenomenal game which he was certain of winning. All he had to do was ask and random money appeared. It was disgusting but he was my only hope and yes, he counted the money and sighed, such a chore, but yes he would do it. I held my breath and would not let him out of my sight, I begged him to allow me to place Hector in the furnace. There was a platform, designed for holding a casket. Hector looked so small as I laid him on it, my sweater under him and I kissed him one last time, whispering, "We got to do this, trust me; trust me."

And there was a loud, industrial sound and a boom, it was the gas element igniting. It had to reach a specific temperature. The undertaker had become very friendly, concerned, perhaps even slightly embarrassed. I had given the greedy hypocrite the equivalent of about $2,000, but I didn't care. It had worked and that was all that mattered. The state of his rotten soul did not concern me.

It was very quick; suddenly there was a sporadic ticking. "It is cooling down," explained the undertaker, "ashes to ashes, dust to dust." All so very final. He offered me coffee and I stayed where I was, aware that I did not trust him to bring me Hector's ashes. Yet he did and with a printed certificate, in French, confirming that these were the ashes of a pet dog, Hector—the "pet dog Hector," was handwritten on what was a blank line. An English translation was underneath, in smaller print. It was useful to have this document said the undertaker, in case of my being questioned at the airport on re-entering the United States. "The American police are far worse than ours; the Americans wave their guns all the time and threaten everyone. This I know from the television," he said. Then he inquired as to which container I wanted, and began reciting off a list of prices. Some of the urns were gaudy, festooned with fake jewels, colored glass, very weird indeed. And a couple of them did resemble time capsules. A small wooden box, with a glass frame in the lid, looked the most dignified and he saw me staring at it. Just as I had figured out that the frame was for a photograph, he cleared his throat for my attention. "It is the most expensive; this box is handmade," he announced it as if a prize-giving was underway. Perhaps I had gazed quizzically at him, I don't know. But at least he had the grace to blush, far more aware than I was at the time of how much money he had made out of Hector, and he said, "Here, take it. Your dog will go home in the best we have to offer."

*

Hector was little yet his ashes which had been placed in a plastic bag almost filled the box. I was glad that I had some photographs that Lone Star had taken. A couple of them were very good and I could recall her bragging about her photographic skills and how her "inspired" use of the light "makes him look about one hundred years younger." Her smarty-pants comments about his age and his blindness had upset me so much that I stopped her taking further pictures but at least I had a few and all thanks to her. The return drive to Amboise seemed much shorter. It was late, well past supper-time. Maman looked worried. She was still there, standing by the table, her son was speaking to Monsieur Gallay and all three paused as I walked in. You would think that they had seen an apparition. Monsieur Gallay studied me and asked me if I was any better. He seemed concerned. I just said I needed to go back to America. "Your father, he is sick?" he asked. That made me pause; if Father was ill, I would have no way of knowing. "Hector died," I said, "Hector died." And all I could do was cry as Maman's son asked in French what it was I had said. Monsieur Gallay explained and almost whispered that he and Laurent, Maman's son, would bury him for me. "Just find a magnificent place, near a tree. How about the rose garden? You like that? We can plant lavender and he will have butterflies . . . Poor Helen, you love your little dog, I am so very sorry." Maman reached up and pushed my hair out of my eyes, my bangs needed to be trimmed so badly by then that I'd taken to scowling at the world from under them. She turned and spoke to Monsieur Gallay. He said that she had offered to bring me supper on a tray to my chalet. I thanked them all and walked slowly to my room, dreading how empty it would be without Hector there to welcome me back.

There was no point in even attempting to sleep. Maman's tray lay untouched, the soup had congealed. The room was so familiar to me and yet it was as if I had never been there before. The large portfolio of the solar system was on display, propped up against the wall on the little table. I had bought the folder at the book stall on the Left Bank, given it for free, in fact, shortly before Hector had found me in the park. Before Hector: life before Hector, life with him, and now, without him.

Gather your things I told myself and leave. That is what I did; just placed everything on the mattress and assessed what I had. My clothes, Mathieu's clothes, books, the portfolio, the riding hat, Hector's white cup, Hector's ashes, and the weatherproof riding jacket Mathieu had given me. Noticing the inflatable made my eyes sting. I would leave it behind. Friedrich's painting of the man gazing out over the mist, into the future, or maybe the past, came into my mind. Caspar David Friedrich, was he a dreamer? Or was he simply despondent? Or perhaps his despondence was far more complicated than that, beyond himself and intended as a universal statement. It spoke to me, it always had. I loved that picture and decided to go and see the painting in Germany, as a sort of quest. That made me gag out loud, a punch to the throat, never even having managed to go back to da Vinci's grave and I had promised Mathieu as I knelt beside his that I would take Hector back to Clos Lucé. I had never gotten round to that. Why I had not even ever swum in Monsieur Gallay's exotic indoor pool sheltered within the hothouse with all those ferns and vines thriving under its glass roof. Never really got around to anything except hoping that Mathieu would love me forever and look where that got me. Had I been really happy with him? Yes, I knew I had and I would have to keep that alive in my shriveled and battered heart.

Far more difficult was the reality of Hector reduced to ash. Hector in a small wooden box, Hector, Hector. His carrier bag which I had dubbed his sedan chair had to become a suitcase. His box took so much less space than he had. Yet Hector had left a gigantic hole I could never fill. The room had become completely dark and I spoke out loud to Billy Bob, asking him and Monticello to look after my Hector dog. I was hungry and sick, and just wanted morning to come quickly so as I could leave. However bad I felt, I could not just slip away in the night, although Billy Bob had.

*

Make a plan, make a plan; some semblance of honor was required and I didn't want to disappear, leaving a cloud of ambivalence. The Gallay people had been good to me. When morning finally seeped in through the darkness I felt numbed not just from being cold and exhausted, but because I had entered a state of dislocation having walked through some doorway into a void. My body stood under the shower; my thoughts were elsewhere. Finally I turned the water off and stepped out, squeezing the heavy wet out of my hair and pulled on some clothes. Maman was waiting for me in the dining chalet, her son was also there, and I knew he was expecting to bury Hector. I said nothing but was grateful for the large bowl of hot chocolate. No one spoke; well, Maman and Laurent could not speak English and I was too drained to even think of French words. Then the son addressed me awkwardly, "Votre petit chien?", causing me to cry and cry.

Maman rushed to my side. Monsieur Gallay appeared and asked very gently had I decided on where I wanted them to put Hector. I told him what I had done and in turn he explained. The son looked surprised but then patted me on the shoulder, kissed his mother, and left for the day. By the time Laurent returned that evening, I remember thinking I too would be gone, probably stuck back in Paris trying to figure out what to do and about to begin another segment of life, the one in Amboise, for me, being over for good. Monsieur Gallay sat down, watching me drink the hot chocolate. He told me to take a few days off, "Go to Paris" he said, and offered me a jeep "or that out there" meaning the station wagon. I could have told him about thinking I would go and see the painting of the wanderer, but decided against that, I was too tired to try and explain that particular piece of madness, so instead agreed to go to Paris, but wasn't sure if I wouldn't just drive to the station and take the train. If I did that, went by rail, I would leave the keys under the front tire, on the driver's side. He nodded and I felt sure he knew that I was not coming back, only he didn't want to ask. He told me that I was welcome, always welcome and that he would always help me. "A moment, a moment," he said, and I sat there, slumped, memorizing the room, the moment. Maman came out with another bowl of hot chocolate, I would be able to drink some more, but maybe not all of it. Monsieur Gallay looked real upset, and he had something in his hands, hastily wrapped in pale-blue tissue paper. It was a delicate little wooden horse, such a lovely thing. It makes me remember so much, the special things in my life, Mathieu and my beloved little dog, and those charmed months in Amboise when it seemed I had finally found happiness and my place in the world.

So many ironies: on that day we had first met at Longchamp racetrack Monsieur Gallay had snarled at me, wishing me to vanish on the spot yet he had not wanted to appear ill-mannered in front of his client, the owner of the horse I'd caught. He'd wanted nothing to do with me. Now he was weeping at the thought that I might not return. He handed me a padded envelope, fat, bulging with francs. More money, so much money and I already had such an amount of it. "A few days in Paris and you will be running home, to here, to the horses. You will forget the train, the car. To flee the city you will race here on your feet, by foot. Shouting 'Let me in, let me in!' And the door will be open wide for you!" He laughed, hoping he could persuade me to return without having to plead. Perhaps I would do exactly that, it might be easier to remain at Amboise, a solitary ghost destined to ride horses until I was old enough to die. I wanted it to be as it had been, me about to head over to the little chalet to settle Hector for the morning, before hurrying down to the yard to find Mathieu waiting, so serious, with his list, ready for me to mount the first horse and walk out on the path toward the indoor. But all that was over and I felt I had shrunk and that my legs would not be strong enough to carry all the weight of my sorrow.

*

Passengers were still boarding the train when an idea so obvious struck me I glanced around for fear I had jumped and spoken aloud to myself. As soon as I reached Paris I would set about getting directly to Berlin, no more idle dreaming. It made complete sense and not for the first time I asked myself why on earth I had so idiotically chosen France when Germany was so much more interesting to me. From my very first encounter with the

Brothers Grimm, I had envied the dark menace of the stories
they'd collected and was drawn to a culture that built gingerbread
houses and had invented Christmas and grasped the deep, abiding mystery of forests. But the fates decided and had I not been
in Paris that day I would never have met Hector and the Amboise
adventure would not have happened and therefore, by further
cruel logic, my heart would not be as shattered.

A bad-tempered whistle sounded with a haughty "Toot,
toot"—how very French. The train lurched forward, causing
briefcases, bags, packages, and some rolled up overcoats to spill
down off the overhead racks. Thud, thud, thud and three oranges
bounced down the aisle in a stately procession followed by laughter. A man's voice swore loudly. There was the usual shouting and
loud exclamations. Made me wonder how much noisier Italians
or Greeks could possibly be. Within minutes the carriage was
filled with tobacco smoke. My eyes began to water and I tried
to open the window. The woman sitting opposite her back to
the engine, actually pulled me by the jacket, hissing at me to sit
down, her bloodshot, operatic eyes glaring with hatred. I gave
her one of Father's stares, allowing me to admire in some detail
her black mustache. She blinked and turned away, two small net
sacks of onions at her feet. Again, how very French I thought. As
for any glimpse of the landscape, there was little to see. Only an
overcast sky, the embankments more like dams were unusually
high on both sides of the tracks, blocking the view. My thoughts
returned to my previous journey, the beginning; Hector on my
lap and me wondering what was facing us. It had been thrilling,
my haphazard adventure still taking shape, or so I remember
thinking. I was nervous, apprehensive about working and also
fretting, wondering if I'd be able to ride racehorses. How different it had all turned out. Would I ever ride another horse?
Perhaps I should just slink back and disappear, live out my life

in Amboise. Monsieur Gallay was an opportunist, not much doubt about that, yet he had an enviable capacity for friendship. He had created a life and was content in his way and in fairness to his methods he was very innovative. A mixture of salesman and guru, he would have thrived in America. Not liking either of his children, he'd just accepted it as something not even he could change. He was tough but also emotional and really kind; a far better person than I had initially grasped. In the time I had been there I had never seen him on a horse although he owned so many—and he did love them, that was plain to see.

The woman with the mustache had vanished. I must have dozed. Her seat was empty, so I made another attempt to open the window. It was jammed tight. The train slowed, clickety-click, clickety-click, squealing and juddering, and the outskirts of Paris loomed into sight, grim and depressing, promising nothing. Then the sky darkened, all I needed in my misery and whoosh, down crashed the rain, hailstones bombarding the dirty glass. It suited my mood. Berlin-bound departures left from La Gare du Nord and a ticket for the night train was soon in my pocket. The journey would take twelve hours and there was almost as long to wait so I walked to Le Jardin des Plantes in honor of Hector and had no difficulty locating the very bench I had been sitting on when he found me. It was devastating and for a moment it seemed I might be about to have a heart attack. I gathered my things and whispered to Hector, "Look what you have done to me, I am just like Billy Bob and people like him and me cannot live on without our special ones." Did humans my age die of grief? Not that I much minded dying, but it would be better to die at home. I wanted to get back to Virginia, and hated the idea of being found dead in Paris. What would they do with me? What would happen to Hector's ashes? Maybe I should forget the train, phone Father, beg his forgiveness, and hurry to the airport.

The only place in which I might feel at ease was the Louvre so I considered stopping a taxi but it was only a short walk, less than ten minutes. Once I reached the river, I knew the way. Rather than leave my bags and Hector in the cloakroom, I would go into the bookstore and look for something about Caspar David Friedrich. That didn't take long, and the large expensive volume I bought had the wanderer, my alter ego, on the jacket. All I needed was hot chocolate and a table to sit at while I began the long wait. It would be easy to pass some of the time gazing at the color plates in the book. The text was in French, how had that happened? It took about three minutes to recognize my mistake: the painting was not in Berlin. *Wanderer Above the Sea of Fog* was held at the Kunsthalle in Hamburg. The other one I wanted to see, the shipwreck scene with the great slabs of ice which was such a graphic representation of my exact state of mind was also there. That Hamburg collection had several of his works. I'd go there instead. No, I would travel to Hamburg and then on to Berlin. I had to see Berlin.

People kept walking by, clockwork toys, so many tourists, moving slowly, bewildered, saturated by Paris, its culture, its history, its arrogance. In among all of it darted the uppity Parisians, shrugs and large, wet eyes, a tribe of intolerant egotists. The people in Amboise had been kind, more human. What was the south of France like, were the people any taller, did they smile like the Spanish? No I didn't much care for Paris, I remembered the Dutch man in the sporting goods store; he had said that everyone was expected to love Paris. Well not me. It was hard to believe that it was the same city I had been in that night at the jazz club with Mathieu. That had been different; that experience belonged to the dream life I might have had . . . Then poof it had up and vanished, gone, snatched away in an instant. So Hamburg, a place to which I had never given a thought, would be my introduction to Germany. What station did I need to get to? More botheration. Then felt a fool, all the northern German trains left from the same station, La Gare du Nord. When I went to change my ticket the clerk asked was I so stupid, could I not make up my mind? He insisted I buy another ticket. I had more money than I needed but the man was so unaccommodating. I leaned in close to his face and hissed, "You change this ticket or I will complain to your superior that you tricked me, me a helpless visitor. You are here to serve the public, not make faces and mock children. You are obliged to help confused tourists. In America, people like you get fired. You should be out there cleaning the trains, Mr. Ticket Person, scrubbing out the toilet bowls. Change the ticket, Hamburg is not as far from here as Berlin. You owe me some money." I had also noticed that he had charged me a full adult fare; I showed him my passport and pointed out my date of birth, "Student, étudiante, étudiante, moi. Comprenez?" The queue behind me was getting restless, he pushed a ticket at me, along with some money and was suddenly looking far less bored, shocked by my aggression. Served him right.

There was a gourmet-quality food stall in the station and although I had little interest in eating anything at all, I bought two very rich, savory, salad sandwiches, chocolate, apples, a bag of grapes, potato chips, candy bars, and a tray of suspect pink cupcakes. Those purchases filled a large brown paper bag. For short term survival, I ate an immense, squashed pastry—it resembled a fungus that would be found attached to a tree trunk, most probably in a swamp somewhere—and also a large cup of watery hot chocolate, so scalding it scorched my tongue. The train was still quiet, almost empty when I decided to board; most passengers were probably still at large, enjoying their final moments in Paris. Bully for them, I couldn't vacate the place fast enough. My first reaction when I saw the berth and its relative height, suspended up over the floor of the carriage, was that Hector would have difficulties, and that made me cry again. I had arranged my things and kicked off my boots. Then, bedlam. More and more people, funny how much noise we make. Loud voices and laughter, followed by screams of glee; enter my countrymen and women. We are not a race known for our love of silence. Someone settling themselves in a nearby compartment had a tape recorder, rock music blasting, ugly and metallic. Was that allowed? Surely not, poised to complain and make another speech, I felt some comfort was to be had in outrage. Aware of all the anger churning away inside me, it seemed likely that if I failed to kill myself, I would eventually become the kind of righteous old lady who regarded complaining as both personal need and a civic obligation. The thudding of footsteps up and down the corridor caused the train to thrum like a boarding school dorm. A long ten-hour journey stretched before me. How I hated humans. How would I endure? Make it stop. The stampede continued. Words began to emerge from the bellowing, "First we take Manhattan; then we take Berlin," over and over . . . Great, except that we were heading for Hamburg, a major port on the River Elbe. I had to smile; of course I remembered the "major European" river upon which the great Hanseatic city was built. I sounded like a guide book, excepting I didn't have one, a guide book that is. In my mind I prepared an image of massive ships lined up along the docks. The train raced through the night, I could feel Mathieu hovering above my carriage; he had become a Chagall-like angel dressed in colored robes, serene and all-seeing, his huge wings shielding me from harm. Our bond would endure.

The first stop was Brussels, we were in Belgium but Belgium did not matter, it was too like France. Then on through Liège, still damnably similar to France; I wanted cannons to fire and trumpets to sound as we crossed the German frontier, it was only when I saw the sign, Osnabrück, that I realized we had sneaked into Germany without my knowing. Osnabrück was the birthplace of Erich Maria Remarque, the author of *All Quiet on the Western Front*. Father had once given me a copy and said that it would touch my soul. He was usually right, about books I mean, and I loved the title, it had a pathos all its own. Father had looked so pleased when I had read it and rushed to inform him that it had become my favorite book, I was ten and he declared, "Good girl, that's a story for a grown-up mind." I was skipping on clouds but went and ruined it all by asking why the writer's middle name was Maria, had he been born a girl? I thought it was an incisive question. Every bit of his approval evaporated as Father rolled his eyes and walked away, muttering, "That's the kind of fool thing your mother would say," and then he turned around and advised me to keep my logical streak under control "lest it destroy your imagination." It had hurt me at the time but there I was, so many years later, imagination intact and suspecting that there would be sea gulls and so overpowering a smell of fish waiting for me in Hamburg that I envisaged becoming seasick on arrival. The train pulled into a commonplace station, not a ship in sight, no crashing waves and the art gallery only a skip across the street. Hamburg Hauptbahnhof, Germany. At last, I was in Germany.

There it was, I stood before the painting, the man with his back to the viewer and his face contemplating the future or the past. Was he lonely or inspired? The first time I had come across it in one of Father's books, I just wondered what mountain it was that he, the wanderer, had climbed. But in time I had recognized the philosophical relevance, a deeper significance. The other great picture, the one dominated by broken slabs of ice, a forgotten ship partially concealed by the devastation, was also there. Larger than I had expected, its size surprised me, and its clarity, pale grays, yellow, bleached-bone colors wan in the stark daylight that Friedrich had created, hit me like a blow. I must have been sitting for more than an hour, perhaps longer in the deserted gallery. Then fracturing the soothing hush, came a voice, "They're just so gorgeous and brave, aren't they?" I looked up at a tall man, heavy, and older than Father, yet his voice sounded much younger and his ravaged, unfinished face was not quite human as if a makeup artist had tried to age him by about thirty years, but not very successfully. His grayish-blonde hair looked dusty while his black polo neck and black jeans suggested upper class bohemianism. It was strange to be speaking with another person; even more unreal, an American, as I felt I had been silent for days, which was not quite true. The man was wealthy, it was easy to tell; his accent, his ease, his self-satisfaction. Having told me that Caspar David, whom he spoke of as if they were close friends, was his favorite artist. "Me too," I replied. He didn't react, only mentioned that he had come to Europe by ocean liner. "So peaceful, I felt it was the 1920s and that everyone was trying to forget the war and just have a grand time."

There was something about the man, that hint of mania I used to sense around Mother. His eyes were very pale, small, and he could have been a German, but only an American would have held court in that way, informing me, a total stranger, how much Caspar David meant to him. "I just got here from Paris," he said, breathlessly, and he mentioned that he had seen *The Tree of Crows* in the Louvre. So had I, only that had been months earlier, I didn't bother explaining but I did say that it had made me think of Poe and that I had been on the same train, the one that had just got in. He had already seen the Caspar David Friedrich paintings in Berlin and then had gone straight to Paris. He looked thoughtful as he said that as if it suddenly dawned on him that he should have traveled to Hamburg directly from

Berlin. "But I don't mind, I like trains and . . ." he seemed distracted and then he looked at me and laughed, shrill without a pinch of humor, saying that he appeared to have left his suitcase on the train. "It's only a small bag, the rest of my stuff is in Paris, I'm staying on for a few months . . . Ah Paris." I smiled blandly. He told me that his Aunt Edith had just died and left him fifteen million dollars. "Would you believe it . . . it's a deal of money, but you know, I've always been rich so it doesn't really matter." He laughed again, the same yelp as before, false and mirthless. The museum guard came over to us, about the noise. The large American was taken aback, and then sheepish, before bowing and speaking in fluent German, accompanied by unexpectedly elegant hand gestures. The guard smiled sympathetically and sighed. I asked him what he'd said that had so tempered the guard's initial rebuff. The multimillionaire became very serious and said that he had told him that he was dying and he had come over from America to see the Friedrich paintings for "the very last time." I said how sorry I was. "Don't be, I'm not, at least I hope I'm not dying; I just find that it's very effective when dealing with pesky officials and such-like, I do it all the time back home. Policemen are such complete numbskulls don't you find?"

Considering his apparent resources he had wretched teeth and I suddenly wanted to get away from him. Perhaps he was lying about everything else as well. Maybe he was insane? Meanwhile, he had been rummaging through a large plastic carrier bag. "Ah, here," another big gesture, then he stood tall, "Let me show you my work." He held out a sloppy scrap book, the pages were covered in mad scrawls that looked like a baby's first drawings. "I'm an artist, you see," he said, deadly in earnest, "Just being here makes me need to work. Please excuse me." And he sat down and began making bold scribbles with a blue marker that must also have been in the bag. I stood staring at him and then he looked

up, suddenly frenzied, and shouted, white spittle foaming on
his fat lips, "Get away, can't you see I'm busy." Well, horrendous
person, I fled, intending to have another look at the paintings
before I left for Berlin. Only I would wait until he had mean-
dered off or been recaptured. I went off in search of postcards.

The Pastoral Symphony was playing on the radio in the first
café into which I wandered, anticipating the ordeal of having
to order, would my German fare even worse than my French.
All around me the customers appeared to be German. Not an
obvious tourist in sight. Lunchtime in a Hamburg café with
Beethoven playing and me jubilant to have finally gotten to
Germany and my first crazy person turned out to be a fellow
American, well I do declare. Was he still at work in the art gallery,
drawing furiously with his blue marker? *Suppe* was on the menu,
I knew what that was. The bread that came with it was fresh, I
could not stop eating it and cleared the plate so fast, the waitress
looked surprised and hurried back over to my table with more.
Her bewildered expression suggested she felt she had given my
first serving of bread to the wrong customer. The hot chocolate
was as good as any I had had in France with the exception of
Maman's, hers was the most chocolaty.

More than an hour passed and I decided to return to the
Kunsthalle, to take a final look at the paintings. The rich man
had left, the Friedrich gallery room was now private, exclusive
and all for me. Again I stood before my friend the wanderer,
wanting to imprint him forever on my mind. Caspar David,
there I go, now I am sounding as if we were personal friends,
frequently depicts his characters standing with their back to the
viewer, as if wholly occupied with his real subject, Nature. What
was going through the mind of the wanderer as he gazed out over
the abyss? His life, the future . . . eternity, or was he just realizing
how far he had climbed?

Approaching footsteps made me turn around, a man and a woman had come in. They looked sane enough, but you never can tell with humans. I sensed they were coming over to look at the wanderer painting so I moved off and went to study the one picture that I had not deliberated over the first time, because it is far less dramatic, almost ordinary and untypical of Friedrich's work. It was a view of his native Greifswald; fields in the foreground, the town itself, windmills and church steeples, outlined in the distance, very peaceful. When I stood in to look more closely, I noticed there were horses in the painting and wept feeble sudden tears at the discovery. Amboise seemed very far away and yet it was there and I could easily return. Reluctantly I moved from picture to picture fearful of forgetting them, but I wouldn't. Caspar David Friedrich understood absolute desolation yet was alert to the beauty of the evening sky. It was possible to feel the fading heat of the setting sun as he had depicted it in a painting of a freshly plowed field. Hours had passed with only a few interruptions as people came in to look at the paintings. Most of them were alone, the best way to experience Friedrich's astonishing moodscapes. Having had so much time, somehow the hours had disappeared, and I had to skedaddle fast to catch the Berlin train.

Why did such a short journey take so long? It was only about 170 miles to Berlin and I had figured on little more than two hours, but it took closer to six. New York to London would have been as quick. But the train had to cross the border into East German territory before it actually reached Berlin. All of this took me unawares. The legacy of the Cold War was all round me and yet again I had proven more aware of events that had taken place hundreds of years earlier instead of within the century I was living. The train progressed so slowly, rattling and creaking, it sounded as if it was about to fall apart. We seemed to have been moving in slow motion for ages but had only gone about thirty miles when the thing ground to a halt. There was a sign, Schwanheide, on the wall beyond the carriage window. At the time I was not sure if it was a command or the name of the place. Later I found out that Schwanheide was a town and that it served as the inner German border crossing point where about five different sets of tracks coming from different directions intersected. The driver went off duty and a new one took over.

Armed men were patrolling. Some of them had German shepherd dogs on leashes. All I could see was barbed-wire fencing. None of the other passengers reacted. Then I heard voices and these armed men, soldiers or police, I'm not sure what they were, boarded the train and then other men joined them. They had more dogs, also German shepherds, the dogs padded stealthily as if they thought we couldn't see them. They were looking at everything, sniffing intently, and passed so close to me I could see their eyelashes and smell their meaty breath. No one uttered a word, no one moved, no one seemed remotely alive, only the guards and their magnificent dogs. The guards had no interest in rail tickets; they were requesting identity papers. All I had was my passport. One guard stopped right beside me, he saw the cover of my passport and just walked on. He barely glanced at me but the dog stared into my eyes. Maybe he sensed I was grieving? Would he have been able to tell it was for my dog and had he detected the presence of Hector's ashes? Would that cause a fuss? Were the guards hunting a spy or was all this just routine, life as lived in the Cold War? Maybe I was about to die in a burst of machine-gun fire. I wanted to go to the bathroom, I felt like getting sick. The carriage was stuffy, airless.

Berlin. Could I be going to die on the way to Berlin? I could not believe that I was finally inching toward a city about which I had dreamed and it had taken the form of a nightmare. Too agitated to sit still, I tried sitting on my hands. The faces around me were impassive. Did they look German I asked myself, did I? Most of my fellow passengers looked more like Americans than the French had. Standard-sized human eyes, not like those tormented wild ones most of the French people seemed to have, all shadows and hollows, even the brown eyes in the German faces looked benign and untroubled, no traces of latent hysteria or emotion.

At first the landscape consisted of flat open fields; we passed about seven equestrian establishments and no towns. And aside from the several stretches of forests, natural woodland, there were so many trees. Black and white cattle grazed and there were many large herds of sheep. Horses were out on grass in the fields and in paddocks, but there were others as well, farm workers. It was the first time I'd ever seen horses pulling plows. Back home it was all machines. I kept my eyes keen, would I spot a rider emerge out of the distance? It would be an omen, and might give me hope. But no rider appeared. The view became much harsher, ordered fields, crops instead of animals. Berlin was a divided city and Germany was a divided country; I was looking at communism and it seemed a very drab reality. Again I studied my fellow passengers and tried to separate the West Germans from the citizens of the East. Imagine getting shot if I was late getting back over the Border. Father would shake his head and ponder the insanity of hearing that his only child, a spoilt runaway, had been gunned down just like Mother but by strangers; communists or border guards or perhaps by members of the secret police, and in Germany of all places.

But I was not intending to seek asylum in East Berlin, just look at some paintings that might comfort me. The Charlottenburg district was the most suitable place in which to stay; Nabokov had once lived there, the entire area or district had been named in honor of a princess who had become the Queen of Prussia. It had been a town unto itself. What would Father say if he knew the extent of my wanderings? There had been a time when he would not even have had to pause for thought if asked about my whereabouts, knowing I'd be up in my room or down in the yard or at school. But that was before all the madness; I was on a train crawling toward Berlin when he probably assumed I was still skulking in France, on the trail of Galileo, the horse he had sold so sneakily from right under me. It still stung.

The Germans spoke softly, I could just about detect a murmuring hum whereas the French sang out their sentences with a competitive edge, as if they were all auditioning for the same role. The men were more substantial, taller. How would I recognize a member of the secret police? How close was the nearest spy? Look for the most banal individual, that much I knew—not the one that looked like a movie star. Would I sense the fear? I guess it would be like walking around New York, which I had never visited, at night, and there I was, about to arrive in a city battered by war and haunted by its own terrible history. Would Mathieu have wanted to see Berlin? The only places he had ever said he dreamed of visiting were the Grand Canyon and Claiborne; he was not overly interested in France, never mind the rest of Europe. Amboise had been his world, and it could still be mine.

Newspapers were being folded, with that dry snapping sound. I could smell the printer's ink. It was sharper than back home, the paper, I guessed, was thinner—thanks to communism. After about an hour, or ninety minutes or so, the guards had exited the train, taking two passengers with them. It was all very quiet; no one could be caught looking, except me who was staring at everything, my eyes ready to fall out of my face. Fascinated, terrified, relieved, and still feeling sick, I wanted to remember it all. Most of all I wanted to remember the moment Berlin, austere and full of purpose, beaten but not defeated, loomed into view. As if the last bow had been taken and the stage curtain closed, the passengers seemed to rise as one and gather their belongings. Bahnhof Zoologischer Garten confirmed the sign in bold letters. I could see through the carriage window; Zoo Station, Berlin. I was in Berlin, well West Berlin, and my heart pounded.

Berlin, all my life I had always experienced a thrill when I heard it mentioned—the same thing happened with Vienna and Leningrad and was even more excited if I came across its old name, St. Petersburg[2]. I'd arrived in central Europe and as soon as I purchased my visitor's permit, I could enter East Berlin. Some of Friedrich's major paintings were in the National Gallery. There were others in Charlottenburg Palace, but first I had to see the ones in East Berlin, for me, they were shrouded in a forbidden glamor. Father was right, aside from horses, it was history. History was the only story worth reading. I saw the bombed tower standing amid the ruins of the Kaiser Wilhelm church, beside which a charmless modern looking structure had been erected and it was an ugly thing to behold. I tried not to look like a tourist, preferring to blend in. There must have been bullet holes on the buildings in Paris but I hadn't looked. In Berlin I put my fingers into them as if they were the nail holes of the one true cross. Making the journey, coming to Berlin might help; the daunting enormity of its past might heal me. Had I remained in France I would have died. There in Berlin I experienced an emotion that seemed to transcend my personal grief; it was like sharing the communal pain of the ghosts that crammed its many empty spaces. Berlin was alive with its dead. It was eerie and desolate; my face felt cold but I was glad to be there with my dead, Mathieu beside me, Hector safe in my bag.

A pair of giant stone elephants guarded the entrance to Berlin Zoo. Elephants seemed incongruous, very un-German.

By following the paths in the Tiergarten I would end up near the Brandenburg Gate and could peer at the Wall beyond which was East Berlin, a mythical Promised Land that had become for the people already there more like a prison; they were expected to stay and help create a mighty new German state. I imagined it was like living in *1984*, the Orwell novel I had read as one of my school library assignments. Eager to experience the reality, I also sought to absorb the menace.

It was late and it made more sense to find a hotel and prepare for my next exploit. No one looking at me could possibly guess at the amount of money I was carrying. The men at the reception of the plush establishment I entered did not even attempt to conceal their inaccurate assessment of my finances. The younger one turned away while the older man, on glancing at my passport, said, in English, that he could direct me to a youth hostel a short bus journey away. "No thank you," I said, deliberately exaggerating my expression of bewilderment as well as my accent. "I wish to stay here. You do accept US traveler's checks and all major currencies such as the US dollar, the French franc?" I continued at my most bombastic, declaring that I'd quite forgotten having a considerable amount of West German marks with me, "Deutsch Marks, that is what you call them?" and assured the clerk that my parents were concluding their European tour in Berlin and would be arriving in a few days.

That was all I needed, a few days, and then maybe I would fly back to my old life, or maybe not. The clerk relaxed at the sight of my billfold. Money seems to make everything possible. A bellhop appeared and remained poker-faced at the sight of my humble luggage. The elevator was slow and I took the stairs. Up two flights and to a room which was blatant old-world pastiche but comfortable. A small box of chocolates had been positioned on one of the plump white pillows. Something made me turn around, the bellhop was standing with his hand outstretched, I went to shake it and then realized he expected a tip. I pulled some coins from my pocket and nodded to him. It was the first time I had ever done such a thing, given a tip that is, and it was unpleasant, making me think of Lone Star's allegations about my being the child of a Southern plantation owner. I hated the way the man fingered the money, indifferent to my standing there while he counted it.

More soul weary than physically tired I assessed my new surroundings; a day begun in Hamburg had finally ended in a West Berlin hotel. Exhausted by the rail ordeal, my mood of celebration had been replaced by many familiar demons; doubts and loneliness along with such leaden despair. Out of habit I yanked the mattress and the bedding down onto the floor and went to run the bath, amazed at how deep the tub was as I had read somewhere that German and Austrian baths were functional, sit-down-and-get-out facilities. Yet that shiny West Berlin bathtub was long with Hollywood-movie star depth   probably intended for US visitors. There I was watching the water flow sedately out of an imitation, old-style but modern chrome faucet which was unusually narrow, and I thought, yet another bathtub in yet another bathroom, I seem to be moving through a series of them. As to further consolidate an impression of affluence, I ordered room service. Soup and baked plaice. It was the same bellhop. Again he stood, waiting. I thanked him and said good night, holding the door for him, but no tip and made it plain I wanted him gone.

And then it was morning, I had slept for hours yet felt groggy, and would have loved to go riding. But I was in Berlin, on a quest, and had come to see the pictures. My worn boots were filthy. There was a shoe polish kit in the wardrobe and the old leather responded. As the shower was a feeble affair, I had another bath instead and succeeded in wetting all of the towels as they tumbled off the shelf and into the steaming water. The hotel clerk had told me where I could purchase a day visa. It suddenly seemed very different from the menace of the border guards on the train. As I combed my wet hair, I studied my face in the mirror. Would the border guards decide I presented a threat to national security? Probably not, I looked so depressed they might mistake me for an East German. No matter how downcast I was, disappointed at feeling tempted to simply get back into bed, the hotel breakfast was indeed an opulent event.

There was so much food on display it was difficult to choose; so many enticing variations of yogurts and cereals, fruits, breads and pastries. A range of juices, cold meats, cheeses, even salty fish . . . I gorged and ate too much. Back in the room I lay down, flat on the floor hoping to settle my stomach. I needed to go to the bathroom and just in time, vomiting into the new white sink. I was sweating and shivering, suddenly hot, then cold, but unwilling to spend my first day in Berlin in bed. After a further polish my boots looked restored, if showing signs of eventual disintegration. I felt a bit better and packed more money than usual into my secret heel. Leaving Hector's ashes in the room with my other things, I took only a notebook and my Caspar David Friedrich volume with me to East Berlin, as proof of my studious intentions.

*

Checkpoint Charlie was no more than a grim little hut at the junction of Friedrichstrasse and Zimmerstrasse. I could have filed straight on through but waited instead in the coffee shop, to observe the people and the contrasting expressions on their faces, trying to distinguish the residents from the visitors; the merely curious like me, compared with the desperate who were attempting to flee. I had assumed that the café was named after the alder tree, but I'd misread the sign, it said "Adler"—the German for "eagle"—nothing particularly imperial about the dilapidated café though. A couple of hardened US soldiers were sitting drinking coffee, so I guessed they were off duty and I asked them what I should do. They were too cool to even pretend to be friendly. "Just you go and git your darn passport stamped like everyone else, costs five bucks and don't you all expect those guys to tell you 'have a nice day' and smile, cos they sure don't spare any welcomes around here. No sir, they don't." He was from the Deep South, what Father, having studied at the University of Georgia, would refer to as the "real South." The soldier was tough-looking, from maybe Alabama or Mississippi, and was what Father enjoyed describing as "the real McCoy." It was surprisingly pleasant to hear that thick an accent after so many months away, I was ready to go home, not quite, but near enough. I ordered hot chocolate, pretending to appear underwhelmed by the setting. The soldiers got up and the other one who had said nothing tossed a packet down on my table. "You have these cookies, I just ate three full packages of them and they're real good. Don't go doing anything dumb over there, causing us an international incident . . . I sure hate having to clean up messes . . ." He waved and off they went. I ate the cookies then stood up, about to enter East Berlin. The border guard took my passport and peered at me, then back at the picture, made a face and stared. He called to his colleague and he too studied my passport photo. Then I remembered, the photograph was of my younger self and they continued to stare, impassive, blue-gray eyes and bad skin, while me? I just blushed redder and redder to a dangerous shade of purple I didn't need to see, I could feel it. Then the first guard shrugged, stamped my passport, leaving a big green square with the day's date on the open page, and he waved me on through.

*

Color seemed to have seeped away in the East. Everything looked different, even the daylight; it was like walking into a world of gray, or the muted, grainy tones of a black-and-white movie. Yet really it was closer to an old newsreel. People appeared to move more slowly; even the Wall was higher, sheer like a glacier. Its eastern face was blank, formidable, impossible to defy. I walked on, waiting for something to happen, a shout, the sound of running footsteps, machine gun fire, frenzied barking or perhaps only a small voice pleading for mercy. But nothing; it was disappointing. The secret police were probably watching every movement, poised to suppress the slightest hint of subversion. They had a name only I couldn't remember it. I felt stupid; tired and stupid. Having at last gotten into East Berlin, instead of euphoria, I was irritated at not being able to recall the name of the secret police. What would happen if I stopped someone and inquired Southern-polite, "Excuse me please; what do you call your secret police force?" Would they think I was trying to be funny, would they even understand me? Then it came to me; "Stasi," like a nickname. Did they wear a uniform, were they like the FBI only even meaner, more organized? Imagine if the very person I decided to ask turned out to be a Stasi agent, what would happen? I could just hear myself, strident and exaggeratedly Southern, proclaiming, "I am a citizen of the United States of America, harm me at your peril," only to be struck in the face with the butt of a machine gun, me falling to the ground, my perfect teeth shattered, the pages of my handsome art book torn and fluttering down the street. The Stasi probably carried Lugers and kept them concealed within an inside pocket. I'd held one. Sheriff Hodge had a considerable gun collection, which included his Mauser Luger, the Black Widow he called it—but that may have been the actual model, not a name he had personally given it. Although not secretive by nature he was careful as to who knew about his firearms. He even had a tall display case devoted to the Winchester rifle which he enjoyed describing as "the Gun that Won the West." Father had no interest in any of it and on more than one occasion had remarked that collecting guns was "indicative of a disturbed mind."

Sheriff Hodge never took offence, no matter how sharp Father was—and he could be real sharp. I missed the Sheriff; he had always arrived on Easter Sunday, carrying a fancy basket of candied eggs for me, with a stuffed toy bunny wearing a top hat or maybe a bonnet and it tidily sitting on the glossy artificial grass, guarding the real treasure, authentic handmade chocolate, all the way from Switzerland. That year in Berlin was the first Easter I had been away, and Easter had been weeks, months earlier, back in France, passed unmarked by me, caught in my air-tight cell of emotion. Was Father still dating his rich widow? Mitzi had mentioned his new association during one of our transatlantic phone conversations, which had returned pretty much to normal once I'd settled in Amboise. She'd asked would I mind if Father got married again. It didn't bother me. But how could he face going through all that a third time? He was a loner and having already lost two wives, this one was just bound to go and get herself killed or murdered, fall off a horse, be struck by lightning, drown in the bath tub, or prick her finger on a bewitched spinning wheel were one suddenly to appear. Father was jinxed, and he had passed that hex on down to me.

Berlin was windy, not particularly cold; just whipped by a penetrating breeze. Fear may have been keeping me warm. I was standing on the famous Unter den Linden, aware that the trees were relatively new, replanted after World War Two and was feeling so lost and aware of the existence of probably about a million hidden cameras raking across the scene like searchlights. How did a bullet feel? Was it like a blow, or did it burn hot as it tore its passage through your body? Could you hear it? Yet again, always, again, over and over, again, I thought of Mother. In all her life she had never once stepped outside of America, she had only almost, but not, gotten to England, and yet there was me, who had spent so many hours contentedly in my bedroom looking at photographs of the night sky, so far away from home, on a crazy odyssey in the middle of Europe inspired by a long-dead artist who had read my sadness 200 years before I was born. That day in Berlin within a few hundred feet of seeing the paintings I had set out to view, I kept imagining the sensation of being shot and felt another of my, by then habitual, nervous breakdowns coming on. The world was spiralling; I was dizzy, my head pounding, my heart sore, and my brain on fire. I could hear my breathing and was convinced my lungs were rotting inside me.

Logic intervened; if I began weeping and was to collapse in a heap it would attract attention and get me arrested. Not that I was frightened though, it was absolute despair that had me in its grip. While the sight of all the German shepherds prowling and sniffing had scarcely impinged upon my consciousness, a little old lady walking her white terrier dog left me distraught beyond words. I went weak and just turned away from the sight of someone whose pet was alive and well. I had left Hector back in the hotel for fear some deranged border guard seeking explosives took it into his fool head to go picking through Hector's ashes and would maybe spill them all over the place. But by then, he was in the hotel safe, along with a letter.

My dreams had returned; sometimes they were delightful, that is, until I woke to the gut-wrenching reality. I would be walking with Hector, or Mathieu would be driving us along in the old station wagon, playing his horrible music, that ABBA tape which I'd kept like some holy relic. We were happy in the dreams and the sun was shining. It always used to shine bright in those dreams; it was always a hot summer's day, although we never did get to have a summer's day together. Marc made an occasional appearance, mocking me as he brandished his stumpy penis, Mrs. Faulkner looking on, lips pursed. Some nights I would see Mathieu falling through outer space, bouncing off the stars and me not able to do a thing, never once managing to catch him, no matter how vigorously I grabbed at him.

At intervals I would again experience the night the Amboise cats had stormed into the bedroom, leaping onto the mattress, terrorizing Hector in his blindness. I could even feel him moving against me, but he wasn't there . . . And then there was another dream, more of an ongoing premonition about the grasping bell-hop. In real life he had taken to sticking out his hand each time he saw me. It was deliberate; just the slightest gesture, engineered to provoke me but easy to deny. I felt like reporting him but I knew he would lie and I'd be left feeling an idiot. I had planned to move on, into one of those small pension-style hotels, boarding houses, similar to the one in which I had stayed while in Paris. It would be a lot more atmospheric than an expensive hotel. I'd get a better sense of daily life as lived in Berlin. Yet I had not gotten around to looking for one and something made me fear that were I to leave Hector alone in the hotel room, that the bellhop would sneak in and scatter his ashes just for spite. That's why I had Hector put in the hotel safe.

Meek and polite, downright unctuous as only I can be, I informed the manager that my parents had been delayed, that Mother had injured her leg skiing—Americans invariably come to grief on mountain slopes, Europeans almost expect it of us— and she could not be moved. Father would be devastated were any mishap to befall our dog's ashes. He would most probably consult his close friend, the Secretary of State, I volunteered innocently, intending to put the manager on red alert, and I asked him to keep the ashes in the safe along with some documents. "Of course, of course," assured the concierge, reminding me of someone I never did remember who, and it all reiterated that coming to Europe had made me into a shameless liar with a previously dormant flair for inventing complicated, fraudulent narratives.

Included among the documents in the safe was a formal letter addressed to Mitzi, a will of sorts, dated the hotel, in which I formally asked her to please look after Hector's ashes should anything happen to me, and if I went missing with no trace of my body to be found, to please bury him in Monticello's garden. I begged her on our blood sisters' bond—and was so happy that I had insisted she submit to that oath even though I knew she thought it was corny and old-fashioned and that she was way too old for it, but I wasn't and had always wanted to make a sacred pact with someone. Lucky I had. My blood had seemed less red than hers and not as thick . . . but perhaps it was only my imagination playing its usual tricks, I'd always felt less consequential than just about everybody else.

Staring at a splendid neoclassical building that seemed to have appeared directly in front of me as if it had just been magicked there, instead of my having drifted toward it in a trance, I could

see that somehow I had been walking and had arrived at the
entrance of the famous opera house. I needed to banish my
various demons and concentrate on what was before me. The
National Gallery was another majestic building, built of a pinkish stone, a Greco-Roman temple, brooding yet looking very
pink indeed, as the overcast sky brightened slightly in welcome.
An impressive bronze statue depicting a king on a horse occupied
prime position on the middle landing of the stairways, some
long-dead Hohenzollern monarch most like. So many momentous events had occurred since he was placed up there, high on
a steed that looked fierce and warrior-like, far more intimidating than the human on its back. On my first visit the long room
in which the Caspar David Friedrich works hung was crowded;
there were three four parties of teenage boys and girls, all about
my age I guess, looking like rival camps, two of which were being
subjected to very solemn lectures. The first group was gathered
before the painting of *The Monk by the Sea*. The large canvas is
overwhelming; dominated by a vast turbulent sky, it looks very
like something by Turner, the famous English painter. The smol-
dering heavens, a narrow strip of sea, and an equally narrow tract
of beach dwarf a tiny human figure, the monk. Is he considering
nature or eternity or both? I couldn't understand the teacher,
who was a skinny middle-aged woman, speaking a rapid, slurred
German that might as easily have been Czech and it would have
been interesting to figure out what she was saying, seeing as she
seemed quite emotional. Some of the students were sniggering at
her from behind their hands and pulling faces. It was comforting though to see her, another human clearly as disturbed by the
picture as I was, in fact disturbed period. I just wanted to hide in
a dark corner and wail, beseeching Caspar David Friedrich's spirit
to come comfort me. Again I recalled that his younger brother
had drowned when helping to save Friedrich who had fallen

through thin ice into freezing water. My artist had understood guilt and I was burdened by mine, consumed by it.

A similar group was gathered before *Man and Woman Contemplating the Moon*, in which a couple are standing beside a contorted, uprooted oak, and have become distracted by the moon. She has her hand on his shoulder and they are together, just them and nature, making me think of me and Mathieu. The teacher with the group read from a binder in a hard, stern voice. I heard my sigh escape loudly into the room and two of the students turned to examine me, their expressions non-committal. Yet they had looked, I still existed and hadn't vaporized with grief. I wanted to absorb the picture, climb into it. I wanted the gallery to be cleared, leaving just me and the paintings as had happened in Hamburg. Footsteps echoed around the space as did an occasional cough. My eyes rested on *Moonrise by the Sea*, two women and a man are gazing out at a dream world of melancholy yearning, making me think of the *Moonlight Sonata* which Father would play tenderly, and exactly as Beethoven intended. It was one of the few pieces that Father interpreted without adding any of his usual digressions. He could play well, much better than I did.

A girl's voice, gentle, almost lilting, startled me with her asking in confused German where had the wanderer painting gone. "Are you Italian?" I responded in English. Her turn to look surprised and ask in American-accented English, "How are you guessing?" All I could say was that she did not sound German and that I did not speak it that well either. She was from Milan and explained that she wanted to show her boyfriend the pictures. He stood, looking blankly at me and then smiled suddenly as if he had decided to take some interest in our conversation. He had the most sensuous dark-brown eyes, not something I'd usually notice. The couple's visit to the gallery seemed to have been her idea, judging by the way she threw up her hands resign-edly in the gesture of a much older person when I told her that the painting was in Hamburg. "Is the ice one there too?" She gave the impression of being able to contain her disappoint-ment. It was different for me, I was on a quest and would have screamed in rage or burst out crying, me having become that new person who seemed to weep all the time. Had I missed out on seeing the pictures I would have sobbed, bitten down hard, teethmarks on my tongue, and then would have devised an alter-native plan . . . She showed no interest in the other paintings; the two she wanted to see were elsewhere, and for her, that was that. "Ciao," she said and they walked away. She with a little waving gesture, just her fingers, her glossy hair swinging loose down her back but for a few strands caught up in her collar.

My legs felt like lead weights. I went back over to the paint-ing of the man and woman studying the moon; I had wanted to sit down but instead I stood memorizing the image. It was very evocative and made me wonder what if . . . Somehow I could not imagine Mathieu standing looking at paintings in a gallery, although he probably would have done it if only to please me. And he did look at things; he would stare at trees and had smiled sadly when the leaves had begun to fall. He had once told me that he dreaded the winter and the death of plants, the withering of almost everything green. Yes I could remember him looking at things in nature; he would have studied the pictures. We could have, together. I didn't even have a photograph of him, just those few of Hector . . .

Suddenly I saw Sophie; cold, beautiful Sophie, clear as if she were standing there before me in the gallery, all I needed in the hell I was in. How boring she would have found Mathieu's gentle, tentative lovemaking after the adulterous romps she had conducted in Paris with men looking for sex, nothing more. I was

glad she'd been left unsatisfied; she had only used him. Mathieu
had been happy with me. I suited him well; I knew that, and
kept that knowledge close to me as some consolation but it did
not comfort me, nothing could. The third group had not moved
and seemed far more animated than the other two. Perhaps their
instructor, another woman, was more involved, less upset than
the older woman, more engaged than the younger one who had
delivered her prepared text like a bored newscaster. The third
teacher was wearing what looked like one of the Chanel outfits
Mother often wore. This woman clearly had foreign connections.
A large smile with expensive, un-East German teeth, and she also
had labor-intensive hair with highlights that would have taken
hours in the beauty parlor. She was from somewhere else, I had
smugly deduced. She certainly looked right pleased with herself,
turning animatedly from her audience and back to the painting,
it was that tremendous mountain scene, *The Watzmann*, the picture that Friedrich had more or less created from something he
had heard about and from other walking tours he had undertaken, as well as from a pupil's picture he had been shown. She
was speaking and the students were responding, asking questions.
I edged closer. It was easily explained why it was different: they
were Americans on a high school tour. This hit me just as she was
mentioning that the artist had never visited Southern Germany,
Bavaria, nor had he ever gotten to Italy, the country so admired
by the German Romantics. She greeted me with a breezy, "Hi
there, are you going to join us?" enunciated slowly and carefully
relying on her welcoming smile to help. Did she reckon I was
an East German with my two braids and forlorn expression? My
face began to heat up; I could feel it burning and I stammered,
explaining that I was from Richmond, Virginia. A girl standing
beside me whistled sharp and high, asking if I had gotten "like
totally lost" and they all laughed at that. The group focused on

me and another girl admitted that she had been trying to figure out how I'd come by the jacket. I was still wearing my shabby tweed one. It was true though, the clothes were different; the East Berliners looked as if they'd been dressed courtesy of the Goodwill, dull, shapeless garments airlifted in by the plane load. The women wearing head scarves and flat shoes looked the same as the wives and mothers, the sisters, the widows, all the bereaved sweethearts in the wartime archive footage used in documentaries. One thing that most of the American students had experienced was longing glances. "At first I thought it was me," said one boy, "and I felt 'wow,' like I don't get this back home, no one ever hits on me." He waited for a reaction; it had obviously become a successful joke. "Then I realized it was my jeans . . . jeans are big in this place, the same in Moscow. Dad said the next time he goes to Russia he's going to take about a ton of Levi's and sell them to the commies."

The gallery guard had finally had enough. The teacher apologized and resumed her talk. It was a school trip from Illinois, made possible because somebody's father worked in the State Department. But East Berlin had proved too grim for the students who admitted they would have preferred Amsterdam and were going to have a race to see who would "hit" Checkpoint Charlie first. "Mrs. Henderson's gonna have a really lonely walk back . . . We were supposed to go and see some opera! Jesus, can you just imagine?"

The teacher looked around and asked if I would like to come along. They were traveling on to Frankfurt for a party at the big US airbase before flying home. It was tempting, they were typical American teenagers, not angry and nowhere as weird as Lone Star but it would have been too easy. I had to stay on and see it out, I was halfway up the mountain as it were . . . Mrs. Henderson saw me as a polite, earnest girl from a good family and she smiled as if she thought I was only trying to please her when I said Caspar David Friedrich was my favorite artist. She probably would have dispensed the same calm welcome to Lone Star, though maybe not. Little in life could upset a woman as in control as Mrs. Henderson. I had planned on going back and forth a few times, from the West into the East just to look at the paintings but also to experience the compelling frisson of being alone in East Berlin. There were other Friedrich pictures to see back in Charlottenburg including one of his most evocative, the view of the harbor; beautiful, masted ships in a golden sunset. It was part of a small, select collection of his works displayed in a summer villa on the grounds of the palace. Even in my loneliness I had no wish to be rescued by a school tour. Just seeing them all together reminded me of my other life. I had been going to be a scientist and while in Germany was aware that I should really visit Regensburg where Kepler is buried, although his actual grave had been lost during the Thirty Years' War. He had died more than a century before Friedrich had even been born and had written his own epitaph: "I measured the skies, now the shadows I measure / Sky bound was the mind. Earth bound the body."

I had had those words printed in Gothic script on parchment-like paper, pinned to the wall above my desk back home. I felt I had entered the shadows.

Kepler's sentiments suited Friedrich as well as me. My legs felt so heavy. I wondered if a horse were suddenly to materialize would I even be able to ride it. No matter how exhausted I felt, horses had always seemed to revive me, as if I somehow drew energy from them. But I wasn't so sure anymore. Friedrich was the one artist, even more than any of the million writers I'd read, that helped me make sense of my turmoil. I would not be able to attend to Kepler until I had completed my Caspar David

Friedrich pilgrimage. There was no fancy gallery shop, not like in the Louvre; you couldn't buy even one postcard or hot chocolate. On I trudged, weary, diminished, and arrived in a large square. It took a moment to realize it was Alexanderplatz. Directly ahead of me was the U-Bahn station, with people coming out. Two figures hurried through the crowd, they were youngish men rushing to catch the tram but it had already started up. High above everything stood the Fernsehturm, a giant TV tower, and I saw the World Clock and noticed that Washington DC was six hours behind Berlin, so was Richmond where Mrs. Faulkner would be busy, vacuuming rugs that never got dirty and making her wonderful pies.

Alexanderplatz was busy and it gave me a chance to take pause and watch daily life, so many people appearing oblivious to their complex history. Germans seemed to huddle over their cigarettes, sucking on them, whereas the French waved theirs slowly like instruments of seduction, exhaling circles of smoke. A greasy smell hung heavy on the cold air and a few customers had gathered around a dubious-looking stall. The only thing on sale was a kind of giant wiener not that I cared much for hot dogs. But the bratwurst was all there was to eat. I bought two, steaming and disgusting, coated thick in mustard which I hate; the first one made me so sick I just threw away the second one and tried to find a bathroom which took some time. I had barely dried my hands when I vomited right into the sink I was standing at, confronted by a blank wall of ugly yellow tiles. There was not even a basic mirror, the type in which you can barely recognize your face. Communists did not indulge overmuch in preening. That sausage thing must have been pork, I decided, wondering where the East Germans ate. Did they all queue up at meal times and hurry into West Berlin which of course was not possible. Yet for such a small country, only eight million, the GDR seemed to have figured at the Seoul Olympics. So at least the East German athletes must have eaten well. The West German equestrian team had won almost everything—Herr Bernhard must have approved, if grimly. How he would have tensed his gaunt, old jaw, gazing into the distance like a mad visionary.

I headed back to Checkpoint Charlie, set on having a long, hot bath in my hotel, and planned on returning to the gallery the next day, which I did. In fact I made several consecutive return journeys, feeling increasingly territorial about the paintings—my artist, my pictures—and gauged the level of emotion they inspired in viewers, most of whom seemed to be from somewhere else. Some visitors barely glanced at them, just ticking them off as had so many of the tourists in Paris who had seemed to jog up to the *Mona Lisa*, look, and scurry away—one more task completed. I wondered if the border guards were keeping count of my many visitations. To hell with their intimidating stares, I'd become brave and defiant, soured and carried my Caspar David Friedrich book as if it were a banner, my proof of purpose. Each evening I returned to the hotel, always to find that someone had pulled the mattress up off the floor and repositioned it on the bed frame, leaving the usual small box of chocolates on the pillow. Before doing anything else, I always took from my pocket the little wooden horse Monsieur Gallay had given me and set it up on the bedside table. Only then would I eat the chocolates, and again haul the mattress back down on the carpet. Candy and cakes, the daily chocolates, and most of the desserts were more appealing than the actual food. The meat was either spicy or insipid and fatty; I only liked the chicken while the vegetables had usually been boiled into submission.

But the breakfasts were wonderland; an open challenge to eat as much as you liked. No one seemed to notice my taking so many pastries away with me each morning. I would gobble my snacks outside the gallery; cake and pastries and chocolate goo-like croissant things that were round not pointy like the papery French ones and I gazed up at the rider who was another Friedrich, Friedrich Wilhelm IV, a king of Prussia who had been not much of a soldier but was a true lover of art and architecture, landscape gardening not battles, and it was he who, while crown prince at the age of fifteen, in 1810, had urged his father, the king, to purchase *The Monk by the Sea* for his personal collection. Friedrich Wilhelm IV had had the gallery built and his father had died exactly a month to the day after Caspar David Friedrich in 1840 . . . Facts, facts, facts, as always, historical detail; enter the class nerd—being in Berlin had reactivated my delight in random information and history's many coincidences and cross references. Would I have gotten bored in Amboise? Maybe, but no, I would have been fulfilled living that other life, the one that was gone.

An unpleasant experience with sauerkraut which had ended violently, leaving me sick, then queasy for a further few hours resulted in my renouncing "serious" food. Grudgingly I had to concede that the cuisine at Monsieur Gallay's was far superior, only not as good as back home. Maman was a great cook. Her Amboise meals had a generous "feeding the troops" quality and were prepared with good humor and affection and after Mathieu died with increased tender compassion. Would I return? I doubted it. Nothing was waiting there for me. Yet I knew I could go back. Monsieur Gallay always seemed able to make things easier, what a gift. Father probably thought I must have run away for good. Only I didn't run away; it was a point of honor that had gone wrong.

After five or six days of visiting the Caspar David Friedrich paintings in East Berlin I decided to see the other collection, the pictures kept in the villa at the Charlottenburg Palace. It would be far more relaxing, maybe "too easy" at the palace and I would probably miss the tension of crossing the border. Perhaps that anxiety was helping me deal with my loss, that and the over-whelming tiredness that made me want to cower in a corner. I hated hearing my heart beat so loudly, I wanted it to stop; I also wanted my brain to cool. Why was my entire body feeling so weak and ailing; earthbound and heavy? Leaden? It didn't matter. Being ill was my new and permanent state and so what? Nothing mattered anymore; nothing that is, except my little quest.

The lady at the desk in the pavilion smiled and said hello, asking in English had I come far? Was I an art student? Her greeting was very different from the expressionless faces at the National Gallery in East Berlin. As for the villa itself, it was cap-tivating, like a doll's house and cluttered with authentic furnish-ings. Each of the rooms suggested having once been a space in which real people had spent some time. It had been a summer residence, a holiday home within yards of the palace itself. The collection included eleven Caspar David Friedrich works and I went directly to *View of a Harbor*. I like to think it depicts an early morning and the clouds are being dispersed by the ris-ing sun. Then again, perhaps it is late in the evening. But no, it is morning. Two modest ships dominate the foreground and there are smaller vessels in the background. As is so characteris-tic of Friedrich, tiny human figures gradually emerge; you don't seem to see them at first. There are three in the immediate fore-ground, aboard a small skiff. It had been quiet in the villa; the only sound was that of the birds outside. Then a breathless male voice approached; it had a wheeze broken every few seconds by a silly giggle. There was a second voice, low and urgent, almost reverential. Annoyance caused me to turn around; all I'd wanted was a few moments of stillness, pure silence, like a raindrop on a rose. It was that need that had kept me going back into East

Berlin; I wanted to contemplate the paintings in complete peace as I had managed eventually to enjoy in Hamburg. It was difficult in Berlin as there was a steady flow of visitors. The villa was unique in that it created the impression of seeing the pictures hanging as they might once have in a private room, not a public gallery. I tensed, willing the voices to disappear. Instead they came closer.

Again that stupid giggle; it spluttered like gas being released and belonged to an enormous human. Sheriff Hodge was fat for sure but the stranger who had lumbered into view appeared to be hiding a small building beneath his long, gray robe. He was a priest, a Catholic, I guessed, wearing a large silver crucifix and a hat like a pope on tour, wide-brimmed and too small to be sitting atop such a gigantic creature. He was maybe about forty-five years old or so, and inclined his head to his adoring companion, a much older woman, as though she were a devoted fool to be tolerated. He kept his sickly white hands up high, suggesting his flipper-like arms were shorter than they should have been as he was tall, about six foot four. He had the biggest face I'd ever seen which included eyes sitting in hammocks of fat and a small, wet mouth filled with tiny teeth. His belly jutted square before him and it was plain that he couldn't see his feet, which were only occasionally visible from beneath his long cassock. He moved as if on wheels and was wearing thick white sports socks and bizarrely ornate purple and gold slippers more suited to an Eastern potentate. There was no disputing that he was right happy with himself. His companion may have been his proud old mother and he kept mentioning Munich. He voiced his opinions about some of the paintings and paused, as I expected, before *Morning in the Riesengebirge*, and no doubt was interpreting the symbolism, a vast landscape redeemed by Christ. Naturally I was staring and the priest made a point of pausing to scrutinize me, and gave me his blessing. It was an audacious thing to do, even offensive. I could have been a strict Muslim or a pagan but he was a performer and dispensed his ritual, making a sign of the cross over me, probably more to impress his companion than to save my damaged soul. They left; he trundling out, the stairs creaking beneath him, her mincing along in his wake and they were gone. What effort it must have taken for him to sit down, aware that he would always have to face the battle of struggling to his feet. Yet he seemed the most self-satisfied of men.

Hours passed and I stayed on, enjoying uninterrupted silence. When the woman from the desk downstairs came up to announce she was closing, she seemed pleased to see me still there. "You love the pictures, as I do," she said, and she mentioned that I should "brave the ordeal" and go into East Berlin to the National Gallery. There were other paintings there she explained helpfully and I thanked her. She may have reckoned on my being too timid to venture across the border and I didn't feel the need to tell her otherwise. I'd return to the villa collection, I said, before going home. "Home" had become a complicated notion.

*

By the next morning I was back in East Berlin, having passed through Checkpoint Charlie as if it was merely a subway station, its severity diminished by having become familiar . . . I had already amassed a small collection of books and tapes from my several trips, but that day I intended to purchase a pair of cheap black nylon tracksuit bottoms and anonymous sneakers, no brand names, not Adidas, not Puma and I soon found exactly what I wanted. There was a reason; they were essential to my plan.

Loss had become a weight across my shoulders; my brain was on fire. Perhaps my head would burst into flames while my legs moved slowly, like an old person's with tiredness beyond my comprehension. I had had the love of Mathieu and Hector, yet for all the horses I had ridden, I'd never had one of my own that I loved and that I knew loved me back. It was not to be, not for me, a special bond with a horse, so unfair and very painful, to have loved horses but not to have loved a particular one, although there was always Monticello, but he was Father's, well more Billy Bob's and I knew what that supreme love had cost Billy Bob. Monticello's death had upset Father more than Mother's had. He had been devastated. Grief had turned his mind and caused him to get involved with those satanic fish of his.

Things tend to drift on. I had often heard that and then something happens, or so they say. For me though it would only continue, dull beat by beat. I felt smaller, shrinking into nothingness, fearing I would never ride another horse, never even touch one or feel all that power beneath the skin. A black pool had formed inside my head or my heart, or both, and it kept getting bigger as if it was an ever-increasing stain. Soon it would fill the space and then what? Would I just evaporate and die? All I could do was wait for the moment. And it had come, not dramatically, just stupidly and it hurt all the same. It was in a small café, near the hotel. I was trying to eat some soup before then ordering cake which was what I really wanted to eat. The soup was tasteless, although it had smelled good but as soon as I had swallowed the first spoonful, I knew it was inedible but I did eat it as if it was a punishment I had to complete, part of my personal atonement for not mourning Mother.

A young man was sitting at a nearby table and he seemed anxious. His hair looked freshly washed and fluffy the way Mathieu's
always had just after a shower. Each time I glanced up from the
soup the man was staring directly at me, wide blue eyes, or maybe
blue gray, and suddenly I thought about what it would be like
to sleep with him and was shocked as I never daydreamed about
sex, only romance, and the tenderness of it—holding hands, I'd
so loved that. Mathieu's hands had been big and solid. Holding
hands was what I missed, a strong, warm hand containing mine.
Mother always said I would develop warts. Lone Star was fully
convinced that I would. But I never had a wart; never even saw
one close up. The man in the café looked a good deal bigger than
Mathieu and was hefty with wide shoulders and a big neck got
from hard work, not by prancing round a gym. His sitting there
was not at all like Marc who had been poised like a predator that
terrible night, hoping to catch someone stupid—and he had.
The young man in Berlin was completely different, wholesome.
What would I say if he spoke to me? Could he speak English?
Would my spoken German sound any more natural than my
French? Who was I fooling? I couldn't speak German either.
Would he notice my creepy eyes straight off? If I spoke to him
would Mathieu's spirit which was staying so close to me, vanish?
I didn't want that to happen, having to choose between the living
and the dead; my dead love and a living stranger, I couldn't make
that choice. Just then the German man's face opened wide into
a smile and I thought he was about to speak to me and I swallowed, preparing to respond. But a blonde girl had come in and
he stood up and putting his arms around her—she was almost as
tall—kissed her right there in front of everyone. She didn't seem
a bit surprised and pulled a flat packet out of her shoulder bag.
At first she presented it to him then snatched it back and tore
the shiny gold paper off it, making him laugh; his face bright

pink. Both looked so in love. How I envied them and felt sick, motioning for the bill, embarrassed and humiliated, aware that such a thing would happen to me again and again, always anticipating something gorgeous only to be left with my hands empty and standing all alone, two odd eyes, marked by God, destined to be an onlooker—an outcast. So that was when my plan had come to me, there in that café, and I knew it was the answer. Perhaps it was Mathieu's idea and he had communicated it to me because he wanted to save me from further pain as much as I wished to be free from grief and loneliness and guilt and pretty much everything.

Standing in line at Checkpoint Charlie as I had several times before, I concentrated on maintaining a neutral expression, ready to argue that "yes that really is me in my passport photograph." And I'd dressed carefully that morning; I was wearing the grungy nylon tracksuit bottoms I'd bought in East Berlin along with cheap sneakers, and I also wore one of Mathieu's sports tops, an old navy windcheater-type thing with black sleeves. It was big on me so underneath it I was wearing the weatherproof riding jacket he had given me. A riding jacket, along with a whole bunch of promises and fantasies for the future; imagine that and then there was nothing.

I wanted to blend in and would; my brown hair, my unremarkable face, my height, my misery. Once I got into East Berlin I would take my farewell of the paintings in the National Gallery and then board a train for Dresden. Caspar David Friedrich had settled in Dresden, establishing his studio and had died at sixty-five, not so very old, following years of ill health—and chronic depression. He was buried there and I realized that as much as I wanted to see the paintings in the gallery, I really hoped to kneel at his grave. It would be fitting for me to die in Dresden, and I was not afraid of dying.

Unrelenting weariness had left me defeated and without hope, all I could do was gather my remaining strength and pay tribute to an artist who had helped me understand what it was like to be human and to love and to lose—and ultimately fail to survive. My objective was to get to Dresden before anyone asked to see my papers. Where did the train leave from? It was easy to stop someone in Zoo Station and just ask. I'd avoided alerting the hotel people in case they took action, eager to please my wealthy parents whom they were still expecting, thanks to my many lies.

Mitzi knew almost everything; I'd phoned her and explained in a no-questions-please call from the hotel and said a letter would follow. All she had to do was wait; and take charge if there was no further contact from me within a week, and there would be none. I wouldn't be phoning her or anyone ever again.

A railway worker dressed in a shabby old uniform, about two sizes too big for her, jumped when I tapped her shoulder in the famous old station to ask how I'd find the Dresden train. Easy; get to Bahnhof Lichtenberg, over at Frankfurter Allee, almost in a direct line east as the crow flies from where we were standing, only on the other side of the Wall. "In East Berlin," she had said with a grimace, suddenly becoming intensely engaged, responsible, advising me to be careful and that all the Russian trains arrived in at Lichtenberg, "and so obviously from there leave also." She said the Russians were always "big and in a hurry," she laughed and was probably a student wearing her father's old jacket, enjoying having me to try out her English on. It was unlikely that she was in the secret police; not standing there, smiling in West Berlin. My mission was safe. She was only a few years older than me and had held out her arms and puffed up her cheeks when she had described all Russians as "big and in a hurry." She seemed happy, what was her life like?

There was of course a complication. The girl had mentioned that all movement inside the East required an internal travel visa which took about six weeks to process. My plan was to get into Berlin on a day pass and then board the Dresden train, without bothering to apply for any permit. I didn't give a hoot what happened; as long as I got to Dresden and saw Friedrich's grave and his paintings. My problems could be finally resolved; I was sick of feeling tired and weak, nauseous with grief whether I ate or not. The food I bought for the journey consisted of a variety of chocolate bars as well as a bag of cakes with a thick, gooey filling. And yes, I had a marzipan and almond loaf, which I really liked and had eaten before the train even pulled out of Lichtenberg. I was very thirsty, the carriage was stuffy, and I had forgotten to bring water with me. Would anyone check the tickets? Would they ask for papers? Let them. Dresden was only 120 miles from Berlin and there was no border to cross, the entire journey took place within the GDR, which was sort of thrilling, even more so as I was breaking the law. And I decided that if I had to continue living, I would have liked to live in Germany. It was quiet and full of forests and lakes, mountains, brokenhearted romantics . . . and all that appealed to me, excepting being ready to die, as I was, killed by love and to think I hadn't cried at Mother's funeral, yet had turned into a person who never stopped sobbing. Endless tears were ready to seep out of me. My eyes were always stinging, tears like pin pricks; so many thorns, blinded by weeping, an honorary character from the Brothers Grimm.

*

It was thick and wet, warm with solid bits. I clutched at my stomach, kneading the stuff, congealed and sticky. How had that happened? I'd been shot but hadn't felt a thing. My eyes opened, the train had stopped and somehow we were in Dresden. Such a shame to have missed out on looking at the landscape; I had fallen asleep, holding my chocolate bars and they'd all melted, making a mess on my lap. At least the thin nylon would be easy to rinse out, if I got to a restroom, one with a sink and hopefully no mirror.

My symbolic arrival in Dresden would be delayed by a minor practicality. Dresden, the great medieval city of Saxony, almost completely destroyed by the Allies during World War Two, how difficult would it be to distinguish the original from the rebuilt? How would I find the grave? It took almost two hours of wandering around in circles but I did locate it, in a graveyard bleached of color, even the pine trees were dusty and the place was so quiet. The only sign was a plain wooden notice board with a few pieces of paper thumb-tacked to it, and among the handwritten notes were two faded postcards, reproductions of Friedrich's paintings. I smiled to myself; I was on the right track but no sign of the grave. Had it been America, there would have been a coffee shop and a hotel, probably a shopping complex, people selling giant posters of his work, never mind hologram postcards. But in a Dresden cemetery, Caspar David Friedrich was just another dead soul, all equal in waiting for the Coming of the Kingdom. Surveying the general area, I began working my way through it, then saw a group of three graves in a slight clearing with a stone bench set at an angle; the middle one was covered in a plain simple slab of stone and there in the old German-style lettering his name, Caspar David Friedrich, and his mortal dates. No flowers, no wreath. I couldn't tell who occupied the graves on either side of his. But there I was at last and I felt Mathieu close to me and remembered his burial place, the earth still fresh, covered in flowers, no stone marker as of yet and all those miles away in France.

Not a person in sight, not a sound. Just the lightest misty rain and I did pray, in my fashion, telling Mathieu that I was there and had traveled to another cemetery as a way of making a pilgrimage for us, for him and me. And that I would also go and see the paintings, pay my respects. I told him that I was awfully tired and sick and alone and that maybe I was about to find out if people really did meet up again in the afterlife. I told him I was Orfeo, come to find him, and that the roles had been reversed and instead of him coming to fetch me back, I was ready to join him and that this great artist had shown me the way. My breathing was louder, kneeling down was making me dizzy and I felt sore all over, sick like always but also hungry, hungry for food that would probably just make me even more ill. Mother came to my thoughts with a force of presence she'd never had in life and I told her that she probably already knew all about Mathieu and that maybe she was glad for us and that I was awfully sorry about what had happened to her but finally did understand her need for love; grand passion and simple affection, a tender gesture which meant so much. Please forgive Father, I asked her, because he had meant no harm. He was damned in his way, cursed to live in his head. Father placed too high a value on intelligence and only existed through ideas and history the way I used to. But I had discovered how to love and how to feel and that it hurt for sure, no denying, but at least I was capable of loving.

Finally, I knew that I had lived and loved; experienced real passion and was suffering true grief—the full immensity of loss. At last I understood Mother's impulsive ways and how she must have felt trapped in a house with two courteous robots, Father and me. Polite and detached, living off facts, gorging on books and always keeping the world at a distance.

Then I spoke to Caspar David Friedrich, thanking him, and told him that I wished that I had known him yet felt that I did and that he could read my mind and had helped me figure out so much through his beautiful, melancholic images and the way he had looked to Nature to find the true meaning of human existence. The world had changed so much since he was living among men and yet the things that were important had remained the same. Mumbling his mantra that a picture must not be invented, it must be felt, I put my hand down on the soil around his grave and felt the dry clay-like powder of it and then rubbed it into my face and took more and rubbed it into my neck and down along my throat, dust to dust.

There is a building in Dresden with a porcelain frieze depicting generations of the kings of Saxony in a procession spanning the centuries. It must be about 300 feet long, and I saw it. Then I walked on the historic Brühlsche Terrasse, named after the man that built it, overlooking the Elbe, the same river that flowed on up to Hamburg, easing its way into the sea. Such continuity I thought, water and time; life and death. Beautiful, mutilated Dresden that had emerged again from the rubble, inspired by its mighty ghosts, was all around me; I wanted to explore it. But no, that couldn't be. I would visit the pictures and then try getting the train back to Berlin and who knew what was going to come to pass. By then I was but marginally curious as to what would happen to me. If I only got deported I could imagine Father looking surprised and probably shaking his head before remarking that he had thought I had been up in my bedroom all along, reading about the planets. No, I would greatly prefer getting shot in the back as I broke free of the border guards. It would be ended quickly, no more problems. But before that, the paintings; the woman in the Dresden gallery proved a fierce custodian; she may as well have been guarding the gates of heaven. There was no welcome in her eyes; she held the ticket close to her chest, staring hard as if I would race in and steal the paintings, all of them. Her attitude was irrelevant; I was impervious to her cranky show of petty authority. It felt like I'd already died and I gazed through her, my need to see those works of Caspar David Friedrich bolstered me for what I saw as a final earthly effort before fate took charge. I had no travel permit; and there was a woman guarding a gallery entrance ticket. If only she knew.

Just the pictures and me, again—no one else. It was a pattern, a gift to me alone. Silence. The first one I saw made me smile; three bare oaks in the snow, two standing straight, one leaning, beaten and weary. Mathieu and Hector and me, the tired one, and in between us, a dolmen, a funeral mound become a monument to us. I loved the picture. And there was a graceful, still landscape, an evening sky just beginning to close over what Friedrich had called "a water meadow." I had seen several reproductions of it in books and on postcards, yet none had replicated the beauty of the colors.

Then I noticed another work and well, it amazed me, new and yet so familiar. It was the painting that articulated it all in such an eloquent image, and I had somehow never properly noticed it before, not in any of the many books about him I had read. Although I felt very familiar with Friedrich's work, he had completed more than 500 pictures of which I had only seen a fraction. But that day in Dresden I stood before a painting that spoke more to me than an ocean of words could have in any or all languages known to man. It is simple and stark; muted, haunting and haunted, the entrance of a cemetery. A pair of tall stone piers stand like sentries, the gates wide open and a ghostly vapor is rising off the graves. Shadowy trees are visible in the background and Caspar David Friedrich somehow evokes a spirit standing there without actually including a figure. Instead there was merely a suggestion so powerful I gasped and felt weak from the sense of loss, my loss, described by an artist whose understanding of the spiritual surpassed that of any preacher I have ever heard. I wanted to stay, but I knew should leave, my quest completed.

Dresden was quieter than Berlin, less dramatic and somehow more real. Berlin by comparison was a blunt, unforgiving theater, challenging a person to respond. Even the checkpoint guards were acting out a kind of role. They were the heavies, eager for action. The people in West Berlin worked that bit harder at appearing more free of spirit than their neighbors to the East; perhaps they were, it wasn't that clear. The station in Dresden was busier than it had been when I arrived. Pushing my way on to the train, determined to be part of the rush, I pretended that I too was an East German and beyond surprising. On sitting down I knew I needed to go to the bathroom but didn't have the energy to get up. About thirty minutes into the journey, I became aware of movement behind me, footsteps and voices moving up along the carriage, and swallowed, maybe shivered too. It was about to happen. A tubby man in a uniform was checking tickets. He seemed very relaxed, unusually slovenly for a German official. His reading glasses were swinging across his face, one of the arms was broken and every few minutes, he stopped to press them down into place but failed to balance them for long. He reached me and my mouth went dry, all I had was the train ticket and he nodded as if to say "and." I showed him my US passport and shrugged. He peered at me and then slowly drew his hand across his throat and made a face as if to say, "You're on your own kid." I smiled to myself, feeling that I had beaten the system and in a different life, reckoned I would have made a good spy. For a split second I felt very smug. Perhaps he'd noticed my smirk, I'm not sure but he clicked his fingers and said something I failed to catch, before growling, "Passport." I handed it to him and he studied it at length before copying down the number on the inside page and he paused. It looked as if he was about to keep the passport. "So this is the end," I said to myself, ashamed of my fear, not so very brave after all. The ticket inspector, if that was what he was, turned and spoke to two men sitting a few seats further up the carriage. I could feel the train slowing. My hands were very sweaty and I was trying not to vomit. An hour seemed to crawl by, in reality no more than five minutes. He laughed at something one of the men said and then, without further comment, tossed my passport back to me without even a glance.

Not once during the rest of the journey did I move my head. Until the train pulled into Berlin, I stared out the window, too nervous to wipe the sweat from my face and the back of my neck, my clothes were damp and I sat there, rigid with dread, waiting to be hauled from my seat. A gun to my head. Click. Boom. But nothing more happened.

On arriving at Lichtenberg my first thoughts were on finding a rest room, I needed to go to the bathroom real bad and whatever about my impending death, I had to hurry. It was late and the cubicle didn't have any bathroom paper, the faucet was stuck and my hands were sticky. I walked on through Checkpoint Charlie. No one stopped me. I was very tired, queasy as usual and aching, feeling very cold. Hungry, yes, and so very weak. The thought struck me that I didn't need a random bullet, I could just drop dead. I was ready.

Back at the hotel I made the mistake of climbing the stairs, too embarrassed to risk taking the elevator because I resembled a hobo and most likely smelled of stale sweat and fear, and possibly, more shame and disgrace, urine. As usual the mattress was back on the bed frame and for once I overlooked the ritual with the little horse and also ignored the chocolates and just fell onto the bed. I needed a bath. The phone rang and such a wave of physical pain came to torment me, it was difficult to answer as I kept dropping the receiver, my hands were shaking. I could hear the manager asking me if I'd had an accident, what had happened to my clothes? All I could muster was that I was awful sick. The knocking came closer and before I realized that it was my door that was being rapped, the housekeeper opened it and came in with one of the young female receptionists. I don't recall what happened right after that, aside from the pillows being moved and a warm, damp cloth gently wiping my face.

*

Early morning light always creeps in as if the day itself wants to sneak up and surprise a body. The hotel room looked different because it was a different room and in an entirely different place. A woman was whispering; she said, "Fräulein, Mademoiselle, Miss," and I don't know how I answered her. I think I asked if she had gotten lost but suddenly felt indignant, demanding, "What are you doing in my room?" She came up close, closer than I felt comfortable with, and she gave me a small package, apparently I told her breakfast usually comes on a tray. She did tell me that later and then we laughed about it but the first thing the nurse had said was that I was a tall girl "for to have such a little baby."

Well, that woke me up to discover that I had landed myself in hospital, and I looked at the doll-sized creature. "Ariadne," I said. "You will be calm and courageous, and kind and happy, and you will have two green eyes or two brown eyes, not one of each,

and you are our daughter." Yet Ariadne sounds aloof, command-
ing, regal, and she was very small, tiny, the first newborn baby I
ever saw, the first I ever held and I was glad that I had so much
money hidden back in the hotel room, in various stashes here
and there under the carpet, and in the safe, and in both heels of
my boots. I could look after her real well. Her entire hand was
smaller than my thumb. Thumbelina. And I told her I would
someday tell her about the stars and the planets and so much
more . . . Maybe she would like horses and that I would call her
Susan. "Your name is Susan," I said, and perhaps she opened her
eyes and saw more clearly than newborn babies are supposed to
see, and saw me. Was Susan the first word she heard? Susan. I
don't know. But I said it again and again, soft as a whisper, "Your
name is Susan; your name is Susan."

THE END

Author's Notes

[1] The famous painting of the stallion, Whistlejacket, by the artist George Stubbs (1724–1806) which was completed in 1762, was indeed later purchased by the National Gallery in London in 1997 for eleven million pounds sterling or about eighteen million dollars. Obviously our narrator, Helen, whose story takes place during the late 1980s, knows nothing of this, although her irritatingly astute father was proved correct by predicting it.

[2] When Helen refers to her thrill on hearing any mention to Leningrad, and her even greater excitement on coming across references to its former name, St. Petersburg, she is again caught within history. The city's name did not revert to St. Petersburg until 1991.

Acknowledgments

Immense thanks to the German writer Rudolf Ditzen (1893–1947), known to literature as Hans Fallada, for leading me to his biographer, Jenny Williams, who supported my efforts throughout as has my great friend and unofficial twin, Mary Sheridan. By intriguing coincidence Ditzen shared a birthplace, the Baltic town of Greifswald in northeastern Germany, with the artist Caspar David Friedrich.

To Mary Cassidy and Mary Mulligan, and also, all love to my dearest daughter Nadia.

Sincere gratitude to John O'Brien, presiding genius of Dalkey Archive Press, whose wisdom is brilliantly well-matched by his intellect, singular wit, and good humor. I continue to treasure the generosity and patience of the remarkable Catarina Koch, also of Dalkey Archive Press. To the wonderful Katesfield horses, dogs, and cats; particularly to sweet, gentle Kingsley the deerhound, whom I found by the roadside; Katesfield Mozart who more usually answers to Josh; to Katesfield Mr. Darcy once a racehorse, always a king; to Katesfield Hermes Nijinsky, "Hero"; to Katesfield Mary Glen; Lady Spec; Ginny and the others. To the tough, little Robin cat and my affable Dickens, also to the mighty Mother Courage Mimi and her family, not forgetting puss.

There is the enduring presence of Caroline Walsh (1952–2011) who so often asked me to write her a story – and I finally did.

My adored guys, Bilbo and Frodo will remain with me forever. Meanwhile, Bilfro is aware of his daunting legacy and looks after his siblings Paddington and Ruth, the children of Aarhus. Always the precious spirits, Ashley, beautiful Nala, my Lord Sebastian, collie brothers Nathan and Loveheart, tiny Holly, the enigmatic Sox; to Can I, the star show jumper, who came to me seriously injured and lived on for another twelve years and rests in peace. Finally, it always comes back to my Kate.

Born in California, EILEEN BATTERSBY is a graduate of University College Dublin. An *Irish Times* staff arts journalist and literary reviewer, she has won the National Arts Journalist of the Year award four times and was National Critic of the Year in 2012. *Second Readings: From Beckett to Black Beauty* was published in 2009. *Ordinary Dogs – A Story of Two Lives* was published by Faber in 2011. *Teethmarks on My Tongue* is her first novel.

MICHAL AJVAZ, *The Golden Age.*
The Other City.
PIERRE ALBERT-BIROT, *Grabinoulor.*
YUZ ALESHKOVSKY, *Kangaroo.*
FELIPE ALFAU, *Chromos.*
Locos.
JOE AMATO, *Samuel Taylor's Last Night.*
IVAN ÂNGELO, *The Celebration.*
The Tower of Glass.
ANTÓNIO LOBO ANTUNES, *Knowledge of Hell.*
The Splendor of Portugal.
ALAIN ARIAS-MISSON, *Theatre of Incest.*
JOHN ASHBERY & JAMES SCHUYLER, *A Nest of Ninnies.*
ROBERT ASHLEY, *Perfect Lives.*
GABRIELA AVIGUR-ROTEM, *Heatwave and Crazy Birds.*
DJUNA BARNES, *Ladies Almanack.*
Ryder.
JOHN BARTH, *Letters.*
Sabbatical.
DONALD BARTHELME, *The King.*
Paradise.
SVETISLAV BASARA, *Chinese Letter.*
MIQUEL BAUÇÀ, *The Siege in the Room.*
RENÉ BELLETTO, *Dying.*
MAREK BIENCZYK, *Transparency.*
ANDREI BITOV, *Pushkin House.*
ANDREJ BLATNIK, *You Do Understand.*
Law of Desire.
LOUIS PAUL BOON, *Chapel Road.*
My Little War.
Summer in Termuren.
ROGER BOYLAN, *Killoyle.*
IGNÁCIO DE LOYOLA BRANDÃO, *Anonymous Celebrity.*
Zero.
BONNIE BREMSER, *Troia: Mexican Memoirs.*
CHRISTINE BROOKE-ROSE, *Amalgamemnon.*
BRIGID BROPHY, *In Transit.*
The Prancing Novelist.

GERALD L. BRUNS, *Modern Poetry and the Idea of Language.*
GABRIELLE BURTON, *Heartbreak Hotel.*
MICHEL BUTOR, *Degrees.*
Mobile.
G. CABRERA INFANTE, *Infante's Inferno.*
Three Trapped Tigers.
JULIETA CAMPOS, *The Fear of Losing Eurydice.*
ANNE CARSON, *Eros the Bittersweet.*
ORLY CASTEL-BLOOM, *Dolly City.*
LOUIS-FERDINAND CÉLINE, *North.*
Conversations with Professor Y.
London Bridge.
MARIE CHAIX, *The Laurels of Lake Constance.*
HUGO CHARTERIS, *The Tide Is Right.*
ERIC CHEVILLARD, *Demolishing Nisard.*
The Author and Me.
MARC CHOLODENKO, *Mordechai Schamz.*
JOSHUA COHEN, *Witz.*
EMILY HOLMES COLEMAN, *The Shutter of Snow.*
ERIC CHEVILLARD, *The Author and Me.*
ROBERT COOVER, *A Night at the Movies.*
STANLEY CRAWFORD, *Log of the S.S. The Mrs Unguentine.*
Some Instructions to My Wife.
RENÉ CREVEL, *Putting My Foot in It.*
RALPH CUSACK, *Cadenza.*
NICHOLAS DELBANCO, *Sherbrookes.*
The Count of Concord.
NIGEL DENNIS, *Cards of Identity.*
PETER DIMOCK, *A Short Rhetoric for Leaving the Family.*
ARIEL DORFMAN, *Konfidenz.*
COLEMAN DOWELL, *Island People.*
Too Much Flesh and Jabez.
ARKADII DRAGOMOSHCHENKO, *Dust.*
RIKKI DUCORNET, *Phosphor in Dreamland.*
The Complete Butcher's Tales.
RIKKI DUCORNET (cont.), *The Jade*

Cabinet.
The Fountains of Neptune.
WILLIAM EASTLAKE, The Bamboo Bed.
Castle Keep.
Lyric of the Circle Heart.
JEAN ECHENOZ, Chopin's Move.
STANLEY ELKIN, A Bad Man.
Criers and Kibitzers, Kibitzers and Criers.
The Dick Gibson Show.
The Franchiser.
The Living End.
Mrs. Ted Bliss.
FRANÇOIS EMMANUEL, Invitation to
a Voyage.
PAUL EMOND, The Dance of a Sham.
SALVADOR ESPRIU, Ariadne in the
Grotesque Labyrinth.
LESLIE A. FIEDLER, Love and Death
in the American Novel.
JUAN FILLOY, Op Oloop.
ANDY FITCH, Pop Poetics.
GUSTAVE FLAUBERT, Bouvard and
Pécuchet.
KASS FLEISHER, Talking out of School.
JON FOSSE, Aliss at the Fire
Melancholy.
FORD MADOX FORD, The March of
Literature.
MAX FRISCH, I'm Not Stiller.
Man in the Holocene.
CARLOS FUENTES, Christopher Unborn.
Distant Relations.
Terra Nostra.
Where the Air Is Clear.
TAKEHIKO FUKUNAGA, Flowers of Grass.
WILLIAM GADDIS, JR., The Recognitions.
JANICE GALLOWAY, Foreign Parts.
The Trick Is to Keep Breathing.
WILLIAM H. GASS, Life Sentences.
The Tunnel.
The World Within the Word.
Willie Masters' Lonesome Wife.
GÉRARD GAVARRY, Hoppla! 1 2 3.
ETIENNE GILSON, The Arts of the
Beautiful.

Forms and Substances in the Arts.
C. S. GISCOMBE, Giscome Road.
Here.
DOUGLAS GLOVER, Bad News
of the Heart.
WITOLD GOMBROWICZ, A Kind
of Testament.
PAULO EMÍLIO SALES GOMES, P's Three
Women.
GEORGI GOSPODINOV, Natural Novel.
JUAN GOYTISOLO, Count Julian.
Juan the Landless.
Makbara.
Marks of Identity.
HENRY GREEN, Blindness.
Concluding.
Doting.
Nothing.
JACK GREEN, Fire the Bastards!
JIŘÍ GRUŠA, The Questionnaire.
MELA HARTWIG, Am I a Redundant
Human Being?
JOHN HAWKES, The Passion Artist.
Whistlejacket.
ELIZABETH HEIGHWAY, ED.,
Contemporary Georgian Fiction.
AIDAN HIGGINS, Balcony of Europe.
Blind Man's Bluff.
Bornholm Night-Ferry.
Langrishe, Go Down.
Scenes from a Receding Past.
KEIZO HINO, Isle of Dreams.
KAZUSHI HOSAKA, Plainsong.
ALDOUS HUXLEY, Antic Hay.
Point Counter Point.
Those Barren Leaves.
Time Must Have a Stop.
NAOYUKI II, The Shadow of a Blue Cat.
DRAGO JANČAR, The Tree with No Name.
MIKHEIL JAVAKHISHVILI, Kvachi.
GERT JONKE, The Distant Sound.
Homage to Czerny.
The System of Vienna.
JACQUES JOUET, Mountain R.
Savage.

Upstaged.

MIEKO KANAI, *The Word Book.*

YORAM KANIUK, *Life on Sandpaper.*

ZURAB KARUMIDZE, *Dagny.*

JOHN KELLY, *From Out of the City.*

HUGH KENNER, *Flaubert, Joyce and Beckett: The Stoic Comedians.*
Joyce's Voices.

DANILO KIŠ, *The Attic.*
The Lute and the Scars.
Psalm 44.
A Tomb for Boris Davidovich.

ANITA KONKKA, *A Fool's Paradise.*

GEORGE KONRÁD, *The City Builder.*

TADEUSZ KONWICKI, *A Minor Apocalypse.*
The Polish Complex.

ANNA KORDZAIA-SAMADASHVILI, *Me, Margarita.*

MENIS KOUMANDAREAS, *Koula.*

ELAINE KRAF, *The Princess of 72nd Street.*

JIM KRUSOE, *Iceland.*

AYSE KULIN, *Farewell: A Mansion in Occupied Istanbul.*

EMILIO LASCANO TEGUI, *On Elegance While Sleeping.*

ERIC LAURRENT, *Do Not Touch.*

VIOLETTE LEDUC, *La Bâtarde.*

EDOUARD LEVÉ, *Autoportrait.*
Newspaper.
Suicide.
Works.

MARIO LEVI, *Istanbul Was a Fairy Tale.*

DEBORAH LEVY, *Billy and Girl.*

JOSÉ LEZAMA LIMA, *Paradiso.*

ROSA LIKSOM, *Dark Paradise.*

OSMAN LINS, *Avalovara.*
The Queen of the Prisons of Greece.

FLORIAN LIPUŠ, *The Errors of Young Tjaž.*

GORDON LISH, *Peru.*

ALF MACLOCHLAINN, *Out of Focus.*
Past Habitual.
The Corpus in the Library.

RON LOEWINSOHN, *Magnetic Field(s).*

YURI LOTMAN, *Non-Memoirs.*

D. KEITH MANO, *Take Five.*

MINA LOY, *Stories and Essays of Mina Loy.*

MICHELINE AHARONIAN MARCOM, *A Brief History of Yes.*
The Mirror in the Well.

BEN MARCUS, *The Age of Wire and String.*

WALLACE MARKFIELD, *Teitlebaum's Window.*

DAVID MARKSON, *Reader's Block.*
Wittgenstein's Mistress.

CAROLE MASO, *AVA.*

HISAKI MATSUURA, *Triangle.*

LADISLAV MATEJKA & KRYSTYNA POMORSKA, EDS., *Readings in Russian Poetics: Formalist & Structuralist Views.*

HARRY MATHEWS, *Cigarettes.*
The Conversions.
The Human Country.
The Journalist.
My Life in CIA.
Singular Pleasures.
The Sinking of the Odradek.
Stadium.
Tlooth.

HISAKI MATSUURA, *Triangle.*

DONAL MCLAUGHLIN, *beheading the virgin mary, and other stories.*

JOSEPH MCELROY, *Night Soul and Other Stories.*

ABDELWAHAB MEDDEB, *Talismano.*

GERHARD MEIER, *Isle of the Dead.*

HERMAN MELVILLE, *The Confidence-Man.*

AMANDA MICHALOPOULOU, *I'd Like.*

STEVEN MILLHAUSER, *The Barnum Museum.*
In the Penny Arcade.

RALPH J. MILLS, JR., *Essays on Poetry.*

MOMUS, *The Book of Jokes.*

CHRISTINE MONTALBETTI, *The Origin of Man.*
Western.

NICHOLAS MOSLEY, *Accident.*
Assassins.
Catastrophe Practice.

FOR A FULL LIST OF PUBLICATIONS, VISIT: www.dalkeyarchive.com

on the Possibility of Literature.

GERMAN SADULAEV, *The Maya Pill.*

TOMAŽ ŠALAMUN, *Soy Realidad.*

LYDIE SALVAYRE, *The Company of Ghosts.*
The Lecture.
The Power of Flies.

LUIS RAFAEL SÁNCHEZ, *Macho Camacho's Beat.*

SEVERO SARDUY, *Cobra & Maitreya.*

NATHALIE SARRAUTE, *Do You Hear Them?*
Martereau.
The Planetarium.

STIG SÆTERBAKKEN, *Siamese.*
Self-Control.
Through the Night.

ARNO SCHMIDT, *Collected Novellas.*
Collected Stories.
Nobodaddy's Children.
Two Novels.

ASAF SCHURR, *Motti.*

GAIL SCOTT, *My Paris.*

DAMION SEARLS, *What We Were Doing and Where We Were Going.*

JUNE AKERS SEESE,
Is This What Other Women Feel Too?

BERNARD SHARE, *Inish.*
Transit.

VIKTOR SHKLOVSKY, *Bowstring.*
Literature and Cinematography.
Theory of Prose.
Third Factory.
Zoo, or Letters Not about Love.

PIERRE SINIAC, *The Collaborators.*

KJERSTI A. SKOMSVOLD,
The Faster I Walk, the Smaller I Am.

JOSEF ŠKVORECKÝ, *The Engineer of Human Souls.*

GILBERT SORRENTINO, *Aberration of Starlight.*
Blue Pastoral.
Crystal Vision.
Imaginative Qualities of Actual Things.
Mulligan Stew. Red the Fiend.
Steelwork.
Under the Shadow.

MARKO SOSIČ, *Ballerina, Ballerina.*

ANDRZEJ STASIUK, *Dukla.*
Fado.

GERTRUDE STEIN, *The Making of Americans.*
A Novel of Thank You.

LARS SVENDSEN, *A Philosophy of Evil.*

PIOTR SZEWC, *Annihilation.*

GONÇALO M. TAVARES, *A Man: Klaus Klump.*
Jerusalem.
Learning to Pray in the Age of Technique.

LUCIAN DAN TEODOROVICI,
Our Circus Presents...

NIKANOR TERATOLOGEN, *Assisted Living.*

STEFAN THEMERSON, *Hobson's Island.*
The Mystery of the Sardine.
Tom Harris.

TAEKO TOMIOKA, *Building Waves.*

JOHN TOOMEY, *Sleepwalker.*

DUMITRU TSEPENEAG, *Hotel Europa.*
The Necessary Marriage.
Pigeon Post.
Vain Art of the Fugue.

ESTHER TUSQUETS, *Stranded.*

DUBRAVKA UGRESIC, *Lend Me Your Character.*
Thank You for Not Reading.

TOR ULVEN, *Replacement.*

MATI UNT, *Brecht at Night.*
Diary of a Blood Donor.
Things in the Night.

ÁLVARO URIBE & OLIVIA SEARS, EDS.,
Best of Contemporary Mexican Fiction.

ELOY URROZ, *Friction.*
The Obstacles.

LUISA VALENZUELA, *Dark Desires and the Others.*
He Who Searches.

PAUL VERHAEGHEN, *Omega Minor.*

BORIS VIAN, *Heartsnatcher.*

LLORENÇ VILLALONGA, *The Dolls' Room.*

TOOMAS VINT, *An Unending Landscape.*

ORNELA VORPSI, *The Country Where No*